Also by Janice Kaplan & Lynn Schnurnberger

THE BOTOX DIARIES

MINE
ARE
SPECTACULAR!

MINE
ARE
SPECTACULAR!

A Novel

Janice Kaplan
&
Lynn Schnurnberger

 BALLANTINE BOOKS • NEW YORK

Copyright © 2005 by Janice Kaplan & Lynn Schnurnberger

Published in the United States by Ballantine Books, an imprint of The Random House Publishing Group, a division of Random House, Inc., New York.

Ballantine and colophon are registered trademarks of Random House, Inc.

Library of Congress Cataloging-in-Publication Data
Kaplan, Janice.
    Mine are spectacular! : a novel / Janice Kaplan & Lynn
  Schnurnberger.
       p.   cm.
     ISBN 0-345-46859-7
     1. Female friendship—Fiction.   2. Divorced mothers—
  Fiction.   3. New York (N.Y.)—Fiction.   4. Pregnant women—
  Fiction.   5. Suburban life—Fiction.   I. Schnurnberger, Lynn
  Edelman.   II. Title.
  PS3561. A5593M56 2005
  813'.54—dc22   2004062799

Printed in the United States of America

www.ballantinebooks.com

9 8   7   6   5

First Edition

Text design by Julie Schroeder

Our children are smart, talented and terrific
and inspire us every day.
To Alliana, Matthew and Zachary—
we admire your quick wits and good hearts.
You are truly spectacular.

ACKNOWLEDGMENTS

We're grateful to our wonderful agent Jane Gelfman whose energy and enthusiam keeps us going. Allison Dickens is smart and savvy—and we're delighted to have her as our editor. Many thanks to editor in chief Nancy Miller for her spirited support. And we endlessly appreciate Kim Hovey, whose passion, commitment and great ideas are boundless.

As ever, we couldn't get through a day without talking to Susan Fine, Joanne Kaufman and Emily Listfield. Emily and Len Blavatnik and Deborah Larkin have been terrific friends and supporters. Primo art dealer Margot Stein has been a fabulous pal and generous art advisor for the book. Lauren Snyder knows everything about being a Manhattan mother and was happy to share. Our very warmest thanks to all of them. We're glad to have you on our side!

To our mothers, Libby Kaplan and Marian Edelman, and to Lissy Dennet, you're our biggest cheerleaders and you made sure that everyone within fifty miles of you knew about our book. We love you dearly.

Our friends are the best. They put up with us and encourage us and sometimes even take us to lunch. A big hug to Stuart, Robert, Anna, Jeanne, Cynthia, Sally, Henry, Allan, Marcia, Linda, Naomi, Peter, Susan, Roseanne, Donna, Jimmy, Martha, Candy, Anne, Jean, Tom, Debbie, Pamela, Maggie, Karen (both of them), Amy, Ronnie and Lloyd, Marsha and David, Nancy and Hugh, Susan and Jen, Anne and

Michael, Leslie and Fred and Ron and Joan. Kisses also to Bob and Chris, Nancy and Frank, David, Lauren, Elyssa, Emily and Lori.

We wake up every morning and look gratefully at our handsome husbands, Ronald Dennett and Martin Semjen. They're smart and sexy and amazing and still know how to make us laugh. We don't know how we were lucky enough to get them. Along with our children, they're the love of our lives.

MINE
ARE
SPECTACULAR!

Chapter ONE

I PEER INTO THE MIRROR in Kate's office, trying to convince myself that the never-before-seen spot on my cheek is a crumb of chocolate cake left over from lunch. Though come to think of it, I didn't have chocolate cake for lunch. I poke at it several times, wondering if it's an age spot. But I'm much too young for that, aren't I?

"What are you doing?" asks Kate, as I lean in closer and start rubbing the blotch with my finger.

"Trying to get this off my face," I tell her. "Come here and figure out what it is. You're a skin doctor." Not just any skin doctor. My best friend Dr. Kate Steele is New York's "Derm Darling" of the moment, if you believe the *New York Post*. And who doesn't?

"What am I looking at?" Kate asks, walking toward me, her four-inch stilettos clicking decisively on the highly polished wooden floor. For a moment I worry that she might slip, but no, this is Kate, the woman who could climb Kilimanjaro in Manolos and make it back to base camp without a wrinkle in her impeccable Escada suit. I love her anyway. Maybe because I've known her since seventh grade when she had braces on her teeth—the last time she was anything less than perfect.

"The spot on my face. It's the size of Texas," I say.

"Don't exaggerate, Sara. It's no bigger than Houston," Kate says, as if that should make me feel better. "Here, let me fix it."

That's my Kate. Can always solve everything. What they didn't teach her at Harvard Medical School, she learned at the Clinique counter. And there's real science behind her beauty tricks—not just smoke and mirrors.

Well, most of the time. Now she simply adjusts a digital read-out on the mirror, and suddenly the offending spot practically disappears.

"I use this for surgery," Kate explains. "It magnifies everything forty times."

"Then let's try to aim it at my bank account," I quip.

Kate laughs, and clears away our empty salad containers and iced-tea cups. We were supposed to have lunch at Nobu but couldn't bring ourselves to move from Kate's cool, comfy office—especially after hearing that the heat-humidity index hit 110. Apparently, New York weathermen figure the actual temperature won't make you feel hot enough, so they invented this new calculation. Personally, I can sweat just fine at ninety-six.

While Kate organizes some files, I surreptitiously flick the mirror back up to forty times magnification, this time to make myself miserable by studying more of my frighteningly flagrant flaws. Crow's feet deeper than Barry White's voice. Laugh lines that aren't very funny. Damn Marx Brothers have aged me by five years. And another five for admitting I watch them.

Kate notices that I'm staring at myself, hypnotized by my reflection. She strides over and with one quick motion unplugs the mirror, swiftly disconnecting me from my source of discontent.

"What's with you?" she asks, looking at me and shaking her head. "You're as insecure as Kennedy airport."

"True," I admit. I had a fair amount of confidence at twenty, but now that I'm twice as old, I seem to have half as much. Despite the fact that the two men in my life think I'm beautiful. Dylan, the most wonderful seven-year-old son in the world. And Bradford, the best—gulp—fiancé in—well, let's say America. After my divorce, I vowed that I'd never get married again. But handsome, Park-Avenue-born Bradford finally convinced me that I was his one and only—the funny, sexy, down-to-earth fifth-grade art teacher he loved. And he threw in a five-carat diamond ring to prove it.

Kate pulls out a gold compact mirror and as she runs a brush through her hair, I notice her licking her lips and smiling. And why not? She could be the only woman I know who doesn't find something wrong with herself every time she looks. Nobody else does either. Glowing porcelain skin, clear blue eyes and a heart-shaped face framed by cascading waves of auburn hair. Not to mention her curvy slim body and her perfectly sculpted arms. And the tiniest waist since Vivien Leigh.

Still, maybe there's something. "Is there anything about yourself you wish you could change?" I ask curiously.

"My address," says Kate, snapping shut the compact and slipping it into the top drawer of her Mies van der Rohe desk. "I love my office, but I wish I were right on Fifth Avenue instead of half a block away. I could charge fifty dollars more a visit."

"I meant anything about your face or body," I say, wondering how Kate could possibly charge any more for a visit than she already does.

"Are you trying to tell me something, darling?" Kate asks. "I know you liked me as a blonde, but I'm not doing that again. I was getting way too much attention. I couldn't walk down the street without tripping over guys." She grins, so I think she's joking. But I'm not sure.

"There are a few changes I'd make," I say.

"In me?" Kate asks, surprised.

"No, in me. Beginning with my boring button nose and going down to my baggy knees."

"So you have no complaints between your knees and your toes," Kate points out optimistically.

"Thanks for reminding me about my toes," I say. "I turned forty and they turned crooked."

I study my feet in the Miu Miu sandals that I bought last week. Why pay full price when they go on sale in July and you still have a whole month and a half to wear them? Of course the only color they had left was purple, but I can compromise. They don't look half-bad with my yellow skirt. Especially if you like Easter eggs.

"There's surgery for that," says Kate as nonchalantly as if she's recommending a new brand of no-chip nail polish. "One of my celebrity patients had it. Jimmy Choo refused to send over any more free sandals unless she straightened out her toes."

"I don't even want to think about what she'd have to do to get a free dress," I say, bending over to play with the little bump on my big toe.

"Nothing wrong with people trying to make themselves look better," Kate says. "I help them do it every day. Collagen, Restylane, a blast of oxygen. When are you going to let me work my wonders on you, darling? You can't be an Ivory girl forever."

"Yes I can. Somebody besides Barbara Bush has to look her age. It's my final stand as a woman of integrity." Kate and I have this conversation at least once a month. Despite my protests, my deepest, darkest secret is that I'm comforted knowing my best friend Doctor Kate is never more than a Botox shot away. And considering how I look this afternoon, I might have to give in and get my first facial. Or my first face-lift.

I sigh and slump down in my chair. "Anyway, your beauty boosters can't cure me today. Those new lines on my face didn't just pop out on their own. I earned them. Worrying."

Kate looks at me quizzically. "Worrying about what?"

"I don't know," I say, wishing I hadn't brought the whole thing up.

"Everything okay with you and Bradford?"

"I guess so," I say, fidgeting with my engagement ring. "Why wouldn't it be?"

"Let's see," Kate says, ticking off the reasons on her fingers. "You have a new man. New house. New stepdaughter. A lot of changes. Puts you at about ninety-nine on the stress meter."

"Maybe the adjustment's harder than I thought it would be," I say slowly. "It's been just Dylan and me for so long that I know how to do life as a single mom. Suburban wife-to-be seems more complicated."

"Yeah, those Lilly Pulitzer outfits you people wear out in the 'burbs are hard to coordinate," Kate teases. "Pink shoes or green? Headband, no headband? Much simpler in the city—just black, black, black."

"Okay, my life's not that tough," I say with a laugh. "And I feel like an idiot complaining. But Bradford's under so much pressure at work and he gets home from Wall Street ridiculously late. He comes in the door, and I find myself griping about every little thing. I wish I could keep my mouth shut and be grateful just to have him."

"He's the one who should be grateful," Kate says. She goes back and leans on the edge of her desk. "Bradford's terrific but so are you. You two are perfect together. You're just figuring out how to be with each other."

"Sure." I look down and play with the edge of my skirt. Which is black. The Stepford transformation isn't quite complete. "But you know what? Starting relationships is easy. It's keeping them that's hard."

Kate eyes me sharply. "Bradford has nothing in common with James."

"I didn't say he did," I snap defensively.

"But that's what you were thinking," Kate says. "You're about to get remarried. How could you not be thinking about your first husband?"

I sigh. "You've known me too long. But you've got to admit not everybody has her first husband run off to Patagonia. He claimed he had to go five thousand miles away to find himself. Six weeks of solitary soul-searching I could live with. But when I told him I was pregnant and he still didn't come back, I figured out that finding himself meant losing me."

"I know, sweetie," Kate says kindly. And boy does she know. How many times have I been over this with her? "But it's been long enough that you can look at the bright side. Most couples who divorce say, 'Oh, we just grew apart.' Your story is so much more interesting."

"Maybe I'll send it in to *Chicken Soup for the Divorced Soul*," I say grumpily.

Kate shakes her head. "Hey, it was tough for you. No way around it. And you know how much I sympathized. Still do."

I manage a smile. "You spent so much time listening to me you could have charged an hourly rate."

"And the support continues," Kate says. "I haven't bought a Patagonia parka ever since. Small gesture on my part, but I switched to L.L. Bean."

"Good thing James didn't run off to Kashmir. That would have been too much of a sacrifice. I can't imagine you trading your cashmere sweaters for Shetland."

Kate comes over and hugs me comfortingly. "It's going to be okay. Really. Bradford's not going to Patagonia. Why would he? The International Monetary Fund never has meetings there. Anyway, he's head over heels in love with you."

"I know, I know," I say. But do I really? Most days, yes. And for me, after all that's happened, that's not bad. "I swear, Kate, we'll never have to talk about James again."

"Yes we will, and that's okay. But what can I do to cheer you up now?" She grins, trying one more time to offer me her own special brand of comfort. "A shot of vitamin C serum? Want to try one of my new lasers?"

"Ooh, yes. Searing off the top layer of my skin sounds like a real pick-me-up. How about lending me your credit card for half an hour instead?"

"If you promise not to go anywhere but Kmart." Kate shakes her head. "Listen, here's something even better. Want to see what my personal trainer has me do every morning to make myself feel good?"

"Whistle a happy tune?" I suggest. "Pop a Paxil?"

"Better," says Kate. She strides over and opens a closet door behind her desk, revealing a full-length mirror. Standing in front of it, she pulls herself up to her full Manolo-enhanced height and takes a deep breath. "First Marco has me stand very straight and tuck in my tummy," she says.

"You don't have a tummy to tuck in," I complain.

Kate ignores me and throws back her shoulders. "Marco says the secret is to tell yourself something enough times that you start to believe it's true."

"I'm rich, I'm rich, I'm rich," I say.

"Stop being silly and come stand next to me," Kate says. As if this whole thing isn't silly enough.

I'm not quite ready to commit. "How much does Marco get for his brilliant advice?" I ask, trying to decide if it's worth dragging myself over.

"Two-fifty an hour," Kate says.

I figure out where the decimal point is and then gasp. "He's rich, he's rich, he's rich," I say. But I sidle over and stand next to her at the mirror.

"Okay," says Kate, "Marco has me warm up with twenty presses, thirty pulls and forty curls. Then he likes me to cup my hands under my breasts."

"He likes that?" I ask, raising an eyebrow. "I bet he does."

Kate shoots me a dirty look, insulted that I'm sullying her personal trainer's pure motives. But Kate's unstoppable. She takes one of her admittedly awesome breasts in each hand, looks herself square in the mirror and with a big smile proclaims, "Mine are spectacular!"

I look at her aghast.

"Come on, do it with me," she says.

I dutifully move closer to Kate and cup my hands on top of hers.

"No, you idiot," she says, swatting me away. "Each to her own."

My own idea would be to get out of here. But Kate was nice enough to invite me here for lunch. And I just can't disappoint anybody. So what the heck, I'll do what she asks.

I point myself—and my breasts—toward the mirror.

"Mine are too small," I complain, going for honesty over ego-boosting . . . "Mine are too big," I add, moving my hands to my hips.

"Well mine are just right," says Goldilocks—er, Kate. "And so are yours. If you'll only say it."

"Okay, I'll say it," I tell Kate, still trying to be agreeable. I stick out my chest, copy Kate's stance, and try to imagine how Pamela Anderson must feel every morning.

"Mine are spectacular," I say in a booming voice. But I immediately start laughing so hard that I collapse onto her couch.

Kate gives up and breaks into giggles alongside me.

"Sorry," I say, still laughing so hard that I have to wipe away the tears from my cheeks. "I'm all for self-improvement. But maybe we should start with my knees."

Four days later, my very pregnant friend Berni, the powerful Hollywood talent agent, is in my house, sprawled across the antique sofa that's been in Bradford's family since the Revolutionary War. Rumor is that after she finished the flag, Betsy Ross stitched the pillows herself.

Berni starts to get up, then leans back and groans dramatically. "It's just too hard to move anymore," she says. "I may lie here until the babies are born."

"You're not due for two more weeks," I say, trying to banish the image of Berni messily popping out two babies in Bradford's—now my—living room.

She groans again. "Just my luck. I'm forty-two and having twins. Who else but me carries to term?" Then she pauses and looks contrite. "I mean, I know that's what you want. The bigger the babies the better. But UPS delivers faster than this, even at Christmas." She tosses back her thick chestnut hair, which she tells me pregnancy has made even more lustrous. Fair trade-off? You get fat, your hair gets fat.

I bring Berni a glass of the alcohol-free punch I'm preparing for her baby shower, which she places on her shelf of a belly.

"Don't get your jacket dirty," I tell her, thinking I've never seen a bright tulip-pink Chanel jacket in quite that size before. Or an outfit quite like Berni's. She's pulled on a pilled pair of stretch black pregnancy pants. And peeking out from under the Chanel jacket is a white T-shirt with a picture of a muffin and the slogan BUN IN THE OVEN! As if anybody might not know.

"I had the people at Chanel Scotchguard it. I had everything Scotchguarded—my clothes, the carpets, the couches, everything. All done. I've baby-proofed the house."

To the ordinary person, baby-proofing involves locking cabinets, covering sockets and fencing off staircases. But I'm finding there's nothing ordinary about Berni.

"Did you get that baby nurse you wanted?" I ask, hitting on our most-talked-about topic of the month.

"No, I couldn't meet her terms," Berni says dispiritedly. "She demanded her own bedroom and bathroom suite. No problem since I have plenty of them. But then she wanted her own driver and a clothing allowance. Honestly, that's a better deal than I negotiated for Sandra Bullock."

"Really? You represented her, too?"

"Well, on her first deal. I discovered Sandy, you know," she tells me.

I carry a platter over and place it down in front of Berni, whom I met just three months ago—when we both moved into the moneyed suburb of Hadley Farms on the very same day. Me, to settle in with Bradford. Berni, freshly relocated from the West Coast with her film-editor husband Aidan, to embark on her new career. Motherhood. Both of us were slightly terrified about starting our new lives and we connected immediately. Berni might have moved three thousand miles, but I was the one on unfamiliar ground—having left my little rent-controlled apartment in Greenwich Village for Bradford's fancy sprawling house. And it wasn't just the shrubs that scared me. Although I still don't know how much you should feed a hydrangea.

"Do you miss Sandy?" I ask, using the nickname as if I, too, have known the plucky actress for years. "I mean, not just Sandy. Your whole L.A. life. It sounds like it was so glamorous."

"It was," Berni admits, looking down and rubbing her beach ball–sized belly. "All those famous clients and fabulous movie premieres. The parties. The private jets. The night Russell Crowe got drunk and told me he had a thing for older women like me."

"Did he follow through?" I ask, probably sounding more like a magazine-reading fan than I should.

"I never gave him the chance," Berni says dismissively. "Besides, all that seems so unimportant to me now. So superficial. How can any of that compare to bringing two precious new lives into the world? I finally know what matters." She breaks into a beatific smile that would give Mona Lisa a run for her money.

I've heard this speech before. Now that she's decided to chuck her high-powered career to be a stay-at-home mom, Berni talks about motherhood as if it's the Second Coming. And in her case, having twins, the Second and Third Coming. She's waited so long to be a parent that she's treating it like her Next Big Project—and she's expecting that heating formula will be as thrilling as creating the formula for the next box-office blockbuster. I'm doubtful, but who knows. There seem to be a lot of overachieving women lately who are trading the fast track for the cul-de-sac. Or in Berni's case, for a ten-room Mediterranean mansion with a pool.

A couple of weeks ago, I asked Berni why she and Aidan—who've been married a dozen years—waited so long to have kids.

"Just an oversight," she said, as if we were talking about how she'd walked out of Stop & Shop without buying a quart of milk. "I was so busy, I forgot."

And now that she's remembered, she's throwing herself into it full throttle. As Berni told me, whining superstars are good preparation for dealing with twins.

"You must be hungry," I say, offering her a fruit platter. "Have something."

"I'm starved, but this isn't going to do it for me," she says, not even tempted by my pretty papaya or perfectly-cut kiwis. "Don't you have any Oreos? Chips Ahoy? Mini Mint Milanos? Really, anything that says Pepperidge Farm on it will be okay. The twins need some sugar."

"No, they don't. How about some cheese?"

"Only if you have Cheez Whiz. At least I know that one's safe. Can't risk anything unpasteurized when you're pregnant."

"Camembert?" I offer.

"No!" she screams, horrified. "Blue veins are the worst."

"They'll go away after you deliver," I promise, deadpan.

"Very funny," says Berni. "You know I can't eat blue-veined cheese. It could carry listeria. Same problem with pastrami. Salmon has PCBs.

Canned tuna has mercury. And don't get me started on cookie dough ice cream. Raw eggs."

I'd forgotten how complicated pregnancy has become. Berni's list of Things to Avoid While Pregnant is longer than Elle MacPherson's legs. And it's not just food. Without waiting a beat, Berni launches into her last-trimester lament.

"I've gone nine months without whitening my teeth, tanning my skin, or bleaching my hair. Staying away from chemicals is harder than you think. I nearly killed the Chem-Turf guy and all he did was park his truck across the street." Berni pauses and squares her shoulders to make her most important announcement. "And don't even talk to me about how I'm going to lose all this weight. Seventy pounds. I know they're twins and a lot of it's water weight. But what am I delivering—the Atlantic Ocean?"

I try to picture what Berni looked like before we both moved to Hadley Farms, our ultra-exclusive gated community just thirty-eight minutes north of the city. Not thirty-nine, as everyone is quick to point out. As if one more minute from Manhattan would be the deal breaker. And who named this place, anyway? How can you call it "Farms" when there's not a thoroughbred or a heifer in sight? Or even anyone making goat cheese. All anyone makes here is money.

"Anyway," Berni continues, "maybe there's hope. Sarah Jessica Parker's giving me her personal trainer as a baby gift."

"I guess that trumps the two silver spoons from Tiffany's I bought for you."

"Oh, stop. Nobody's better than you," she says, getting up and coming over to give me a generous hug. "You're throwing me this baby shower. Way beyond the call. I can't believe how lucky I am. I feel like we've been friends forever."

"It's just that last trimester that feels like it's been forever," I say, laughing and hugging her back. "But I feel the same."

A chirping noise sounds in the apartment and Berni instinctively reaches for her cell phone. She holds it out and looks disappointed. "Not mine. I used to get sixty calls a day, but nobody calls a newly retired talent agent." To me, that sounds like an improvement. But from Berni, it could be a complaint.

The chirping continues. Doorbell? Intercom? Smoke detector? Nothing so mundane. I head to the kitchen. Maybe it's Bradford's high-tech refrigerator that has Internet access, a DVD flat-screen and beeps when the tomatoes are overripe. Or the self-propelling Roomba robot vacuum cleaner that bleeps when anything gets in its way. It could be any one of a hundred gizmos since everything in Bradford's designer kitchen chirps. The only thing missing is a parakeet.

Then I figure it out—the timer on the Viking stove. I rush over and pull out a tray of cheese puffs that haven't puffed. Instead they're flat and burned at the edges. I stare at them in disbelief. "This never happened to me before," I tell Berni, who's traipsed in behind me and is leaning against a wall in the breakfast nook that's bigger than my whole West Village apartment. "In my old kitchen I had to bake in the toaster oven and everything was always perfect."

"What you've sacrificed for love," Berni says, making fun of me. She comes over, pops a puff in her mouth and makes a face. "Gross," she says, spitting it out into a napkin. "In this case the sacrifice might have been too great."

"I don't think we'll starve," I say, dumping them into the garbage disposal and looking around at the counters piled high with trays of food I've spent two days preparing and managed not to burn.

Another chirp. Again Berni reaches for her phone, but over the intercom, from the main gate half a mile away, booms the voice of the guard. Not that we're allowed to call him that. The Hadley Farms Community Handbook requires he be addressed as "The Doorman." I thought I was moving out of Manhattan, but apparently everyone in this McMansioned community wants to pretend they're still living on Fifth Avenue.

"Hey, girls, it's Enrique," says the doorman. "How ya doin'? Party's about to begin. Two hot ladies here for you."

"Send them over," I say, back into the intercom. "And you don't have to call for the rest."

"If the next batch look like this I'm coming over, too," he shoots back.

Berni looks amused. I turn away from the intercom and start to giggle. "Next to you, Enrique's my favorite thing about Hadley Farms so far," I tell her.

I go to the door to welcome the first arrivals. Enrique's "hot women" turn out to be Berni's sixty-four-year-old mother Erica and an agent colleague of Berni's named Olivia Gilford, who's decked out in a black python suit and enough gold chains to stymie Houdini.

"My god, you're the size of an elephant," Olivia says, greeting Berni and throwing her arms wide open to emphasize her point. "How can you stand being that big? Are you having second thoughts?"

"It's a little late for that," says Berni.

"Good thing you quit. If your clients saw you this way they'd die," says Olivia. She heads over to grab a glass of wine from the bartender, hired for the afternoon from the hip New York employment agency Actors Behind Bars.

"What a bitch," I whisper to Berni. "I can't wait to meet the rest of your friends."

"This one's not a friend," Bernie whispers back. "Rival. I invited her so I can keep an eye on her. If she's here, she's not out stealing my clients."

"But . . ." I start to say.

"I know," Berni interrupts. "I'm out of the game so I shouldn't care anymore. But old habits die hard."

Guests keep arriving, and the house starts to fill. Well, the foyer, anyway. The entire Rose Bowl Parade could march through this place and you'd hardly notice. The women grab for the Rosenthal china and begin filling their plates.

"What fabulous food," says our pencil-slim Hadley Farms neighbor and community board president Priscilla, who looks like this could be her first meal in years.

"Yes, fabulous. Who catered?" asks another equally slim and aerobicized woman as she forks down my pesto pasta. It used to be that skinny women waltzed through parties nibbling a celery stalk or the occasional carrot stick. Now the bar's higher. To be truly admired, you have to be a size two while still wolfing down everything but the custom drapes. Once upon a time the crème-de-la-thin wouldn't be caught dead eating in public. Now they do nothing but.

Before I have the chance to take the credit for the catering, Priscilla interrupts. "I'd know this pecan chicken salad anywhere," she says smugly. "It's got to be Barefoot Contessa."

"I would have said the same," says the other woman, now intently nibbling at a beef teriyaki skewer, "but I detect just a hint of Glorious Food."

"No, no," says a third woman, now joining the fray. "The peach aphrodisiac salad just screams Colin Cowie. He sent something just like it to Barbados last year for our New Year's party."

By now I'm too embarrassed to admit that my hands have touched the food, but I am thinking there may be a career in this for me.

When we get to dessert, I invite the women to bring their plates into the library, where I offer a choice of coffees—Tahitian brew, Samoan simmer, or Costa Rican nugget. Talk about a coffee break. Feels like each cup should come with frequent flyer miles.

Berni sinks into the oversized winged-back chair ready to attack her enormous pile of presents. I'm expecting to see a lot of Baby Gap booties and stretchies. But as paper and ribbons go flying, it quickly becomes clear that Berni's unwrapping a whole new level of baby must-haves. Two cashmere Burberry baby blankets. An eighteen-karat gold David Yurman bunny bracelet. A Swarovski crystal box for the tooth fairy—who apparently would never think to look under a plain pillow in Hadley Farms. A Louis Vuitton diaper-changing bag. Then come the alphabet blocks. Finally something the babies can play with—if you trust your toddler with Steuben crystal.

"My gift's a little late," says Olivia, looking worriedly at her watch and hurrying out of the room. Berni finishes opening her presents and somebody suggests making a hat out of the ribbons.

"Or we can play pin the rattle on the donkey," offers Berni's mother Erica energetically. "I did that at a baby shower just last week."

But Olivia has another game in mind.

"Look who's here!" she calls out gaily from the foyer, as she ushers in a six-foot-tall blond policeman.

"Did I do something wrong?" I ask, jumping up nervously. I can't think what it would be. Maybe it's against the law in this zip code to cater your own party.

"Not yet," he says slyly. "Now where's the birthday girl?"

"This is a baby shower," I say, confused.

"Okay, the *birth*-ing girl," he says jocularly. And then he tosses his hat in the air and bends over to grab something from his belt. Oh my god, his gun? Reflexively, I fling my hands into the air.

"Don't shoot," I plead. "I'm innocent."

"But I'm not," he says. And as if on cue, the house fills with P. Diddy wailing from a mini-CD player, "Girl I'm a Bad Boy."

Our trusty patrolman starts unbuttoning his shirt and twirls his club in time to the music. I watch agog as the top comes off and he sends it flying into the crowd, revealing his bare, bronzed chest. Pretty buff, too—though why the heck are we looking at it?

Olivia has the answer.

"Happy shower!" she shouts to Berni, above the music. "My baby present to you—Patrolman Pete! The Cop Who Rocks!"

"Thank you, ma'am," says Pete, who in one swift motion rips the Velcro seam on his pants and steps casually out of them. He sidles up to nine-month-pregnant Bernie and swivels his hips—and his red bikini underwear—as close to her as he can get. He winks broadly, plays provocatively with his nightstick and makes his intentions clear. "This officer is not a gentleman!" he says, removing the leather belt that's still at his waist and snapping it suggestively.

I look around at my thirty guests. It's a defining moment. One group, led by Olivia, is grinning, swaying to the music and waiting eagerly to see what happens next. Preferably to them. Next are the women who have a sudden need to clear away wineglasses, retrieve wayward wrapping or pick the lint off their skirts—anything but look at Pete. And then there's Berni's mother, who was only bargaining on a spirited game of pin the rattle on the donkey. But a spirited game of being pinned by Pete apparently has a certain allure, because she makes her way over to the edge of Berni's chair, claiming her maternal right as heir to the throne.

Pete, catching her drift, bends over suggestively and places his hat jauntily on her head.

"You go, grandma!" Olivia cheers from the sidelines.

"Nobody feels like a grandma when I'm around!" Pete promises, letting out a whoop. He wiggles to the edge of Berni's chair and grabs mother Erica onto his dance floor. He grinds his pelvis in time to the Maroon 5 CD now blaring, bumping hips with Berni's mom on every rotation.

"Whooo!" she yelps, raising her own arms above her head. Then she drops them around Patrolman Pete's neck and wriggles closer to his well-tanned body.

"I'm *lovin'* this woman," Pete hoots, pressing against her tightly.

Apparently, Berni thinks he may be doin' too much lovin', because she gets out of her chair. Up until now, Berni's been a good sport, but this is her mother we're talking about. The woman she'd like to think of as a virgin. And who no doubt feels the same about Berni, despite all evidence to the contrary. Daughters don't want their mothers having sex and mothers don't want their daughters having sex. And still we have a population explosion.

"Nice dancing, mom," Berni says. And then in an effort to break up the happy couple, she uses her stomach as a wedge and plants herself between them. Patrolman Pete, though, misinterprets her move and thinks he's scored a threesome. So what if the mother's sixty-four and a little scrawny and the daughter's nine months gone. By the time he recounts the afternoon's activities to his buddies, those little details will drop by the wayside.

"Lovin' this, loving both of you!" he says grinding lustfully now in all directions. Erica shimmies her hips, but Berni stands there like a stick. Or in her case, an oak tree.

"Loving time is just about over," Berni says firmly. She takes the patrolman's cap off her mom's head and hands it back it to Pete. "Time to call it a wrap. Thanks for the memories." And with that, she loops her arm through Pete's elbow and escorts him toward the door. Make that drags him to the door, since he's in no rush to leave.

"I paid for a full hour," says Olivia petulantly. "Pete doesn't have to go."

"Yes he does," says Berni. "You gotta know when to hold 'em and when to fold 'em."

Olivia, who definitely comes down on the side of wanting to hold him, instead hands Pete her card. "I'm a talent agent. If you need anything, call me. Anything at all." And I swear she bats her eyes.

For once, Berni doesn't parry that she's a talent agent, too.

With Pete gone, Berni's mother and several other women head over to the bartender. Whether Pete's gotten them interested in the only other man left in the room or they need to dull their senses is anybody's guess. Olivia grabs a cosmopolitan and saunters over to Berni with a smug grin plastered on her face.

"This is soo good," she says taking a long sip of her pink drink and pointing out just one more deprivation Berni must suffer in the name of motherhood. "It's a shame you can't drink. But didn't you just love Pete? I figured a stripper was just what you needed since you probably can't have any sex these days."

"At least I did once," Berni says, coming to her own defense.

"And she'll have plenty more," says Hadley Farms' own Priscilla, joining the conversation.

"Not living here," Olivia says scornfully. "From what I hear, everyone was upset when *Sex and the City* ended because sex in the suburbs ended a long time ago."

"Not in this suburb," Priscilla says with a wink. And then whispering to me, "Now that you live here you'll find out what I mean."

Maybe I should have studied the Hadley Farms Handbook more thoroughly.

A stream of women begin coming over to say their good-byes and linger to look one more time at the pile of gifts.

"My goodness, I just realized nobody gave you *The Mozart Effect* tapes," one woman says in a concerned voice. "I'll send some over as soon as I get home. You've got to start playing them the *moment* the babies are born if you really want to raise their IQ."

"I'm not quite sure I want babies who are smarter than I am," Berni says. "I was just planning on propping them up in front of the washing machine and seeing what happens."

The woman doesn't know whether to laugh or call the authorities. But Berni breaks out into a big grin. "Of course I have the Mozart baby tapes. I've been playing them to my tummy since the second trimester," she says. "I swear one of the babies is already kicking in time to the harpsichord."

After the bartender has packed up and all the guests have finally gone, I plop down into a chair. I feel a little guilty thinking about the sticky plates and mounds of pots piled up in the kitchen, but I'm too pooped to look at them.

"Did you have fun at the party?" I ask Berni, putting my feet up on the ottoman next to hers.

"So much fun. I can't thank you enough. But that Olivia is some piece of work, huh? See why I'm glad to be getting out of the business? I'll never know if she thought I'd like the stripper—or if she did it to torture me."

I laugh. "I thought he was kind of cute," I say. "But were you really upset?"

"Not by that," she says with a sigh. "The party was perfect. I couldn't be happier." But she sighs again, this time even deeper. "It was a nice group of women, wasn't it? I guess I was just disappointed that Cameron Diaz was a no-show. I know she's in town and she said she'd stop by. In fact, none of *Charlie's Angels* came. Olivia's right. I guess I'm out of the game. Leave L.A. for five minutes and you're off everybody's speed dial."

"You're still on mine," announces a bright voice from the hallway.

We both turn around to see Kate striding into the room in a sexy but still professional Michael Kors tulip skirt. She kisses me on the cheek and then deposits the huge cellophane-wrapped wicker basket she's carrying next to Berni. Ever since I introduced them, they've become fast friends.

"Darling, I'm so sorry I'm late. I have the best reason. But I'll save it," Kate says, her porcelain skin looking slightly flushed.

"Tell me," Berni says, cheering up. "Except if it involves good sex. I don't think I can bear to hear about that right now."

"Then I'll definitely save it," Kate says with a devilish laugh. "Now open your presents. You'll need every one of them."

Berni fumbles with the oversized pink-and-blue ribbons tied at the top. After the third try, she pushes the basket across the sofa. "Damn, you do it," she says to Kate. "Even my fingers are bloated."

Kate's long, perfectly manicured hands make short work of the ribbons, revealing a tower of fancily packaged boxes, bottles, unguents and ointments.

"What are they?" Berni asks, picking up a shiny silver tube and looking at it quizzically.

"That one's the beeswax belly salve," says Kate. "Really good for stretch marks."

"Wow," says Berni. "Terrific. You can't imagine how much I need that. Or maybe you can." She laughs and picks up another bottle. "And this?"

"Eighty percent pure shea butter. For stretch marks. Lavender belly oil, ditto. And my very own concoction of aloe with vitamin E and extract of tamarind root. Doesn't smell very good, but it's really great . . ."

". . . for stretch marks," Berni finishes.

"Right," says Kate happily.

I look at Kate dubiously. "So which one of them really works?"

"For stretch marks? Nothing," she admits. "But rubbing lotions on your tummy three times a day is better than sitting around worrying about the delivery. Oh, and Berni, I also gave you some fabulous lotion for the babies. Keeps their skin soft."

I thought that was the point about babies—they have naturally soft skin. But maybe without proper intervention, it's all downhill after the first three months. No wonder I'm in trouble. I didn't start using moisturizer until I was twenty-six.

I pick up a pack of teeny bottles with graceful stoppers in the lids. "What are these?" I ask.

"Aromatherapy," Kate says. "Keeps the babies stress-free. Want to try?"

"Stress-free sounds good," I say, dabbing a drop of oil on my wrist. "Could use some of that around here. Next time, bring some extras for Bradford."

Berni looks up sharply at me. "Don't tell me you're having problems with Mr. Wonderful," she says.

"Definitely not," says Kate, answering for me. "No trouble in Paradise. Sara's the happiest woman in the world."

I nod. She's right. Of course I am. Bradford's the love of my life.

Chapter TWO

TWO DAYS LATER, I'm in the Harrison Hotel, which Kate has assured me is the chicest new spot in New York. I can see how the squiggly fuchsia sofas made out of poured cement and the wobbly free-form three-legged tables pass for hip, but I wonder why the dermatologists didn't pick a place with better lighting for their annual "FIGHT AGE!" conference. The yellow fixtures make everyone here look like fugitives from the ICU. And when did "age" become a call to arms anyway? I've tried to Save the Whales, Save the Earth, and Save *Family Guy* from being cancelled. But this is the first time I've rallied to save my face from the demon wrinkle.

Kate's drawn a standing-room-only crowd for her keynote speech, and since I'm sitting uncomfortably in a backless acrylic chair, I think of offering my seat to someone older than I am. If only there were someone. The place is packed with twenty- and thirty-somethings who've barely graduated from Clearasil. Instead of fighting age, shouldn't they be fighting to get into graduate school?

Kate strides to the podium to begin her talk. She's professional and charming, and the audience hangs on her every word. One woman scribbles notes on the palm of her hand—how good can that be for your skin?—and others have brought tape recorders so they can listen to Kate's speech again and again. Maybe they'll replay it when they're jogging in the park, trying to lower their cholesterol. Though I'd worry that listening to an anti-aging tape is more likely to raise their blood pressure.

For over an hour, Kate makes the case for the latest scientific break-throughs that will eliminate brown spots and even out your skin tone. You can even give up sex—though who'd want to, Kate jokes—because the newest LED laser gives your cheeks that rosy post-coital flush. And unlike an orgasm, it lasts all day. She touts a cream that costs four hundred dollars an ounce and comes from dehydrated test-tube-cloned lizard pancreas. Or something like that. The exorbitant price and the exotic ingredients convince most of the audience they've found a gift from God.

During the question-and-answer period, a few women ask high-minded questions about clinical trials and FDA approval. But the main thing on most people's minds is—what are your office hours and how long do I have to wait for an appointment? I hope nobody's having a freckle emergency, because I happen to know that Kate's booked for the next four months. She's made believers of us all.

Well almost all. There's always a naysayer in the crowd who needs to be converted.

"I think all this is a bunch of hokum," says a fair-skinned fortyish year old woman, standing up and identifying herself as Alva. "I don't believe in all this age-defying, age-denying hocus-pocus. You're a doctor so you should know physics. You can't turn back the clock unless you're traveling at the speed of light. And even Einstein couldn't do that."

"That's because Einstein didn't have lasers," Kate says, dismissing the Nobel Prize winner's work as unimportant—relatively. "And trust me, lasers turn back the clock. Come on up here and let me show you a little technological whiz-bang. A miraculous resculpting facial that can give you a fabulous face-lift in five minutes."

Maybe when it comes to beauty, even a skeptic wants to believe, because Alva hesitates for barely a moment before making her way up to the small platform in the front of the room. Kate smiles at her and turns on one of the machines she'd been describing during her lecture. Lights flash and the device emits a buzzing, sizzling sound.

"You're welcome to sit down," Kate tells her genially.

Alva looks at the blinking contraption—and cautiously lowers herself into the chair next to it. Kate gets busy connecting some long wires with saucer-sized electrodes to Alva's forehead, cheeks and double chin. The crowd is suddenly very still. Is this a facial or a scene from *The Executioner*?

"I promise nothing really shocking's going to happen," Kate says, turning to the audience and giving a little wink. She smiles at her subject. "Are you ready to go ahead?"

Alva nods solemnly, and Kate flips the switch. When the lights on the machine start flashing furiously, Alva stoically grips her hands on the armrests and leans back in her seat. If electricity were pulsating through my body, I'd at the very least be worrying about the Con Ed bill.

Kate spends five minutes explaining to the audience how the electrical pulses cause muscle contractions that tighten the skin. The gentle flow of current reduces puffiness, increases circulation, and should give Alva an instant lift.

"So what do you think?" Kate asks the audience as she flips Alva's face from side to side, checking out her work in progress. "Is it going to work? Ready to see the unveiling?"

The audience lets out a few hoots of "Yes!" and "Let's see!" I definitely want to see, because I'm still looking at Alva, whose eyes are closed. And whether she's fallen asleep or dead, I can't really tell.

"Okay, then," Kate says dramatically, her voice deepening. "The big moment." With a flourish, she turns off the machine, removes the electrodes, and strokes her fingertips across Alva's face, patting here and there as if molding a big lump of clay. Finally Kate nods approvingly and hands her patient a mirror.

At first Alva says nothing as she stares at her reflection. Then she breaks out into a big grin and pats her now-tauter cheeks. "My gosh, I really do look better," she says.

"Yes, you're beautiful!" Kate exults.

The audience is on its feet applauding. Loud cheers of "Me next!"

and "Where can I get that?" fill the room. Everyone wants to be the re-
cipient of Kate's next bolt of beauty. The crowd starts pushing toward
the stage, whooping and stomping. If Hewlett-Packard stock had inspired this much enthusiasm, Carly Fiorina would still have a job.

The women gather around and one touches Kate's sleeve as if she
were the pope. Another asks for an autograph. When we were kids Kate
used to say she wanted to save the world. Who knew she'd be doing it
one pimple at a time.

Thirty minutes later, the potential patients are finally out of questions and Kate's out of business cards. She excuses herself and I follow
her as we make a graceful exit.

"So what'd you think?" she asks me happily, on a high from her
worshipers' adulation.

"I feel like I should kiss your ring," I say, laughing. "That woman
really did look good."

"And that's just a sample. The whole process with the dermabra-
sion, collagen and vitamin serum takes at least a couple of hours. It
costs a fortune, but for you, my dear, I'd do it for free."

"I'll add it to the list," I say with a laugh. "How long do your mira-
cles last?"

"A full twenty-four hours."

"And after that your Cinderellas turn back into pumpkins?"

"At least they look good for the ball. Or the Oscars."

"As long as the show doesn't run late," I say.

Kate laughs and links her arm through mine.

"Come on, I promised you lunch. I owe you a Harrison Hamburger
for coming to my speech. Specialty of the house. The chef makes them
with foie gras and caviar."

"Caviar?" I ask. "Hasn't anybody here ever heard of Hamburger
Helper?"

"Yes, they have," Kate says, holding the door open for me. "And
that's why they use caviar. Let me introduce you to my favorite lunch."

But it's not the hamburger I get to meet. As we head toward the
forty-dollar sandwiches in the wildly overpriced hotel restaurant—
modestly billed as The Cafeteria—Kate suddenly comes to a dead halt.

She self-consciously tugs at the hem of her tight Gucci shirt. If she pulls it any harder, I'll get to see that three-hundred-fifty-dollar La Perla bra she swears by. I follow her gaze and see a man rushing across the lobby in our direction, waving at Kate with one hand and scrolling through his Blackberry with the other. He's wearing an expensive wheat-colored linen shirt that amazingly hasn't wilted in the humidity. His crisp olive pants are equally wrinkle-free, and there are no creases on his face, either. Maybe he's been resculpted. I suddenly have a brainstorm. Can Doctor Kate make over any guy so he's the man of her dreams? If so, she might have made the biceps on this one a little bigger.

"I'm here," he says, tucking away his Blackberry and planting a light kiss on Kate's cheek. "Sorry I missed your speech, babe. I was buying a building on Thirty-third Street and it took longer than I thought."

Buying a building? No wonder he's late. Given the price of Manhattan real estate, it would probably take forever just to write all the zeros on the check.

"Let me introduce you. This is Owen Hardy," says Kate, never taking her adoring eyes off of him. "My dear new friend, the fabulous and famous Owen Hardy."

The very tan man in question looks at me expectantly, tapping his foot and waiting for a reaction. He's clearly miffed when he doesn't get one.

"*Owen Hardy,*" he repeats, saying it slower and more loudly. He could announce his name in American Sign Language and Koko the gorilla might get it, but I still won't be able to place him.

Kate tries to come to my rescue. "Owen Hardy. You must see his name all over the city," she prompts. "On buildings. H-A-R-D-Y. Hardy."

So then it hits me. Those great big twenty-foot-high bronze letters on top of half the skyscrapers in New York. Owen Hardy is one of New York's most prominent real estate moguls. Ads for his buildings say *He Trumps Trump!* Owen definitely trumps Donald in the hair department. But I wonder if he can say "You're fired" with as much élan.

"Nice to meet you," I say, shaking his hand.

But my audience with the fabulous and famous Owen Hardy is apparently over, because he glances at his watch and raps his finger on the dial. Is he hyperactive, or is that how he winds his fifty-thousand-dollar Patek Philippe? He grabs Kate's elbow, clearly ready to lead her away. "Sorry to rush, but we better get going. I only have an hour for . . . lunch."

"We were just heading into The Cafeteria," I say innocently. "Why don't you come along."

"Not the kind of lunch I had in mind," he says looking meaningfully at Kate. "I already stopped at the front desk and got us a suite."

Oh, that kind of lunch. And why not? A rich, powerful, well-dressed man about town with his name on dozens of New York buildings. He seems like a pretty good match for my Kate—who might as well enjoy her afternoon tryst without worrying about me.

"Listen, you guys, I just remembered I have to . . . go." Great excuse and very clever. Maybe I can get a job as Dick Cheney's speechwriter. I look at my watch for emphasis and try rapping it. But that's apparently not how you wind a Swatch.

Kate and I say hasty good-byes and she promises to call me later. She and her real estate mogul head to the elevators, and I go in the opposite direction, through the revolving doors and out of the hotel. If I'm buying my own hamburger, it's not going to involve foie gras. But this must be an upscale neighborhood because I have to walk a whole two blocks before hitting a McDonald's. At the counter, I turn virtuous and order a chicken Caesar salad. While I'm eating, I study the nutrition information and let out a gasp. A zillion calories in the Paul Newman dressing. This is as big a con as he pulled off in *The Sting*.

I'm taking another stab at my salad when I feel my cell phone vibrating in my pocket. I see the words I LOVE YOU flashing on the screen, the message Bradford programmed into my phone months ago along with his number.

"So you'll know how I feel every time I call," he'd said, handing it back to me and kissing me gently on the lips.

And kissing him is still the best part of my day. Even when he comes home from work at midnight, exhausted, he still cuddles next to me before falling asleep. And he swears that once the deal he's working on now is done, he'll be more relaxed. Or—as he says—as relaxed as a man who was born in a three-piece suit can possibly be.

"Hi, honey," he says now when I answer the phone. "Where are you?"

"Having lunch," I say, wiping the last incriminating trace of salad dressing from my mouth. As if my cell phone might suddenly turn into one of those camera models.

"Someplace good?" he asks.

Here's a dilemma. Bradford usually eats broiled fish and steamed vegetables for lunch, whipped up by his company's executive chef and delivered to his desk on Limoges china and a silver tray. Should I tell him I've been eating plastic fast food with a plastic fork? Not exactly his style. But I can't lie.

"I just became McDonald's hundred-billionth customer," I say. "I'm hoping I won a free apple turnover."

"Go buy yourself one. My treat," he says with a laugh. "Is Kate with you for your fancy lunch?"

"Nope. Turns out she had other plans."

"So do you, if you can manage it," he says cheerfully. "Can you meet me in an hour? I'm taking your advice and working hard to be more relaxed."

I laugh. "What do you have in mind?"

"A little surprise."

He tells me where to meet him and ten minutes later I'm in a cab, zipping down the FDR Drive. I look appreciatively at the cityscape, glowing in the sunshine, and suddenly HARDY seems to be looming everywhere. When did that happen? Once something hits your radar screen, it seems to pop up all over. I'm pretty sure the family didn't acquire fifty new buildings since lunchtime. Especially since Owen's tied up at the moment.

Owen. So Kate's got a new guy. Good. She's the most gorgeous woman I know but it's been a long stretch between boyfriends. If this works out maybe we can have a double wedding—since I don't seem to be doing anything about planning one on my own. But I don't care what Kate says, no way that fancy pastry chef Sylvia Weinstock is making us one of her famous eight-layered confections. Unless she jumps out of the wedding cake, I'm not spending the twelve hundred dollars.

Still, I'm getting ahead of myself. Owen seems interesting. But does he deserve Kate? Is he good enough? Nice enough? I need more details. I start dialing Kate's number, but then snap my cell phone closed. Occurs to me that she might not be done with . . . lunch. And I know she wasn't having a Caesar salad.

I arrive at Wall Street in record time, and Bradford's waiting in front of a large, corporate-looking building. I see him before he sees me and feel my heart skip a beat. The tall athletic body, curly dark hair and sparkling green eyes get me every time. And that dimple in his right cheek—that God surely put there so he could get away with anything— makes me melt. With the rush of anticipation I still feel every time I see him, I bound over to give him a hug.

"You look great," he says. He gives me a big kiss and flashes the dimple. Melting, part two. Will I still feel this way once we've been married twenty years? It's a risk I'm willing to take.

He takes my hand and gives it a squeeze as we walk toward the elevator. What are we doing at this Wall Street enclave, anyway? Maybe it's Take Your Fiancée to Work Day. Well, I don't care. Whatever Bradford has in mind, I'm game.

When we reach the twenty-third floor, I'm half expecting to see rows of cubicles and computer screens, but instead the door opens into a jungle with a huge cascading waterfall, a thicket of towering elephant-eared plants and the whooshing, hooting and chirping sounds of a rain forest. If this is an office, the workers must swing through trees.

A barefoot woman in a leopard-skin miniskirt bounces toward us with miniature martini glasses filled with a brown, bark-colored liquid.

"Pomegranate cocktails!" she says cheerily. "Filled with anti-oxidants—protects you against cancer, and just as important, every sip makes you look younger!"

Bradford chugs his down immediately but I eye the murky potion more warily. What is this with pomegranate juice? A month ago, I'd never heard of Pom and now it's the Fruit of the Month. Whatever happened to the purported healing powers of grapefruit, blueberries and cranberries? And given the rising cost of health care, shouldn't we all just stick with apples, which at least keep doctors away?

The leopard-clad woman of the forest takes a gulp of the drink herself. "By the way, I'm Jane," she says. As if I couldn't have guessed. I look around the room for Tarzan, but he must be off getting his diptheria shot because he's nowhere in sight.

We dutifully follow Jane into another part of the rain forest, an intimate dimly lit room with two huge lengthwise logs topped with thin foam padding.

"So is this a good surprise?" Bradford asks, taking my hand again and grinning.

"Probably—if I knew what we were doing here," I say, laughing.

"We're in Shangri-La," he says, kissing me as Jane discreetly disappears. "Our chance to relax."

Relax, huh? If we're here for our own nooner, I would have picked the Ritz Carlton. At least the minibar has some unhealthy drinks in it. And I'd like something larger than those twin logs. Not to mention softer.

The luscious Jane comes back, followed by a heavyset gray-haired woman who looks like her job in the jungle might be leading guerrilla warfare.

"Couple's massage," Bradford whispers, coming over and gently unzipping my skirt.

"Do you need robes?" Jane asks perkily.

"No, it's warm in here," says Bradford, unbuttoning his Brooks Brothers shirt and strolling over to a log massage table. He's getting into that ol' relaxed spirit faster than I would have imagined, and seeing Jane eye him appreciatively, I'm thinking that uptight has its upside, after all.

Jane positions herself by Bradford's side. "I'll take him, you take her," Jane announces to her colleague, Olga, who's old enough to be her grandmother.

Feeling not quite so blithe as Bradford, I take my place on the other massage table. From my perch, I see the comely Jane lining up small bottles of aromatic oils for Bradford to choose from.

"Mmmm," Bradford sighs blissfully as Jane wafts one sensuous scent in front of him. "That's heaven."

"We're just starting," she coos, leaning across him to dab a droplet of another fragrant oil on his wrist. "Do you prefer this one?"

What I'd prefer is for Jane to be a little less attentive. But I'm deciding which of the warm oils I'll choose for myself when a dollop of cold, stinging lotion lands square on my back.

"Ouch," I say. "What are you doing?"

"A deep tissue orthopedic myofascial release massage," declares the muscular Olga. "Not that wimpy touchy-feely treatment that Jane gives. You're lucky you got me."

And I'm feeling oh-so-lucky. Another squirt of cold lotion, and then she begins pounding my back as if she were trying to tenderize a too-tough side of beef.

"Could you go a little easier there?" I ask.

"You'll get used to it," Olga says, grinding her elbows into my back and pummeling harder.

The tweet-tweet-tweeting on the background tape that's meant to be calm-calm-calming is definitely not-not-not. Still it's not nearly as annoying as the other noise that's filling the room—the blissed-out moans of my lover being satisfied by a woman. A woman who's not me.

"Honey, you okay?" I call over to him.

"Mmmm. Mmm-hmmm," he replies, apparently too ecstatic to articulate an actual word.

Great. My lover has reached the Seventh Level of Happiness and I'm going ten rounds with Evander Holyfield's mother.

And she won't let up. "Ugh, Ugh. Ugh!" I pant in pain.

Meanwhile, Bradford's sighing happily. "Mmmm-mmmm-mmmm," he murmurs.

"Urgh. Urgh. Urgh," I wheeze, raising the decibel level. Olga won't quit.

"Mmmm-mmmm-mmmm," Bradford sings back contentedly under Jane's gentle hand.

"UGH. URGH. AARGH," I yelp, hitting a louder pitch with each punch.

Finally, Bradford realizes that our mating call is a little off-key.

"What's going on over there?" he asks, raising his head to look over at me. "Everything all right?"

"No. Not all right. This hurts," I say petulantly. I sit up and turn to the mighty masseuse. "Sorry, but I think I'm done. Appreciate your efforts."

"Lie back down," Olga barks, pushing me back toward the table. "You can't leave with half the toxins still trapped in your body."

"Yes she can," Bradford says, marching over with the sheet wrapped around his waist. "If Sara says it's enough, it's enough."

That's nice. The hero coming to my rescue. I'd almost forgotten how lovely the whole white knight thing can be.

But Olga's not giving in that easily. "I can't stop now," she says, firmly positioning her hands back on my shoulders.

Bradford gives Olga an icy stare. "We're done. You're done. Please leave now," he says quietly. But his tone leaves no room for doubt.

"Fine, I'll go," Olga says haughtily. She turns on her orthopedic heel to stomp out of the room. "But don't come back complaining that all your free radicals haven't been freed."

I'm not worried. The only free radicals I complain about are the ones who tie up traffic at the World Economic Forum every year.

"You can leave, too, Jane," Bradford says in a softer tone.

"You sure?" Jane purrs seductively. "I like to finish what I started."

"No, I'm done," Bradford says. "Thanks. But we'd appreciate the use of the room for a few more minutes."

Once Jane's gone, Bradford wraps his arms around me and lets the sheet at his waist fall to the floor.

"Sorry that didn't work out as well as I'd hoped. Looks like I still owe you a massage," he says, sweetly kissing my ear. He guides me back to the table and begins caressing my shoulders.

"Would you like the warm patchouli oil?" he asks, rubbing a few drops between his hands.

"Whatever you suggest," I say, suddenly more in the mood.

He slowly moves his hands from my shoulders and slides them around my waist. Drawing his own body closer, he begins sensuously caressing my back.

"Now this is the kind of massage I like," I say. I close my eyes and leave myself entirely in his hands. Which is where I should have been in the first place.

"Aaaaah," I say, letting out a long, luxurious sigh. I turn and wrap my body around his, feeling his muscular thighs pressed against mine.

"Aaaaah," he sighs happily. "Aaaah."

The mating call is back in sync. And "aaah" trumps "mmm" anytime.

The next morning, I put Dylan on the bus for day camp, checking his backpack for the requisite towel, two bathing suits, change of shorts, suntan lotion, sunburn cream (in case the counselor forgets to apply the lotion), granola bar (in case he doesn't like what they serve for lunch), tennis racket, baseball cap, baseball glove and goggles. Incredibly, we've gone through only four pairs of goggles and it's already the last week of camp. Dylan must be getting older. But not that old. As the bus pulls up, I'm still allowed to give him a big hug good-bye in full view of his buddies.

I want to make a special dinner for Bradford tonight to thank him for the massage. My first impulse is to go in to the city and head down to the friendly Italian butcher at my old West Village neighborhood. But no, I'm a suburbanite now, so I climb into our Volvo SUV. Being from Manhattan, it's my very first car, and I still consider driving an extreme sport. ESPN isn't covering the event today because I'm only heading over to our local Gourmet Meat Designs. A whole different competitive sport. At least I'm properly attired for shopping there— although where else in the world do you have to dress up to buy a chicken? Even free range.

Still, the little storefront is packed, and given how the man behind the counter ignores me, maybe my clothing's not up to the job after all.

Next time, high heels. Finally, he deigns to look at me, and I quickly ask, "How much veal do I need for three people?"

Without bothering to answer, he begins slicing and quickly hands me the wrapped package—clearly ready to help someone with larger ambitions. I miss my old butcher. At least his apron wasn't designed by Gucci.

I stop by the local fancy carb emporium S.U.G.A.R. to pick up a D.E.S.S.E.R.T. I look at the Sacher torte, so small that Dylan would probably polish it off before dinner. For thirty-six dollars, I'd rather have it mounted and hung on the wall. Maybe cookies, then. Although at five dollars apiece, one late-night snack attack and I could bankrupt even Bradford.

A couple more errands and I head back with lots of packages and an empty wallet. Given what the Gristedes up here charges for Ultra Charmin, it better be ultra-ultra. No telling what the local post office charges for thirty-seven-cent stamps.

When I open the door to the house I'm hit by an icy cold blast of air. I shiver and check the air conditioner thermostat, which is set at a frosty fifty-eight.

"Consuela?" I call out, trying to figure out what's going on.

Our housekeeper trudges out of the kitchen, wearing a parka and wool mittens. Bradford's black lab Pal comes trailing dutifully behind her, dressed in a royal blue doggie sweater. I wouldn't say Pal is spoiled, but he does have a dog walker who comes in three times a day. When he gained two pounds, she insisted on taking him to the gym and working him out on the treadmill, but we drew the line at putting him on Atkins. The other day, she reprimanded me for taking Pal along on my morning bike ride.

"Now he's too tired for a proper walk," she chided. "What will the other dogs say?"

I wanted to tell her they probably wouldn't say a single word. And if they did, she should stop walking them and start booking them on David Letterman.

"Miss Berni is here again," Consuela says now, shaking her head and pointing toward the living room. "Those twins better get born soon or we're all going to freeze to death."

Berni has assumed her usual position on the Betsy Ross couch, and she's flipping through a Victoria's Secret catalogue.

"I stopped getting these at my house," she says. "Even the mailman can't imagine that I'll ever wear a teddy again."

"Oh come on, even pregnant you're still hot," I say.

"You have no idea how hot," Berni groans, now using the catalogue as a fan. "How did I let my husband convince me to move to New York in the summer before the house was finished and with no air-conditioning? He gave me some song and dance about sea breezes. What did I think? We were moving to Bali?"

I laugh and wrap a blanket around my shoulders.

"Thank God for you and your central air-conditioning," Berni continues. "My internal temperature's at a hundred and ten, but we can't even put a temporary window unit in the bedroom. The community board says it'll destroy the integrity of Hadley Farms. Oh please. All anybody cares about around here is how things look from the outside. I didn't have to leave L.A. for that. Doesn't anybody care about the inner me?"

"Sure they do. Your husband and your nutritionist," I say. "Not to mention your obstetrician." I pull the blanket a little tighter around me. Is it my imagination, or is it so cold in here that I can see my breath?

"Oh, shit," says Berni. She brings her hand quickly to her mouth. "I didn't mean to say 'shit.' I meant 'damn.' I promised myself I wouldn't swear in front of the twins." She pats her stomach and looks down remorsefully. "Sorry, guys."

"What's wrong?" I ask, less concerned about her language than her going into labor. "Are you okay?"

"Yeah, but I forgot. My client Kirk. Or former client. I said I'd meet him at a photo shoot today in Manhattan to lend my support. He's going to be one of *People* magazine's Fifty Sexy Young Stars. Do you want to come?"

"Which one is he?" I ask, trying to click through the clients Berni has told me about.

"The hunk I discovered working in a Santa Monica car wash. He had his shirt on but I could still recognize his talent. Now he plays Dr. Lance Lovett on that medical soap opera. You know the one—*Days of Our Knives.*"

"Then let's go," I say, jumping up. Even a sweaty car on Metro North would be more appealing than this Arctic igloo. The place feels like the set for *The Day After Tomorrow.* Now that I know global warming makes the world colder, I might stop using hair spray.

Consuela comes in with the hood on her parka pulled up tightly now, carrying a silver tray. "Hot chocolate?" she offers, holding out steaming mugs.

"Thanks, Consuela, but we're going out," I say, trying to stifle a laugh.

"Right," says Berni. She gets up and looks longingly one more time at the Victoria's Secret catalogue before tossing it into the wastebasket.

Berni and I hop on the train and arrive at Grand Central Station in the advertised thirty-eight minutes. We head down to a huge studio loft by the Hudson River, where dozens of photo assistants, lighting assistants, and cappuccino-fetching assistants are all busily scurrying around. At the center of the activity is a beautiful dark-skinned girl with multicolored hair wearing a tight white sparkly dress.

"That's Eve," Berni whispers to me. "Very happening rap star."

But what's happening with Berni right now is that she's already exhausted and goes across the studio to sit down. I stay mesmerized where I am, watching in fascination as Eve poses in the light box, three feet from the photographer. Her skin glistens and a makeup artist rushes to dust her face with powder and polish her arms and shoulders.

"Is this the place for the Sexy Stars?" someone behind me asks in a deep, masculine voice.

I turn around, and find myself looking into a chiseled face framed by blond, spiky hair. "Apparently," I say. The hunky guy in front of me is broad shouldered and muscular. When he gives a little smile, his liquid-blue eyes twinkle.

"Are you one of the stars in the photo shoot, too?" he asks, flashing a bright grin.

"I'm . . . I'm . . ." apparently I'm stuttering. "I'm just a friend," I say, collecting myself.

"Sorry, I thought you were one of the sexy stars," he says.

The man must have a PhD. from the George Clooney Charm School. But I find myself smiling.

Just then he spots Berni, who's sprawled in a canvas-backed director's chair.

"You're here!" he says, rushing over and throwing his arms around her. "And you look fabulous!"

Berni waves her arm dismissively but still looks pleased. What is it about a handsome guy slinging a compliment? Even fake flattery is a better mood enhancer than two Zolofts and an Entenmann's coffee cake.

I come over to join Berni and she quickly introduces me to Kirk.

"We've already met," Kirk says, smiling and turning to me. "Sorry if I'm a little sweaty. I didn't get to the gym today so I power-walked over from the set of *Knives*."

Power walking usually means going fast—but with a soap star, it could mean he got to walk with the director.

Kirk's supposed to be next up with the photographer. The frazzled wardrobe mistress—dressed in a silver Mylar micromini layered over tutti-frutti tights—comes over and, completely ignoring Berni and me, grabs him by the arm.

"We have to get you into some clothes," she says hurriedly, pointing across the studio to the five wardrobe racks she has ready for him.

"Aren't these clothes?" Kirk asks, holding out his faded black T-shirt. "My favorite jeans. I'll just wear these."

Seems like he's a regular guy with no posse and no pretentions. I like that. But the wardrobe mistress doesn't.

"No jeans. No T-shirts. No black," she says, ruling out just about everything that Kirk probably owns. "We have to make you look sexy."

That shouldn't be hard. Is the woman blind? Nature already took care of it. Still, Kirk amiably agrees to follow the wardrobe mistress to her racks across the room. Though given the way she's dressed, I wouldn't let her outfit a Barbie.

"You go, too," Berni tells me, sighing. "I can't move. Make sure he looks good."

Since there's no dressing room, Kirk strips down to his gray spandex Calvin Kleins and begins flicking through the clothes. While he's checking out Armani, Versace and some pretty cool Hugo Boss, I'm checking out his well-cut abs. Much better than Patrolman Pete's. I sure have seen a lot of nearly naked men lately. And I don't even watch Bravo.

Kirk holds up a buttery-soft brown leather jacket. "Do you like this one?" he asks, slipping it on over his bare chest and skivvies.

"It's great!" I say, thinking it looks particularly good without pants. Kirk could single-handedly destroy Seventh Avenue since the less he wears, the better he looks.

Berni suddenly appears behind me and clutches my arm.

"Water," she says in a hoarse whisper.

I turn around and notice beads of perspiration dripping down her forehead. "Let me get you some," I say. "There's some Pellegrino over there."

"Not that kind of water," Berni says, looking like she might pass out.

"I don't like Pellegrino either. Too many bubbles," Kirk says, digging into his backpack for his private stash. "Here—try my Vitamin Water."

"I don't need vitamins. I need an ambulance," Berni moans. "Water. My water broke."

"Oh my god!" I scream. I look around wildly, trying to remember what I'm supposed to do. Call the doctor? Call her husband? Call Pratesi to see if the damn layette ever came in? But the nearly naked Kirk is quickly at her side.

"Let me help. I'm not a doctor, but I play one on TV," he says calmly, putting his arm around Berni and ushering us all toward the exit.

"Are you going to deliver her right here?" I ask, ever more panicked.

"No, I'm going to deliver her to the hospital," Kirk says with a smile. He pulls on a pair of pants, exchanges a few quick words with one of the photo assistants and by the time we get downstairs, a cab is waiting. We all pile into the backseat.

"Let's time those contractions," Kirk says as the driver speeds off, diving through a few potholes and scoring a near miss with a pedestrian. "How far apart are they?"

That mellifluous voice in a doctor—or in this case, an actor—is a real plus. With one of Kirk's big, strong arms around her Berni seems to relax. When the contractions come, he talks her through the breathe-in breathe-out that everyone forgets in the crunch. In between, he has her laughing and licking a lollipop that he has with him. "Part of the actor's emergency kit," he explains. "Keeps your lips moist at auditions."

By the time we get to the hospital, Berni's forgotten that Kirk's medical license came with his SAG card, and she's more than a little disappointed when the nurse wants to call in a certified MD.

"Kirk's doing fine," Berni argues. "Six months on that soap and he can deal with anything. Can the obstetricians around here do a heart transplant? Separate Siamese twins? Has any one of them ever brought a cadaver in the morgue back to life? Because Kirk has."

Berni's so passionate, she's even got me convinced that Kirk's the man for the job. But the nurse decides otherwise. She gives Kirk a lascivious glance, but in the end professionalism gets the better of her. Either that, or his bare chest under the leather jacket is undercutting Kirk's authority.

"It's okay, Berni," Kirk says, giving her a kiss on the cheek as the nurse prepares to wheel her to the maternity floor. "Delivering twins is easy. So easy, we never do less than triplets on the show."

"The show," calls out Berni, suddenly remembering that she has at least five minutes left as an agent before she turns into a full-time mom. "As soon as I'm finished here, I'll call the producer. From now on, you don't deliver anything less than quints."

Chapter THREE

I STAY WITH BERNI for close to an hour until her husband Aidan rushes in, holding a bedraggled bunch of daisies he obviously picked up at a Korean market on his way, and the Kate Spade overnight bag that Berni had packed for the hospital weeks ago.

"How are you?" Aidan asks, kissing Berni and stroking his hand across her brow. "Sorry it took me so long. I left the edit studio as soon as you called. But I was way downtown and the guy at the garage had jammed ten other cars in front of mine." He pauses, flustered, trying to figure out what he's supposed to say now. Unlike Kirk, he's not working from a script. "Anyway, wish I got here faster."

"Maybe you can get these babies moving a little faster," Berni wails, shifting from one side to the other, unable to find a comfortable position. "When the hell am I getting the epidural?"

"Soon," Aidan says patronizingly, stroking her forehead again and trying to distract her from the clicking monitors, the clucking nurses and the contractions that are coming closer and closer together. "Very soon."

"How do you know?" Berni asks, agitated. "You just got here."

Aidan looks at me, and I can see he's at a loss. So I chime in.

"Good news," I say cheerfully. "The doctor says the labor's going well. Right now it looks like it'll be a natural delivery. No C-section."

"How's that good news?" Berni roars. "I'm forty-two already. I don't have much time. The least they could do is get these babies out of me. Isn't anybody going to do any work around here but me?"

"I've been working on the movie," Aidan says defensively, trying to elevate cutting a film to the same league as cutting the umbilical cord. "And guess what? The set designer offered to come by the hospital and feng shui the room. He said not to deliver before he gets here."

"I'll just hang on until he can rearrange the furniture and paint the door red," Berni says irritably.

"He said he wouldn't charge us," Aidan says, as if the bargain will ease the pain. "Volunteered his services."

"Well I didn't mean to volunteer mine," Berni screams at her husband. "I don't want to do this anymore. In fact, I'm not sure why I agreed in the first place. If you ever want more babies you can do the whole thing in a test tube. Or find somebody else. Preferably somebody with wider hips."

Aidan resists making the obvious point that at the moment, when it comes to size, Berni's hips are unsurpassed. Instead, he squeezes her hand and gives her another kiss. Thank goodness for Lamaze class. It teaches women how to count their breaths during labor and teaches men how to count to ten during their wives' predictable rants.

"I'm here for you, honey," Aidan says. "Fifteen hours, twenty hours, however long it takes. I'm yours."

I worry that Berni's reaction to the time line will blow the roof off the place, but instead, she sighs and puts both hands into Aidan's. "I'm glad you're with me," she concedes. "This could be a long night. How many years have we been married? Twelve? I hope you have a few stories left I haven't heard."

He laughs. "It's not going to be so bad. The whole thing's like directing a movie. Long hours and a lot of junk food, but it doesn't matter because you create something great."

I'm hoping Berni's delivery doesn't end up at the Loew's Cineplex or in reruns on TNT. But Berni seems happy to think of herself as Orson

Welles in a maternity gown. She looks into Aidan's eyes and lies back peacefully. Given the way the contractions have been going, I'm figuring her bliss could last another four minutes and twenty-seven seconds.

Before time runs out, I blow Berni a kiss and tell her I'm heading out. There's not much more I can do around here unless the feng shui guy arrives and needs help hanging crystals and spreading his good chi.

"You've been great, Sara," Berni says, giving me a feeble smile. "You're a terrific friend. Thanks for getting me here."

"Actually, I'm the one who got you here." Aidan laughs, rubbing her belly. "But Sara, you really are great. Once the babies are born, you'll be our first call."

"Second call," Berni says. "Right after the admissions office at Yale."

Outside in the fresh air, happy to be alive and not in labor, I turn my cell phone back on. The signs in the hospital had warned that making calls would interfere with vital equipment. Oh, please. Millions of dollars' worth of monitors and EKG machines are going to be screwed up by my twenty-buck Nokia? Just how much faith can you have in a hi-tech ICU if it doesn't know the difference between a call coming in and a patient on his way out?

Three text messages are waiting for me, all from Kate. One insists I call immediately. The second gives an address where I should meet her. The third sounds an alarm. "Emergency! Get here right away!" and gives a few words of explanation. As a doctor, Kate is trained to recognize a traumatic situation—and she's certainly in the midst of one right now. No woman should have to face buying a tankini on her own.

I walk briskly over to meet her at Sunshine Beach, the famous bathing suit boutique where you can get less fabric for more money than anywhere else in New York. I push through the fingerprint-free glass door—somebody must be on Windex duty 24/7—and gingerly step inside. The store is so chic that I've heard Winona Ryder has given up Saks to shoplift here exclusively. The music is blaring, the lights are white-hot, and so many mirrors are scattered at different angles in the room you'd think someone was trying to solar-power a rocket to Mars. Preening in front of those mirrors is a gaggle of model-beautiful customers, all long-haired, long-legged, and short on flaws.

I sigh and turn away. These are not my people. The whole scene is enough to convince me that the only reasonable place to try on a bathing suit is in a dark cave far, far away from the other villagers. Or to buy one online late at night while eating Mallomars. Sure, you can use the Internet for research, communication, and creating a global community. But it's made an even bigger contribution to humanity. I can digitally try on a Lands' End bikini without ever having to look at my thighs.

Kate is nowhere to be seen, so I call her on my cell phone to tell her that I'm at the store.

"You are? Thank God. I'm just in the fitting room." I catch a glimpse of her face peeking out briefly from behind one of the satin curtains. Then she disappears. "Owen's taking me for a romantic weekend and I need something sexier than last year's La Blanca. I'll be out in a sec."

While I'm waiting, I saunter over to peruse the limited edition bathing suits, each hanging importantly on its own individual rack. Most of the gossamer mesh and gold-grommet confections look like they'd dissolve in a swimming pool faster than a Listerine breath strip. There's not a swim-friendly Speedo or a black one-piece Anne Cole in sight. And nothing with Lycra panels to hold in extra flab. Sunshine Beach patrons must do all their tummy tucking at the plastic surgeon.

Kate emerges from her dressing room wearing her trademark spike heels and a lace eyelet side-tied bikini.

"Looks good," I say, truly impressed with Kate's forty-year-old body.

"You're right. Not bad," Kate agrees, pivoting in front of the mirror. But she pauses midspin and pinches the back of her perfect thigh. "Is the cellulite too disgusting? Like cottage cheese?"

I look for some evidence of lumps, bumps or even a grain of sand that might be stuck to Kate's thigh. Nothing. "Smoothest thing I've ever seen. More like pasteurized Velveeta than cottage cheese. Owen will eat it up," I add.

"Maybe Owen would like a halter top better," she says. Then giving me a little wink, she adds, "I figure if I look good enough, I can get him to give me a full-service massage. Like yours."

It definitely won't be as good as mine. But I'm glad to have given

Kate some ideas. That's what best friends are for. No secrets. We tell each other everything.

Kate disappears into her dressing room, and I continue looking through the racks for a bathing suit that's compatible with chlorine. Or even salt water. I stop at one hanger that has two identical strings, each sporting three very small black crocheted squares. I hold the pieces in front of my body and start turning them as if they're a Rubik's cube. But I can't line up the squares to cover the requisite body parts. I wouldn't even know how to wear this thing to a nude beach.

Giving up, I wander to the seating area in the back of the store. Half a dozen men are comfortably lolling on deep-cushioned leather couches, having generously decided that just this once, they can skip the baseball game to come shopping with their girlfriends or wives. What a sacrifice. I figure a guy deserves points if he's at your side buy-ing the shower curtain at Ikea. Not when he's waiting in front of the bikini-modeling mirror.

I rifle through a *New York Times* on the table, and since the front page is too depressing and the Home section has already been stolen— now I'll never know what happened at the Milan Furniture Expo—I reach for the Metro section. And there above the fold is a familiar face. I look again, suddenly excited. It's Owen Hardy, beaming and looking handsome in a tux. He's standing in a floral-filled tent at some glam-orous affair, surrounded by equally glamorous admirers.

I smile smugly. Pretty neat. My best friend's boyfriend, right there in *The New York Times*. I'm just two degrees of separation from a celebrity. I grab the section and start to walk toward Kate's dressing room. "Kate," I call as I get closer. "Did you see this? Owen's in the paper and . . ."

My voice trails off as I read the caption and stop dead in my tracks.

I go back to the couch and read the caption again. Maybe the paper got the ID wrong. Could be they'll print a retraction tomorrow. But no, this is *The New York Times*. Ever since the Jayson Blair scandal they don't declare that the world is round unless they can fact-check it with Christopher Columbus. Still, I read the article, hoping that the attrac-tive woman with the diamond necklace and her arm snaked around Owen's waist is really his sister. Or, given today's plastic surgery mira-

cles, his mother. Anything but what the paper claims. That the sophisticated blonde standing next to Owen is his wife.

I keep reading and it's even worse than I think. Owen and his wife
weren't just attending the party, they were hosting it. A little charity
benefit at their upstate retreat. Twenty acres including a team of race-
horses, a pond stocked with exotic fish and a brood of champion golden
retrievers. Everything but a dancing bear.

I put the paper down. So where does Kate fit into this pretty picture? It doesn't sound like there's a lot of room. Does she even know
about this? She must.

Across the store I see her flouncing out of the dressing room
wearing the same bikini bottom but a striped halter top. I rush over
to her.

"Kate," I blurt, the moment she's in earshot. "Owen's married. Did
you know? Did he ever tell you?"

In the mirror, I see Kate's pale face redden.

"Of course he told me," she says carefully.

"When were you going to mention it to me?" I ask, thinking how
pleased I was a few minutes ago that we never keep secrets from each
other.

Kate fiddles with the halter top. "Sorry, Sara," she says apologetically. "I wanted you to have a chance to get to know him. Because it's
not the way it sounds."

"It sounds bad. Bad like a fourth-grade cello concert. But this one
probably won't improve."

"It might," Kate says, turning around to look at me with her big
saucer eyes. "The situation with Owen's more complicated than you
think."

Complicated? Seems pretty simple to me. Married men are right up
there with carbs, Easy Stride shoes, and blind dates arranged by your
pastor—or with your pastor—as things every single woman should avoid.

"All right, tell me all about it," I say, trying not to be judgmental.
First I'll listen to my best friend's story. Then I'll tell her why she's ruining her life.

"Owen and his wife aren't getting along all that well," Kate says, launching into her defense. "They've talked about a separation. Or he's thinking about talking about it. Something like that."

"What do you expect him to tell you? That they're building their dream house in Tahiti?"

"Owen tells me the truth," Kate says.

"The truth is he's not leaving her," I say firmly. "They never leave. You should know that. Don't you watch *Oprah*? 'Married Men Talk But Never Walk.' "

"Make it into a bumper sticker and I'll put it on my car." Kate sighs. "Look, it doesn't matter to me. Owen and I care about each other and we have fun. That's all that counts. What we have is exciting—and pretty damn sexy."

I'm sure it is. An affair with a married man has so much intrigue. All those whispered conversations. All those clandestine meetings. All those chocolates the hotel maid leaves when she turns down your bed mid-day. But that's not the point.

"Married men are lethal," I say. "I'm worried about you."

"Don't be," Kate says. "Owen's definitely non-toxic."

"Also non-single, non-marriageable and non-available for Christmas dinners or family events," I say, trying to make my point. Though I have to admit there's an upside to missing Christmas dinner with in-laws.

Kate picks up a pair of Persol sunglasses and a sparkly hair clip that the salesgirl has discreetly left in front of the mirror, right next to the flowery sarong, jeweled mules, Louis Vuitton beach bag, and matching Christian Dior towel. All de rigueur accessories when buying a swim-suit. These days you need more equipment to lie out in the sun than to climb the Himalayas.

"I don't care about non-marriageable," Kate says, looking me squarely in the eye. "I really don't. I've finally given up looking for Mr. Perfect. I've been around long enough to know there's more than one way to live your life. I have a great practice, great friends and now I have a great guy. How many women can say that? I'm happy."

"You can't be happy," I say. "Admit it. Secretly, you want to get married. You think he's going to leave her."

"Nope," Kate says resolutely. "I don't expect him to leave his wife and it doesn't matter." She looks carefully at the glittery hair clip and uses it to pull back her perfectly cut, perfectly shiny hair. Then she comes over and rubs my arm. "Listen, I'm not against love and marriage. I think it's great that you and Bradford found each other. But Owen and I have something terrific going. I don't know where it'll lead. I'm just going to enjoy."

I'm sure she will. At least for a while. Kate's in that first flush of infatuation where the relationship seems inviolable, the guy can do no wrong, and rationality goes out the window. Reasoning with her at this point would be as impossible as trying to disconnect a teenager from her iPod. For now, I might as well give up and go for a more neutral topic.

"So where's Owen taking you this weekend that you need this new bathing suit?" I ask, looking at her in her teeny-weeny halter bikini. "I hope it's Rio, otherwise you might get arrested."

"Do you think it's too skimpy?" she asks, looking in the mirror, and tugging at the bottom.

"No, you pull it off brilliantly," I say honestly, realizing that Kate, at least, didn't forfeit her right to wear a bikini when she traded in Bonne Bell Lip Smackers for Bobbi Brown concealer.

"Not too young for me?" she asks, still hesitating.

"You look better in that suit than any twenty-year-old possibly could," I confirm.

Kate glances over at a young blonde who's parading around in the Rubik's cube bikini—and all the squares are in the right place. The girl has a great body—and she obviously knows how to solve algorithms.

"Maybe not any twenty-year-old, but you do look pretty darn good," I say, laughing. I peek into Kate's dressing room and see three more suits waiting. "Want to go try on the others?"

"No, this one's just right," Kate says, taking one last appraising glance.

"I don't mind waiting," I tell her.

"I like this one," Kate says, heading off to change.

What other woman could find the right bikini so fast? And be confident enough that it *is* just right—without fussing and trying on thirty others? I've got to say this about Kate. She knows what she wants. Unfortunately, at the moment, she seems to want Owen.

I call over to the hospital three times, but by seven o'clock at night, Berni still hasn't delivered.

"Do you want me to come over?" I ask Aidan, when I reach him on the phone.

"No, that's okay. The room's already pretty crowded. The nurses. The doctors. The drummer."

"The drummer?" I ask.

"Mood music for delivery," Aidan explains. "Gets you back to your basic primordial rhythms."

"Is it working?" I ask.

"I can't tell. You could probably bring in the whole London Symphony Orchestra and it wouldn't make a difference right now."

"And the hospital doesn't mind having Ringo playing on the maternity ward?" I ask.

"We didn't get Ringo," Aidan apologizes, not realizing that I didn't really expect the hallways to be crawling with Beatles. "The drummer came with the deluxe package. It was one of the reasons we picked this hospital. Berni showed you the brochures, didn't she?"

She sure did. When I delivered Dylan, the only goody I got was a take-home bag with Pampers and Pond's cold cream. Now with so much competition for the baby business, choosing a hospital is like deciding between luxury hotels. Choice of Frette sheets or Anichini. Reflexologists or accupressurists. Not to mention birthing bed or birthing pool—which shouldn't even be a choice. Some crazy expert or other decided that since the baby has already spent nine months in a womb full of water, why not deliver her into a pool of water? Berni nixed the suggestion. She decided Mommy and Me swim class would be quite enough.

"So are you eating?" I ask Aidan, remembering that Berni had pre-ordered a lobster and steak dinner for him.

"There's a great spread here, but I don't dare touch it. It doesn't seem fair. Berni's on ice chips, I'm on ice chips," he says supportively.

"Well, if you faint from hunger, at least you're in a hospital," I say. "Hang in there. Call with any news." I decide not to add that I'm on my way to have dinner at some fancy Chinese restaurant in midtown that Bradford has suggested we try.

Twenty minutes later, I pick up Dylan in the West Village from a play-date with his best friend, and we head to Sianese Palace. It's supposed to be the new hot place, but it sounds to me like a hoity-toity name for a nasty nasal infection. The white-gloved doorman opens the restaurant's heavy gold door, and I wonder what Bradford could possibly have been thinking. Has he forgotten what it's like to have a seven-year-old? Given that there's a noisy, kid-friendly Chinese joint in New York on every corner, did Bradford have to pick an elegant room where the loudest sound seems to be the ping of Perrier splashing into crystal goblets?

Dylan looks around the hushed, child-free room, tugs at the collar on his polo shirt worn especially for the occasion, and looks dubiously at the maître d'.

"Do you have fortune cookies?" Dylan asks hopefully.

"Pardon me, sir?" The maître d', dressed in a tuxedo and bow tie, looks at him uncertainly.

"Fortune cookies. The Chinese restaurant we used to go to had a big bowl in front."

"This is *not* a Chinese restaurant," the maître d' says haughtily. "We're Chinese-Thai-French fusion." He lays down the menus grandly and holds out a chair for me.

What could possibly happen when you fuse all those cuisines? General Tso's chicken paté? Moo goo gai pan bouillabaisse? Must have taken a host of green cards to open this place.

We sip on lemonades for a while, waiting for Bradford. But when he still doesn't appear, I order rice wontons for Dylan, who's thrilled by the rainbow-colored crackers and works his way happily through the bowl.

I order another round. Starved myself by now, I absentmindedly munch on a pink one.

"Eew," I say, tossing it onto the table. "Tastes like Styrofoam. How can you eat those things?"

"I like them," he says, grabbing another handful. Then he yawns. "I'm full. Can we go?"

The waiter has stopped refilling our water glasses since he's now figured we're making a dinner out of the crunchy Styrofoam wontons. At $4.95 a clip, I think the tab's running up just fine, but he has other ideas. He can't expect that everyone will order the hundred fifty dollar per person Taste-of-the-World Tasting Menu, but he had to be hoping we'd spring for at least a couple of egg rolls.

I'm getting as pissed off as the waiter. Where is Bradford? At least I can keep Dylan amused in the meantime. I pull out two pens and a piece of white paper and put it on the table between us.

"Tic-tac-toe or battleship?" I ask.

"Battleship!" Dylan says with a grin, grabbing a pen.

I draw six rows of six evenly-spaced dots and we take turns making connecting lines. The beginning goes quickly, and then it comes down to some hard choices. Dylan triumphantly closes the first box and claims it with a "D."

"I'm winning!" he hollers.

"Got a long way to go, buddy," I tell him, laughing.

He closes three more. "Still winning! Killing you, mom! You're so lame!"

The elderly couple at the next table eyes us disapprovingly, as irritated as if we were playing roulette in the middle of the Metropolitan Opera House.

Bradford, finally coming up behind us, shares their displeasure. Not realizing there's a paper on the table, or that I'm drawing as well, he grabs Dylan's pen from his hand.

"We don't draw on tablecloths, young man," he says sternly.

Since he hasn't bothered with hello, I don't either.

"Why not?" I say, jumping up and jumping to Dylan's defense.

"Lots of great artists have drawn on tablecloths. Picasso did it. And so did Dubuffet."

"That was different. They were famous."

"Maybe Dylan will be famous, too," I say.

"We weren't drawing on the tablecloth, anyway," Dylan says, since we've both missed the point. He holds up the now-checkered sheet of paper. "See? Look."

Bradford looks contrite. He tosses me a wan smile and tousles Dylan's hair. "Sorry, guys," he says, slumping into a chair. "It's been a rough day. I need a Diet Coke and then I'll feel better."

I try to smile, but I'm still vaguely annoyed at Bradford. Forty minutes late and the first thing he does is snap at us. I've got to say this for Bradford, though—when he knows he's wrong, he immediately tries to make amends. He takes the paper Dylan's still holding and looks at it carefully.

"All those D's are your points?" Bradford asks, impressed.

"Yup," Dylan says, nodding.

"You're really killing your mom, Dyl, huh?"

"Just what I told her!" Dylan crows.

"You guys want to finish the game?" Bradford asks, loosening his tie, and then, remembering where he is, tightening it back up again. "I'll referee."

"Are you kidding?" I say. "No way I can make a comeback. Thanks for the save."

Bradford takes my hand. "That's what I'm here for," he says, and then he mouths, "Forgive me?"

I squeeze his hand and Bradford kisses me on the cheek. The waiter comes over, sizes up Bradford and looks relieved. Finally, someone at our table who might order the Peking duck. Bradford reads the funny French-Chinese-Thai food names from the menu and lets Dylan pick his favorites. Fortunately, the food's not quite as exotic as I'd feared.

"I like the one with the 'dragon' in it," Dylan says, leaning over Bradford's shoulder to look at the menu.

"Me, too, Dyl. Let's get it. And how about the one named after the emperor." All in all, they pick out six dishes and two appetizers and Bradford asks the waiter to bring the chopsticks.

"For three," he says.

"Nope. I need a fork," Dylan says, looking slightly abashed.

But when the chopsticks arrive, Bradford has a plan. He secures a rubber band from the now-fawning waiter—ordering eight expensive dishes guarantees our water glasses are quickly refilled—and expertly wraps the top of two chopsticks so they click in unison.

"Try this," Bradford says, placing Dylan's fingers around the chopsticks and showing him how easily they now work. "It's how my daughter Skylar learned. She mastered it before our trip to China."

"Can we go to China?" Dylan asks, excitedly clicking away. "I think I've got it!"

"Sure. We'll go all sorts of places. Ever been to Paris?"

I give him a raised eyebrow. Bradford knows how I feel about giving kids too much too soon. Just because you can afford to do everything doesn't mean you should. Catching my drift, he adds quickly, "Maybe we'll start with a trip this fall up the Taconic to go apple-picking. Ever done that?"

"Yup," Dylan says disappointed, dreams of the Great Wall dashed by visions of manual labor. "Mommy and I do it every year. Last year I ate so many apples I threw up in the car on the way home."

"We won't let that happen this year," Bradford promises. "Skylar can keep tabs on you."

"It's going to be fun having her," I say. "We're so excited Skylar's coming home from her summer trip in two days. It'll be great to be all together."

Dylan grunts. Maybe I'm the one looking forward to it. Well, mostly. I'm a little wary of the arrangement—Skylar will be alternating weeks at her mom's house and ours. But I know we'll make it work. I have this cockeyed image of a happily blended extended family, with Skylar good-naturedly offering me back-to-school fashion tips. And she'll be my ticket into all those bubble-gum movies I secretly love but am embarrassed to go see myself. Teens need an adult to get into

R-rated flicks. And any self-respecting adult needs a thirteen-year-old girl in tow to fully enjoy *The Princess Diaries*.

"Skylar called from Rome today," Bradford says, clicking his own chopsticks. "She liked the Vatican, but she had more fun at Prada."

"I wouldn't worry," I say. "Some people consider Prada a religious experience."

"We'll get to hear all about it," Bradford says. He looks at Dylan, who's avidly working his way—with chopsticks—through a plate of Peking duck. Then he turns to me and shakes his head. "I'm a little worried about Skylar," he admits. "After two months in Europe with her mother, she sounded sort of nasty about you and me when she called."

I nod. "Don't worry, I'll win her over," I say bravely.

Bradford takes my hand. "Thanks, honey. I'm glad you're ready for this. Because Skylar may not make it easy."

Chapter FOUR

THE PHONE RINGS at two A.M. and Bradford doesn't stir. What is it about men? Women wake up in the middle of the night because they hear leaves falling off the trees. Guys can sleep through Armageddon and never shift sides.

I lean across Bradford to pick up the phone. I'll let him sleep for another fifteen seconds, but I know it's going to be for him. Probably one of his firm's brokers in Japan or London or wherever the heck they trade when it's the middle of the night here, calling with an urgent message. Talk about making money in your sleep.

But it's not business. At least not Bradford's business.

"Hi," Kate says when I grab the receiver. "What's up?"

"Me, I guess," I say groggily, rubbing my eyes. "But I wasn't up before."

"Glad you are now," says Kate. "I've got a great idea."

I sit up and punch the pillows behind my back to settle in. Undisturbed, Bradford rolls over in his sleep and flops a warm arm across my thigh. I lower my voice so as not to wake him, but who am I kidding. He lets out such a loud snore that Kate anxiously asks, "You okay?"

"Of course," I say. "I'm in bed. Where are you?"

"Tortola, British Virgin Islands," she says, as if I should have known.

And I probably should have. How could I have forgotten the bathing suit? My synapses don't work as quickly as they should at two A.M. Or at forty-one.

"How's Owen like the bikini?" I ask.

"Liked it," Kate says curtly. "For the few minutes he got to see me in it. He had to leave right after we got here. Annoying, really. I'd just slathered myself in Bain de Soleil SPF ninety-eight so we could go to the beach. Instead, he was on his way to the airport."

I don't know what could have sent Owen to the airport, but at least I understand how Kate maintains her perfectly smooth skin—super-strength sun protection in a number high enough to be a basketball score. Though come to think of it, Kate used to have cute freckles sprinkled across her nose. She must have zapped them away when they went out of style. But what if they come back in vogue? After all, nothing stays chic for more than a nanosecond. Wax your eyebrows into a fashionably thin line and suddenly *Elle* declares bushy is back. Finally start drinking Bellinis and everybody's switched to ginger daiquiris. Suffer through eight hours of Japanese hair straightening and you can almost guarantee the return of the Afro.

"Owen left? How come?" I ask, getting myself back on track. "Something happen?"

"His wife called," Kate says grumpily. "She cut short her weekend at Canyon Ranch and had to come home immediately because she'd had an allergic reaction to an apple-and-oatmeal scrub facial." Kate pauses and adds snidely, "Apparently 'natural' doesn't agree with her."

I ponder what Owen the real estate mogul can do about an allergic reaction to a facial. Bring roses? It might have been better if Doctor Kate had gone. But then again, maybe not. There must be some AMA regulation against a doctor treating her lover's wife. I think it may even be covered under the Geneva Convention.

"What are you going to do in Tortola for the rest of the weekend?" I ask.

"Follow Owen's advice. Stay in our luxurious cottage by the ocean, order margaritas, and damn well enjoy myself," Kate says firmly.

I bite my tongue. This is not the time to point out the disadvantages of having a married lover. The words "I told you so" will never cross my lips.

Next to me, Bradford, still half asleep, starts making small circles on my thigh, and I stroke his cheek and gaze at him appreciatively. He pulls his whole body closer to mine.

"So here's my great idea," Kate continues. "Why don't you fly down for the weekend and join me? You've always said you want to learn how to windsurf. This is your chance."

Bradford, now more awake, is playing with my hair and softly kissing my shoulder. I stir as his warm lips move sweetly across my neck.

"I can't get away," I say, thinking about my weekend plans with Bradford. And what appears to be Bradford's more immediate plan for the proverbial roll in the hay. I'm not passing that up for a roll in the surf.

"Too bad," Kate says. "Are you sure I can't tempt you?"

I put my arm around Bradford's waist and stay mum about what's really tempting me.

"I almost forgot to tell you," I say instead. "Berni and Aidan called. They finally delivered the twins. Aidan's a little hungry, but everybody's healthy and doing well."

"Good for them," Kate says. Then she immediately comes up with a new brainstorm. "If she's done delivering, maybe Berni'd like to join me. She could probably use a weekend at the beach."

"She probably could, but the doctor said no windsurfing for another twenty-four hours." I laugh. "Then there's the whole problem about being around to breast-feed."

"She could bring the babies," Kate suggests, ever flexible. But even she doesn't sound convinced.

"Maybe the twins should leave the hospital in a stroller, not a 757," I say.

Kate sighs. "Doesn't matter. I know how to spend a weekend on my own. I'll just enjoy my one hundred hours of solitude. Maybe I'll write a book about it."

Worse things can happen than spending two days on a beautiful stretch of island, reading beach books and searching for seashells. And if Kate strolls the sand in that sexy new bikini, she won't have to be alone for long. Though meeting new guys doesn't seem to be on her agenda. Maybe Owen's momentarily stepped out of the frame, but he's clearly still in the picture.

When we hang up, Bradford rolls on top of me with a little smile and a long kiss.

"I need your full attention now," he says.

"You have it," I say, closing my eyes and savoring the sensation of his strong body against mine.

I hear a sound from the living room and start to sit up.

"Don't worry," Bradford says, his strong hands on my shoulders as he gently shifts me back against the bed. "Just Pal."

As if he's heard his name mentioned, Pal gives a little bark. Which seems strange. I've never heard him do that in the middle of the night before. But then all's quiet again and Bradford's smothering me in kisses. We're moving together now, lost in the moment, our bodies finding the same rhythm. My breath is coming fast and I gasp with pleasure.

And I'm not the only one gasping.

"Oh my god, Daddy! What are you doing?" calls out an indignant, high-pitched girl's voice.

For an instant, my eyes lock with Bradford's and we're both too startled to move. Then Bradford leaps off me, snatching the crumpled sheet from the bed to wrap around himself. I grab for my abandoned T-shirt and a pillow. No way I'll find the panties.

"Skylar!" Bradford says, looking into the dim room and seeing the outline of his lanky soon-to-be-fourteen-year-old daughter standing at the foot of the bed. Sounding more cheerful than most men could in the same situation, he adds, "Great surprise! We didn't expect you until tomorrow."

"Well, I'm here," Skylar says petulantly, shrugging out of her Prada backpack and flinging it on the floor.

And apparently the party's just starting. Walking into the bedroom now, accompanied by the faithful panting Pal, is a perfectly coiffed

Louis Licari blonde, dressed in a hip-hugging blue pantsuit with an expertly knotted Hermès scarf at her neck. It's the middle of the night, but she looks like she stepped out of an ad on the back cover of *Town and Country.*

She pushes aside the duvet and sits down primly on the edge of the bed. She doesn't look at me, but I swear she sniffs the air. "Bradford, what kind of homecoming is this for your wife and daughter?" she asks.

Bradford's ducked into the bathroom and emerges now in a pair of jeans. He tosses me a terry bathrobe. "You're not my wife. My ex-wife, if memory serves," Bradford says.

"Whatever," Mimi says, tossing her head. "Who's your latest girlfriend?"

"You've met Sara and you know she's my fiancée, not my girlfriend," Bradford says sharply.

Mimi looks me over. And at this moment, I'm at a distinct disadvantage, cowering in a Yankees T-shirt and Bradford's too-big ratty robe. For a man who dresses in Savile Row suits and Loro Piana cashmere sweaters, he sure doesn't pay much attention to what he puts on after a shower.

"So you're his fiancée. Big deal. Risky business, if you ask me," she says sarcastically. "You got the diamond and moved in. But you haven't exactly sealed the deal. Have you thought about that?" She looks approvingly at her own well-manicured fingernails and smiles secretively. "Things can change, you know."

"Wrong again, Mimi," says Bradford. "The only reason Sara moved in before the wedding is so Dylan could start the school year. But this is a done deal."

"Are you at least using condoms?" Skylar asks.

Mimi smirks and cocks her head in my direction. "Do you play tennis well enough to be invited to the country club doubles tournament? Do you know how to be a trophy wife?"

"Do you even have a personal shopper at Bergdorf's?" Skylar volleys.

"Has Bradford told you he doesn't like sex in the morning?" Mimi fires at lightning speed.

Whoa. The two of them are shooting questions faster than Tim Russert on *Meet the Press*. But with these topics, any network censor would demand a five-second delay. Skylar sits down on the bed next to her mom. We're certainly an intimate little family group. Maybe I should make some tea.

But Bradford isn't waiting for crumpets. He strides over to the bed and puts his arm around Skylar. "Mimi, cut it out. What are you possibly thinking of, barging in at this hour?"

"You weren't happy that I took Skylar away for so long," she says, adjusting the gold circle pin on her scarf, "and you said you wanted to see her the moment we got back. So this is the moment. We came here straight from the airport."

"And I'm tired," Skylar complains, yawning dramatically.

I get up and offer my hand to Skylar. "After that flight, you must be exhausted," I say sympathetically. "Come on, let's get you to bed. I'll take you to your room."

"I don't need your help. I know where my room is," Skylar snaps, standing up and grabbing her backpack. "This is my house, not yours."

"Skylar, dear," Mimi clucks approvingly. "That's not a nice thing to say to this . . . woman."

"Well, it is my house. I've been here longer than she has. A lot longer," Skylar says, her voice getting louder.

"And you'll be here long after she's gone, dear," Mimi says.

"You can bet on that," Skylar shoots back.

She storms out of the room and I see Bradford set his jaw. "I'm not going to let you do this," he growls to Mimi in a low, controlled voice. "It was your decision to walk out two years ago and run off with that sleazy CEO. Now you have to live with the consequences."

"What consequences?" Mimi asks, feigning innocence. "I had a little fling. I'm back. Now you're having a little fling. Come on, darling. How long can yours last?"

"Forever," Bradford says, taking my hand. "Sara and I are getting married. That's permanent. You and I are divorced. Also permanent. Why doesn't that sink in?"

"Because I've decided I want you back," Mimi says coyly. "And what Mimi wants, Mimi gets."

"What Mimi wanted was a CEO who had more money than me, as I remember," says Bradford. "I can't help it if he was indicted and went to jail for fraud."

"He'll be out in two years," Mimi says. "But I never liked him anyway. The sapphire-and-diamond necklace he gave me turned out to be fake."

Bradford shakes his head. "I'm not going through this old history again. Thank you for bringing Skylar over. It's great to have her here. We'll resume our usual custody arrangement—one week our house, one week yours." He glances at his watch. "Do you want us to bring her back at three A.M. next week, or should we pick a more civilized hour?"

Mimi plays coquettishly with her Elsa Peretti earring and offers Bradford a winning smile. She leans in and territorially puts her hand on his shoulder. "Oh darling, whatever you want. I wasn't trying to upset you. Skylar's missed you and so have I. It's been too long apart."

Too long apart for what? Or for whom, more to the point? For Bradford and Skylar or Bradford and Mimi? Lord knows I haven't been missing Mimi. And I'm hoping Bradford hasn't either.

"Look," says Bradford, his tone softening. "Skylar's welcome here any time of the day or night. The door's always open. Or at least she has the key. But next time you're coming over, I'd appreciate it if you used the doorbell. And some advance warning wouldn't be a bad idea, either."

"You used to like it when I surprised you," Mimi says, flirtatiously strumming her fingers on his shoulder. "You know what I mean, don't you, darling? That night in Vienna. The black lace garter belt. I know you remember."

Bradford looks momentarily embarrassed. Okay, so he does remember. Mimi notices Bradford's expression, too. "I still have that garter belt," she says, rubbing her hand seductively along her hip.

The woman is shameless—and appropriately named. For her, life is all about Me, Me, Me. But I refuse to let myself be jealous of Bradford's ex-wife. Mimi's the past and I'm the future. Bradford's told me a million times that he made a mistake marrying the slick, social climbing Mimi. This time around, he wanted something real. Someone real. I pinch myself. Yup, I'm real all right. Though the situation is feeling a little absurd.

Luckily, Bradford's not falling for Mimi's charm act. "I've got an important meeting in the morning," he says, putting an end to the conversation. "I'm heading out early, but Skylar can sleep in. Sara will be here when she gets up."

"Sure will," I say chirpily, happy to prove to Bradford that despite the midnight intrusion, I'm glad Skylar's here. "I'll make breakfast. I whip up a pretty good banana pancake."

"Aren't you the good little housewife," Mimi says, releasing Bradford's shoulder and reverting to her snarky self. "Your little flapjacks. How quaint. Let's see how they measure up to the soufflés Skylar ordered every morning in Paris at the George V. When she was with me."

Turning on her heel, Mimi reaches for her alligator purse, pulls out a gold compact and powders her nose. As if leaving with a shiny nose at three A.M. will blind the doorman.

Bradford follows his ex to the front door and throws the dead-bolt lock as soon as she's gone. He comes padding back into the bedroom and climbs into bed.

"We'd better get some rest," he says, kissing me amiably. So much for our post-midnight passion. Within seconds he rolls over and falls into a sound sleep. I lay awake for the rest of the night—or what's left of it—watching the pulsating digital numbers click toward dawn. Come to think of it, Mimi's right. Bradford doesn't like sex in the morning. Wonder what else she knows about him.

Dylan is already eating a grilled cheese sandwich for lunch when Skylar sleepily slouches into the kitchen. He barely looks up when she flops down at the table, dressed in skin-tight white shorts, an orange halter midriff top, and a chain-link belt wrapped around her tiny waist. If she were one of my students, I'd send her home to put on some clothes. I look protectively at Dylan. But fortunately, he's still at the age when he doesn't notice girls and he thinks Britney Spears is famous for her singing.

Dylan peels back the top of his sandwich and starts cheerfully making little Swiss cheese balls which he shoots across his plate. Across the table, Skylar stares at him disdainfully.

"Good morning!" I say brightly to my almost stepdaughter. "Or I guess, good afternoon! Sleep well?"

"The bed didn't feel right," she says huffily. "Don't you know that anything less than three-hundred-count sheets makes me break out in hives?"

Dylan looks up, finally interested. "Do you want to count to three hundred by threes?" he asks. "I can do it. Three . . . six . . . nine . . . twelve . . . fifteen . . ."

"You're such an idiot," Skylar says, rolling her eyes.

"Eighteen . . . twenty-one . . . twenty-four . . . twenty-seven," Dylan continues, undeterred.

I put my hand on his. "That's great, honey, but let's finish counting later." I turn to Skylar, ignoring both the idiot comment and her idiotic comment about the sheets.

"Chocolate chip pancakes?" I offer Skylar, deciding on the spot that past noon, a well-balanced lunch can include Hershey's. And a little dash of sugar might sweeten her mood.

"Gross," Skylar says disdainfully, wrinkling her nose. "You want me to get fat? You want me to get pimples? I get it. You're trying to make my life hell, aren't you."

Wow, we got there fast. I figured I'd have to confiscate her gold MasterCard, delete her AOL buddy list, and marry her father before I could actually destroy her life.

"How about some Cheerios?" I ask, trying not to take the bait. And thinking that something with the word "cheer" in it might have a sub-liminal effect.

"My mother always gives me Special K," she says. "No sugar. No fat. And get it? She thinks I'm special."

"Yeah, my mom thinks I'm special, too," Dylan pipes in, now eating the grimy little cheese balls he's done playing with.

Skylar stands up, scraping her chair loudly against the terrazzo tile floor. "I'm going over to Heather's house. I'll be back whenever," she says, popping one of Dylan's cheese balls in her mouth and heading to the door.

"Wait," I say, trailing after her. "Who's Heather? Where does she live? Can I take you?"

"Don't bother," Skylar says, sailing past me. "Heather lives in Manor Haven."

Hadley Farms. Manor Haven. Why do all these suburban communities sound like rest homes?

"Heather's sister's picking me up in the Mustang convertible," Skylar continues, grudgingly giving me more information. "She just got her driver's license."

Now I'm stumped. Is Bradford's daughter allowed to get in the car with a sixteen-year-old? I don't even know what I should be more worried about—Skylar in the car with a newbie driver or nubile teenagers driving with the top down. Hopefully the car's top, not theirs.

"I have some errands. I'll drive you instead," I say, grabbing for my wallet.

"Over my dead body," Skylar retorts, slamming the door behind her.

Dylan looks up at me with a big grin. "Now what are we going to do, Mom?" he asks happily. He's never had a sibling before and Skylar seems to be providing a certain level of entertainment.

I take a moment to think who I can ask about this, and in a burst of inspiration, I rush to the intercom.

"Enrique?" I entreat.

"At your service," says the friendly doorman from his guard post at the gate. "What can I do for you today?"

"Skylar's driving with her friend Heather's sister over to Manor Haven. Can you tell me where that is? I'm thinking about following them."

"Don't bother," Enrique says soothingly. "I'll keep an eye on them.

It's just two gated communities over. All private roads between here and there and the speed limit's ten. Cops at every corner flag anybody going over fifteen."

Who says suburban children are overprotected? "Thanks," I say, sighing in relief. Enrique knows everything. Next I'll have to ask what he suggests about Skylar's too-tight shorts.

Exhausted, I slump down next to Dylan and nibble on the crusts he's left on his plate. Amazing how many people one little grilled cheese sandwich can feed.

"So now can I count?" Dylan says. "Thirty . . . thirty-three . . . thirty-six . . . thirty-nine . . . forty-two . . ."

I don't care how long it takes him to get to three hundred. At least I haven't ruined his life yet.

When I get to Berni's hospital room an hour later, I edge my way past baskets brimming with flowers and three king-sized orange trees. So many helium balloons are pushing toward the ceiling, I feel like I've wandered into the Macy's Thanksgiving Day Parade. In a corner, the drummer is still on duty, though now he's switched to a keyboard, abandoning primitive primordial rhythms for easy listening.

Aidan is swaying in place to the music, cradling one baby in each arm. And darned if they aren't cooing instead of crying at Neil Sedaka's greatest hits. Poor kids. When they're older, they'll never understand why they feel so happy in elevators.

"They're just gorgeous," I say, smiling into their sleepy sweet faces. "Who do they look like?"

"Robin Williams," says Berni groggily from her bed.

I do a double take, and push up one of the baby's teeny sleeves, rubbing my finger gently along the soft, smooth arm. Nope. Not hairy. Sweat's not pouring down his face, and he's not compulsively spewing jokes, either.

"I don't see the resemblance myself," I say.

"No, really. The three orange trees came from Robin Williams," says

Berni, who's apparently misheard my question over the strains of "Love Will Keep Us Together." "Wasn't that fabulous of him? I love Robin." She shoots a sidelong glance at Aidan. "Maybe we can name one of the babies after him."

"We could name them both Robin," says Aidan. "With an 'i' for the girl and a 'y' for the boy."

"Or an 'i' for the boy and a 'y' for the girl," counters Berni.

Aidan signs and turns to me. "We can't agree on names," he says, in case I hadn't guessed. "We've been through six books including the Manhattan telephone directory and nothing seems good enough. We may have to go with working titles. Baby Project A and Baby Project B."

"Better than your idea of Hannibal and Clarisse," says Berni.

"*Silence of the Lambs* was a great movie," growls Aidan. "One of my favorites."

It's a good thing Aidan's not a Jim Carrey fan. I wouldn't want him naming the babies Dumb and Dumber.

I hold out a finger to one of the infants, marveling, as everyone does as he (or is it she?) clenches it tightly. I extend a finger to the other baby, who has an equally strong grip. Funny how two little beings who weigh less than six pounds each can take over a room. Not to mention your life.

"How about naming them Ben and Jerry?" I suggest. "It might entitle the kids to a lifetime's free supply of Chunky Monkey."

"If we're going for endorsements, why not 'Mercedes' and 'Benz,' " suggests Aidan.

"I like it," Berni says, thinking about the deals she could make. "If the company doesn't send new cars, at least one kid could become a rapper, Ben-Z."

At this point, Baby Project A and B is sounding pretty good to me.

Just then, a tall doctor in hospital scrubs and surgical mask strides in.

"How are the most gorgeous babies in the world!" the doctor sings out loudly, pulling out a digital camera and madly snapping away. Then he spots me, puts his arm around my waist and swings me around. "We did it!" he says. "What a team, hey?"

Surprised, I look into the doctor's eyes and realize it's Kirk, in full soap-opera regalia.

"I came over as soon as we finished shooting," he says, pulling off the mask, hugging Berni, then going back to the door and dragging in the two biggest, fluffiest stuffed animals I've ever seen. "One for each of the baby's cribs."

"What a great gift," Berni says warily, eyeing the animals worriedly. Nine months of trying to have the perfect pregnancy may be over, but new mother mania has kicked in and a hazard lurks behind every teddy bear. Is the stuffing safe? Is the fur flame-retardant? Are the button eyes sewn in securely so the kids won't swallow them? Buttons are already Berni's biggest bugaboo. She swore off normal blouses a month ago and had Chanel custom make a dozen shirts with Velcro.

Kirk's gift reminds me that I have a little something for Berni, too. I pull out a pretty box and plop it next to Berni.

"Chocolate truffles," I tell her.

"Ooooh. How perfect." Berni pops one in her mouth, savors it for a moment, and breaks into a smile.

"Three flavors," I say proudly. "I made them for you last night. I've been playing around with the recipe for weeks."

"Aidan, honey, come take one. I've never tasted anything this good," Berni says.

Aidan sidles over, still holding one baby in each arm. He shifts a hip forward and tries to snatch a chocolate without dropping a baby. Doesn't work. He jiggles around, reconfiguring the babies, one higher, one lower, but he's still not any closer to a chocolate.

"Put Baby A down," Berni says helpfully.

"I've been wanting to for the last half hour," Aidan says mournfully. "I can't quite figure out how."

Kirk and I step forward and each rescue a baby wrapped in a yellow blanket from Aidan's aching arms. "Aren't these babies the cutest?" Kirk says, jiggling his baby and smiling at me.

"The cutest," I beam, rocking the bundle in my arms. But since there's no pink or blue blanket to tip me off, I have to keep the compliment generic. Berni is intent on raising egalitarian, non-sexist, politically correct babies. She wants her kids to grow up free and unbound by stereotypes. It's a good idea and it might work, at least until the twins see their first Mattel commercials.

Aidan laughs and flops on the bed next to Berni. "Look at our friends Kirk and Sara," he says, cuddling next to her. "What a cute couple. Maybe we should let them be the godparents."

"I'd be honored," I say, intoxicated by the sweet baby smell that White Linen could never match. "Be a nice balance for that teenager I have at home."

Kirk steps back and eyes me appraisingly. "You couldn't have a teenager," he says. "You're way too young for that."

"Not too young," I say, secretly pleased that he'd think so. "But she's not exactly my teenager either. My stepdaughter-to-be."

"You're getting married?" Kirk asks.

"Yup," I say. "If I ever order the invitations."

"Then there's still hope for me," he teases. "Picking a typeface has sunk many a marriage. If the wedding doesn't work out, call me."

The baby in my arms starts fussing and I hand her over to Berni. Kirk does the same, and then puts his arm around me.

"I'm heartbroken you're getting married," he says with a wink. "But don't forget. Everyone needs a last fling."

We both laugh. Kirk isn't serious, but it's fun to have someone flirting with me. Is that because I've gotten older? I used to be outraged to hear wolf whistles as I walked by a construction site. Now if a guy in a hard hat screams out after me, "Nice butt, lady!" I secretly murmur, "Thank you."

Across the room, Berni is happily breast-feeding and making her way through the entire box of truffles. The hospital room phone rings, and Berni hits the speaker button with her elbow. Half-a-day into motherhood and she's already mastered multitasking.

The voice of her rival agent pal Olivia booms into the room.

"So you delivered," says Olivia. "Good. That's a load off, huh? How much do you weigh now?"

"You're supposed to ask how much the babies weigh," Berni says.

"Why, are they fat, too?" Olivia asks.

"They're perfect," Berni coos, so infatuated with A and B that even Olivia can't get a rise out of her.

"Enough about them," Olivia says briskly. "You can finally do something for me. I'm having an important dinner party Friday night. My caterer ate his own gazpacho and has food poisoning, so he's bailed. *Basta. Finito.* Gone. I need someone fast. You have to get me the chef who catered your baby shower. Your food was actually decent for once."

Berni smiles and gives me a thumbs up. "Decent" in Olivia's lingo probably ranks three stars in the Michelin guide.

"My chef is pretty in demand," Berni says, "but I think I can get her. She'd only do it as a favor to me, though."

I start shaking my head wildly and mouthing "No," but Berni pays no attention.

"Here are the terms. No negotiation," Berni says, pleased to be cutting a deal fourteen hours after giving birth. "Whatever you were paying the gazpacho guy, she gets double. She charges a full day for shopping and another full day for menu preparation. You pay for hair and makeup. And she doesn't do cleanup."

Olivia knows when she's over a barrel and hesitates only briefly before muttering, "Fine." Still, she needs to make at least one demand of her own. "No tofu," she decrees. "In anything."

Figuring this will have no effect on soybean futures, Berni concedes on the tofu and they make final arrangements.

"Hey, Sara, not bad, right?" Berni hoots triumphantly when they've signed off. "Who's the better agent, huh? Even breast-feeding I can one-up Olivia any day of the week."

I'm so stunned by the whole transaction that I barely know where to begin.

"Hair and makeup?" I ask in a weak voice.

"You're right. I should have demanded Frederic Fekkai," Berni says. "Want me to call back?"

"Yes, I want you to call back. And tell her I won't do it," I say. "I'm not a caterer."

"You are now," Berni says, as if my protests are just an annoying detail. "Besides, I never go back on my word."

"You have to listen to Berni," Kirk says. "She's the best agent in the world. She's always right."

"I can't do all this alone by Friday night," I gripe, thinking about the shopping, the chopping, and the whopping mess I'll probably make out of the whole production.

"I'll help," Kirk volunteers. "I'm a pretty decent chef. The first role Berni ever got me was in a Red Lobster commercial."

"Then I guess we'll serve seafood," I say. "And we'll put up little 'All You Can Eat' signs."

"That settles it," Berni says. She leans back against the pillows and closes her eyes, still holding the twins who are now peacefully asleep in her arms. "One more thing," she adds before drifting off to sleep herself. "Just don't make those awful cheese puffs."

Chapter FIVE

"AM I CRAZY to be getting a house?" Kate asks exuberantly when I stop by her office late Monday afternoon. She swoops down in her white lab coat to give me a kiss on the cheek. "You're wonderful to come look at it with me on such short notice. I'm not quite ready yet. Can you wait a couple of minutes?"

"Sure," I say. I look dubiously around the busy waiting room, where I spot five patients, and I instantly recognize three of them from television shows. The new route to stardom—first you get an agent, then you see Kate, then you date Colin Farrell.

I figure that for Kate to finish with all her clients has to take at least an hour, but I don't mind. Her coffee table is stacked with women's magazines whose cover lines promise advice on "4 Ways to Have a Better Orgasm," "5 Ways to Give a Better Orgasm," and "6 Ways to Have 7 Simultaneous Orgasms." What they don't say is how many men all this will require.

Kate disappears back into her office and I start to make my way through a copy of *Marie Claire* that heralds "587 New Looks For Fall." I figure they're offering more bang for the buck. By the time I look up again, the waiting room has emptied and the last patients of the day— a mother and her teenage daughter—are emerging from Kate's inner sanctum. For a moment, I wonder which one is the patient, and then I realize it's probably both. The mother is furrow-free and the daughter has zero zits. And I bet it costs a small fortune for each to get what the other has naturally. Kate follows behind them, jingling her car keys on their Cartier chain.

"We'll both see you next week," the mother says. "Same time, as usual."

They come in every week? How much Retin-A does one family need? And where does a dermatologist fit in with the usual New York City kid's lineup of after-school consultants? Tennis coach, self-esteem guru, SAT I and SAT II tutors, college essay expert—also known as the ghostwriter, therapist, herbalist and the ever-important orthodontist. Because whether or not your children have crooked teeth, giving them braces shows that you care.

"One more thing," says the mother, pausing at the door. "My other daughter Kimberly's turning four next week. I'm thinking of bringing her in. I want to make sure we don't wait too long."

"Don't need to see her yet," Kate replies. "Wait until she's six."

Ah yes. Odds are little Kimberly's skin will still be peaches and cream pure at that point. But the stress of first grade and all her mother's expectations will probably make her break out in hives.

Once the derm-addicted duo leave, we head out to the sidewalk where Kate's zippy new Z-4 convertible is parked. Top down, and not even so much as a fire-engine red Club on the steering wheel to protect against thieves. It would never occur to Kate that anything could go wrong in her life. And somehow it hasn't.

We pull away from the curb and Kate revs the engine as she weaves her way through heavy traffic.

"Zero to sixty in five-point-nine seconds," she says proudly. Even though we haven't broken twenty. "Mapquest says we'll be in Bedford in sixty-eight minutes. A quick commute."

Since we haven't moved an inch, I wonder if Mapquest allowed time for the traffic-stopping pothole repair crew that's blocking all of 88th Street. And I also wonder why my city-loving Kate suddenly wants to commute in the first place. Maybe my moving to Hadley Farms has started a trend.

"When did you decide to buy a house?" I ask Kate. "Last I heard, you were buying the Birkin bag. Nobody should be able to afford both."

"I'm still on the waiting list for the Birkin," Kate says. "The house is instant gratification."

When I need instant gratification, I buy a Mars bar or a Milky Way. Kate buys a mansion. If this is what she does on the spur of the moment, I'm afraid to ask about her long-range plans.

But when we finally arrive in Bedford and cruise up the driveway past rolling lawns and a thick hedge of perfect trees, I see the hidden white-gabled house with hunter green shutters—and I understand the appeal.

"Come on in," Kate says eagerly, hopping out of the car and sprinting up the stone path in her stilettos without ever missing a beat. I try to follow and immediately catch my flat Cole Haan loafers on the edge of a rock. But even a stubbed toe can't distract me as I step inside and take in the charming Georgian rooms with wainscoting and cozy crown moldings. Through the bay window I spot what appears to be a black-watered pond surrounded by boulders. It takes me a minute to realize that it's really a man-made swimming pool, decked out with jagged rocks and a small waterfall.

"Don't you love the pool?" Kate asks eagerly, following my gaze. "The designers put wildly expensive onyx stone on the bottom to make the water look murky."

Great idea—pay extra to muddy up crystal blue water. Does the Sierra Club know that the swampy look is now soigné?

I turn back from the window and walk around slowly. I stop to take in the living room fireplace. Pretty, but what exactly is she going to do with it? I can't picture Kate getting a fire going even if she had a butane torch and a Duraflame log. On the other hand, it's a darn good place to store books or beauty potions.

"What a great spread," I say finally. "You're really going to buy this?"

Kate hesitates. "I'm not actually buying per se."

"That's smart. Rent for a season. See if you like it."

Kate turns around and sighs. "Okay, I'll give you the whole story. Owen wants to buy it as an investment and I'll stay here so we can spend more time together. He felt really bad about having to run out on Tortola."

"Generous apology," I say. "Couldn't he have just sent Godiva chocolate?"

Kate puts her hands on her tiny waist. Oh, that's right. She doesn't eat Godiva chocolate.

"Owen thought this house would be perfect for us. I mean, for me. I came up last night to look and I wanted you to see it right away. Isn't it amazing? Owen just stumbled on it yesterday when he was out jogging."

Suddenly a light dawns. Owen was out jogging around here because it's close to his country mansion—where he lives with his wife. And it would be convenient to install Kate nearby.

"You're going to give up your whole life to move here and be at Owen's beck and call?" I ask incredulously.

"Don't be ridiculous," Kate says. "This is a little weekend place. I'll come up when I want. If I want. Besides, I'm dying to learn how to garden."

"Come on, Kate, I can't picture you hoeing. You don't even like potted plants. You have silk geraniums in your waiting room."

"At least I'll have a lawn. And open space. And a little peace and quiet."

"A lot of peace and quiet," I say disapprovingly. "You'll be sitting around all by yourself waiting for Owen to call. Don't you see what's going on? You're talking about gardening. What's really happening is you're trying to put down roots. And face it, in a situation like this, nothing's going to grow."

Kate ponders this for a moment. Maybe she's impressed with my metaphor. Got to admit that I am.

"You don't understand," Kate says in a small voice. "I'll take Owen however I can. However much I can. I've found my soul mate."

Her soul mate? This relationship with Owen—the married Owen—is ratcheting up faster than the national obesity crisis. I'm about to launch into my list of fifty reasons why she needs to rethink it when I'm distracted by a noise in the driveway. Through the window we both spy an oversized silver Hummer pulling up, the wide car trampling a bed of late-blooming hibiscus roses.

"Be nice," Kate implores, a look of panic crossing her face. "It's Owen."

"Am I ever *not* nice?" I ask, with an edge in my voice, thinking "not nice" is exactly what Owen deserves. Still, I'm Kate's best friend. I'm not going to embarrass her. I'll save embarrassing people for back-to-school night with Skylar.

Owen bursts through the door, cradling a magnum of champagne and two glasses.

"So what do you think, babe?" he asks, putting down the champagne and grabbing Kate for an endlessly long kiss. I keep myself busy counting by threes to three hundred. Smart kid, that Dylan. I'll have to thank him for the tip.

Finally, Kate pulls back. "You remember Sara," she says, her arm still wrapped tightly around Owen's waist. "I wanted her to see the house with me."

"It's great, isn't it?" Owen asks, patting the wainscoting as if it's man's best friend.

"I love it," Kate says. "What do you think, Sara?"

"Great house. Lousy situation," I blurt out bluntly. Oh damn. I said I'd be nice.

"*Saaara,*" Kate whispers pleadingly, sounding like an eight-year-old. "You promised."

"What did she promise?" Owen asks.

"Not to bring up any problems," Kate says with a sigh. She settles into the white damask sofa and pats the cushion next to her, inviting Owen to sit down.

"Problems?" Owen asks. He looks sharply around the room as if the only trouble he can imagine is with the chandelier, which we've all just noticed needs three new lightbulbs.

"I'm not thrilled with this whole situation," I say frostily, standing with my arms crossed firmly in front of my chest. "You're married."

"That's not your business," Owen says, crossing his own arms and matching my icy tone.

"Sure it's her business—she's my best friend," Kate says. She plays with the fringe on a throw pillow next to her and looks anxiously at Owen. He glances at his watch—this is a bigger commitment than he'd planned—but then sits down next to Kate.

"Okay, let's talk," he says briskly to me. "I care about Kate so I don't want you unhappy. What do you need to know?"

I uncross my arms and sit down. If he's willing to be straightforward, I will be, too.

"You're married, so why are you sleeping with my friend Kate?" I ask. There. Straightforward.

Owen pauses, puts his arm around Kate's shoulder, and then turns back to me. "Because I'm in love with her," he says.

I wasn't expecting that. And from the look on her face, Kate wasn't either.

"Then you're leaving your wife?" I ask. My bluntness knows no bounds. But it doesn't seem to upset Owen. He strokes Kate's cheek gently.

"I don't know," he says carefully. "This is new territory for me. I wasn't planning to get emotionally involved. But Kate's special. I feel like a lovestruck kid."

Kate leans forward and fixes her gaze on Owen. "But we're not kids, and that's why this means so much," she says, turning from Owen to me. "We're both old enough to know life doesn't go on forever. You have to make your own happiness. Be open to new adventures. Take a risk or two. If not now, when? After all, I'm thirty-eight."

That's interesting. Kate and I were the same age in seventh grade and I thought I'd already passed forty. I'm glad to hear I'm younger than I think.

"It's so very nice to have adventures, but where does all this leave you?" I ask.

"With somebody who cares for her very much," Owen says, taking

Kate's hand and kissing her fingertips. "Other than that, I'm not making predictions for the future. I can tell you that my wife and I don't have much of a relationship anymore. We've drifted apart."

That's original. Where do married men come up with these lines? Are they written on a TelePrompTer in the sky, visible only to the Y chromosome? I'm not sure why men think "drifting apart" gives them permission to stray, anyway. What they really need is a map home.

Owen brushes back Kate's hair and looks soulfully into her eyes. "Being with you has brought me back to life," he says.

I can guess which part of him she's brought back to life. But right now, Kate and Owen both look so content that I want to believe against my better instincts—and all warnings from Oprah—that there'll be a happy ending.

"You're the most amazing man I know," Kate says, kissing him.

"I hear that a lot," Owen admits. "But back to the real issue. The deal. Do we have one? I told the owners if you liked the house, I'd sign the papers tomorrow."

"I like it," Kate says decisively.

"Then it's done," Owen says. "Now where should we go for dinner?"

That was fast. I guess when you're used to dealing in skyscrapers, buying a little house—or even a big one—isn't any more important than whether you're eating Japanese or Italian.

"How about that champagne first?" Kate says.

Owen reaches over for the magnum of 1975 vintage Dom Perignon that he'd brought along for the occasion and pops the cork.

"Here we are," he says, pouring the bubbly champagne into the two Baccarat flutes and handing one to each of us. Then he goes to the kitchen and comes back holding a flowered Dixie cup. He pours his own champagne into the paper container and swirls it around.

"To the new house, and many happy times here," Owen toasts, raising his paper cup and clicking—or trying to—Kate's crystal goblet.

"And to good friends," Kate adds, graciously lifting her glass to mine.

I take a little sip. Good stuff. I guess vintage really is better, at least when it comes to champagne. I still won't wear vintage clothes, though.

No matter how many times you send that original 1960s Pucci to the dry cleaner, it still smells like mothballs.

Owen starts affectionately nuzzling Kate's neck and I go for another gulp of champagne, then think better of it. I put down the glass, spot Kate's Fendi bag on the floor and grab it to rifle around for her car keys.

"Time for you two to christen the house, and I should be getting back now," I say to Kate. "Can Owen get you home in the Hummer?"

Kate nods distractedly and for a moment seems to like the plan. "Sure, take the Z-4," she says.

"Great," I say, happily twirling the car keys around my finger.

Then Kate suddenly remembers. "Wait. You hate to drive. You only get into that armored Volvo to go half a block to the train station."

"I know," I say, tossing the keys in the air and catching them with a flourish. "It'll be really cool. What's life without a few risks."

Amazingly, I get both myself and the Z-4 back to Hadley Farms intact. Not a scratch on either of us. My first time driving on a major highway and boy was it fun. Hair blowing in the wind. A truck driver giving me a honk and a thumbs up. CD player blaring Outkast's "Hey Ya!" Good song, bad English. I don't let the kids in my art classes say either "hey" or "ya." But strung together, the title hit the charts and rocketed to number one. Listening to it, I hit the gas pedal and broke the speed limit. Rocketed to fifty-six.

I fling open the door to the house, eager to tell Bradford about my highway adventure, but as I rush into the living room, I come to a dead halt. Bradford, my beloved Bradford, is holding a stepladder. And his grinning face is two inches away from a shapely red-skirted butt—which is attached to an equally shapely pair of bare, long legs. The woman is giggling and hammering a nail into our ecru wall.

"Hi, honey," Bradford says ebulliently to me. "Isn't it great? Mimi brought back my Campbell's soup. Hot Dog Bean. And Tomato Beef Noodle O's."

What is the man talking about? I look from Bradford to the blonde on the ladder. So it's Mimi who's invaded the living room. At least she's not making another guest appearance in the bedroom.

All of a sudden, Mimi squeals as her kitten mule slips off the top rung.

"Whoops!" she cries, leaning into Bradford to steady herself. She giggles some more, holding onto his broad shoulders. "We shouldn't have had that glass of wine."

"Let's get you down from there," Bradford says, wrapping his arms around her waist and lifting her down from the ladder.

I stand there speechless, trying to figure out what's going on. And how to close my mouth, which seems to be locked open in surprise.

But Mimi, ever the gracious hostess, takes over. "It's Sally, isn't it?" she asks, walking toward me and extending her hand, as if welcoming me into my own home.

I wait for Bradford to correct her, but this time he doesn't seem indignant that his ex-wife can't remember the name of his soon-to-be new wife.

"Mimi, try to get it right," he says with a laugh. "It's Sara."

"Oh that's right. Sara. I'll remember next time. Sara, plain and simple. Bradford dear, wasn't that gorgeous redhead you dated before this one named Sally?"

"No, that was Stephanie," Bradford corrects, laughing again.

What, was he working his way through the S's? Good thing I met him before he got to the T's. But I have more pressing concerns.

"Why is Mimi here?" I ask. "And why is she standing on a ladder in the living room to bring us soup?"

Mimi and Bradford exchange a knowing glance.

"Andy Warhol's soup cans," Mimi says condescendingly.

Oh, of course. I knew that. I'm an art teacher. Though a slightly upset and distracted one.

"Warhol's soup cans were always my favorites," Bradford explains. "But in the divorce settlement . . ."

". . . I selfishly took them," Mimi says. "Which I shouldn't have, because I always liked . . ."

". . . the de Kooning lithograph better," Bradford says. "And Mimi's been feeling so bad about it that tonight . . ."

". . . I just took the Warhols off my wall and came right over here to put them back where they belong."

I'd like to tell Mimi where she belongs. Which isn't here, looking adoringly at Bradford and coquettishly finishing his sentences. And it gets even worse. She tucks her arm into Bradford's. "I'm just trying to do the right thing," she says.

I take a deep breath. Any second, the woman's going to lift her leg and leave her scent. But this is my territory now. And it needs protecting.

"The right thing for you to do right now is leave," I say, trying to keep a nasty tone out of my voice. And failing.

"Tsk, tsk, Sara," Mimi says in a suspiciously honeyed tone. "We're all one family, after all."

One family? I'm pretty sure the law in this state allows only one wife per household. And I didn't hear anything about our joining the Mormon Church anytime soon. Still, I'm the one coming off badly here. How did Mimi the bitch suddenly become Mimi the benevolent? I think I liked her better in the bedroom a couple of nights ago. At least then Bradford seemed annoyed to see her.

"*Nyam hey renga calm,*" I hear myself blurt out.

Darn, I didn't mean to say that out loud. I was just trying to relax myself with a mantra. But I think the instructions in *Ladies' Home Journal* were to say it to yourself.

Still, the mantra works—though not as advertised. Mimi's so startled that she steps away from Bradford. And Bradford comes over and solicitously puts his arm around me.

"Are you okay?" he asks, concerned that I'm suddenly speaking in tongues.

"I'm fine," I say. In English. I even make myself smile. "I'm glad you got the painting back. It looks great on that wall."

"It does," Mimi says smugly. "As Bradford can tell you, I'm good at decorating. And other things. I have a nice touch."

I let that one go since Mimi is collecting her pink toolbox and seems to be heading toward the door. She throws Bradford a kiss.

"So we'll rendezvous tomorrow to pick out Skylar's birthday present? I still can't decide between the Links charm bracelet and the Tiffany pavé pendant."

Nice choice for a soon-to-be-fourteen-year-old. Maybe they can buy both and give one to me.

"I'm sure I'll like whatever you pick," Bradford says. "But of course I'll come. Four o'clock?"

"Perfect," Mimi says, sailing past me and out of the house. I slam the door, but I can't get rid of her. The mandarin overtones of Mimi's J'adore perfume linger. And I pause for a moment, wondering who j'adores who.

When I turn back to Bradford, he has a smile on his face—but I'm determined to believe it's because of the returned Warhols, not Mimi. As if to prove me right, he comes over and gives me a big hug.

"So how was your evening with Kate, honey? You two do anything interesting?"

"It was fine," I say with a shrug. I put down the car keys, which I'd been holding in my hand all this time. Somehow, I've lost the impetus to tell Bradford about Kate's new house and my escapade in the Z-4. My road trip no longer ranks as the big risk of the day. Frankly, Mimi's cozying up to Bradford seems a lot more dangerous.

Late Friday afternoon, I'm standing in the kitchen of Olivia's luxe Manhattan apartment, sweating. How did I let Berni railroad me into this? Sure I can pull off a little lunch for a baby shower. But catering a fancy buffet dinner for forty where the guest of honor is Harrison Ford? When I'm stressed, I usually start gorging, but today I can't even do that. What if I don't have enough food for the party? Is fifty pounds of Ghirardelli chocolate enough for forty people?

Fortunately my new assistant Kirk is unflappable, and it looks like he'll be as good a sous-chef as he is a doctor. As a little joke, he got the wardrobe mistress from *Sweeney Todd* to provide matching aprons for us. So what if they're splattered with fake blood.

I'm scurrying around the kitchen, fussing with my hors d'oeuvres, appetizers, salads and three main courses. Not to mention my one spectacular can-always-count-on-it chocolate soufflé. Meanwhile, Kirk is unhurriedly unpacking the eight boxes of produce that we carefully culled from the shelves at Whole Foods. And he's giving loving attention to each piece.

"Is this the most beautiful tomato you've ever seen?" he asks, holding it aloft and rapturously turning it full circle.

Since this is the fourth tomato he's admired, I'm getting a little suspicious. "They can't all be the most beautiful," I say, busily trying to separate egg whites for the soufflé.

"You're right. I just want each tomato to feel special," he says. "That way they'll be at their juiciest best."

"We're talking beefsteak tomatoes here," I say with a laugh. "Not those cute little tomatoes you date." Though I bet any variety of tomato is at its juiciest around Kirk.

"Many tomatoes around." Kirk grins, looking at me. "But you're the most beautiful of the crop."

"Cut it out," I say, wiping my brow with the back of my hand. "I'm feeling a little overripe."

"Not at all," Kirk says thoughtfully. "Unlike tomatoes, women get better as they age."

"Very profound," I say, rolling my eyes but enjoying his banter. And not wanting to tell him that the reason we get better is that winning combination of insight, experience and alpha-hydroxy.

"I majored in philosophy in college," Kirk explains proudly. "It's been really important to my career as an actor. Helps me understand the motivation of my characters."

Right. Because everything you need to know about why Dr. Lance Lovett dumped the young nurse to sleep with the evil twin of the cardiac-transplant patient is right there in Plato's *Republic*.

"Philosophy's also good for picking up girls," Kirk adds with a smile. "I'll show you how it works." He pauses and then regales me with his best come-ons. "Want to talk some Nietzsche? Or are you too busy making the gnocchi?"

"Definitely too busy," I say, kneading the pasta dough and looking for a rolling pin.

"Sorry. I don't want to distract you. We'll get to Spinoza after you cook the spaghetti." He stands up very straight and pretends to be serious. "And no Kierkegaard until you've cut the cantaloupe."

Now I put down the rolling pin and just laugh. "Okay. And let's save the Rawls until I've baked the rolls."

"Good one," Kirk says, and he raises his hand to slap me five.

I meet his hand and grin. Somehow, he's managing to make cooking this dinner fun.

"Back to work," I tell him, trying to remember how many eggs I've already separated. Must have been six. Or maybe it was seven. How much difference could a yolk or two make anyway? This recipe is foolproof.

Kirk's slicing his way through a hunk of sashimi-quality tuna when Olivia bustles into the kitchen, dressed in a sleeveless black satin shell, hot pink capri pants, and jeweled sandals with four-inch spike heels. She glances at me just as I'm digging a shard of eggshell out of the bowl with my pinky.

"Fingers out of the food," she says imperiously, treating me like the help. Which I guess I am. Given what Olivia's paying for my services, I'm not going to complain.

Having thrown her weight around with me, she now changes direction and throws herself at Kirk.

"Oooh, I've never seen such gorgeous tuna," she says, leaning over his shoulder and hugging him from behind. Is she trying to seduce him or give him the Heimlich maneuver?

"Wait until you see the tomatoes," Kirk says proudly. "Talk about gorgeous."

Yes, Olivia would like to talk about gorgeous. But the foodstuffs aren't the only objects of her affection.

"I'm so lucky to have you here," she says, stroking his arm. And his ego. "Kirk Hudson, soap star extraordinaire, right here in my kitchen. Darling, you're just too wonderful to be doing this for me."

"I'm not doing it for you," he says, wielding the chef's knife like a pro. "I'm here for Sara. I'm hers for the night."

Olivia spins around to look at me.

"What he means is he's staying for the whole party," I explain.

Olivia looks relieved. "Then he's really mine for the night. My party. I'm paying."

Three hours later, the payoff begins. The guests are arriving, the waiters are circulating with hors d'oeuvres, and Kirk is helping me get forty filleted quail legs into the oven. He carefully studies the broiler pan.

"Pretty small legs," he says.

"But they're firm and perfectly shaped," I say, having personally stuffed each one with my spinach and cheese mixture.

Kirk winks. "You're right. And as they always say. Size doesn't matter."

"One of the great lies of all time," I say flippantly.

Olivia bursts into the kitchen, her face flushed in excitement. This time she ignores me completely.

"You're done in the kitchen," she tells Kirk, untying his apron. "No reason to keep a treasure like you hidden away. Come be my escort. A lot of important people are out there that I want to introduce you to."

Kirk, torn between catering and his chance for connections, throws me an apologetic glance. "Why don't we get Sara out front, too?" he suggests.

"That's okay," I say. "I've got to keep an eye on things here."

"And nobody wants to meet her, anyway," Olivia says brusquely.

For once I know the perfect thing to say. And I know it on the spot, rather than coming up with it six hours from now when I'm lying in bed.

"Don't worry, Kirk," I say as Olivia hustles him out of the kitchen. "We can finish talking about my shapely legs later."

A few minutes later, I peek out through the swinging door. Either I haven't been watching enough *Hollywood Squares* or Olivia hasn't pulled in quite the crowd she was hoping. Harrison Ford is invisible—or he hasn't shown up yet—and soap stud Kirk seems to be the main attraction. Women are hanging on his every word and a sexy brunette is hanging on his bicep. Any doubt that daytime hunks are now the Masters of the Universe is erased by an investment banker across the room who's shooting Kirk menacing glances.

I undo the top two buttons on my white cotton blouse. The party scene is steamy, but that doesn't explain why the kitchen's so hot. Could be the vent on the Garland range isn't working very well. Or maybe I'm having a hot flash. I could be in perimenopause—though who has any idea what that means. Is it when you start losing estrogen? Or collagen? Or men? Maybe all three. Best I can tell, it's something doctors dreamed up so you spend your forties panicking about going into menopause in your fifties. And buying any beauty product that promises to make you look like you're in your thirties.

But this particular hot flash won't go away. And I'm starting to see phantom flames. Help! The flames are real. The oven. I grab the fire extinguisher and start spraying in the general direction of the smoke. But instead of hitting the flames, I manage to knock over two bottles of wine, which smash noisily to the floor. Before I have a chance to make the Pepsi bottles explode, I fling open the door to the living room.

"Kirk," I holler urgently into the crowd, "come quick! My legs are on fire!"

Harrison Ford turns around. So he did make it after all. But he's no Indiana Jones—at least off the set. He stands frozen in his spot as Kirk rushes to my side and assumes the heroic starring role, snatching the extinguisher from my hand. In one swift move, he slams the oven door closed and turns off the gas.

"Fire should go out in a second," he says reassuringly.

He's right. No gas, no oxygen, and suddenly the flames are gone.

But I have a new problem. "The dinner's ruined," I say, sniffling.

"It's not ruined," Kirk says comfortingly, reaching into his back pocket and handing me a perfectly ironed handkerchief. Once I would have thought the crisp hankie meant Kirk was either gay or lived with his mother. Now I know it's a white flag that he's a true metrosexual— the newly coined term for a guy who sleeps with a woman and then joins her at a day spa for his very own facial. Nice, but I prefer a relationship where I'm the only one who exfoliates.

I wipe my eyes on the hankie, blow my nose, and start to hand it back to him. Then I think better of it. I'll give him back a clean one. Wonder if he prefers starch?

"We'll just tell everyone blackened quail legs are a delicacy," Kirk says, improvising happily.

"Blackened doesn't mean burnt—it's a spice," I say, stuffing the handkerchief in my pocket.

Kirk grins. "And who's supposed to know that? Olivia the epicurean?"

Kirk helps me whip the quails onto platters, then drizzles some Grand Marnier on the side and lights a match.

"Flambé," he says triumphantly, as the waiters whisk the flaming platters to the buffet table. "The crowd will love it."

And amazingly, he's right. Next time I peek out, I see that everyone is actually eating and the food seems to be a hit. A few more stars have arrived and Olivia is busy accepting accolades for our fabulous flambé.

I go back to the stove to check on the vanilla custard sauce for the soufflé. I beat the egg whites until they're stiff but glossy, delicately fold the mixture and pop the molds into the oven. Done. I pour myself a glass of Chardonnay and sit down to wait for them to rise. It always makes me laugh that people think soufflés are so complicated you have to be Richard Feynman to get the formula right. I flunked physics and still I've never gotten it wrong.

The kitchen fills with the endorphin-inducing chocolate aroma coming from the oven, and I'm finally relaxed. In the homestretch now. All I have to do is get the irresistible dessert out there and then I'm out of here. Sure enough, when I take out the soufflés, they're perfect. I can already hear the oohs and aahs. I look at them admiringly for thirty seconds—and then they start deflating faster than Jeff Gordon's car after a blow-out at Nascar. The soufflés are sinking lower and lower, and all of a sudden my delicate dessert is a sorry second to a dish of no-cook instant My-T-Fine.

I stare into the chocolate disasters and tell myself I'm not going to cry again. I'm really not. I down another glass of Chardonnay. Good wine. Though two glasses on an empty stomach might be too much for me. Still, I'm feeling calmer. How upset can I get about questionable quails and soggy soufflés? I've pulled off a pretty good party, but the officious Olivia isn't going to be grateful for anything I've done—except bringing Kirk. And maybe Berni secretly wanted me to ruin her rival's party. Why else send an elementary school art teacher to cook anything you can't fit into an Easy-Bake Oven?

Suddenly I have an idea on how I can salvage the dessert. If the wine's making me feel better, just think how it can improve the pudding. I transfer the goopy chocolate mixture into a large ceramic bowl and grab the Grand Marnier again. That might help. I search Olivia's cabinets and pull out some Amaretto and Frangelico and liberally pour them over my fallen masterpiece—adding a dash of Remy Martin for good measure. I should probably mix in some Tylenol to prevent hangovers. What else is in Olivia's pantry? Mmm—chocolate sprinkles. A small bag of M&Ms. Chocolate-covered raisins. Reese's pieces. The woman really can snack. I dump them all into the bowl.

For a final touch, I snatch a bag of mini-marshmallows from a shelf and sprinkle them over the top of my creation. Nice, but needs a little color. With a flourish, I grab a bag of gumdrops and plunk down all the pink ones. Then I add the yellow. And green. My first—and farewell— performance as a professional chef will be truly memorable. I hand the bowl to a waiter and tell him to bring it out. Then, leaving the scene of my culinary disaster, I make a swift getaway down the service elevator.

Chapter SIX

THE NEXT MORNING, I'm the one with the hangover. My eyes are puffy and my head is aching—whether from the wine or embarrassment I can't tell. And worst of all, I have lines on my face from the pillowcase. I can't even put my head down at this age without my face turning into a road map.

I roll over on the pillow to try to get back to sleep. I might as well make sure both sides of my face are equally etched. Is this what they mean by turning the other cheek?

"Saaa-raa," calls Berni from outside my bedroom door. "Are you there? Come on out."

Is there anybody who doesn't barge into this house? I pull on a pair of shorts and wander out in my T-shirt and bare feet. When I get to the living room, Berni's lying flat on the floor, knees up, a baby balanced like a barbell above her head.

"What are you doing?" I ask, rubbing my eyes sleepily.

"One . . . two . . . three . . . four," Berni counts out loud, the baby wavering in her hands. Berni inhales deeply, then lowers her arms slightly. Next she exhales and lifts again, picking up the pace. "Up . . . down . . . up . . . down," she says, moving her baby barbell more vigorously.

I'm barely awake, and Berni's already bonding with the babies while using them to build her biceps. What the heck. Looks like more fun than my Thursday afternoon spinning class. I lie down on the floor next to Berni and take the other twin from the Jolly Jumper.

"Make sure you lift slowly but don't shake," Berni warns. "And keep one hand under his head and the other under his butt."

In unison, we raise our babies and count together. I kind of like this. Better than a Nautilus machine, though frankly, this baby doesn't weigh enough to put a muscle on a mouse.

"Now arm curls," Berni says, sitting up and repositioning Baby A. She stretches her arms straight in front of her, curls the baby to her face, kisses her, and brings her back. Curl, kiss, curl, kiss. I can do that.

But four repetitions later, my barbell is starting to get a little soggy. Something that never happens at Crunch.

"I think he needs to be changed," I say, abruptly ending my exercise session and trying to hand the baby back.

"Diapers are in the bag," she says. "House rule. Whoever's holding the baby last gets to change him."

Could make for a mean game of hot potato. I try to pass Baby B back to Berni but she's not taking. I dutifully go over to the bag figuring I'll change the little tyke quickly—but instead of Pampers, Berni has cloth diapers and it takes me forever to figure out how to fold one. I probably should have guessed Berni would go for something complicated. She didn't quit a full-time job to pat down a piece of Velcro.

Berni watches me for a minute and then laughs. "You need a degree in origami to do this right," she says, taking over and finishing the job with a flourish. And looking at her handiwork, I wonder if she actually got one.

Berni turns to me, cuddling the now happy baby.

"So what happened at the party last night?" she asks. "Olivia called. Such an uproar."

"You heard from Olivia?" I ask guiltily.

"First thing this morning. Ken Chablis, head of the Food Network, called me, too."

Was he at the party? Maybe I poisoned him. Or maybe he choked eating a gumdrop. Or choked just looking at it.

"That dessert's usually foolproof," I say, ready with my excuses. "But I never made it for so many people before."

"It's all anybody can talk about," Berni says.

"If Olivia's upset, that's just tough. She's awful and she had it coming." Wow. Where did all this false bravado come from?

"Why would Olivia be upset?" Berni asks.

"Because . . ." I hesitate. Seems like I'm missing something here. "Why did Ken Chablis call you?"

"Olivia told him I'm your agent. It must have killed her to have to say that." She grins gleefully. "That Chocolate Surprise dessert you made knocked him out."

"Are we speaking literally or figuratively here?" I ask.

"Sounded pretty awful to me," Berni continues, "but he loved it. Said retro-chic could be the next big trend."

He must know. This is the network that discovered Emeril and the Iron Chef. Though given what they sometimes make, my Chocolate Surprise deserves a James Beard Award.

"So he wants the recipe?" I ask nervously. God knows what I threw in there. Because I certainly don't.

"He wants the recipe and wants you," Berni says. "He asked if you'd come in for an audition, but I said no. I played hardball and told him no tryouts. Either he books you or not. And he did. Two weeks from tomorrow, you're on live."

"Berni, you can't keep doing this," I say, exasperated. "I mean, I appreciate it and all, but you can't run my life."

"Of course I can," Berni says, nonchalantly. "That's what agents do. I'm good at it, too. Listen, Sara, this is a big deal. People love that network. Think of the future. You could end up endorsing a grill."

Ah, the American dream. I could marry a prince. I could live in a castle. I could endorse a grill.

"But I've never done anything like this before," I say.

"Exactly the reason to do it," says Berni, looking tenderly at her babies. "Trying something different is the whole point. Nobody expects doors to open at our age. But look at us. Isn't it amazing? New husband for you. New babies for me. And new careers for both of us. We've zipped past forty, but we get to start again. Who would have thought?"

Not me, for one. But Berni's convincing.

"So how much would I get paid?" I ask, apparently ready to buy into the dream.

"Nothing," Berni says putting down Baby A, who's now blissfully asleep. "You do this to build your career."

"Clothing allowance?" I ask hopefully. Berni's a barracuda. Her negotiations must have gotten me something.

"Are you kidding? This is cable. You'll get an apron. With a logo if you're lucky. Ken said to bring your own bowls and spoons to the set. And sugar. Just in case."

"Hair and makeup?" I ask.

"Sure. If you do it yourself." She picks up Baby B and begins wagging her head in his direction, leaning in closer until she's rubbing his nose with hers.

"Boo-ful, boo-ful baby," she burbles, fully forgetting about me.

So much for the art of the deal. Bring my own sugar? Maybe I should call Olivia.

Kate has convinced me to come with her to a chic Madison Avenue day spa for the latest South American Wrap. I thought I'd be getting some Nuevo Latin chicken with salsa on the side. Instead, I'm the one getting wrapped. Apparently, the very same Brazilians who sent us the bikini wax have devised a new form of torture. This time for weight loss. Your targeted body parts are covered in a plaster cast, and after just one session you end up thinner and cellulite free. Or you vow never to go skiing again.

Right now, the white-uniformed Felita is carefully bandaging my calf. The material is slowly snaking its way up my leg, and I'm starting to get an itch somewhere above my ankle. An area that she entombed five minutes ago.

"When you get to the thighs, wrap really tight," Kate commands, waving her fingers excitedly. Her fingers are about all she can still move, since her own plaster casts reach from shoulders to wrists. With her encased arms extending straight out in front of her, she looks like a sleepwalking Egyptian mummy.

"Very tight," Felita agrees, without a break in her wrapping rhythm. English doesn't seem to be her first—or even second or third—language, so I'm not sure how much faith I can put in her assent. But she smiles pleasantly.

"Is good?" she asks, finishing one leg and starting on the other.

Oh yes, is good. Nothing makes your day like double casts, an itch you can't scratch, and interrupted blood flow.

I look down at my legs, now thoroughly trapped in white plaster. I can't even ask anyone to send me an FTD bouquet or a Hallmark "Get Well" card because this is my own fault. What was I thinking? I can't be this desperate to lose five pounds before my television debut. Oh yes I can.

"Are you feeling thin yet?" Kate asks, staring at her own plastered arms.

"I'm feeling like a refugee from *M*A*S*H*," I reply.

"But a thin refugee, right?" Kate suggests.

A strange aroma starts to waft up off the cast. Either the fat is disappearing or the herbs and algae that were mixed into the plaster are marinating on my sweaty legs. Kate claims one hundred and sixteen secret ingredients, all flown in fresh daily from South America, go into the mix. Sounds like we could have had lunch here after all. The Brazilian comes over and shakes something from a container over the top of the casts. Salt and pepper?

She pats the casts, then pings the flesh on the underside of my arms. "Wrap arms?" she asks.

I watch mesmerized as she pinches an inch of flab. Guess those curls with Berni's babies didn't do the trick. Maybe Dylan would make a better barbell. But I can't bear to have my arms wrapped, too. In fact, if Felita doesn't stop playing with that too-soft upper arm flesh, I'm going to use one of my leg casts as a battering ram.

"How much longer do we have to stay like this?" I ask Kate when Felita finally leaves.

"Fifty-nine minutes," she says, trying to look at the watch on her outstretched wrist. "Some people leave the casts on for days, but it's not recommended."

As if this shorter stint has the *Good Housekeeping* seal of approval. I can't imagine that researchers have run any double-blind studies on this little procedure yet. Or even any animal studies. And come to think of it, if anybody did to a dog what we've each paid the Brazilian three hundred fifty dollars to do to us, they'd end up on PETA's hit list.

I'm trying not to think about a second itch I can't scratch when Felita comes back with a worried look on her face.

"*Problemo!*" she says excitedly. "Big *problemo!*"

Damn. I knew something would go wrong. I'm going to be really embarrassed if I end up dying because she put the wrong herbs in the plaster.

But she has something else on her mind. "*Problemo,*" she repeats. "Is a man. Come."

It should be pretty obvious that we're not exactly in a position to handle problems right now. Or men, for that matter. But Kate has already jumped off the table.

"I'm sure it's Owen," she says smugly. Since she can't run her fingers through her hair, she tosses back her head and shakes it a few times. "Nina has been my secretary forever and I love her. But if she doesn't stop telling Owen where I am every second of the day, I'm going to kill her."

I'd be mortified to have anybody see me this way, never mind a lover. But Kate gives a little smile, secretly pleased that Owen can't bear to be without her for a minute, and heads confidently out the door. I hope the emergency isn't that he needs a dose of affection because there's no way she can give him a hug.

Whatever Owen wants must be pretty important because the meeting takes longer than I would have thought. I wiggle my toes to make sure they're still moving and decide that maybe I should get a pedicure someday, after all. Kate finally comes back, looking shaken. She glances at me briefly and takes a moment as if deciding what to say. Then she takes a deep breath.

"You better sit down," Kate says.

"How can I sit when I can't even bend my knees?" I ask. I'm sprawled across the table, but if this requires my total attention, I can make an effort. I prop myself up with my elbow.

"I just meant for you to steel yourself," Kate says. And then she seems to do the same. "Sara, there really is a problem. The man outside. He wanted to see you, not me. It's James."

So it isn't Owen who showed up. It's not Dylan. Not Bradford. It's James. The name doesn't make any impression for a moment.

"Oh my god," I say, suddenly jerking so abruptly that my elbow slips and smashes against the side of the table. "*The* James? My James? I mean not 'my' James. My ex-husband James? It can't be. He's in Patagonia."

"I know it can't be, but it is," Kate says consolingly. "He's here and he hasn't changed. Or maybe just a little. He looks even better."

This is helpful. Without thinking, I massage my injured arm, then run my fingers through my own hair. But what am I doing? I don't want to see him. Not now, not ever. Although if he waits a few more minutes, at least I'll be thin.

"Tell him to leave," I say vehemently. "I want him gone. Gone, gone, gone."

Of course gone is what he's been. The real question is what's brought him back. Maybe he knows I'm finally happy and he figured he'd show up and try to screw up my life. Again.

"He says he came back to New York a week ago," Kate explains. And then she adds quietly, "He wants to see Dylan."

I fly off the table—casts and all—and land flat on my face. I scramble back up and tentatively touch my nose. Not bleeding. Probably not broken. But at least there are plenty of bandages if I need them.

"He's never wanted to see Dylan before. And he's not seeing Dylan now," I say, trying not to get hysterical. "Go tell him that."

"Tell me yourself," James says, striding into the room.

In an instant, the whole world stops. Adrenaline is pulsing through my body and every nerve ending is on alert. My heart is pounding and I can even feel the blood vessels throbbing in my forehead. But somehow I'm frozen in place, staring at the man in front of me.

James's sandy blond hair is as thick as ever, but instead of the long ponytail he sported last time I saw him, he's cut it short and neat. The beard is gone, too, and his skin is deeply tanned and smooth. The slim shoulders have gotten more solid—maybe carrying a backpack through the mountains does that to you—and he's added some ropy muscle but no fat to his arms. The deep blue eyes are still piercingly sharp, and right now, they're focused intently on me.

How many nights did I lay awake over the years, imagining this moment of coming face to face with James again? How would I feel? Would I still be in love? Now I have the answer.

I can't stand the sight of him.

Maybe I should use these casts as a battering ram after all. One good hard kick to send James right back to Patagonia.

"As usual you've picked a bad time and a bad place," I say, my voice trembling. "Get the hell out."

He sits down on the therapy table I've just abandoned. "Sorry to startle you," he says. "I've been trying to track you down for a week. I finally went to Kate's office and got sent over here."

"Nina," Kate mutters. "Can't keep a secret. Too bad she doesn't have the combination to Harry Winston's safe."

"I didn't want to waste another minute," James says, looking down at his Merrell hiking boots and shifting his weight from side to side. "I figured there's no time like the present."

"The present was a long time ago," I say. "Eight years, to be precise. You missed it."

A soft chime sounds and the Brazilian comes back in. "Time up," she says. "Unravel." She starts to nudge the edge of the cast with a tiny knife. As if I'm not unraveling enough.

"How should we do this?" James asks, ignoring the treatment going on and forging ahead with his plan. "Should I come to your house? Or do you want to bring Dylan somewhere like the zoo or Central Park? Maybe that's an easier way for him to get to know his father."

"You're not his father," I say stalwartly. "And you're not seeing him."

For a full minute James stands absolutely still, as if mustering his resolve. "I'm moving back to New York to be near my son," he says. "If you need me to say I made a lot of mistakes in the past, I'll say it. I did. But I'm ready to make up for it now."

"Well, you can't. You don't just waltz back in here after all these years and expect things to be the way you want. You left me and went off to hike. I went on to be a mother."

"I wasn't just hiking," James says defensively. "I was doing important work. I've been part of the international team trying to rescue the Patagonian language."

"Only you, James," I say bitterly. "You go off to some dangerous mountains in a godforsaken country and you're not even rescuing people. You're rescuing a dead language."

"The Endangered Language Fund has put Kawésqar on the critical list," he says grandly. "Only six people still speak it. We're preserving it for the children of future generations."

"Then go back to focusing on those children," I suggest angrily. "And keep away from my child. Dylan's happy. And he doesn't need you."

"I just want to see him," he says quietly. "Take a day or two to think about it. I know we can work it out."

Felita continues scissoring her way from thigh to ankle on both casts. When she finally gets the plaster off, I can't tell if my legs are thinner but they're definitely an odd shade of green. Maybe too much basil in the mix. With my legs finally free, I should feel as if a huge weight has been lifted. But with James hovering, an even greater weight seems to be pressing down.

James starts to walk out of the room, but then turns back. "Sara, you have every right to be angry at me. I understand. It took me a long time and a lot of years in Patagonia to grow up. I'm not trying to get our old life back. I'm just trying to make a new one."

I'm distracted from answering since Felita is now rubbing my legs with soft chamois cloths that must be soaked in fifty other secret ingredients, because the green is coming off and my legs are glistening.

James watches the procedure for a moment. "One more thing," he says, smiling slightly for the first time since he came into this Brazilian beauty chamber. "You don't need any of these crazy treatments. You look even prettier than I remember."

As soon as James is gone, Kate holds out her arms so Felita can remove her casts, too.

"It's going to be okay, Sara, it really is," she calls out to me gently.

"No, it's not," I say, grabbing my things. "This is a nightmare. Everything is a nightmare where James is concerned. Sorry to leave you. But I have to get out of here and find a lawyer. Right away."

I rush out of the dim spa and into the bright sunlight. I blink a few times and dash madly down the block, as if I expect to find Johnnie Cochran standing on the corner with a sandwich board, looking for new clients. But I pull myself together enough to shakily speed dial Bradford who immediately hears the tremor in my voice. He doesn't even ask what's wrong. He just asks if I need him. I feel a flood of gratitude.

"Yes, I need you," I say, choking back tears.

"Then you have me. I'll drop everything," he says, making a quick plan to meet me at the understated private club where he's a member. "See you there in fifteen minutes."

I start walking toward the club, trying to keep my knees from buckling. All of a sudden my neat little world is falling apart. James can't be back now. I have a fiancé. I'm supposed to be getting married. Everything's in place and under control. But what's that old expression? If you want to hear God laugh, make plans.

My head is spinning as I try to think how James's reappearance could change my life. What will happen next? This being New York, I may not have to wait long for an answer, because right in front of me on the steamy sidewalk is a huge purple sign proclaiming, LEARN YOUR FUTURE! MADAME ROSA KNOWS ALL. FOR $15 SHE TELLS. I pause in front of the grungy storefront and try to peer in. A round-figured woman in a gypsy headscarf and flowing flowered robes comes with unexpected speed to the door.

"You unhappy, I tell you good future," she offers, grabbing my arm and trying to hustle me inside.

"I could use a good future," I say, sniffling, but still not making a commitment.

"For you, ten percent discount," the gypsy woman says, figuring that the buck and a half is the only thing between me and her tarot cards. "I promise, only good things in my crystal ball."

"Only good things, that's right," I say, suddenly remembering that this is one of those scams the mayor cleaned up. Psychics were predicting terrible futures—and then charging a fortune to lift the spell. "It's illegal in New York City now to give bad news, isn't it? I wish CNN had the same policy."

Madame Rosa looks askance. "An educated consumer is my worst customer," she says, abandoning me on the sidewalk and walking back into her den of tea leaves. Green tea, no doubt, for the antioxidant effects.

With even a psychic turning me away I walk several more blocks and slip into the discreetly marked club. The moment I see Bradford, I fall into his arms and burst into loud sobs.

"Come on, we need a quiet place to talk," Bradford says, taking my hand and leading me up to a private conference room. But I notice the RESERVED sign on the door and start sobbing even louder.

"Nothing's working out today," I cry. "Where else can we go to talk?"

Bradford smiles as he opens the door. "It's reserved for us," he says.

We go into the carpeted room outfitted as an old-fashioned library with large wooden tables and oversized chairs. I collapse onto a leather sofa and before Bradford says anything or even asks me what's wrong, he tilts my head and kisses away my tears.

"Whatever it is, we'll fix it," he says reassuringly, leaning against me and continuing the kisses.

"I don't know how to fix it," I say, sitting up abruptly. "James showed up this afternoon and he wants to see Dylan."

I've told Bradford enough about James in the past that he doesn't need to hear any more. He can fill in the blanks by himself.

"I won't let James into Dylan's life," I tell Bradford furiously. "I'll fight him. I need a lawyer. An expensive one. We'll take it to the Supreme Court."

"They may be busy this week," Bradford says calmly, taking my hand. "And getting involved in a court battle is never a good plan."

"Ruth Bader Ginsburg would be on my side," I say.

Bradford smiles. "She probably would. But so would my old friend Joy Brown. You know who I mean—the psychologist who has a radio show. When Mimi ran off, Joy reminded me that no matter how angry you are at your horrible ex-spouse, you have to focus on what's best for your good kid."

"I was focused just fine on my kid until James came back from Patagonia. Tierra del Fuego. Also known as the End of the Earth."

Bradford rubs my hand sympathetically. "Okay, but this isn't the end of the world."

I stand up and start pacing around the room. "I have to do something," I say.

Being a man of action, Bradford picks up a portable phone from the corner table.

"Should I call Joy for you? I have her private number."

"You might as well," I say with a shrug. I'm hoping she's bound by the same rules as Madame Rosa and can't give me any bad news.

Bradford dials and, after a brief pause, exchanges pleasantries with someone on the other end. He quickly explains he's a friend of Joy's and outlines the situation. Then he passes the receiver over to me.

"Her assistant said Joy will be on the line in a second," Bradford says.

I take the phone, but I'm on hold and plugged into a radio news station. Traffic out to Kennedy airport is backed up for seven miles and there's a thirty percent chance of thundershowers this afternoon. A commercial for Pizza Hut offers a free loaf of garlic bread with every jumbo order. And the next spot, for a weight-loss pill, guarantees to help you lose twenty pounds in a week. Though probably only if you don't order from Pizza Hut. Someone in scheduling isn't paying attention. Or else has a sense of humor.

Finally there's a staticky sound on the line, and then a click.

"Hello, Sara, this is Joy," says a friendly voice. "We don't have much time so let's get right to it. What's your question for me?"

Doesn't have much time? If she's a therapist, shouldn't I get an hour? Or a fifty-minute hour? Apparently not. So all I have to do is describe my life in thirty words or less. I give it a shot.

"I'm engaged to be married," I say, carefully thinking this out. "My ex-husband has just come back after nearly a decade to see the child he's never met."

Hey, that was pretty succinct. Maybe I could get a job at *Reader's Digest*.

"Where was he?" asks Joy Brown, as if in certain situations it would be acceptable to be missing for eight years. Like if you're Tom Hanks stranded on a desert island talking to a Wilson volleyball.

"He was in Patagonia," I say.

"Is he with the Endangered Language Fund? Wonderful project," Joy burbles.

How does she possibly know about the Endangered Language Fund? Maybe she's one of the last six speakers of Kawésqar. Bradford said she was smart.

But Joy is still talking. And apparently not only to me. "If any of our listeners don't know about the Fund, I'll give the phone number for donations later in the show," she announces.

Wait a minute. Our listeners? The show? If Joy's a radio psychologist, am I on the air?

"Am I on the air?" I ask in a panic, my voice suddenly shaking.

"Of course, cookie. Just take a deep breath. I know it's thrilling to get me on the phone. But pretend it's just you and me talking."

That's just what I had been pretending. Or assuming. Now what do I do? Hang up or hang in? Or just hang myself?

"I'm on the air," I hiss to Bradford.

He looks stunned. "How could that happen?" he asks. "I thought this was her private number."

"So let's get to it," Joy says briskly, moving her show along. "The husband who dumped you has come back and wants to see the kid. First impulse is to string him up. Or get a lawyer. Practically the same thing. But at the end of the day, you've got to figure out what's worse— your kid seeing his father. Or your kid seeing his mother and father fighting over him."

"I think of James as a sperm donor, not a father," I say, irritated.

"At least he had a strong swimmer. Something good to say about him," Dr. Brown quips. "Look, I know how you're feeling right now, but you're going to have to be the grown-up. Work out something with him. I'm not saying he gets to move in, or gets custody, or even gets a tie on Father's Day. But your son must have questions. And it's good that even at this late date, dad wants to be part of his son's life."

I start crying again because of course Dylan has had questions. And I haven't been able to answer them. I can never forgive James and he doesn't deserve to be Dylan's father. But Joy has a point. Maybe I shouldn't keep Dylan from meeting him just to get my own revenge.

"James said we could meet him at the zoo but Dylan's afraid of lions," I say, looking for any excuse.

"Hypnosis is very successful in dealing with phobias," says Dr. Joy, our endless font of information. "But you could just take Dylan to the sea lions. Feeding time is four o'clock. It's adorable. But don't be late, it gets crowded."

Bradford was right. Joy's rational and she knows how to lay out a plan.

"Thank you, Dr. Joy," I say, meaning it.

I hang up and give Bradford a hug. I'm grateful for my new perspective—though totally humiliated that I've been on the air and the whole world now knows my problems.

"Very helpful," I admit to Bradford. "But embarrassing. Talk about airing your dirty laundry."

"Don't worry, Joy's been complaining her ratings are down. Nobody listens," Bradford says reassuringly.

I'm comforted by that thought for exactly five seconds—until my cell phone rings.

"Did I just hear you on the radio?" Berni asks.

"I hope not," I say. What must Berni think of me, that I'm calling a radio psychologist? On the other hand, why was she listening? Maybe all that diaper folding doesn't quite fill her day.

"It was me, but I shouldn't have called," I say, embarrassed.

"That's right," says Berni, not mincing words. But her complaint isn't quite what I would have expected. "You shouldn't have called. You're a TV star now. And if I'm your agent, you clear all media through me."

Chapter SEVEN

FOR THREE DAYS, I'm depressed about James. I manage to keep my-self going, but every evening, I eat my way through a pint (or two) of Rocky Road. On one particularly bad night, I can't sleep at all and check the TV listings at two in the morning for something to watch. *The Sorrow and the Pity* sounds good.

When James tracks me down on the phone, I manage to pull my-self together and call on my Dr. Joy–inspired maturity to stay calm. We launch into two days of nonstop negotiations over what I'll tell Dylan, when we'll all get together, and where the big meeting is going to take place. Kate calls almost hourly, falling back into her old role as best friend and marriage counselor. Or in this case, ex-marriage counselor. She's too polite to complain about my endless whining, but by mid-week, even I'm getting tired of it. Time to change the subject. So when Kate mentions that she's going to an auction at Sotheby's to buy Owen a birthday present, I offer to tag along and give her some advice. As long as she's not buying soup cans.

I arrive early and stand on the sidewalk outside of Sotheby's, wait-ing for Kate and watching a steady procession of art patrons going in. The men, carrying expensive T. Anthony briefcases and dressed in con-servative pinstripe suits from Louis of Boston, glide confidently to the front door. The women, all outfitted in tasteful St. John summer knits, are well-heeled—literally—in their boring but reliable pumps. As they walk by, several glance in my direction and then quickly look down at their Ferragamos. Either they're checking that the buckles are on straight or they recognize that in my twenty-eight-dollar H & M cotton-polyester sundress, I'm not one of the club. Though frankly I think the dress is adorable.

"Your dress is adorable," says Kate, coming up to me with a kiss a minute later and patting the full skirt admiringly. "You're so lucky that you look good in cheap clothes. I've never been able to wear them. They just don't fit."

What a compliment. I have hips made for polyester. But how could anything not fit Kate's perfectly slim body? More likely that cheap clothes just don't fit her image. And it's just as well, since her sophisticated John Galliano suit fits like it was made for her, which it probably was.

"I've been poring over the auction catalogue," Kate says exuberantly, as we enter the elite art emporium and walk through the intimidating granite-and-glass lobby. "I know exactly the right print to buy. Red Grooms has this huge, wild New York picture that I swear has one of Owen's buildings in it. And Grooms is Owen's favorite artist. It's perfect."

"Sounds great," I say, wondering where a married man hangs a litho from his lover. The bathroom? The basement? The back of the closet? Or maybe he just gives it to another girlfriend.

We head upstairs to sign in.

"You should get a paddle, just in case you want to bid," says Kate. And while that's about as likely as George Bush giving the keynote at Planned Parenthood, I give my name and relevant information to a haughty sixtyish-year-old woman with too-pale makeup and a helmet of too-black hair. She types my vital statistics into the computer, makes two whispered phone calls and hits a few more keys on the iMac.

"Apparently your credit was approved," she says snottily, making it very clear she personally would never give authorization to someone carrying a LeSportsac tote. Reluctantly, she hands me a paddle for bidding.

"I need a paddle, too," Kate tells the woman. "I should be in your computer already."

Miss High and Mighty types in Kate's name and breaks into a welcoming smile. "Ah. Dr. Steele, what a pleasure," she says sycophantically. "Good to have you here again. I'll seat you and your friend right in the front." And then, lowering her voice, she adds, "Perhaps after the auction, I could have a word with you about liposuction."

I roll my eyes. Ever since Kate's name has become known, everyone wants to give her things, hoping to get a magic makeover in return. This woman apparently believes a good seat at the auction is worth a pound of flesh—surgically removed by Kate.

We walk quickly away, stroll down a long hallway and take our second-row seats. Furtively, I practice raising and lowering my paddle. What if I sneeze, go to wipe my nose and accidentally raise the paddle by mistake? I could end up buying a Julian Schnabel—one of his broken plate paintings. I've never liked those. They remind me too much of the summer I was a waitress, which was not a thing of beauty.

Once we're seated, Kate flips through the catalogue and points out a few affordable prints that I might consider. She checks the lot number for the Red Grooms she wants and dog-ears several other pages.

The auctioneer, a debonair older man in a bow tie, ascends the podium, and the buzzing in the room quickly subsides. In cultured English-accented tones, he welcomes the audience and I immediately feel more at ease. Maybe it's because he reminds me of that guy who used to host *Masterpiece Theatre*.

Bidding begins on the first few artworks and prices escalate quickly.

"Just another thousand dollars and we'll set a new price record for this," encourages the auctioneer, peddling a Jasper Johns flag. For some reason, that inspires more spirited bidding.

"A new high!" he announces happily, when he finally bangs down his gavel, and the audience breaks into applause. Apparently, the higher the price, the happier rich people are. They brag about paying outrageous sums for private school tuition, East Side co-ops and hunks of chevre at Zabar's. Personally, I only clap my hands when things are on sale.

The auction continues, and the bidding is fierce. Though when I look around, I realize the big action comes from the nod of a head, the tapping of an index finger, or the polite semi-raising of a paddle. I'm busy trying to decide whether the man at the end of our row rubbing his forehead is making a bid or needs two Advil when there's a slight stir in the room. Miss High and Mighty herself—or Miss H & M as I've laughingly come to think of her—comes in a side door with a couple trailing behind her. She gets them settled in reserved seats and effusively fusses over them. Once she steps away, I try to get a good look at the tony twosome who've rated all this attention.

And then I see them.

Stunned, I spin back in my seat and grab Kate's arm. In my panic, my paddle falls to the floor with a loud thud and going to pick it up, I bang my head on the armrest and let out a small yelp.

"You okay?" Kate whispers.

"No," I hiss, grabbing for my LeSportsac tote. "We have to leave."

Kate looks surprised. "The Red Grooms litho is next," she says. "We can go after that, if you want."

I want to get out right now. And to get Kate out. Because I can't bear her noticing the couple who just walked in arm-and-arm, chattering sweetly. The cozy couple who are now seated just four rows away. Owen and his beautiful blonde wife.

Up on the stage, the large colorful Red Grooms comes out and Kate sits up in her seat. She holds her paddle tightly and gives me a little nudge.

"This is it," she says, excitedly. "Remember, I'm relying on you. Whatever happens, don't let me go over my budget."

"Will do," I say. But as far as I can tell, Kate's already over budget. She's invested way too much in Owen.

The auctioneer announces the floor price and the bidding begins. It advances at hundred-dollar increments, and Kate's paddle moves up and down so quickly it looks like she's competing in the Ping-Pong

Olympics. But it soon becomes clear that an equally determined opponent is vying for the Grooms. As the price escalates so does the auctioneer's enthusiasm. He seems to relish the battle, and at every bid his head bobs back and forth from Kate to her adversary, who's sitting a few rows away. Kate keeps her eyes forward, focused on the auctioneer, but I've already figured out that the woman bidding against Kate is Owen's wife. One way or another, the real estate mogul is going to get what he wants for his birthday.

"Getting close to your limit," I murmur anxiously to Kate. "Probably time to stop."

"One more bid," Kate says. But when the bidding keeps creeping up, Kate doesn't quit. Like a gambler at a Las Vegas slot machine, Kate's sure she's going to hit the jackpot on the next round. Her budget be damned, she wants to win.

"You have to stop," I entreat, as the price keeps climbing. "This is ridiculous."

"I don't care," she says. "I want to do this for Owen. He's worth everything to me."

Whatever Owen's value, the picture seems to be going for a lot more than Kate expected. Her opponent blithely tops every one of Kate's bids, and it soon becomes apparent that she's not going to give in. Kate doesn't get the message until she's gone three hundred percent over her budget. Then she reluctantly puts down the paddle.

"Going once, going twice, gone!" the auctioneer announces gleefully, banging his gavel against the podium. "Sold to Mrs. Owen Hardy!"

Not used to losing, Kate doesn't register the name for a moment. But then it hits her and she turns ashen. She looks at me in shock, then half leaps out of her seat, turning around in disbelief.

"Owen?" she blurts out, catching the eye of the man for whom just a moment ago she was willing to break the bank.

The powerful Owen Hardy, known for his negotiating skills with the toughest unions in New York, has only one response when caught between his wife and his lover. He looks embarrassed and offers Kate a little shrug.

Kate sits down, not looking to make a scene. But there's some murmuring around the audience and a few people crane their necks to try to see the woman who called out Owen's name.

"Come on, let's go," I say, tugging at her sleeve.

"No," says Kate resolutely. "If someone's going to leave, it's not going to be me."

I sit back. I was secretly hoping the sight of Owen and his wife together might bring Kate to her senses. Make her realize that the marriage isn't quite as finished as Owen hinted. Instead, Kate's more determined than ever. She straightens her back, squares her shoulders and flips her hair. The color even returns to her cheeks. "I'm not skulking out of here. We're going to say hello to them."

We are? What else are we going to say? That side exit's looking pretty good to me right now. But as soon as the auction is finished, Kate tucks her arm firmly around mine and heads us toward her married mogul.

"Hello, Owen," Kate says calmly, smiling at him.

"Oh hello, Kate," he says. With his girlfriend standing next to his wife, his voice rises an octave higher than I remember.

Kate doesn't wait to be introduced. She extends her hand to his wife. "Hi, I'm Kate Steele."

"Tess Hardy," the elegant blonde replies, shaking Kate's hand. I'm just hoping the eight-carat rock Tess has on her fourth finger doesn't pierce Kate's palm. "So how do you and my husband know each other?"

Intimately, comes to mind. As does, *In the biblical sense.* Although I seem to remember God had something to say about this subject. He came down against it.

"Kate's my dermatologist," Owen says, his usually booming voice now approaching high C.

"Oh, *that* Kate Steele," Tess says, turning to Kate with new admiration. Then she furrows her brow and frowns disapproving at Owen. "You go to a dermatologist? You never told me that."

So the woman gets upset if her husband doesn't reveal everything. I can't wait until Tess finds out that not mentioning doctor visits isn't Owen's only sin of omission. Or his only sin.

"I don't go often," Owen says defensively, shifting his weight from one foot to the other.

"What do you do there?" Tess asks him, not letting up.

Good question. I've been curious about the same thing myself.

Now Owen and Kate lock eyes. And I notice an amused little smile dancing on Kate's lips.

"Peel," Kate says playfully.

Tess hesitates, then comes to her own conclusion.

"Those lunchtime peels are supposed to be wonderful," she says, stroking Owen's cheek. "You've been glowing lately. Now I know why."

Yes, the glow does have something to do with Kate. And with peeling. But not in the way Tess imagines.

Just then a young blue-blazered Sotheby assistant taps Tess on the shoulder and asks her to come take care of the paperwork for buying the Grooms.

"Of course," Tess says. And then turning to Kate, she adds, "You put up quite a fight for that picture. But I had to get it. Owen wanted it for his birthday."

Tess goes off with the attendant, and as soon as they're out of sight, Owen takes Kate's hand. "I'm sorry. I had no idea you'd be here," he says.

"Not your fault," Kate says forgivingly.

Not his fault? As far as I can tell, all of this is his fault. Everything's his fault. Including acid rain.

"You're an incredible woman. I really do love you," he says, happy to be off the hook. He gives her hand a tight squeeze, then lets go in the name of discretion.

"I love you, too," Kate says.

"I know," Owen says, grinning. "You must love me. You wanted to buy that lithograph for me, didn't you?"

"I want to do a lot of things for you," Kate teases, letting Owen fantasize for himself about what she might have in mind.

Owen gives her a hug, and they rapidly make a date to meet the next afternoon. Kate triumphantly leads me out of Sotheby's and I'm steaming as we stroll down York Avenue.

"Do you finally get it?" I ask Kate, wondering if the day made any impression on her. "Owen has a wife. And you've got a problem."

But Kate just shrugs. "Only problem I see is what to get him for his birthday now."

"A card would be too good for him," I say.

"Don't be like that," Kate says. "Owen loves me. He's just in a tough situation. He hasn't made his separation official yet, but at this point it's just semantics. Nobody's going to get hurt. He and his wife lead separate lives. They're friends but they haven't had sex in years. They even belong to different country clubs."

No sex is one thing, but different country clubs? Maybe the marriage is shakier than I thought. People do move on, as I well know. But not without a lot of heartache.

"Listen, Kate, all I want is what's best for you. And seeing you as the third wheel doesn't make me happy."

"Me either," Kate admits. "But things can change." She starts walking faster, and in another block or so, I'm practically running to keep up. By the time we get to her office, Kate's New York stride—maybe the high heels help—has me sweating. At her office door, Kate stops to throw me a kiss and give me a brave smile. "Don't worry, Sara. Tess Hardy may have won the painting. But I can still win the man."

Late that night, I'm waiting for Bradford to get home and distracting myself watching the eleven o'clock news. If they show one more fire in Brooklyn, I'm going back to reruns of *Everybody Loves Raymond*. But at least I'm not eating Rocky Road. I've stepped down to chocolate sorbet. By the end of the week I should be at lemon.

I'm clicking around the remote when Dylan pads into the room, wearing his Harry Potter pajamas and clutching Bunny, the stuffed bear he's loved since he was a baby. Dylan's knowledge of the animal kingdom has improved since he was one, but the name stuck. I open my arms wide for Dylan to come over and he jumps onto the bed and cuddles close. I stroke his soft hair and take in that yummy little boy smell of bubble gum, rocks and No Tears shampoo. How long will my sweet boy stay this lovable? Forever, I hope. "What's the matter, honey, can't sleep?" I ask him. "Want a story?"

"Okay," Dylan says.

I reach over to my night table where I keep a collection of Shel Silverstein books for occasions just like this. But when I pull out his favorite, Dylan doesn't seem interested.

"Is my real daddy really back from Patagonia?" he asks, folding his legs and sitting up next to me. "Is it true you saw him? And I'm going to see him soon?"

Daddy? Patagonia? Where did all this come from? I'm completely caught off guard. Did James call when I wasn't around? I'll kill him. But I can't let on to Dylan that I'm upset. I'm going to stay calm even if I have to go back on Rocky Road.

"Dylan, why are you asking?" I ask in as measured tones as I can muster.

"Skylar told me," he says happily. "She talks to me now. She knows everything."

And how does she find everything out? Standing outside the bedroom door when I'm talking to Bradford? Listening on the extension when James calls? Doesn't matter. Right now, that's not what's important.

I launch into part of the speech that I've been working on for days.

"Well yes, Dylan, guess what!" I say with forced enthusiasm. In fact, too much enthusiasm. I tone it down a notch. "Your birth father James happens to be in New York. I've always told you he loves you but couldn't be with us. Now he's here and we can all go to the zoo together. But only if you want."

"I want, I want, I want!" Dylan says, jumping up and down on the bed. "My real dad. That's so cool. Are we going back to Patagonia with him?"

"Of course not, honey," I say. "We live here now, with Bradford."

"But Skylar says we're leaving soon and her mom is moving back in," Dylan says. "And she knows it for absolute sure."

Now there's a news flash I hadn't heard. And I'm hoping Skylar hasn't really heard it either—from Mimi or Bradford. She probably just made the whole thing up. On the other hand, her information about James being back was dead on. And she got that from someone.

I want to give Dylan a hug, but my heart is pounding so hard, I'm afraid he'll feel it. So I just rub my fingers over his hand. "We love Skylar, but she's not right about everything. From now on, only mommy gives you information, okay?"

"Okay. But I'm a little scared." He snuggles closer to me and I hold him tight.

"I'll be with you. I'll always be with you. But if you're scared, you don't have to see James."

"I want to see Daddy," Dylan says, clutching Bunny bear. "But you said we're going to the zoo and I'm afraid of lions."

Nice to have something specific to be afraid of instead of what I'm feeling—an overwhelming sense of dread, and no place to direct it. I could focus it on James, of course. But why do I also have a sense of foreboding about Bradford? Somehow the comment of a snotty almost-fourteen-year-old, repeated by an innocent seven-year-old, has me worried. But that's ridiculous. Bradford and I love each other.

Dylan falls asleep in my arms and I carry him back to his own bed. I stand gazing at him for a while and tuck Bunny into his arms, so he'll be there when Dylan wakes up. Back in my own room, I have nothing to hold on to. I crawl into bed and stare blankly at the TV. I'm hoping Bradford gets home before two A.M., because I don't want to spend another night with Jimmy Kimmel.

I'm so preoccupied worrying about Bradford, Mimi, James, Dylan, Owen, Kate, Skylar and—what the heck, whether Berni's twins are eating—that the first few days of school pass in a haze. At least by now I'm used to the routine. The binders outlining school regulations are thick enough to soundproof a room and my class list has so many asterisks on it that it looks like the Big Dipper. Two of my art students are on Prozac, three on Ritalin, and twelve can't eat peanuts. I know it's a real problem, but how can so many kids suddenly be allergic? Mothers have started to treat Skippy, once standard lunch box fare, as a national threat. It's gotten so out of hand that my students aren't allowed to smell peanuts. Or see peanuts. Or even read anything by Charles Schulz.

The third day of school, I get back to my house late in the afternoon, toss down my tote bag and take out the highly-prized student directory. Having the home phone number of every girl who goes to our exclusive Spence School means instant access to some of New York's most illustrious parents. (Although the Brearley directory is more prized since it contains Caroline Kennedy's private number.) Still, Spence regulations insist that the list be used for school business only. Which doesn't explain why someone spent nine hundred dollars last year buying a copy on eBay.

"How was your day, dear?" calls out a friendly voice.

I laugh and head into the next room where Berni is sitting on the Betsy Ross couch, knitting. The heat wave is over and so is her pregnancy, but my living room has become her Starbucks. Great hangout, and I even have wireless Internet access. Though she's been pressing me to serve mocha frappuccinos.

"Since when do you knit?" I ask, looking at the silvery-spun yarn that's zig-zagged across her lap and slowly becoming—well, I don't know what. Maybe booties. Or a baby blanket. Though they're not usually trapezoidal.

"Everyone in Hollywood knits," Berni says, making a few more slightly crooked stitches. "I've got to keep a hand in the business."

Berni leans over her handiwork and clicks her needles.

"How are the babies?" I ask, glancing over at the laptop Berni has propped next to her on the couch.

Berni pauses in her knitting to look at the screen and grin. The faces of her two little sleeping angels fill the frame. "I don't know how people lived without remote video," she says. "The nanny is with them but I still like to watch every minute. And the babies can watch me, too."

I look around my living room to see if Berni's installed a camera so the infants can enjoy a live feed of her knitting. Nope.

"Paste your picture onto the crib?" I ask, thinking I'm making a joke.

"Better. Infant Recognition Video. The babies have a DVD in their nursery that flashes my picture next to the word 'Mommy.' "

Gee, I didn't know the kids could read yet.

"I used a photo that's about ten years old and very glamorous," Berni continues cheerfully. "I want my children to get to know me at my thinnest."

The good headshot might be a bad idea. If the twins think that thin glamorous woman is "Mommy," what will they call the nice lady who breast-feeds them every day?

I sit down next to Berni on the couch and take the knitting from her hands, quickly picking up the three stitches she carelessly dropped while her eyes were on the monitor. Berni looks at me in amazement, as if stunned that anyone who's never been invited to the Oscars knows how to knit.

"I've been doing this since I was a kid," I say, quickly getting back into the rhythm and clacking away.

"You're good at it," Berni says, sitting back, happy to watch me work. "You'll have this finished in no time."

I'd love some clue about what it is I'm finishing, but it's a relief to be sitting here mindlessly putting one needle in front of the other. I almost forgot how relaxing this is. Instead of taking a honeymoon in Tahiti, maybe Bradford and I will stay home and knit.

"So are we going to the Hadley Farms' party this afternoon?" Berni asks. "Priscilla told me it's a very supportive group."

"What could they possibly do at a suburban newcomer's party?" I ask. "Write letters to Martha Stewart? Discuss the pros and cons of Burpee seeds?" I finish a row of knitting, switch hands and begin again. Hmm. I'm not exactly spending the afternoon at the Metropolitan Museum myself.

"Priscilla promised it would be fun," Berni says. "And I need to get out of my house."

I think about that one. "You are out of your house," I say.

"Technicality," Berni says. "I'm getting a little tired of your four walls, too."

I guess we could move into the den. Or the library. Or the family room, the study or the media room. Not that I've really figured out the differences among them since each one has a couch, bookshelves and a plasma screen TV.

"Then let's go," I sigh, putting down the knitting. "At least I'll get a cookie."

But a cookie isn't the first thing that Priscilla, the perfect hostess, offers five minutes after I've stepped into the crowd of pink-and-green-clad women who are singlehandedly keeping Lilly Pulitzer in business. There are enough pearl earrings in the room to have depleted the oyster beds of Oyster Bay. And from the welcoming smiles the women generously offer, I'm pretty sure the local pharmacy must be sold out of Crest Whitestrips.

"What can I get you?" asks Priscilla, hurrying over to greet us warmly. "The vodka martinis are at the bar. And the vibrators are on the table."

That's an interesting way to break the ice. And apparently it's working because across the room, the Lilly Pulitzer ladies are giggling and trying the vibrators against their wrists as if they were perfume samples.

"I'm fine with a Diet Coke," I say nervously, trying to figure out what's going on.

"Me, too," says Berni.

"Come on girls, loosen up," Priscilla says genially. "I can't wait to show you what we've got. Neon vibrators. Underwater vibrators with twelve speeds. And a new one that works by remote control. All here courtesy of the PTA."

"The PTA is providing vibrators? Progressive school system," I say. The only thing the Spence PTA provides is brownies for the bake sale.

Priscilla laughs. "Gotcha. Great name, isn't it? Stands for Playtime Toys for Adults. When we have these parties, we don't even have to fib to our kids. We just tell them we're going to a PTA meeting."

So much for my stereotype of uptight suburban women. I thought I was so cool when I lived in Manhattan, but I couldn't even get my book group to read William Burroughs's *Naked Lunch*. They didn't want any-body seeing them on the subway holding a book with that title. And forget Henry Miller's *Tropic of Capricorn*. They were even more embar-rassed that people might think they were into astrology.

"Are we starting soon?" asks a pretty woman coming over to join us. "I'm dying to see the new edible panties. I'm hoping for dulce de leche. My husband's sick of raspberry." She adjusts her pink velvet headband and tucks a strand of hair behind her gold earring.

"You'll love the new crème brûlée," says Priscilla. "But you're right, we should start." She taps a martini glass with a Tiffany butter knife. Amazingly, the genteel tinkle commands everyone's attention and the women quickly seat themselves around the room. Priscilla strolls over to take her place behind the vibrator table.

"I hope you all had a great summer," says Priscilla brightly, using the same opening line as the principal at Spence the other morning. "And I hope every one of you has put the lickety-lube vibrating bath loofah from the last PTA meeting to good use." Definitely a line the principal didn't use.

Priscilla rubs her hands, getting down to work. "Okay neighbors, let's start with sharing time," she says, sounding frighteningly like Mr. Rogers.

One woman stands up from her seat on the chintz sofa. I almost didn't see her before because her summer sun dress is the same floral print as the upholstery. "Hi, for our new friends I'm Lizzie," she says, smiling over at Berni and me. "And I'd like to share that the Magic Mood Cream was fabulous."

That's nice. I guess we can all learn a thing or two from each other. Maybe when we're done with this, somebody will tell me the name of a good Hadley Farms dry cleaner.

"If you haven't tried it," Lizzie says, looking straight at me, "Magic Mood Cream puts you in the mood for sex. Even if you're grumpy and you think you're too tired. Much more efficient than lighting a bunch of candles. For an amazing tingle, all you have to do is apply a quarter of a teaspoon directly to your clitoris."

Funny, I remember going to parties where "clitoris" wasn't the first word someone said. Even parties where clitoris never came up at all. And come to think of it, I've been in bed with men who as far as I could tell never heard the word "clitoris." And wouldn't have a clue about where to find one.

"It worked for me, too," says the only woman in the room dressed in black. "And I hadn't been in the mood for about three years."

The women burst into applause. "Three cheers for Margaret," one calls out.

"And three orgasms!" cries another.

Margaret blushes and Berni raises her hand. Oh no. I can't believe she's actually participating. Maybe she has been in the house too long.

"Right now it'd take more than a quarter of a teaspoon for me to want sex," she says boldly to the audience of avid advice givers. "I could bathe in the stuff and I wouldn't be in the mood. How long after babies until you want sex again?"

The women give knowing looks to each other look and exchange giggles.

"About eighteen years," one offers.

"If you're lucky," adds another.

But Priscilla isn't allowing any negative thoughts to invade her meeting. "You can buy some Wild Whipped Cream right now and your marriage will be better in a week," she says optimistically.

With the variety of vibrators here, marriage seems like it could go out of style altogether. Why put up with snoring, shared bathrooms, and the marriage penalty tax when you could replace it all with a ten-speed Sweet Satisfaction power tool? For now, though, I'm sticking with Bradford. That model doesn't look like a very good cuddler.

Like any good Tupperware saleswoman, Priscilla holds up the whipped cream and squirts a bit onto her finger. "Mmmm," she says, sensuously swirling her tongue over it and batting her eyes. "Deee-licious. Deee-lectable. And definitely worth the twenty-four fifty."

Okay, maybe yummy. But what could possibly be in her can that's better than Reddi-wip? Maybe it's carb-free.

Several more women in the group share their triumphant sex stories and then a few have questions. Priscilla seems briefly stymied when asked whether the cervical tightening cream can also be used for tightening under your eyes.

"You wouldn't want to waste it," pipes in the ever-helpful Lizzie. "I'd stick with Preparation H for undereye puffiness. It's proven."

"That's one I'll add to my shopping list," Berni whispers to me. "And trust me, I'm not thinking about my eyes."

Sharing over, Priscilla announces she has a surprise for all of us. "Outside on the deck!" she says buoyantly, pointing us toward the large outside area overlooking her sumptuous gardens. "Grab your favorite color!"

The women head to the flagstone deck without hesitation, and following behind, I realize I'm getting into the spirit. I'm a little disappointed when the only props I see waiting for us are long silk scarves. Even from far away, I can see they're not Missoni, so I wonder why any of the women in this group would be interested.

"What do we do with these?" I ask, vying with Lizzie for the pale purple one.

"Sexercise!" says Priscilla cheerily, holding her own scarf behind her hips and tightening the ends between her outstretched arms. "Swing those beautiful butts, PTA newcomers! Get that pelvis moving!"

Unembarrassed, the women begin swaying against their brightly colored scarves, following Priscilla's lead and simulating the moves they'll use—she hopes—for an erotic night in bed. Nice. Forty women learning how to fake an orgasm. Though most of them probably knew how to do that on their own.

Down on the lawn, I see the gardener glance up at the action on the deck. But apparently women wiggling in demure Lilly Pulitzer shifts is about as exciting as crabgrass. Without so much as a second glance, he goes back to trimming the hedges. Maybe we should offer him some mood cream.

"Close your eyes, ladies," commands Priscilla. "Swivel those hips and imagine you and your husband having sex."

"I can't remember," says Berni. She stops gyrating completely and drapes the scarf around her shoulders. Behind me, two women also take Priscilla's directive to heart and stage a little re-enactment of a wild night in bed.

"The Dow dropped fifty-eight points today," says one, dropping her voice to imitate her husband.

"But thank god the NASDAQ rallied," says the other, breaking into giggles.

I don't have to imagine a thing. I just start to remember how good it feels when Bradford's body is close to mine and we dissolve into each other. No lickety-lube loofah in the world could be more gratifying than that. But when the exercises are over and we all troop in to make our purchases, I plunk down my twenty bucks for the crème brûlée panties. Good deal. I won't have to make dessert tonight.

Chapter EIGHT

SO THIS IS what it feels like to be famous. Or semi-famous. Or at least making a single appearance on a cable channel. When I walk into the cavernous Chelsea Market, home of the Food Network TV studio, I have my very own entourage. Kirk, Kate and Berni are all with me to lend me moral support—and to help carry the M&Ms.

I don't know how long they usually keep Emeril waiting, but nobody comes out to greet us for twenty minutes. When someone does come, it's an AA—assistant's assistant—a perky pony-tailed blonde in blue jeans who's barely older than Skylar.

"I'm Kerri, and let's see, you must be Sara," she says, glancing past me and making a beeline for Kate, whom she clearly judged Most Likely To Appear on TV. "You're much prettier than your picture."

"The picture wasn't of me," Kate starts to explain.

"You sent someone else's picture?" the AA asks, baffled.

"Sara sent the picture, and Sara's right here," Kirk says, putting his arm around me and bringing me center stage. "Meet your star. Sara."

The young girl swings around, and seeing Kirk in front of her, lets out a little squeal. "Oh my god! You're Dr. Lance Lovett!" she exclaims, looking starry-eyed at Kirk and identifying him, as most fans do, by his TV persona. "I love you! You're the heart surgeon with a heart!"

Kate, who never watches daytime TV, looks quizzically at Kirk.

"My soap role," he explains sotto voce to Kate. "I wanted to be the brain surgeon with a brain, but that role was written for a woman."

I giggle, but quickly cover my mouth so Kerri won't think we're making fun of her.

"Let's get into the studio," Berni says, glancing at her watch and assuming her natural role as field marshal.

Kirk, Kate and Berni pick up the shopping bags stuffed with my brand new bowls from Williams-Sonoma and my mixing spoons from Gourmet Garage. At first I bought the bowls at Broadway Panhandler and the spoons at Macy's Cellar, but then I returned everything and started again. The curse of living in New York. So many choices, it's hard to settle for what you have. You're sure that somewhere out there is a better spoon, a better gym, a better job, a better house, a better spouse. Or at least a different one. If you live in a place where there's only one housewares store, does that also keep the divorce rate down?

The bright-eyed Kerri, who's now had dealings with everyone in the room but me, does what Berni suggests and heads us toward the studio. We push through a set of heavy double doors that say WARNING: CLOSED SET and into the gleaming studio—stocked with enough mixing bowls, measuring cups, gizmos, gadgets, plates, pots, pans and provisions to outfit the *Queen Mary 2* on a six-week voyage.

"Why did I have to bring my own stuff?" I ask Kerri.

"Because you're not on the list," she says enigmatically.

"But you'll get on the list," Berni promises energetically.

"You bet she will," says Kirk enthusiastically.

"Soon!" Kate chimes in encouragingly.

I have no idea what list anybody's talking about, but I'm suddenly dying to be on it. And secretly thrilled that I have an energetic, enthusiastic and encouraging entourage.

I move over to the granite counter, and an attractive young man in frameless glasses strides over. He looks about six months older than

Kerri. Another assistant's assistant, or is he an actual assistant? Probably an actual one—or maybe even better—because Berni rushes over and gives him a Hollywood hug.

"Darling, fabulous to see you. Fabulous to be here. Fabulous studio," she gushes. It's been a while since I've heard her use the f-word three times in a row. Her first full day away from the twins, and she's sounding like an agent again.

Now Kerri decides to step in and make her introductions. "This is Sara," she says efficiently to the man in glasses, barely glancing at me. And then, her voice dropping and her eyes batting, she coos, "And this is the famous Dr. Lance Lovett. I watch his soap every afternoon."

The young man looks pleased to have a real star in the mix and quickly walks over and shakes Kirk's hand.

"Pleasure to meet you, Lance. I'm Ken Chablis, president of the Food Network."

He is? No wonder I didn't notice him at Olivia's party. The guy's so young that if I had seen him, I probably would have thought he was somebody's son. And I guess he is. I just didn't realize we'd end up working for our children so soon.

"You have a great network here," Kirk says. "Sometimes I stay home just to watch. I loved your series on choosing melons."

"Thanks," Ken says modestly, adjusting his glasses. "I heard from a lot of grateful viewers. We're planning a sequel."

"On what?" Kirk asks, trying to imagine what could top cantaloupes.

"Thin-skinned fruits."

No one in the room says a word about thin-skinned fruits. But the phrase does hang in the air for a moment.

Ken throws a casual arm around Kirk and looks over at Berni.

"I've got to hand it to you," he says to her exuberantly. "This is why you're my favorite agent. Another brilliant idea. Bringing me a soap star to put on the show with Sara. I smell a real winner."

Actually it's the Tobler Bittersweet chocolate melting on the double burner that smells so good. But am I really going to have a costar? Berni takes a moment to realize why Ken Chablis thinks she's so brilliant.

Then she winks at Kirk. She's clearly surprised that she has two clients hosting, not one, but she's not letting on.

"You're right, Ken. Sara and Kirk make a great team. But before we start shooting, you should know Kirk doesn't come cheap."

"Sure, no problem. We'll work out the details later," Ken says, waving his hand dismissively. "Whatever he costs, he's worth it. Star power."

Okay, I'm not a star. But who knew I had this little power? I'm thinking of walking off the set but I'm worried nobody would notice—not even Berni. And the truth is, I'm glad to have Kirk by my side when we start rolling. A few days ago, he tried to give me a few TV tips—explaining that I should just talk to the camera as if it's a friend. But my idea of a friend is something more animated than a hulking black box with a blinking red light.

Kirk casually strides over to join me behind the studio kitchen counter. He undoes one more button on his pale denim shirt, slicks back his hair and points his index finger at the cameraman, cowboy style. "Shoot anytime, pardner," he says. "I'm ready."

Just like that? How could he be ready? I've spent four days practicing how to stir batter and say "Now add the egg whites" at the same time. I kept looking into the mirror, repeating "Chocolate, chocolate, chocolate," and wondering why nobody ever told me before that my mouth makes a funny shape when I say that word. Then there was the problem of what to wear. Yellow pantsuit? Too Hillary Clinton. A red jacket? I'd look like I work for Avis. Black or white? Not on color TV. I settled on blue, but everything this season is pink, so it took hours in Bendel's, Bloomingdale's and Bergdorf's to track down a cerulean blue V-neck top that wasn't too V. After that came the sleepless nights trying to recreate the recipe so my Chocolate Surprise wouldn't be a Chocolate Shock. And I still haven't mastered pouring milk without splashing. This whole TV thing is harder than it looks.

"Should we rehearse?" I ask Kirk anxiously.

"Nah, let's keep it fresh," he says, grinning. "You know the recipe and I'll play along. Always works if you just relax and be yourself."

"But I'm nervous," I whisper to him.

Kirk takes my hand and gives it a squeeze. "Take this. Actor's trick to calm you down." He reaches into his pocket and hands me a tiny tablet the shape of a Tic Tac. Without asking any questions, I swallow it whole.

"Two minutes and you'll feel better," he promises.

I take a deep breath, but my heart is still beating so hard I don't know how I'll be able to talk.

"It's not working," I mutter.

Kirk casually pulls out another magic pill. "What the heck. Your debut. Take two."

He reaches over to straighten out my earring, then steps back to check me out. "Perfect!" he declares.

And amazingly, holding his hand, I start to feel a lot better. Calmer and even excited about this whole thing. Heartthrob heart surgeon Kirk somehow has my heart under control. Either that or the double dose of drugs has kicked in.

I pull out a compact mirror to make sure that the makeup Kate carefully applied before we came over to the studio is still intact. What a friend. She spent an hour putting on four layers of foundation, concealer, bronzer and blush so my skin could look natural. Now Kate bustles over with a powder puff. "To get rid of the shine," she says, efficiently patting down my nose.

Kirk watches, then taps her on the shoulder. "Mind doing me?" he asks.

Kate goes over with her powder, then steps back and takes an appraising look. "Has anyone ever told you that you have perfect skin? And you're gorgeous?"

"Yes, many people," Kirk admits, and somehow, coming from him, it doesn't sound like bragging. In his case it's like saying the Sears Tower is tall. Or the Mona Lisa is smiling. Or four out of five dentists prefer sugarless gum for their patients who chew gum. It's just true. Though what were the dentists going to say? Chew Bazooka?

A stage manager comes over and reels off instructions about time cues and hand signals and tosses around various other technical terms that I don't understand. I look in panic at Kirk.

"All you have to know is the camera with the light is the one that's on," he tells me, patting my arm.

An audio tech comes over with a clip-on microphone. "I have to snake the wire under your top," he says eagerly.

"I'll do it for you," says Kirk, stepping forward. He takes the wire and does the job with gentlemanly discretion.

"I shouldn't have let you do that," grumbles the audio guy, walking away. "Union rules."

I can just imagine the Teamsters negotiating that contract. They were willing to cut their pensions but demanded exclusive rights to under-the-blouse wiring.

The stage manager calls for quiet on the set and blindingly bright stage lights immediately shine into my eyes.

"Rolling!" the stage manager cries out. "We have speed."

"We have speed?" I ask, looking up. "What's that mean? Where are we going?"

"Cut!" says the stage manager, disgruntled. He stomps over to me. "What's the matter? You're acting like this is your first time on TV."

"It is my first time," I say in a small voice.

"Christ," he says, shaking his head. "Well then just make your damn pudding and I'll worry about everything else. They let anybody on TV these days."

He's right. Between the Bachelors, the Apprentices and the Survivors, so many people are on the air, it's amazing anyone's left in the audience to watch. Still, this is my big chance. The least I can do is crack an egg properly.

I pull myself up straighter, and this time when the red light goes on, I do successfully crack an egg. And a joke. In fact, several. And when Kirk pretends to take a swig from the Amaretto bottle, I grin and grab it from him.

"Dr. Lovett, no drinking," I say with a laugh. "Aren't you doing heart surgery this afternoon?"

"I'll bypass the bypass," he quips, in his deep doctor's voice.

I groan and he grins, but we're really cooking. The on-air chemistry is working. While I'm blending and beating, Kirk and I banter so easily we actually do sound like TV hosts. With Kirk by my side, I feel as comfortable as in my own kitchen. Or maybe it's those pills. Might want to take one before I see James.

But it's a mistake to let any thoughts about James cross my mind, because just as everything's going so smoothly, I start beating a little too furiously with my wooden spoon. My other hand slips off the edge of the bowl and lands smack in the middle of the sticky batter. Well that should make a quick end to my TV cooking career.

But no, I won't let it. Without missing a beat, I turn and raise my chocolate-covered hand and wiggle it in front of the camera.

"A few fingers in the bowl just add to the taste," I say, laughing into the lens.

"In fact, it's the best part," says Kirk, coming behind. He grabs my hand and starts licking the chocolate off my index finger. "Mmm, yummy!"

I giggle. "I promise it's even better when it's done," I tease, taking back my chocolate fingers. On the other side of the set I see the formerly surly stage manager laughing and Berni giving me a thumbs up.

We finish the segment effortlessly, and surprisingly the gumdrop-studded dessert looks good enough to eat. As the cameraman counts down the last ten seconds of the segment, Kirk and I say our good-byes, then dig in and feed each other spoonfuls.

"That's a wrap!" calls the director. "Nice job, you two."

"In fact, terrific!" says an exuberant Ken Chablis, coming over. "I want you both back as soon as possible."

The whole staff crowds around to offer their congratulations—and I proffer spoons so everyone can taste the Chocolate Surprise. Amazing that I've become a star on a liqueur-infused sunken soufflé, though I have to admit that my revised recipe isn't bad.

"What do you think, Ken?" asks Berni, striding over. "Weekly show for my duo?"

Pondering the idea, Ken cups his hand and strokes his smooth chin. Someone should tell him that gesture's more meaningful once you're old enough to have a beard. "I can see it," he says. "We'll call it . . ." He pauses for a moment and snaps his fingers to herald a brainstorm. "Afternoon Delights!"

Kirk and I look at each other.

"Great, isn't it?" says Ken, pleased with himself. "All those double entendres. The show'll be on in the afternoon. Kirk's already an afternoon soap star. And you'll be making delightful desserts."

"How disappointing," Kirk whispers to me. "I thought an 'afternoon delight' was a romp in the hay."

"Please, it took me a solid week just to get ready to *cook* on TV," I say, laughing. But I'm flushed, and caught up in the excitement. Am I really going to be a TV star? Will strangers on the street ask for my autograph? Will Stila name a lipstick after me?

I'm still fantasizing about my acceptance speech at the Golden Globes—do I thank Kirk first or Bradford?—when Berni moves into action. "We'll go for it," she says to Ken, as usual speaking on all our behalfs. "When do you want to hammer out the deal?"

"No time like the present," he says. "Come on over to my office."

But Berni suddenly realizes that the present is not a good time at all. She's been away from the twins too long and her breasts must be leaking. She glances down and we both notice that a small stain on her blouse is quickly getting bigger and bigger.

"Excuse me, but I'm going to run," Berni says. She picks up her jacket to mask the mess, but it's already too late. Her shirt looks like it could be used for target practice. Double bull's-eyes. Berni throws air kisses all around.

"Sara, you were great," she says, rushing toward the studio door. "You too, Kirk. Ken, I love you, but we'll negotiate later. Right now a couple of really important clients need my attention."

In a flurry of clacking heels and flying hair, Berni's gone—and Ken Chablis looks miffed. "More important clients," he grumbles, misunderstanding her quick departure. "She's wrong. You two are going to be her biggest stars."

That won't take much, given that the only other stars in Berni's life at this moment are under ten pounds. But Ken doesn't know that. And I'm flattered that he sees celebrity potential in my pudding.

Kirk, Kate and I pack up and say our good-byes. Out on the street, Kirk hails a cab and just before he ducks in, he grabs my hand and kisses the top of my finger. "Tasty, even without the chocolate on it," he says, flashing me a big grin. I laugh and kiss him on the cheek.

"By the way," I say. "I was incredibly calm throughout that whole show. Amazing pills you gave me. Bring them next time because I think I'm hooked."

"They're pretty potent," he says, nodding gravely. "You've got to be careful."

Now I'm worried. One day on a TV set and I may have taken my first step toward rehab.

"What were they?" I ask, concerned. "What's in them?"

Kirk gravely pulls a small box out of his pocket and shakes it. He tosses a handful of the pills into his palm and pitches them into his mouth.

"Tic Tacs," he says, smiling and tossing me the rest of the box. "I've taken them for years. The orange work best."

Kirk's cab pulls away and Kate laughs as we wait for the light to change.

"Now I'm embarrassed," I say as we cross the street. "It just takes a breath mint to calm me down. An Altoid would probably put me in a coma."

"Don't feel bad, the placebo effect is real," Kate says, still laughing. "Anyway, I'm glad to hear your friend Kirk isn't dispensing dangerous drugs without a prescription. You two were terrific on that show together. And by the way, he's awfully cute."

I brighten. "He is, and he's funny. And smart. And single. And he majored in philosophy. You should go out with him."

"I'm taken," she says.

"Not this afternoon," I point out. "And not tonight, I'm guessing."

"My heart belongs to Owen," she says, sounding like a bad country-and-western song. Or maybe a good one. "Anyway, you're the one Kirk likes, in case you didn't notice."

"He's a pal," I say. "He thinks of me as a sister. An older sister."

"Good thing, since you have eyes only for Bradford," says Kate.

"But does Bradford have eyes only for me?"

Kate pauses and looks at me to see if I'm being serious. "What the heck is that supposed to mean?" she asks. "Bradford would never fool around."

"I don't know if you'd call it fooling around." I take a deep breath. "But Dylan tells me that Skylar told him that Mimi told her that she and Bradford were getting back together."

Kate looks relieved, but she refrains from telling me I'm a complete idiot. "You're not exactly hearing it from the horse's mouth," she says dismissively.

"But what if it's true? Everyone seems to know about it."

"Right. And 'everybody' knows a lot of things that are wrong."

I sigh as we approach Sixth Avenue. I guess Kate didn't believe last week's cover story in the *National Enquirer* about the crop circle made by the two-headed alien. I bang the button on the pole to get the light to change. Then hit it again.

"Don't bother," Kate says. "Those buttons were all disconnected years ago. The city just leaves them there to make you feel like you're doing something. Traffic placebo."

"Well, I do need to do something," I say, slamming my finger into the button one more time. We stand there for another minute, and the WALK sign finally flashes. "Any advice for me about Bradford and Mimi?"

"Talk to Bradford," says Kate. "He's going to say you're a nutcase, but that's okay. Make it a romantic evening. Bring it up in bed."

I can do that. Skylar's at Mimi's tonight and Dylan has a sleepover. And if I do say so myself, I did pretty well at sexercise class.

Bradford promised me he'd be home early, and sure enough at eight o'clock—early for him—I hear the front door swing open. Upstairs in our bedroom, I give a secret smile and adjust the thin strap on my pale silk nightgown—an upgrade from the Yankees T-shirt I usually sleep in. Only downside to this plan is I don't get to see the thrilled look on his face when he takes a look around and realizes what's in store.

I've pulled out every romantic trick I could think of—turned off all the lights in the house and filled the foyer with dozens of flickering candles that lead up the staircase and directly to our bedroom. I've tossed rose petals everywhere and filled the air with the scent of my own Annick Goutal fragrance. Nora Jones is softly crooning her siren songs from the CD player, and there's a bottle of white wine chilling in a silver bucket by the side of our bed. A little old-fashioned compared to mood cream, but reliable.

I flutter around the room, trying to decide where I should be posed when Bradford comes in. Too bad nobody smokes anymore—holding a cigarette seductively between my fingers would give just the right decadent touch. Instead, I grab one of the fluted wineglasses—there's no time to open the bottle, so I just hold the empty glass and sprawl languidly on the satin settee. I'm so filled with anticipation that my heart's pounding harder than it did on the set of the TV show. I wish I had one of those Tic Tacs to calm me down.

I cross and uncross my legs at least a dozen times and lean my head sexily against the palm of my cupped hand. But it's taking Bradford so long to get upstairs that my hand falls asleep and I sit up abruptly to shake out the pins and needles. Okay, I'll lean against the pillows.

But what's keeping Bradford? Maybe he's slowly stripping on the way upstairs. Very slowly stripping. Finally, I see under the door that the hallway light's snapped on—didn't I leave enough candles there?—and Bradford bursts in.

"What's going on, honey?" he asks, slightly put out. "I came in and there were no lights anywhere. I figured something was wrong so I went to the basement to check the fuse box. Banged my shin. Then I came upstairs and saw all the candles. Somebody trying to burn the house down?"

"I thought it might be pretty," I say mildly, my previously pounding heart now sinking.

"They were a little close to the curtains," he says, tossing aside his Canali suit jacket and pulling off his tie. "And I cleaned up all that stuff on the stairs so nobody slips and falls. Oh, and by the way, somebody left the CD player on. Did the remote get lost again?"

My plan has definitely made an impression on Bradford. But not the one I intended. I'm looking for romance and Bradford's figuring we need a new housekeeper.

"Have a hard day, sweetie?" I ask, trying to get things back on track.

"You bet," Bradford says. He turns around and finally notices me in my nightie. "You're ready for bed," he says in surprise. He glances at the clock on the side table and then looks at me with concern. "It's early. I figured we'd have a nice dinner, but are you feeling sick or something?"

Sick is exactly what I'm feeling. And kind of stupid. I pulled out all the stops to make a perfect night, and instead I've made a perfect mess.

"I wanted tonight to be special," I say. "Candles. Music. And the stuff on the stairs was rose petals. I picked them myself." I flop down on the bed. Right now I feel so ridiculous I just want Bradford to go away. But instead, he comes over and puts his arms around me, holding me tightly and massaging my shoulders.

"I'm so sorry," he says, obviously feeling equally ridiculous. "This is wonderful of you. I don't know what I was thinking. I guess my head was still at the office."

Bradford's strong, comforting hands on my back are definitely doing their job.

"I'm liking the sexy nightie," he says, running his fingers over the strap. "Maybe I'm dense, but I finally get it."

"A little late," I say, teasingly tossing the pillow at him.

"But never too late," he says, tucking the pillow behind me and unbuttoning his shirt. "What if I make myself so irresistible that you can't keep your hands off me?"

"And how would you do that?" I ask.

"Maybe with something like this," he says leaning over and letting his tongue play softly on the edge of my lips. Then he nibbles the corners of my mouth and only slowly, slowly, moves in for a long kiss that—he's right—is irresistible.

I start to reach for him but he says, "Not yet, still my turn. You set the stage. Now I get to play." He gently pushes me back on the bed and kisses my neck, and starts moving slowly down my body. "As much as I like this pretty nightgown," he says, "I think it's time to take it off." I slip the straps off my shoulders and he helps me slither the silk down my body. But when it gets to my hips the slithering turns to tugging. And pulling. I sit up, the soft fabric scrunched uncomfortably around my midsection.

"Maybe we should pull in the other direction," I say, immediately breaking the mood that I worked so hard to create. "My butt's too big."

"Your body's perfect," he says, kissing my now bare breasts.

"You're at the good part," I admit.

"They're all good parts," Bradford says, grasping the nightie in his hands and lifting it smoothly over my head.

I start to tell him that he's wrong and that the thighs are even bigger than the butt. Then I stop myself. Bradford likes my curves. He's told me a million times. And the way his hands are now caressing my hips, I have to believe him. I can worry about those few extra pounds when I'm trying to fit into my old Levis, but not when I'm alone in bed with my lover. What a waste that would be.

I lie back and instead of thinking about everything that's wrong with me, I abandon myself to Bradford's sensuous touch, and enjoy the pleasure he takes in my body. His hand strokes my thigh and as he folds his body into mine, I just revel in everything about the moment that's right.

A little while later we're contentedly lying in each other's arms. "I love you," Bradford says, stroking my hair.

"I love you, too," I tell him.

I cradle my head against his warm shoulder and rub my finger back and forth across his broad chest, thinking about why I set up this whole night in the first place. My worries about Mimi seem so silly now. I'd like to just forget about them. But something tells me that if I do, they'll still be with me tomorrow.

"Am I allowed a foolish question?" I ask, snuggling even closer, and knowing there's nothing you can't ask the person you love. Especially after you've both just had earth-moving orgasms.

"Let me guess," Bradford says, stretching his arms playfully above his head. "You want to know how I could be such an amazing idiot when I came in and such an amazing lover afterwards."

"No," I tease back. "But I do want to know how you became such an amazing lover."

"Years of experience," Bradford says.

Just banter, I know, but still I recoil slightly. Bradford feels my back stiffen.

"That was a joke," he says, rolling over to kiss me.

"I know. But it's actually kind of the subject I wanted to ask you about," I admit. I bite my lower lip. "Honey, maybe this is ridiculous, but you and Mimi seem to be friendly again. Spending more time together. It's making me uncomfortable."

Now Bradford's the one whose back stiffens. He brings his arms back down and slowly crosses them in front of his bare chest. "I don't ever want you uncomfortable," he says carefully. "But I do think you're making an issue where one doesn't exist."

"Mimi certainly exists," I say, trying to keep my voice light.

"Yes, and she's Skylar's mother," Bradford says. "We still have a lot of parenting to do. I'm glad that Mimi and I are getting along again. It's the same thing I was trying to tell you about James."

"But Mimi's acting like it's more than that," I say. "She's made it pretty clear she wants me out and you back."

Bradford swings his legs over the side of the bed, hesitates for a moment, and then gets up. "I'm not worried about what Mimi wants, and you shouldn't be either."

"But you have this whole life that I'm not a part of," I say, sitting up and getting more agitated than I should.

"So do you," he says, heading into the bathroom. "You were right the first time. This is ridiculous."

"You don't even want to talk about it?" I call after him, surprised.

I hear the water running and after a few moments, he comes back and sits down next to me, looking weary.

"Sara, you want to talk about this, so let's talk. Here's what I have to say. You and I both have children and exes and past histories. At our age, love is complicated. Maybe it's better and deeper, but it's complicated. I'd like to tell you that we'll hold hands and walk into the sunset together and nothing will ever go wrong. And as far as I'm concerned, we will. But the road may have some detours."

If this is supposed to make me feel better, it's not working.

"What does that mean?" I ask plaintively. "While we're walking into the sunset, will you be taking little side trips now and then over to Mimi?"

Bradford takes a long time to answer. He looks at me and then looks away, and I see his jaw tightening. "Is that what you really think?" he asks.

"I don't know what to think," I say.

He stands up and starts pacing around the room. "If you don't know what to think about me by this point, what can I say? I've spent a year and a half telling you that I love you, I'm not going to leave you, I'm not James. If you still don't believe it, maybe I'll never be able to convince you. Either you trust me or not."

"Of course I trust you," I say softly. "I'm sorry I brought the whole subject up in the first place."

Bradford hesitates, but then he comes back and wraps his arms around me. "It's okay. We have to be able to talk about everything. But you have nothing to worry about. You need to have a little more confidence in me. And yourself." He kisses me.

"Okay, starting right now. The new me. Fearless and unafraid," I say, kissing him back, thinking how safe I feel in his strong arms.

"Good." He hugs me. "So not to switch topics, but tell me how your TV show went this afternoon."

"Brilliantly," I say, determined to show him that I really can be a secure and confident woman. "It may even become a weekly gig."

"That's great," he says with a big smile. "I'm proud of you. So I'm going to be married to the next Katie Couric?"

"No, she's not as good a cook as I am," I say airily. This whole confidence thing is pretty easy. All you do is pretend.

"Well, my good cook, would you like to make dinner for a hungry husband-to-be?"

"I can do even better than that," I say, innocently wiggling closer to him. "Let's skip dinner and start with dessert. I just happen to have a very tasty crème brûlée."

Chapter NINE

BERNI GREETS ME at her door with baby spit-up all over her baggy gray sweatshirt. Attractive. And even more appealing since she's paired the sweatshirt with orange nylon warm-up pants that have a white racing stripe down the side. I guess even a Scotchguarded Chanel was no match for a drooling baby.

"Nice outfit," I say with a grin, stepping inside her empty foyer.

"Think so?" she asks. "I've already changed three times this morning."

"I can see that look would be hard to achieve on the first try," I say, taking Baby B from Berni. Baby A is sleeping—well, was sleeping—in the Snugli on Berni's chest. Now she opens her eyes beatifically—and spits up more of her breakfast.

"Should I get you another sweatshirt?" I ask helpfully.

"No, I'm starting to like them this way," she says. "Very Jackson Pollock. I might frame them and save them as the babies' first masterpieces."

I study the interesting pattern of splatters and decide she's right. Novice museum-goers always complain that Pollocks look like they were done by a three-year-old. Who knew they could be done by a three-week-old.

"Maybe you could submit the shirts to the Whitney Biennial," I suggest.

"No, I've decided not to push the twins to be stars. At least until they're five."

"You're right," I say. "Everybody deserves a childhood."

I follow Berni into the twins' room, the only part of the house that's actually furnished yet. Berni seems to have had the entire Wicker Garden catalogue shipped, including the ultra-padded custom-designed bumpers—which sound like they belong at Nascar, not a nursery. I don't know how good the babies' vision is at this point, but six colorful mobiles are hanging from the ceiling. At least I think it's a ceiling—it's been painted to look like a blue sky filled with puffy white clouds. And the moon probably comes out at night.

Berni tucks the babies into their respective cribs and motions for me to follow her into the empty room next door. It's not hard to guess what the room will eventually become since there's a wall of still-empty bookshelves and a stack of boxes marked "Berni's Study." Though when she'll get to unpack is anybody's guess.

"The babies always sleep for an hour in the morning," Berni says, settling into one of the two folding chairs set up in the middle of the room.

"Good time for you to catch a nap, too," I say, the experienced mom.

Berni closes her eyes briefly. "I need it. They wake up every morning at four A.M. And anyone who says you can change a baby's schedule never had a baby."

"Being a new mom's exhausting," I say sympathetically.

"Not to mention being an old new mom," says Berni. "I probably wouldn't have been this tired if I had them at twenty. Then again, at twenty, I couldn't have afforded the service for twelve Lenox baby tea set or the toy Jaguar. Or the class I'm taking on how not to spoil your children."

She holds out her sweatshirt and starts picking away at some of the crusty stains.

"Don't tamper with the artwork," I say lightly.

"Lots more where this came from," she says. "And then there are the water paintings. Every time I take off Baby B's diaper, he turns into a fountain."

I chuckle. "They do grow up," I promise her.

"I know," she says fervently. "And I swore to myself that I'd be here for every one of those moments—first words, first steps, first fight we have over what to wear to the prom. That's why I hung up on Edie Falco when she called this morning."

I blink trying to follow Berni's logic and figure out what Edie Falco has to do with Baby A's prom.

"You hung up on Edie Falco?" I ask. "From *The Sopranos*? Aren't you afraid Tony will send a hit man?"

"I was more afraid that if I talked to her, I'd take her on as a client. She asked me to be her agent. But I can't do it. It's enough that I have you and Kirk."

"Well, yes, I can see why you'd ignore Edie Falco in favor of me," I say sarcastically. "Why have a client with a mantel full of Emmys when you can have one with an oven full of raspberry tarts?"

Berni rolls her eyes. "I'm stuck with you two," she says affectionately. "And by the way, I did your deal with Ken on the phone. Got you great terms. And I had a terrific time watching you guys shooting the show the other day. It almost made me wish I could go back to agenting again for real."

"You can if you want," I say.

"No, I can't. I took an oath," Berni says. "I promised the babies that I'd stay home with them."

"Did you cross your heart and hope to die or just pinky swear?" I ask.

"I'm serious," Berni says, sounding as sanctimonious as one of those teenagers who vows to remain a virgin until marriage. "Would you like to see the letter I sent all my clients explaining that I'm leaving the business? Everyone was shocked. I was the best, you know. Studio heads were terrified of me. The only way to get what you want in Hollywood is to make them think you're stronger than they are."

I always thought I could get people to do what I wanted by being nice. And wearing lipstick. But maybe Berni has a point. I practice setting my face in a scowl and giving off some don't-mess-with-me attitude.

Berni leans back until the chair tips and she's rocking on the rear two legs. Just the way Dylan does, although I always tell him to stop.

"You know what's funny?" she asks, not even noticing my fierce face. I guess I'd better keep practicing. "I've never thought of myself as anything but an agent. Now it's like starting from square one. I don't have interesting work and glamorous stories to tell. When I got that call this morning I realized it would be so easy to fall back into the role I know. But I'm not going to do it." She brings the chair forward and the front leg lands with a decisive slam.

"It doesn't have to be either-or," I say. "You're always going to be second-guessing yourself anyway. What is it someone told me? Don't stay home with your kids and they end up on drugs. Stay home with them and *you* end up on drugs."

"At the moment, the only thing in my medicine cabinet is Baby Tylenol," Berni says.

"Should be enough," I say. "I'm convinced there are lots of ways to raise a kid that work out just fine. I've always had a job and look at Dylan. He's perfect."

"Yup, Dylan is perfect," Berni agrees with a laugh. "And I'm pretty confident I could keep working and raise great kids. But I'm staying home as much for me as for them. I'm kind of curious to find out what I'll become if I'm not an agent."

"Depressed?" I joke.

Berni shrugs. "Sometimes I feel a little lost. The babies are wonderful but I've got to tell you, the days seem long. And sometimes even"— she lowers her voice—"boring."

"That's the part nobody tells you," I confirm.

Berni suddenly looks worried. "I'm not trying to jinx anything," she says, looking around for some wood to knock on, and, not seeing any, rapping on the cardboard box. "I'm lucky. Two beautiful, healthy babies. It's just such a change in pace."

"It's okay. You can count your lucky stars every day—and still miss those Hollywood stars you used to hang with. They were probably better conversationalists."

"Not all of them." Berni laughs. "You spend a lot of time in Hollywood kissing ass. So now I'm wiping tushes. Fair trade."

"It gets easier," I tell Berni, remembering my own fraught, frazzled days when Dylan was an infant and James was long gone. "And at least you get to share it with your husband."

"Careful, the husband is listening," says Aidan, overhearing me as he rushes past in the hallway. He pauses and comes into the room, bending over to kiss Berni.

"Staying home today?" I ask Aidan, who's wearing well-worn jeans with a hole at the knee and scuffed sneakers. I guess these babies haven't been good for either one of their wardrobes.

"Not if he's in his work clothes," says Berni, looking over admiringly at her husband in his film-editing uniform. His T-shirt says *The Manchurian Candidate,* his windbreaker advertises *About Schmidt,* and his baseball cap is from *Freaky Friday.* Bradford wouldn't even dress that way to play softball. He once tried to take off his tie for a summer casual Friday, but said he felt like he was going to work naked. Obviously, Aidan would go to work naked if not for the freebies from his films.

"I hate to leave you and the babies, honey," Aidan says to Berni. "But Steven's really pushing hard to get the movie finished."

"Steven Spielberg," Berni explains to me proudly. "Aidan's having an amazing time working for him."

"It's really a fabulous project," Aidan agrees happily. "Steven's a great visionary. The film genius of our generation. And the only director I know who stocks the edit room with Devil Dogs."

Aidan kisses Berni on the top of her head and heads out the door.

"Does it bother you to see Aidan heading off to make movies while you stay home?" I ask Berni, getting up to leave myself.

"A little," she says. "I can cope with the identity crisis. But Devil Dogs were always my favorite."

* * *

Kate invited me to the Yankees game, and I've never had seats like this in my life. Owen's season tickets are in the front row, next to the Yankees dugout. I've already bought a soda that cost me five dollars and seventy-five cents, including the souvenir cup. If I get to enough games—or drink enough soda today—I'll have service for twelve.

I'm hoping Kate and Owen get here soon, but I'm not betting on it since they're probably indulging in their own pregame activities. I turn my attention to the field where just twenty feet away, Derek Jeter is warming up. He casually catches a ball and turns around and smiles in my direction. But probably not at me since Mayor Bloomberg is sitting one row behind. Then Jeter exchanges waves with a man in sunglasses and a Yankees cap who's walking down the aisle, accompanied by an usher. They stop directly at my row and the attendant flips down the seat right next to mine and dusts it off. The baseball-capped man says, "Thanks, buddy," offers a ten-dollar tip and then settles in.

I idly glance over at my new neighbor and suddenly realizing who he is, jerk back in my seat, stunned. In my excitement, the soda spills and my pretzel goes flying. Oh my gosh. Yankees fan Billy Crystal is sitting right next to me.

The best thing to do is ignore him. Pretend it's no big deal to have the funniest man in America—okay, the funniest man after Jerry Seinfeld— inches away. I casually toss my hair back and take the sunglasses from the top of my head and readjust them on my nose. I look straight ahead, eyes focused on the ground crew who are preparing for the game rather than risk turning to my right and saying something stupid to my favorite celebrity in the whole world. I am cool. I am confident. I am Woman.

"Excuse me, miss," says my next-seat-over-mate, tapping me on the arm. "Is this yours?"

I muster the courage to turn and see Billy Crystal holding a jumbo soft pretzel in front of his face. Did he steal my pretzel? I wouldn't blame him. Same vendor that ripped me off for the soda charged three seventy-five for it.

"Uh, could be. No way of knowing. They all look alike," I say flustered.

"I found it in my lap," Billy says.

So that's where it landed.

He holds the pretzel in his palm, studying it as if it were Yorick's skull. "Alas, poor pretzel, she didn't know you very well," he says, taking a big bite.

I finally laugh. "Okay, maybe that's my pretzel."

"Not anymore," he says, munching away. Then he grins and puts out his hand.

"By the way, I'm Billy Crystal," he says.

"I know," I blurt in a rush. "I love you. I love every movie you've ever done."

"Well thank you," he says, smiling sweetly.

"I loved you in *Mr. Saturday Night.*"

"You did?" he looks surprised. "Nobody's ever said that to me before. Even my wife hated it."

"You've made much worse movies," I say encouragingly. "Think about *My Giant. Throw Momma from the Train.* I loved all of them."

"You should be the movie critic for *Variety,*" he says, obviously pleased with my terrible taste.

I shrug. "Anybody can like *City Slickers* or *When Harry Met Sally . . .* Making it through *Forget Paris* takes real devotion."

"I see your point," he says, finishing the pretzel and licking the salt off his fingers.

The usher sidles up to our row again and flips down two seats, readying them for Owen and Kate, who are holding hands and bounding down the aisle behind him. From the spring in Kate's step, they must have had some pregame warm-up.

Owen thanks the usher and slips him a twenty-dollar bill. Ten from Billy and twenty from Owen. This guy's got it better than the pretzel vendor. If my gig at Food Network doesn't work out, maybe I can set up shop here.

"Hi, Owen. Good to see you at another game," Billy says affably, reaching over to shake Owen's hand. But he's staring straight at Kate.

"Hi, Billy." Owen looks as embarrassed as a kid who has just been caught cheating on a math test. Or as a man who has just been caught cheating on his wife. "I didn't think you'd be here today."

"I wanted to see the game, so I postponed going to L.A. until tomorrow."

There's an awkward pause as Kate looks at Owen expectantly, waiting to be introduced. But Owen just takes his seat and motions for Kate to do the same. She ignores his signals and leans across Owen to give me a kiss on the cheek. Then she smiles at my seatmate and says "Hello, Mr. Crystal, I'm Kate Steele. A thrill to meet you. *When Harry Met Sally . . .* is my favorite movie."

"Really?" Billy says, tugging at his Yankees cap. "My true fans prefer *Mr. Saturday Night.*" He looks at me with his impish smile, and then I see him looking quizzically again at Kate.

On the other side of me, Owen purses his lips and hisses to Kate, "Don't talk. Billy and I sit next to each other at every game and he knows Tess. I wouldn't have brought you if I realized he'd be here."

Kate's happy demeanor disappears. "Well, I'm here," she says.

"And we should probably leave," Owen says, looking around, as if plotting an escape route.

"No, I want to see the game," Kate says tersely, holding her ground. Kate, the big baseball fan who asked me this morning if it's three strikes you're out or four.

We all stand for the national anthem and at some point after "rockets' red glare" and before "Play ball!" Billy whispers to me, "So who's Owen's friend?"

"She's my friend, too," I say, trying to provide even the flimsiest of covers. "I think it's wonderful when men and women are friends, don't you? Friends, friends, friends. Old friends. You've got a friend. With a little help from my friends. Be kind to your web-footed friends. Amazing how many songs there are about friends, isn't it?" I'm burbling over like a Coke on a hot day, but I can't seem to stop myself. "And come to think of it, you know all about friends. That's the whole story of *When Harry Met Sally,* right? They're friends."

"They sleep together," Billy reminds me.

Now that's a problem. "But not in every scene," I say, trying to support my case. And deciding I won't mention my favorite speech in the movie, where Harry explains to Sally that friends or not, men want to sleep with every woman they meet.

We sit down, and on the other side of me, I see Kate putting her hand on Owen's arm. And him brushing it away. We're barely into the first inning and things are tenser here in our little row than in the bullpen during the World Series. Or in George Steinbrenner's office anytime.

Owen, used to getting his way, isn't giving up on getting Kate out of the stadium. But ever the businessman, he's now putting a new deal on the table.

"Let's go shopping. I'll buy you whatever you want. If we leave now, we can get to Armani before it closes."

Kate gives him an icy stare.

"Okay," he says, upping the ante. "Versace. Fendi. Dior. Your choice."

I listen in fascination, wondering how many minutes it will take him to get to Van Cleef & Arpels.

"I don't want you buying me anything," Kate says. "We invited Sara to spend the day with us. She wants to see the game."

Now wait a minute here. I'm flexible. If he wants to take me to Armani, I can always listen to the Yankees on the radio.

Kate and Owen are trying to whisper, but their heated voices are louder than they think. Now Billy jumps in.

"Hot dogs, anybody?" he asks, calling over the vendor. With no olive branches in sight, he's hoping a Hebrew National will calm things down. He cheerfully passes hot dogs, napkins, and little packets of mustard to each of us.

"Thanks," Kate mutters.

"If you're hungry, we can leave and go to Cipriani's," Owen says, not willing to quit. There's a reason the man owns half the real estate in Manhattan. "The one in Venice. We'll take my plane."

"I don't care if NASA's sending a rocket ship. I'm not leaving," Kate says, folding her arms. She turns plaintively to Owen and lowers her voice. "You keep telling me you're in love with me. That you and Tess lead separate lives. You want to be together with me forever. Why should it matter if somebody sees us?"

"I do want us to be together," he says, trying to mollify Kate. "Just not in front of Billy Crystal."

"Then you've been lying to me," she says.

"I'm getting out of here," says Owen, cornered and cutting off the conversation. "You can take the subway home with Sara."

Whether it's the public humiliation or the threat of public transportation, Kate's had enough. Owen's gone too far and Kate explodes.

"You're an ass," she mutters, throwing her hot dog at him and hitting his white polo shirt. The mustard lands in a splat across the Ralph Lauren logo.

Owen's face turns crimson—and I'm not the only one who gets to see it. Because the TV camera that has just panned from Mayor Bloomberg to Billy Crystal and put their larger-than-life images on the huge stadium screen has just focused in on New York real estate mogul Owen Hardy. And is beaming his fight with the pretty woman next to him to fifty-five thousand stadium fans. Not to mention the million television viewers at home.

A loud cheer goes up from the fans who, as usual, are watching the screen instead of the game.

"Food fight!" comes the cry from one section.

"Food fight! Food fight!" the crowd in the bleachers chime in.

And suddenly the entire stadium is erupting. "Food fight! Fight fight! Food fight!"

Beer is spurting and popcorn is popping into the air as Kate's little hot dog toss goes global. Burgers and buffalo wings come pelting down on us from the tier above and there are so many flying French fries that Owen may need a Lipitor to recover just from seeing them.

In the frenzy, Owen escapes, leaving Kate and me to fend for ourselves.

"I hate him," Kate says, bursting into tears.

"Well that's a good start," I say comfortingly.

Kate wipes at her eyes and glares at me. "How can you be so cruel, Sara? I love him. It was all supposed to be so simple."

Billy leans over then and hands Kate a mustard-smudged napkin so she can blow her nose. "Love him—hate him. Love him—hate him," Billy says, reeling his head from side to side as if someone were slapping his cheeks. "I feel like Faye Dunaway in *Chinatown*."

Kate finally laughs. How come he can cheer her up and I can't? Oh, that's right. He's Billy Crystal.

"It's all my fault. I should have known something like this was going to happen," Billy says with mock seriousness. "I never should have bought the hot dogs. They always give you heartburn."

When I finally get home after dropping off Kate, the house is quiet. Consuela's gone for the day, Skylar's out with friends, Dylan's asleep, and even the dog doesn't come to the door to greet me.

"Bradford?" I call out hopefully.

But there's no answer. I see low lights twinkling on the patio and step outside into the moonless night.

"Anybody here?" I ask.

"Over here, honey," Bradford calls out from across the lawn. "Come join us."

I hear some splashing and as my eyes adjust to the darkness, I realize that Bradford's in the hot tub. That's not like him. And here's something even stranger. He doesn't seem to be alone.

I walk carefully over to the wooden deck and notice several heads bobbing above the water. "What's going on?" I ask. "Who's there?"

"Me," says a familiar voice. "Kirk."

"And me," sings out another voice. I stop, stunned. How can this be? The dreaded Mimi.

"Kind of a long story," Bradford says nervously as I step closer. "I played tennis and my back hurt, so I hopped in the hot tub just as Mimi was bringing Skylar home. They both jumped in with me, and then Skylar left to meet her friend and Kirk arrived so you two could rehearse for your next show but you weren't home yet so here we all are." He pauses for breath, and to gauge my reaction. Didn't he ever learn that you should always keep your cover story simple?

"Bradford's become such a prudey-prude since he's been with you," Mimi says, lolling against the tub and kicking her legs. "He insisted we keep our bathing suits on."

"I alas didn't have a bathing suit," says Kirk, looking down at—I'm not sure what.

"This is heaven for me. Surrounded by handsome men. I don't know which way to turn first," says Mimi. She extends a long leg, trying to tickle Bradford with her toe, but he sidles away and pulls himself onto the ledge.

"Probably time for you to go," he says to her coolly. I can see he's being careful about my feelings. After our conversation about Mimi the other night, he knows that seeing her here, I might overreact.

And I do. But not the way he might expect. I strip off the Guess jeans and Juicy Couture tee I wore to the Yankees game, revealing my best Victoria's Secret push-up bra and bikini panties in pink floral. I figure it can pass as a bathing suit. I slither into the water and settle down next to Kirk.

"Wow!" says Kirk. He puts his arm around me. "Hey, Bradford. If you want to keep your girl, you'd better get back in here."

"This girl's all grown up," I say. And it feels good to act that way. Bradford was right when he said that love and life are complicated. But I don't have to let that make me insecure. Or let a complication like Mimi come between us.

I playfully duck under the water to wet my hair. While I'm here, I might as well find out if Kirk is at least wearing the same Calvin Kleins from the photo shoot. Nope, looks like basic white Fruit of the Looms. Even Bradford's underwear is racier than that. I wonder what got between Kirk and his Calvins.

I come back up and shake out my hair and tug at Bradford's leg to pull him back in. Bradford hesitates, but seeing that despite Mimi, I'm being a good sport, he decides it's safe to come back in the water. I'm not going to drown him.

He slips in beside me and starts playing footsie with me under the water. "You didn't tell me your costar was so good-looking," he says, now rubbing his calf against mine. "I'd better send a chaperone on your next shoot. I like it much better when you're teaching at that all girls school."

Yes, all my students are girls, but I keep mum about the new male gym teacher who's so ripped that attendance in phys ed class is at an all-time high. I know Bradford's only teasing, but it's nice to have the tables turned. And to have Kirk continuing to make me seem like the most desirable woman on earth. Or at least in the hot tub.

"I must say I'm enjoying this more than I'd expected," Kirk says, eyeing me. "If you dress like this for all our rehearsals I'll never be late." He runs the back of his hand across his forehead. "Is the water in this tub overheated? Or am I just feeling all hot and bothered from being near you?"

I giggle, even though I'm pretty sure that line's from an episode of Kirk's soap. The kind of cutting-edge dialogue I've learned to expect from *Days of Our Knives*.

Bradford gets into the spirit. "Something's making me hot, too," he says, pulling me onto his lap. "And I'm sure it's my sexy fiancée."

This is fun. I could get used to it. I look gloatingly over at Mimi, who decides to make one last-ditch effort at getting some attention.

She shimmies over to one of the water jets, raising herself on her hands so its full blast is squirting at her bikini bottom.

"Ooh, ooh that feels so good," she moans, writhing on the water jet, and enacting a little drama, all by herself. I'm briefly stunned, but then remember my new resolve. No reason to be jealous when I have the real thing under me.

"Mmm, Bradford, you feel good," I say, wriggling around on his lap.

And talk about getting attention, I certainly have his. A little spontaneous bouncing got his interest a lot faster than roses and candles.

Kirk paddles over. "Hey, Bradford, I'm a star. I'm not supposed to lose the prettiest girl in the pool."

I laugh and so does Bradford. But Mimi doesn't find it at all funny.

"Harumpf!" she says. I've never actually heard anybody say that word before. I thought it was something you only see in a bubble in *Doonesbury.* But Mimi's genuinely miffed that she's being ignored by two men. She gets herself out of the hot tub and grabs her clothes. "I'm leaving," she says dramatically. "I wouldn't dream of staying where I'm not wanted."

Coming from Mimi that's a new policy. One that definitely gets my vote. I'm perfectly happy to see her unhappy, but Bradford's too kind-hearted to enjoy Mimi's chagrin.

"Don't be upset," he says to her, standing up to offer a few words of comfort and unwittingly dumping me off his lap in the process. "Let me get you a towel."

"I have one," she says, drying her feet. "Why don't you just walk me to my car."

Bradford looks at me. "Do you mind, honey? I'll be back in a minute."

"Go ahead," I say, splashing some water with my feet, determined not to be jealous. Ever again.

Bradford and Mimi walk toward the front of the house, and I make an effort not to watch them. He's just walking to her car, not out of my life. I'm going to stay rational. No need to sign up for match-dot-com if Bradford's not back in six minutes. Though I'll think about it if he takes seven.

But as if on cue, Kirk picks up the slack. "Alone at last. I get you in the end after all," he says happily. "Whoo-hoo."

How bad can life be if Kirk is pitching woo? Literally.

He puts his hand against a water jet and sends the spray in my direction. "Finally just the two of us."

"And what should the two of us do?" I ask.

"We could rehearse our cooking show," he says. "Or better yet, you can help me practice my scene for tomorrow's soap. Where I make passionate love to a beautiful woman." He leans in and gives me a soft kiss on the lips.

"We'll stick to the cooking show," I say with a laugh. And I kiss him back lightly on the cheek because I know we're just joking around.

Chapter TEN

WHEN I TOLD James he could meet Dylan two weeks from Saturday, I meant to pick a day so far away that it would never come. But now here it is. Dylan and I are standing at the bottom of the steps at the Bronx Zoo, looking up at the fountain—where I expect James is already waiting. He and I agreed that if the weather was bad, we'd put this off until tomorrow, so I search the blue sky hopefully for clouds. Cumulus, cirrus, stratus. Anything will do. But all I can see is a helicopter.

"You don't look happy, Mommy," Dylan says as I bend down to tie his sneaker. Admittedly, it's not really untied, but if I stop to fuss with the laces on his Nikes, I can put off our meeting James for another thirty seconds.

"Of course I'm happy," I say, standing up and trying not to sigh. Or at least too deeply. "I'm always happy when you're around, sweetie." I ruffle his hair, then pat it down, and do the same to my own.

"Then come on," he says impatiently. "I want to meet my real daddy."

And I want to throw up.

I go to take Dylan's hand, but he races ahead of me and bounds up the steps. At the top, he turns around to grin down at me. "Slowpoke!"

he hollers. Once I'm next to him, he dashes toward the fountain. And then comes to a complete halt.

I catch up to him and put my arms around him. "Everything okay?" I ask.

"I'm scared. There are lions here," he says, tears springing to his eyes. And then he adds more quietly, "And what if my daddy doesn't like me?"

I hug him close. My first impulse is to grab him and run away. And why not? That's what James did to us. But this isn't about James. Dylan deserves to find out about his father. And to feel secure while he's doing it.

"Who in their right mind wouldn't like you?" I ask, kissing the top of his head. "In fact, who wouldn't love you? Just the way I do."

He looks up at me with trusting eyes, and I feel a lump in my throat. Then I notice James, standing on the other side of the fountain, watching us. I don't approach him. Maybe it will be like one of those scenes in a movie where he spots us from afar, realizes what a perfect duo we are, and decides just to disappear again.

But no such luck. He's waiting for us to come over. I take Dylan's hand in mine. "Honey, that's James over there," I say. "Let's go say hello."

Dylan hesitates and then follows my gaze. "The man holding the balloon animals?" he asks, his face brightening.

I nod and Dylan lets go of my hand to rush over. James walks toward him, a big smile spreading across his face. He holds out what's probably meant to be an elephant, made from I don't know how many blue and green balloons, and Dylan accepts it eagerly.

"Daddy, this is great! Did you make it yourself?" Dylan asks.

Daddy? It took me eleven months, two hundred sleepless nights and two thousand diaper changes to hear the word "Mama" for the first time. All James has to do is make a lousy balloon animal and he's "Daddy."

I approach them slowly. James and Dylan are already laughing together and talking and for a moment, I'm the one who feels like an outsider.

James gives me a shy smile. He's not sure whether to kiss my cheek or shake my hand, and he settles on a little wave, avoiding all bodily contact.

"Can we go to the children's zoo?" asks Dylan, heady with excitement.

"Sure," says James, leading the way. We start down the road and Dylan reaches to take James's hand. I'm walking awkwardly next to them and think of taking Dylan's other hand. But will that make us look too much like a happy little family? Give Dylan the wrong idea of what he can expect? I don't have to worry about it for too long, because after just a few minutes, Dylan groans and looks down the endless path in front of us.

"How much more do we have to walk?" he asks, leaning heavily on James's arm.

"Not far, almost there," says James, ever the encouraging hiker. "But do you want a ride?"

Dylan, my city-raised son, looks around for a taxi.

"On my shoulders," James explains. And when a wide-eyed Dylan agrees, James crouches down and says, "Hop on!"

Dylan grabs onto James's sandy hair like he's riding a pony and from his perch high above, looks down and gives me a big grin. "How cool is this, Mom!" he says, bouncing along.

"Really cool," I say, offering a weak smile. I haven't been able to carry Dylan since he had that growth spurt at four, but I'm glad— should be glad—that he can get a treetop view of the world from James's shoulders.

At the petting zoo, James puts Dylan down and gives him a quarter to get a bag of animal feed. Dylan confidently holds out a handful of nuggets for a billy goat, but when the horned animal lowers his head to start munching, Dylan lurches back and drops the feed on the ground.

"Let's try it together," James says, putting his palm under Dylan's. "Secret is to keep your hand flat. He wants the feed, not your fingers, so just keep them out of the way."

With James at his side, Dylan successfully provides lunch for two billy goats and three baby sheep. James has endless fun facts to tell about the animals, and Dylan seems thrilled with his steady stream of stories. I have to admit that even I'm enjoying myself listening to James's easy banter. After the children's zoo, Dylan wants to see the penguins, and who could say no? We go to observe them and James makes the usual joke about their looking like maître d's. Dylan giggles. He seems to have accepted James at face value—a nice man who knows his way around a zoo. I keep hoping Dylan will at least ask James an awkward question or two, but he never does.

We'd agreed to an hour and a half visit for the first meeting, but we're all having so much fun we let it slide into two. Finally, James walks us back to the parking lot.

"Where are we going next time, Daddy?" Dylan asks, dragging his feet.

James glances at me uncertainly. "Some place great," he says. And then turning seriously to me he adds, "If it's okay with Mom."

I'd like to take my time to answer. In fact I'd like to take about eight years. But I've done the right thing. This has been a good afternoon for Dylan and he deserves more.

"Sure, we'll have more great afternoons," I say. But I keep the what and where vague. It took all my emotional reserves to deal with today and I'll have to restock before the next meeting. I hustle Dylan into the backseat and when I buckle him in, he quickly reaches for his Game Boy. I wish Dylan had gone for a book instead of the electronic toy. Maybe that would be proof that I'm a good mother. But apparently his skill with the control button is impressive enough.

"You've raised a terrific kid," James says, after he's high-fived Dylan and said good-bye. He walks around to the other side of the car with me and opens the door. Then he startles me by taking my hand. "In fact, you're both terrific," he says. "Thanks for letting me back into your life."

I step away from him and slide behind the wheel. Finally, I turn on the ignition. "Back into Dylan's life, not mine," I correct him.

"Enough for now," James says. He waves to both of us and stands watching for a long time as I drive away.

* * *

"So it doesn't sound like it was that bad," Kate says as we push our way through the lobby of the Empire State Building the next day.

"Not so bad. He was good with Dylan. And that's all that matters," I say, finally summing up my visit with James. Bradford got the abridged version of the story, but as usual I put Kate through the whole play-by-play. She even nodded encouragingly when I got to the part about which billy goat was cutest. That's what best friends are for.

"I don't know if I could have been as mature as you were," says Kate supportively.

"You don't know the half of it," I say, thinking proudly of how I handled the situation with Mimi and the hot tub. "I'm acting so grown up lately that by the end of the week I may be eighty."

"Don't worry, I have a new DNA skin cream that can make you look seventy," says Kate.

"Thanks, but I'm pretty sure I can do that all on my own." I laugh.

We hit the button on the elevator and breeze up to the twenty-fourth floor and through a door marked METRONAPS. Most people come to the Empire State Building to stand on the observation deck and take in the city. Kate and I have come to escape from everything and catch a snooze. Some genius decided he could charge people to come here and sleep for twenty minutes in plastic padded cocoons. And I guess he is a genius, because here we are, plunking down our money.

"Tell me again why you want to do this," I ask Kate.

"Because it's Tuesday," she says, looking at me meaningfully. "Used to be my regular day with Owen at The Waldorf-Astoria. Or the Four Seasons. Or the Plaza. We always had great sex and even better rooms. And then we'd take a nap. Have I ever told you about the naps?" She pauses. Yes, she has told me about the naps and I'm convinced that the best part of having an affair is getting to lie down in the afternoon.

"I'm glad you're not seeing Owen today," I say. "You're making the right decision."

Kate looks dubious. "I don't know if I am. He's still the most wonderful man I know. But after the Yankees game I decided we should take a break. He got me so mad that day. We both need time to think things over."

I worry that while Kate needs time to decide whether Owen's still a fling or her future, Owen's just working on how to get the mustard stains out of his shirt.

I take in the strange room filled with rows of sleeping pods. Pods. The whole thing feels very sci-fi. Something out of *Invasion of the Body Snatchers*. Though if somebody's going to snatch my body, I hope they bring back a thinner one. I wouldn't normally go to a place like this. Still, I'm here for Kate. If Owen can be replaced by a commercial sleeping station, I'm all for it.

I climb into my personal sleep capsule and notice several businessmen dozing nearby. Only in Manhattan could people be convinced that instead of simply putting their heads down on the desk when they're tired, they need to pay good money to take a nap. And maybe they do. After all, this is the sleep-deprivation capital of the world. Sleeping no more than five hours a night is a badge of honor, and four hours proves you deserve to be mayor. Although you shouldn't necessarily operate a car.

In the next pod, Kate is fiddling with the lighting controls, and her pod plunges into near darkness. I busy myself adjusting the speakers, which offer a dozen choices of relaxing sounds. I flick between lapping waves, which make me slightly seasick, and the gushing waterfall, which makes me want to go to the bathroom.

"You sleeping?" I ask Kate, trying to keep my voice low.

"No," she says.

"Me either. And guess what I just thought of?" I say brightly. "You and me. Here. We're like two peas in a pod."

"That's really what you were thinking about?" she asks, probably disturbed that when her best friend lets her mind roam free, this is where it ends up. "I was thinking about Owen. How much I love him. And that I should have been more understanding."

I practically jump out of my capsule. "Understanding of what?" I ask.

"Shhh," says a man a few cocoons away. "People are trying to sleep in here."

What does he think this is, a library? Feels to me more like a pajama party. Where the whole idea is to talk. And talk about boys.

But Kate's closed her eyes, so I lie rigidly in my shell. How embarrassing to admit that I got eight hours of sleep last night and don't need a nap. I switch the white-noise speakers past the sounds of wind rustling and rain pattering to the very realistic bees buzzing. What's relaxing about a bee that's about to sting you? Good thing I don't need any sleep, because I'd never get any.

Nobody else in the room can get much sleep either, because Kate's cell phone starts ringing shrilly. She abruptly sits up and answers it, but with the white noise machine still on in her pod, she doesn't realize how loudly she's talking.

"Oh darling, I love you, too!" she says, practically screaming. "No really, it was me. My fault. All my fault. Yes, I know it's Tuesday. Of course I want to be with you."

I turn down my speakers so I can listen to every word.

"Owen, of course, yes. Forever." She turns up the lights over her head, and from the happy look on her face, I guess that three seconds of Owen is better than twenty minutes of dreamy sleep. If Kate was taking a break from Owen, it turned out to be shorter than Britney Spears' first marriage.

Kate gives me a thumbs-up sign and mouths, "Owen!" As if the whole room doesn't already know. She points to the door and I gladly abandon my pod to follow her out.

"Darling, wherever you want. I'll be there in ten minutes." There's a brief pause and then she makes a face. "The Plaza again? Didn't we have better sex at The Carlyle?" She giggles. "Well, yes, your empty warehouse was definitely the best. Or maybe the penthouse on the top of that office tower you're buying. And I love it that you're bidding on that former church in Brooklyn. That pew was the most fun!"

The pew? Some details I could live without knowing. Guess when Owen is thinking about location, location, location, real estate's not the only thing on his mind.

* * *

I wake up in the middle of the night and realize I'm not being a good friend. Instead of standing by Kate no matter what, I should be dragging her away from Owen. Kate's not seeing the handwriting on the wall, but I am. Every story ends the same way. Fly down to Tortola? Owen rushes back to his wife. Auction at Sotheby's? He's there with his wife. Yankees game where we're sitting with Billy Crystal? He wants to get out of there, because he's a married man. Is there a theme here?

Maybe they had make up sex at the Plaza yesterday, but no amount of sex can make up for what Owen's doing. And as it turns out there wasn't that much sex anyway. Kate called me at five to say she was back in her office. Owen forgot he had to hightail it over to Cartier to pick up a little anniversary present. For guess who?

I lie staring at the ceiling for half an hour trying to figure out how I can help Kate. Or when I can get the ceiling painted. Maybe I can ask Berni who did her little clouds. As long as I'm wide awake I get out of bed and pad down to the study where several sample wedding invitations are spread across the desk, exactly where they've been sitting for three weeks. The standard engraved one is too stuffy. The hand-printed calligraphy is impossible to decipher. I toss them all into the wastebasket. Maybe I can create my own. Even better, make it a project and declare next Wednesday Design a Wedding Invitation Day at Spence. Or maybe that sends the wrong message to eleven-year-old girls, who should be thinking about becoming world leaders, not wives.

Better to focus on someone else's problems than your own. I put my mind back to solving Kate's married-man crisis, but I need help with this one. I slip out of the house, and walk through the quiet streets of Hadley Farms over to Berni's. I know she and the babies will be awake at this hour because it's feeding time. Then again, it's always feeding time. I knock softly on the door, and Berni doesn't seem at all surprised to see me. She's up, so why wouldn't the rest of the world be?

"Kate needs our help," I say, skipping past hello and getting right to the point. "She has an addiction."

Berni seems unfazed. "Who doesn't have an addiction? With a

client list like I used to have, I've seen 'em all. Let's see, there's alcohol, cocaine, heroin, Percoset, sex, shopping and chocolate." She reels off the classics as casually as she would this week's grocery list. "What's Kate's problem?"

"Owen," I say.

"That's all?" Berni asks. She sounds disappointed. It's hard to impress a woman who's visited so many clients at Betty Ford that the clinic named a bench after her.

While we've been talking, Berni has been holding Baby B over her shoulder and patting his back. Now he lets out a contented burp and Berni breaks into a big smile.

"My smart boy. My wonderful boy." She rubs his back happily. "Wasn't that the best burp you ever heard?" she asks me.

"Good burp, but not the best burp," I say critically, as if I'm judging an Olympic competition. High marks for length of emission, but points off for volume. Most new moms think their baby's every burp qualifies for a gold medal. But aren't we setting unrealistic expectations if a baby grows up thinking that whenever he burps or poops, the world is going to cheer? Let the kid try either of those things in public when he's six and see what happens.

"So a substance abuse problem. Kate. Owen. It's simple," says Berni, sounding professional as she puts down Baby B. "We need to do an intervention."

It doesn't take her more than a couple of minutes to clue me in on what she has in mind. Asking Berni what to do about an addiction is as efficient as asking Anna Wintour where to buy sunglasses. She's done it a million times and knows exactly how to proceed.

"Let's head over to Kate right now," she says. "No time like the present."

"What about the babies?" I ask.

"The baby nurse is here. And Aidan. And my mother." Berni snaps her fingers. "My mother. Erica should come with us. As many people as possible should confront Kate. The whole idea of an intervention is to make the addict realize that everyone in the world sees her problem."

I'm starting to feel a little bad about turning Kate into the poster girl for addiction. Just because she won't leave Owen doesn't mean she's the new River Phoenix. Still, Berni seems to know what she's doing. And it's starting to sound like a party. Maybe I should call ahead to make sure Kate has enough food.

Berni grabs her half-asleep mother, who thought she was here for a visit with her grandchildren but has now been enlisted into the Leave Owen Now army. We get into the car to race over to Kate's new upstate house and storm the barricades. Or in this case, the white picket fence.

"Surprise is everything," says Berni, as we get to Kate's front door and she expertly picks the lock. Something else she learned from one of her clients? But even Berni's no match for Kate's alarm system. Loud wails and flashing lights scream into the dawn, along with a deep, masculine recorded voice. "The perimeter has been breached. Police have been called. Leave the premises immediately." You'd think we were breaking into the National Gallery.

With the alarms and warnings ringing, Kate dashes down the staircase in a panic, and when she sees us, she looks relieved. Why she came down if she thought she was interrupting a crime in progress is beyond me. A bell goes off, and everyone's first impulse is to run right into the arms of the robber.

"What are you doing here?" Kate asks, turning off the alarm system. And then looking alarmed herself as the three of us circle around her.

"It's an intervention, dear," says Erica kindly. "I'm not sure what that means. But you do have a lovely place here. Thank you for having us."

Kate, who hadn't intended to have us at all, looks baffled and turns to Berni for help.

"We're here to make you see the truth," says Berni.

"I can't handle the truth," says Kate flippantly. "I still refuse to believe that butter is bad for you."

"You have to handle this," I say adamantly. "We're here to get you to break up with Owen. He's bad for you. It's never going to work. You have to leave him."

Kate ducks away from our circle and stamps into the living room. "Is that what this is about?" she asks incredulously.

Before we have a chance to answer, three policemen walk through the still open door, hands poised on their pistols.

"Dr. Steele, are you okay? We got a call from the security company." He eyes us suspiciously. "These people bothering you?"

Kate spins around, looks at us, and then putting her hands on her hips turns histrionically to the policeman. "Yes, yes!" she says. "Definitely bothering me. They're up to no good."

"Are you filing a complaint?" asks one of the other cops, pulling out a pad.

"I certainly am," says Kate, flouncing over to lean against her grand piano. Which in her case, is best used for posing, not playing. I once heard her pound out the "Minute Waltz" when we were kids and it felt like it took an hour.

Berni goes over and puts her arm around the shortest policeman's shoulder. "Honey, it's just a domestic dispute," she says. "We'll take care of it." She artfully steers him toward the door and the other two follow without even a backward glance. These guys are less effective than Patrolman Pete. And not nearly as cute. I kind of wish we'd set off the smoke detector. Firemen are always adorable.

"I need a drink," says Erica, once they're gone.

"Coffee? Tea? Milk?" asks Kate, happier to play hostess than hostage.

"A nice Chardonnay would be good," says Erica.

At seven-fifteen in the morning? We could be focusing on the wrong addict here.

Kate comes back with an open bottle of white wine, and in deference to the hour, four juice glasses. She fills each glass to the brim and hands them out. When Kate sits down, we each grab a chair to gather around her.

"We're here because we love you," says Berni, kicking off our intervention.

"And because we're worried about you and want to help," I add importantly.

"So let's start with the fact that you're dating a married man," says Berni.

"You are?" asks Erica, who up until now hasn't known the details and is suddenly interested. She sits up, takes a sip of her wine and gives a knowing smile. "Aren't married men the best? I had one myself. They're so passionate. So attentive. Shower you with presents." She settles back into her chair, lost in her own memories.

Berni whips around. "Mom, you?" she asks. "I thought you'd never been with anybody but Daddy."

"This was before I met your father," Erica says. "Why would I have told you?"

"Why would you tell me now?" Berni asks.

I clear my throat. "We can discuss this another time," I suggest. "But thank you for sharing, Erica."

"It's been a pleasure. I'm glad you appreciate it," she says, patting me on the knee. "We can only help dear Kate if we're honest."

Kate swigs down her wine and refills her glass.

"All right, I'll be honest," says Berni, turning back to Kate and getting straight to the point. "You're being an idiot. Owen's a shit. I personally can't bear the sight of him."

"You've never seen him," Kate fires back.

"None of your friends get to see him," I say. "Including you half the time. Owen only gets together with you when it fits into his schedule."

"Which is fine, because I'm very busy myself," says Kate.

"Right," I retort. "Busy waiting in Tortola. Waiting by the phone. Waiting for him to introduce you to Billy Crystal. Waiting in this house for him to come by for a quickie."

Berni said I had to be confrontational if we're going to bring Kate to her senses, but I might have gone too far. There's a palpable silence in the room. Erica rushes in to fill the void.

"Nothing wrong with a quickie," she says cheerfully. "Some mornings when Doug's in the mood and I'm not, I tell him just to go ahead anyway. And you know what? Makes us both feel better for the whole day."

Berni looks thoroughly horrified. "Doug?" she asks.

Erica smiles. "Dear, I loved your father very much. But he's been gone five years. He would have wanted me happy, don't you think?"

"No," says Berni.

"You're wrong. Sex was very important for both of us. And what I've learned is that a quickie today will allow a man to be patient and loving tomorrow."

We all stare at her. It's encouraging to know that at sixty-four, she's still having great sex. I make a mental note to ask her out to lunch next week. Who knew that feisty Erica Davis was the Dr. Ruth of Poughkeepsie?

"Okay," says Berni, turning back to Kate. "We've established that Owen's a shit. That he's ruining your life. You spend too much time waiting for him. And my mother's a slut."

"You've only hit it right on one of those," says Kate haughtily.

"Which one?" asks Erica, more curious than worried about whether she's being branded with a big red S. Even a designer one.

Kate uncorks a second bottle of wine and pours us all another round. "I do spend too much time waiting for Owen," she admits.

"Good start," says Berni approvingly. She pulls out her pad. "That'll be number one on the list of three things you hate about Owen. Now tell me two more."

Kate takes a long time. "I can't think of any," she says.

"Sure you can," I say helpfully. "The sandals."

"He stopped wearing those the minute I asked," she says. "He does everything I ask."

"Except leave his wife," I say.

"Oh, they never leave," says Erica, who obviously knows. Because we now know that Erica knows everything. "Is that what you were hoping for?"

"Not at the beginning," Kate says, squirming in her chair and pouring herself yet another refill. This is more than I've seen her drink in the last twenty years. If she wasn't an addict before, the intervention could turn her into one. "But now that Owen and I are so close, I guess it hurts that we can't be together all the time."

"And you'll never be together all the time," I say. "I know you're in love and I'll even believe that he is, but he's never leaving. It's just going to get more and more painful. Worse than waiting for the Birkin bag."

"Supposed to be arriving next week," says Kate. She takes a little nip of wine straight from the bottle.

"Promises, promises," I say.

Suddenly, Kate bursts into tears. "I don't know why I'm crying," she says. "I never cry."

"You never drink, either," I tell her, putting my arm around her comfortingly.

"He's the most wonderful man I've ever been with," Kate says. "A little of him is better than a lot of most guys. At least I thought it was. I'm still convinced it's a good theory. But dammit, I hadn't planned on getting so emotional about him."

Now we all get emotional. Erica dabs at her eyes with a tissue and even Berni sniffles a little. Hard to bring Kate to this point, but it's been worth it. Maybe Kate's hurting a little today, but we've saved her years of heartache.

Kate stands up and looks pointedly at each of us to make her important declaration. "I have to give Owen up because he's never leaving his wife," she says. "He's never leaving."

"Never leaving," says Berni firmly.

"Never leaving," I chime in.

"Never leaving," agrees Erica.

We all rush over to Kate and in a moment we're all crying and hugging. In the midst of our group embrace, none of us hears the front door fling open.

Owen bursts into our gathering, holding a big bouquet of flowers and a Tumi suitcase. He charges over with a cocky smile on his face.

"I've done it," he says pushing us all aside to give Kate the only hug she really wants. "Thank you for never losing faith in me. I've done it, darling. I've left my wife."

Chapter ELEVEN

AS FAR AS INTERVENTIONS GO, I'd have to say ours was a bust. But upbeat Berni has a different take.

"We did it!" she boasts as we drive home. "We changed her life!"

"We did?" I ask.

"Maybe not the change we planned on," Berni concedes. "But after this morning Kate's whole life has turned around. A success is a success."

No wonder Berni was such a hit in Hollywood. She's mastered the art of spin-doctoring. I decide to give it a whirl.

"If Owen's moving in with Kate, maybe now she'll get more than quickies," I say, going for the only positive thing I can think of. I was wrong that married men don't leave. But there's a bigger problem. Owen was fine for a free-spirited dalliance, but how will he be to live with day-to-day? From all evidence, he doesn't seem like good husband material.

"I think we've had a wonderful morning," chimes in Erica from the backseat.

"I bet you can't wait to call Doug and tell him all about it," says Berni. Who may need her own intervention after learning that her mother gets more than a glass of warm milk every night before bed.

Berni drops me off and I see the door fling open while I'm still fumbling for my key. Skylar appears and watches me come up the front steps, her hands on her hips and her head cocked to one side.

"Your boyfriend's here," she tells me in a challenging tone. "Just because my mother's sleeping with my father again doesn't mean you should be dating."

I open my mouth but I hardly know which part of this multiple bombshell to address first.

"Which boyfriend?" I blurt.

"A cute one and he's waiting for you," Skylar says. She eyes me with a little more interest than usual. "How many boyfriends do you have?"

I brush past her to see who could possibly have arrived. In the living room I find Dylan happily jumping up and down. And next to him, running a Lego truck across the Aubusson carpet, is James.

"Hi, Mommy, look what we built!" Dylan calls out excitedly. "Come see!"

From where I'm standing I can see quite enough. One trip to the zoo and James thinks the welcome mat is out? Time for me to set some ground rules. But before I have a chance to say anything, James unfolds his long legs and stands up abashedly.

"Hi, Sara," he says. "I didn't mean to barge in. I was just dropping off a present for Dylan." He points to the brand new Lego—the one Dylan's been dying for and I decided not to buy until his birthday.

"He was going to leave but I asked him to stay," says Skylar, who's traipsed in behind me. "Everyone's always telling me I should have better manners."

And what a time for her to follow advice. Although I'm thinking that her real motive was stirring up trouble, not earning an etiquette award.

"Really, this wasn't my plan," James confirms.

"Best I know you've never had a plan," I say, a bit too tartly.

James nods solemnly. "I'm not going to argue that, believe me."

From his spot on the carpet, surrounded by a pile of still unconnected red, blue and yellow plastic Lego blocks, Dylan calls out to James, "I want to build the spaceship next. Can you help me?"

James looks uncertainly at me, and I take in Dylan's bright, expectant face. I'm pretty good at making up games to play with him. And Bradford's been a champ about teaching Dyl to kick a soccer ball. But Bradford's not home—which is becoming a constant refrain—and eager James is right here.

"Go ahead," I say to James with a half shrug.

Skylar, standing in the doorway, looks disappointed. "That's all that's going to happen?" she asks. "Aren't you going to get mad at him? Or me? Or somebody?"

"Nope," I say, clearly foiling her plans for an earthquake in the middle of the living room. Or at least a few tremors.

"Fine," she says, stomping out of the room. "I'll go watch some ice melt. More exciting than anything else going on in this house. Not like my other house."

Skylar's probably hoping I'll run after her to ask how exciting the days are at Mimi's house. Or the nights. And whether any of them really do involve Bradford. But I'm not going to buy into it. If Skylar's looking this hard for attention, maybe I should see if Berni can get her a screen test.

For once Dylan's paying no attention to Skylar's theatrics. He and James have already snapped together half a space station and Dylan's intensely sorting through piles of blocks looking for the next piece they need. "Anybody seen a red with six holes?" he calls out. Without thinking, I kneel down to join him in his search. Before I know it the three of us are working as a team. James is reading the instructions, I'm finding the pieces and Dylan is gleefully constructing his rocket and feeling like a junior astronaut. He's so animated that he seems like he's already in orbit.

I slip off to the kitchen and bring back a tray of lemonade and my own homemade chocolate chunk cookies.

"Delicious," says James, nibbling his second. "I remember what a good baker you are."

"She cooks on TV. Mom's famous!" pipes up Dylan, my own personal publicist.

"I'm not surprised," James says admiringly. "You have a really special mom." Dylan grabs his empty lemonade glass and then runs into the kitchen for a refill.

The room is suddenly silent. James fiddles idly with some of the Lego blocks, still strewn around the room. "You're doing well for yourself, Sara," he says without quite meeting my eye. "I always knew you were going to be okay. But it's good to see just how awesome you are."

I feel that usual flash of anger at James. "You knew I was going to be okay?" I ask, my voice tightening. "Is that what you told yourself when you decided not to come back? Sara will be okay? Everything will be okay?"

"I don't know what I told myself," he says quietly. "It seems like so long ago. Amazing how you can screw up your life. You think you're doing something free and wonderful and then one day you wake up and you realize you've blown everything."

Despite myself, I feel a pang of understanding. What I'd always loved best about James was his wild spirit that took me out of my own tightly-wound world. I was cautious and James wanted adventure. He swept me along and made our world exciting. But I guess it really is true that what attracts you most to someone is exactly what you most end up hating.

I stand up and kick some of the scattered Legos into a pile. I've spent eight years hating James. And that's enough. A part of me will never forgive him, but it's time to move on.

"I'll never really understand what you did, or why," I tell him. "But we can't change the past. All we can hope is that we do better in the future."

"That's what I'm trying for," James says. "Do you think you can forgive me?"

"No, but we can get past that," I say with a weak smile. "It feels good not to hate you."

James stands up and puts his hands on my shoulders. "It feels good to be back," he says, locking eyes with me. He's standing a little too close for my comfort.

And apparently for Bradford's comfort, as well.

"What's going on here?" asks Bradford, coming into the living room and tossing down his briefcase.

James takes his hands off my shoulders and steps back, guiltily.

"Who are you?" asks Bradford.

I move farther apart from my ex-husband to make the proper introductions. "Bradford, James, James, Bradford," I say nodding from one to the other and running their names together until it sounds like a fancy hotel in Washington, the James Bradford. Or in London, the Bradford James.

"So this is James," Bradford says, offering a curt hello but not reaching out to shake his hand. I'm guessing walking in on our cozy little makeup scene has upset him. But sure enough, being a man, he focuses his distress on something he thinks he can actually change.

"What are all these Legos doing here?" he asks, looking around the messy room.

I bend down to scoop some of the pieces back into the box. "We were playing," I say.

"That's why we have a playroom," says Bradford—rather sternly, it occurs to me. "Everything in its place."

I don't look over at my freewheeling ex-husband, whose only rule used to be anything goes. Place for everything? James always insisted that for every time we had sex in the bedroom, we had to have sex twice somewhere else. Preferably on the same day.

Hearing slightly tense voices, Skylar prances back into the room expectantly. Maybe there'll finally be some natural disasters. Or one she can cause.

"He's been here for a while," she tells her dad, pointing a finger at James. "He told me that he used to be married to Sara. They used to sleep together."

"I didn't tell you that," says James, taken aback.

"But you *were* married to Sara," says Bradford.

"A long time ago," I interject, trying to be reasonable. "But nobody told anybody anything about us sleeping together."

"Sometimes I sleep with mommy," says Dylan, innocently entering the conversation.

Finally Bradford laughs. "Me, too," he says, coming over to put his arm around me. I give him a light kiss, glad to have everyone else in the room see us together.

But Skylar's not happy about it.

"Well, I sleep alone," she says petulantly, finding a whole new way to stir up trouble. "And frankly, I'm the only person in the whole ninth grade who does."

Bradford and I just gawk at her, but James turns and gives Skylar a little smile. "Don't bet on it," James says. "What you have to remember about the ninth grade is that ninety percent of what a third of the kids tell you is fifty percent untrue."

Skylar tilts her head to one side, as if she's trying to absorb this nugget of information. Since she got a C in math, I'm figuring this tricky equation will keep her busy for a while. And hopefully keep her away from sex even longer.

I sneak a look at my watch and realize I have a new problem. Despite the fact that my fiancé's in a snit, my ex-husband's camped in the living room, and Dylan's rocketing around like he's halfway to Mars, I have to make a hasty exit. "Guess what," I say brightly, figuring I'll be cheerful rather than apologetic. "Kirk and I are shooting another show this afternoon. So while I'd love to stay, I have to get into the city."

"On a Saturday?" Bradford asks, removing his arm from around my waist. "You're working?"

"We have to shoot on Saturday because I'm at school all week," I reply.

"Looks like you were working today, too," James says, pointedly staring at Bradford's briefcase and instinctively coming to my defense.

"I came home early," Bradford says. Then realizing he doesn't owe James an explanation, he says to me, "I was hoping we could do something together this afternoon."

"I'm sorry about this afternoon, but we have all day tomorrow," I tell him.

Bradford pauses. "Actually I don't," he says a little awkwardly.

"Ha ha, no he doesn't!" Skylar gloats, finally triumphant. "My mom got theater tickets for the three of us. Another birthday present for me. Just the three of us. You're not coming."

"Good!" says Dylan, going over to James again. "That means you can visit again tomorrow! Do you know how to play Sim City?"

Bradford nailed it that night when he said we have complicated lives. Right now, I'd need a scorecard to know who's up, who's down, and who's miffed. Though the one thing that's clear is that we're all feeling a little strained. And nobody seems to be winning.

"Listen, I really do have to get going," I say, looking furtively at my watch again. "Kirk's waiting for me at the studio."

"That's right, your other boyfriend," says Skylar, thoroughly pleased with herself. She's having a much better afternoon than she thought she would.

But Bradford has apparently had enough. "I'm going upstairs to change," he says, putting an end to the proceedings. "See you later, Sara. Have a good shoot."

I go into the kitchen to collect the props I need for today's show. I'm finally allowed to use the Food Network's mixing bowls, and if I do well today, next week I get a time-share on the Cuisinart. Everything gathered, I head outside to go to the train station. But James is waiting for me by his car—an energy-conserving, environmentally-friendly Toyota hybrid Prius. The same model Jennifer Aniston drives when she's not tooling around the Hollywood Hills in her gas-guzzling SUV.

"Can I give you a lift into the city?" James asks.

"No thanks," I say, hesitant to get in the car with him. "I'm short on time. I'll take the train."

"I can get you there faster," James says. And then he gives me a wry, knowing smile. "Don't worry, I won't go off track. I finally know how to stay on course and end up where I want."

Okay, I hear him. And I decide to join him. The show starts taping in less than an hour and my prop bag is heavy. "If where you want to get is Ninth Avenue," I say, "I'm with you. Let's go."

* * *

For today's show, Kirk and I make a key lime pie. Or at least our version of it. After the success of our Chocolate Surprise, we've learned that America loves anything with packaged marshmallows, gooey chocolate, or gumdrops. Preferably all three. So our pie includes a creative crust of Kit Kat bars and a filling healthy with fruit Skittles. Lime ones, of course. As usual, network president Ken Chablis is beside himself with joy. Or maybe he's just on a sugar high.

"You two are brilliant," says Ken, gobbling down a hefty slice of pie after the shoot. "This crust! Pure genius!"

I've heard there are eight new ways to measure intelligence, but who knew that choosing Kit Kat bars over Snickers was one of them.

"Sara's the genius," says Kirk. Which isn't exactly true. He's the one who suggested we do an international recipe next week. We're using Swedish fish.

"This show's doing so well, I have a big surprise for you," Ken says, now scooping more of the pie directly from the serving dish. "I'm putting you both on a bus."

Berni's really slipping. A limo might be a lot to ask, but couldn't she at least get us a Town Car?

"A whole ad campaign," Ken goes on, explaining. "Pictures of you two on every bus going down Lexington Avenue. Keep up your numbers and we'll move over to Madison Avenue, too."

Ken licks some Kit Kat crust off his fingers, and Kirk gives me a secretive thumbs up. He doesn't want Ken to see that even a big soap star is excited about having his face plastered on the M101 that regularly passes by Bloomingdale's. With the possibility, if all goes well, of being upgraded to the Barney's line.

"An ad campaign. Terrific!" I say, wondering how my crow's feet will look blown up to poster size. Or if getting rid of them will deplete the world's supply of airbrushing.

"Photo shoot's the Tuesday after next," Ken says. "You two are so fabulous. You're going to look amazing." He starts to walk out, then turns around. "Sara, we should do something about your hair color before the shoot. My treat. You can expense it. Shouldn't be more than nine dollars. Why don't you stop by Duane Reade and pick up the L'Oréal Preference."

My preference would be to keep my own color. But when Ken leaves, my hands fly instinctively to my hair, which I long ago convinced myself was shiny brown, not mousy. Now I'm not so sure. Kirk comes over and tousles a few curls. "It wouldn't hurt to put some highlights in," he says, kindly. "I'll take you to my guy, Phillip."

I study Kirk's spiky blond hair, which looks like it comes from long afternoons surfing. Though now it occurs to me that there's not a beach around, and Kirk spends most of his days under hot lights, not hot sun, anyway.

"You're an actor," I tell him. "I'm an art teacher. The only color I do is on poster board."

"Hey, you're a big-time TV star now," Kirk teases. "You even have a beauty budget."

"And how many strands of hair will your guy dye for nine bucks?"

"Don't worry, he owes me a favor," Kirk says with a laugh. "I fixed him up with Roger, the makeup artist on our soap, and they've been together ever since."

Hair and makeup in one family? I hope they adopt because their kids will have everything.

Half an hour later, I'm sitting in a chair in Phillip's salon as he's telling me how lucky I am that I got here in time. And I don't think he means before his next appointment.

"I can't imagine how they let you on TV this way," he says, as he paints a smelly white concoction onto chunks of my hair and methodically wraps them in tinfoil. "When I'm done, you'll finally look like you."

"And who did I look like before?" I ask.

"Ugh, darling, don't make me say," Phillip insists, shaking his head and wanting to spare me the pain.

Kirk has taken the opportunity of our little salon excursion to have another colorist tend to his eyebrows. Which, I find out, he likes to have exactly two shades darker than the lightest spike in his hair. This is a whole new world. I barely remember to tweeze my eyebrows, and now I'm finding out that people dye them. And that's the least of my discoveries.

"I want my pubic hair very, very blonde," says a woman's voice from across the salon.

Pubic hair? I look into the mirror and notice a scrimmed-in area behind me. Is nothing left untouched? Are there no virgin areas anymore?

"I want it white-blonde, not yellow-blonde," the woman directs loudly. "Whatever you do, no red."

And why no red? Lucille Ball had plenty of admirers. But this is a woman who's taking color-coordination to a new level. Bad enough to be her hair stylist, I'd hate to be her housepainter.

Hearing her demands, Phillip chuckles. "One of our more difficult clients," he whispers to me, wrapping another chunk of my hair. "She's trying to get her ex-husband back. I can only imagine what else she's trying."

"This has to be perfect!" the woman commands arrogantly. "I'm not leaving until it's right."

It sounds like she should be worrying about her personality, not her shade of pubic hair. But then again, what would I know? Until today the only highlighter I used was a pink one to underline my textbooks.

"I have a big theater date tomorrow night," says the woman. "And it's going to end in bed."

I clutch the arms of my chair and half stand up. I suddenly realize who the pubic-dyer really is.

"Mimi!" I hiss.

Kirk comes over, his eyebrows now a dreamy sun-kissed shade.

"Mimi," I repeat again in a panic.

Kirk immediately recognizes the name from the hot tub, and not being a stranger to soap operas, he understands we have a little drama on our hands. He pulls the scrim around my chair. "Just talk softly and she'll never know you're here," he counsels. "You're safe."

Safe from being spotted. But will I ever really be safe from the conniving Mimi? First she leaves and breaks Bradford's heart. Now she wants to steal it back. And break mine.

Kirk puts his hands on my shoulders, currently covered by a brown plastic cape, and rubs them gently. "You're the star and Mimi's the wannabe," he says reassuringly. "And not just on TV. In life. No matter what she does, Mimi can't possibly compete with you."

Phillip picks up the drift. "Don't worry, honey," he adds supportively. "I've seen her pubic hair. You have nothing to worry about." And then he turns to Kirk. "But if there's a competition going on, I should make Sara a little blonder than we planned, right?"

"Right," says Kirk.

And blonde is what I am, when Kirk and I are finally ready to leave the salon almost two hours later.

"Is it too much?" I ask, taking a final glance in the mirror and trying to figure out how the person looking back could be me.

"No it's perfect," says Phillip. "I used Marilyn Monroe base and Madonna highlights and a little Reese Witherspoon thrown in for good measure."

With all that talent going for me, maybe I should set my sights higher than a cooking show.

By the time we step outside, the sun is going down and it's magic time in New York, when the city glistens and a strange silence seems to descend. You can almost feel a pause in the usually manic bustle—the sea of Saturday shoppers have gone home and the night people haven't come out yet.

"Isn't it beautiful?" Kirk says, taking in the city and the last rays of sun gleaming from the art deco spires of the Chrysler Building. "Let's grab something to eat."

I'm starved. I didn't even have a bite of the key lime pie we made—not that I wanted one. The last thing I remember eating today was a handful of Skittles.

"Thanks, but I should get home to Bradford," I say.

"So you can warn him about his predatory ex?" asks Kirk.

"No, I don't want to talk to him about Mimi. I've been there, done that," I say. "It just ends in a fight."

"How can I help? Want me to play detective tomorrow and follow them after the theater?"

"Not a bad idea. But how about an even bigger favor. Why don't you just marry her."

Kirk laughs. "I'm not sure even that would get her off your backs."

I think about it for a minute and realize that in a way he's right. No matter what happens, Mimi's going to be part of our lives forever. I have to decide to get used to that—or not.

"Come on, let's be wild," Kirk urges. "My regular hangout is two blocks away."

I give in, figuring that if I don't eat now I'll be munching potato chips all the way home on the train. "Okay," I say. "A quick bite."

Kirk's hangout turns out to be an unassuming coffee shop with standard booths, a two-tone linoleum floor, and some fifties-looking fixtures. But from the lanky, long-legged women and buff-bodied men draped languidly around the room, I can tell Kirk isn't the only actor-model type who calls this place his own. The drop-dead gorgeous hostess, who probably bothers with this job only when *Vogue* hasn't called, gives Kirk a welcoming hug. She leads us to a table, and as she drops the menus in front of us, she actually smiles at me. "Great hair color," she says. "Who did it?"

"Phillip," Kirk answers for me.

"Should have guessed," the hostess says, tossing back her own waist-length blonde hair and walking away.

We order omelets and a carafe of wine and I touch my hair self-consciously.

"I'm still not sure about this color," I say, stretching a lock of hair in front of my face so I can see how yellow it really is. "I thought it would be a little more subtle."

"It looks amazing," says Kirk. And to prove it, he beckons over some of his buddies for a straw poll about my straw-colored hair. "What do you think?" he asks each of them. When the comments are in and the ballots are counted I have three "Fabulous!", two "Phillip definitely outdid himself!" and one "Very glamorous. Even for an older woman."

"Not bad," Kirk says, pleased. And I have to admit that a vote of confidence from this crowd can't be all bad. Even the remark about my being an older woman doesn't bother me. At least I was called "glamorous" by a stud who couldn't be a day over eighteen.

Kirk's pals pull their chairs over to our table, telling funny stories from on and off the set. I'm laughing and enjoying myself, and somehow our quick bite turns into a whole night. I call home a couple of times, and when nobody picks up, I leave a message on the machine that I'm running late. And then it gets even later than I'd planned, because when I finally rush over to Grand Central, I miss the train to Hadley Farms by about forty seconds.

"Can you wait?" I scream, dashing down the platform as the whistle blows and the train starts to pull away. But the commuter train waits for no man or woman. Even a blonde one. Frustrated, I head back into the mostly deserted station. By now, only Starbucks is open. What the heck, I'll eat again. Given that it's Saturday night, the next train won't come for an hour. So much for my thirty-eight-minute commute.

When I finally stumble in the front door of our house, it's close to midnight and I'm tired and irritable. But nothing compared to Bradford.

"Where were you?" he asks, putting down his *Financial Times* when I walk into the bedroom.

"In the city," I say, stating the obvious.

"Seems like it took a long time to shoot a thirty-minute show."

"I went out with Kirk afterwards to get something to eat. Then I missed the stupid train," I say, too tired to give a more amiable explanation.

"Where'd you go to eat?"

"What difference does it make?" I snap, wondering why he's grilling me. And realizing that for once, the shoe is on the other foot. Bradford's not used to sitting home waiting for me.

"I just wondered," he says. "You spent the morning with James and the rest of the day with Kirk. Any other dates I missed?"

Whoops. Apparently it's not just the shoe that's on the other foot. It's a whole boot.

"I did have a little rendezvous with someone named Phillip," I say, trying to be lighthearted.

"Is that supposed to be a joke?" Bradford asks, looking down again at his newspaper. There must be something fascinating going on with corn futures since he seems captivated by the headlines.

"I did spend time with a Phillip," I say, now more annoyed myself. "He's a hairdresser. And you'd know what I meant if you'd put down that paper and look at me."

Bradford does just that—though not to the effect I'd hoped.

"You're right, your hair. What have you done to yourself?" he asks unhappily, clearly not casting his vote with either "Fabulous!" or "Very glamorous." And I'm not about to ask him how he feels about "Older woman."

"I did it for the TV show," I tell him defensively. "And everyone else I saw tonight thought I looked gorgeous."

Bradford fixes me with a long stare. "The TV show. Kirk. James. Phillip. I don't get it, Sara. Sometimes I feel like I don't know who you are anymore."

"Just because I'm blonde?" I ask, trying not to get upset. "This will grow out. It's still me underneath."

"Is it?" he asks. "All of a sudden, you're a TV star, running around the city all night. The woman I fell in love with was a down-to-earth art teacher. Funny and fun and in love with me."

"I still am," I say. "Why would you think otherwise?"

Bradford pauses. "Because you seem to be moving ahead with everything in your life except me. If you really want us to start our lives together, why aren't you planning the wedding?"

Now I could use a *Financial Times* to study. Because Bradford's probably right. I'm terrified about the thought of getting married again. But I can't admit that, so I go on the offensive. "You could plan the damn wedding, too," I say. "Calling florists and picking the table linen isn't for me. I never know what I want."

"When it comes to not knowing what you want, I think we're talking about more than table linen," Bradford shoots back. "It's hard to keep up with what you're thinking. First you accuse me of being too friendly with Mimi. Next thing I know James is hanging around."

"That was your idea," I say. "You're the one who thinks we should all be chummy with our exes."

"And Kirk? How does he fit into this little picture?" he snipes. "Hanging around in our hot tub."

"Let me remind you who else was in our hot tub," I snipe back. "Or maybe I should say 'your' hot tub."

"What does that mean?"

That stops me for a moment, since I don't actually know. So instead, I go for the kill.

"Your lovely Mimi has been busy preparing for her theater date with you tomorrow. She spent the afternoon dying her pubic hair."

Now Bradford's the one who stops. "How the hell do you know that?"

"It doesn't matter but you'll find out tomorrow that I'm right."

"Meaning that you still think I'm sleeping with her," Bradford says accusingly. "Here we go again. No matter what I say you'll never trust me. And I've got to tell you my trust's being a little tested these days, too."

Our tempers are rising and so are our voices. If Skylar's within earshot she's probably breaking her arm patting herself on the back. I take a deep breath and try to be reasonable.

"You were the one who said we have complicated lives. Did you mean just yours?" I ask, sounding angry and not quite as calm and reasonable as I'd hoped.

"Maybe this whole thing has gotten too complicated for both of us," Bradford says, slamming his fist into his *Financial Times* hard enough to rip through half a dozen pages. He grabs what's left of the paper. "I'll spend the night in the study," he says. "I don't want to fight with you."

"You already have," I say, tears springing to my eyes. I'm so angry that I can't wait for him to get out and leave me alone. But if he really loved me, wouldn't he realize how upset I am and come over to comfort me?

He stands at the door for a moment, possibly equally torn. But his anger wins out. "One more thing," he says, "You look ridiculous. You weren't meant to be a blonde."

The door slams behind him and I can't help myself anymore. I fall onto the bed crying. My whole body is shaking and I crumple the king size pillow, burying my head into it to muffle my sobs. In a minute it's soaked through with my tears.

"Maybe I wasn't meant to be your wife, either," I whisper. But there's no one next to me in the bed to hear.

Chapter TWELVE

I WAKE UP early the next morning, but Bradford and Skylar have already left. Dylan heads off soon afterward because today is Community Service day for his second-grade class, and the children are supposed to be helping the poor. Since there are no actual poor in Hadley Farms, they've settled for helping the middle class by planting bulbs in front of the Wal-Mart in the next county. I tried to volunteer for the outing, but so did every other mother in the class who's trying to prove to her kid—and herself—that she's the Best Parent in Town. I worked hard on the three-hundred-word essay "What I Can Contribute as a Chaperone," but I didn't even make the waiting list.

With everybody gone, I head into the bathroom to splash some water on my puffy face and relive the highlights of my fight with Bradford. But when I look in the mirror, a different set of highlights catches me off guard. Crumpled, matted, tangled hair looks worse in bottled blonde than it ever did in plain brown. And judging from my admittedly short experience, I'd have to say that the answer to the eternal question: "Is it true blondes have more fun?" is a resounding no.

Kate calls me when her Owen is in the shower to tell me what an amazing twenty-four hours they've had together. Now that Owen has left his wife and officially moved in with her, they've taken a bubble bath, made love five times, and best yet, lay in bed together watching TiVo.

"We never had enough time to watch TV together before," Kate giggles.

I sigh, not sure if I'm more envious of the sex or the cozy companionship. But I know that I didn't have either of them last night. I congratulate Kate on the start of her new life.

"My new life may be about to end," I tell her. "So one of us might as well be happy."

"Oh no, what happened?" Kate asks, always ready to spring to my support.

"Bradford and I had a fight last night."

"People fight. It's part of relationships." Kate's been living with Owen for one whole day and she's already a sage.

"I know. But this one just felt bad. We weren't even trying to understand each other." I launch into a quick outline of the battle, and then to make sure she knows how serious it was, I conclude by repeating Bradford's final remark about how he hates me as a blonde.

"You're a blonde?" Kate asks in surprise.

"Yeah, but it doesn't matter. I think he's going to leave me."

"You always think that," says Kate, "but it's not going to happen. Let's talk about it over lunch. Owen says he has a craving for Cajun. We'll pick you up."

"There's a new Cajun place on Seventy-sixth," I volunteer. "It's supposed to be pretty good."

"Owen has a better idea. He wants to take his new plane for a spin and go to New Orleans. Or N'awlins as they say there."

"New Orleans? Isn't that a little far?" I ask, startled.

"It'll be fun, and it's what Owen wants," Kate replies firmly. "Owen says nobody makes jambalaya like they do on Bourbon Street."

Kate has started to proclaim "Owen says" with the same reverent tone a Southern Baptist preacher uses when quoting what "the Lord says." But going to New Orleans sounds like a pretty strange commandment.

"I can't possibly," I say, thinking I'm not the type to fly off to another city for lunch.

"Why not?" Kate asks.

I start to answer, but realize I don't have a particularly good reason. Dylan's Wal-Mart outing will last all day, and then he's going straight to a new friend's house for a playdate and sleep-over. I don't have any plans myself, and I'm not looking forward to knocking around this big house all alone. Maybe I *should* be the kind of person who goes to New Orleans for lunch.

"I guess I could join you," I say hesitantly. "But I'm a little afraid of small planes."

"It's not small," Kate says. "Nothing about Owen is small."

She hangs up and I step into my oversized walk-in closet, trying to decide what to wear. Now that I have all this space, I need to fill more than a measly two dozen hangers. Especially since half of them hold almost identical pairs of Banana Republic black pants. I grab one and then go for a top—considering pullovers in cherry red, lime green and raspberry. Ever since I've become a TV cook, I can't even get away from food in my closet. I settle on a turtleneck—in lemon yellow.

Kate calls me from the car and I step outside into Owen's stretch limo. It's bigger than the one I rented for my senior prom—and there were eighteen of us sharing that one. I don't know why Owen needs such a big car since he and Kate are huddled together in a corner and Kate's draped over his lap.

Kate nods happily when she sees my hair—either she genuinely likes the color, or she's just glad to have me doing anything in the name of beauty. After our brief exchange, she turns back to Owen and he resumes his usual place as the center of attention. We spend the ride extolling his prowess—this time in business—and listening to a litany of his latest deals. I try to bring the subject around to Kate, who's just landed on *Vogue*'s list of Top Ten Medical Magicians. Number six. Right after that guy who claims you'll have clear skin if you eat salmon three times a day. Either that or you'll grow gills.

"I don't want to talk about me," Kate says, stroking Owen's arm and eager to get back to stroking his ego. Apparently she's given up trumpeting her own horn so she can blow his full-time.

I sit in amazement, listening to how many variations Kate can come up with on "Honey, you're so wonderful." But it passes the time, and when the car stops, I'm not completely sure where we are. I'm surprised when we step out onto a tarmac, where a pilot and two attendants are waiting. Next to a gleaming Gulfstream.

"Luggage, Mr. Hardy?" asks one of the attendants with a big smile.

"No, we're just going for lunch," Owen says, bounding up the steps to the plane.

Kate follows him confidently and I hesitate just briefly. I look at the pilot, dressed in a snazzy blue uniform with gold wings that look suspiciously like the ones Dylan gets from the flight attendant when we fly American. The pilot takes my hand, walks me up the stairs, and settles me into my seat.

"Comfortable?" he asks.

I'd probably be more comfortable if he were in the cockpit checking his flight plan, communicating with traffic control, fiddling with gizmos or reading through the instruction manual. No, scratch that last one. Better if he memorized the instruction manual—several years ago.

I buckle in, but nobody shows us the usual safety movie on how-to-use-your-seat-cushion-as-a-life-raft. Not that I'd ever want to bet my life on a two-inch rayon-covered cushion. Instead, the pilot turns around from the cockpit and with a convivial grin asks, "Everybody ready?" I expect the attendants to come by and threaten us about keeping our seats and tray tables in an upright position, but instead they're busy asking us if we'd prefer our mimosas with or without pulp in the orange juice.

After takeoff, Kate and Owen only seem to want the same thing they wanted before takeoff. They paw each other until we're at cruising altitude, then get up and head toward the back.

"Owen outfitted the plane with a bedroom," Kate whispers to me. Seeing my stunned look, she adds, "Nicely decorated with a queen-sized bed."

I've always had my own fantasy about making love on an airplane, thirty thousand feet above the ground. When I imagine the scene, my lover and I are squeezed into the tiny coach bathroom on a commercial flight, our backs pressed against the aluminum sink, with an anxious passenger who needs to use the facilities banging on the door. Risky and uncomfortable and probably illegal—but isn't that what makes it sexy? In my view, Kate and Owen's antics are too cushy to qualify for the real Mile High Club.

But I'm a little miffed. Why did Kate invite me to come along? She and I can't exactly talk about Bradford if she's going to spend all her time lip-locked with Owen.

I fiddle with my new iPod—I'll never get the hang of this—until Kate finally comes back by herself, adjusting her La Perla bra strap. "That little blow job cost Owen five million dollars," she says proudly.

"You're that good?" I ask.

Kate laughs. "A building he was negotiating for. He said he was going to top out at twenty-five million. But he got a call about it while we were in the midst, and I didn't stop what I was doing. Before you know it, Owen was going, "Oh, Oh, Oh . . . Okay." And he agreed to pay thirty." She giggles again.

"How much sex do you two have anyway?" I ask.

"A lot," Kate says happily.

"What's a lot?" I ask. "Do you think there's some national sex average? I heard a study that claimed a third of married couples have sex three times a week, a third three times a month, and a third three times a year."

"So does three times a day get me an award from the Kinsey Institute?" Kate asks with a sly smile.

Owen comes from the airplane bedroom, tugging at his belt and looking happy.

"That was amazing," he says, sitting down next to Kate.

She winks at me then lowers her eyes modestly. "I'm glad," she tells him.

"Four other developers competing and I got the building," Owen boasts.

Kate pokes him. "That's all that was amazing?"

He rubs the nape of her neck and gives her a kiss. "You're right. I got the girl, too."

Kate and Owen manage to sit in their own seats long enough for the plane to land. We taxi to a graceful stop, and when we get off the plane another stretch limo is waiting two steps away. How do rich people stay thin if they never have to walk more than three feet?

I'm expecting Owen to take us to some famous New Orleans restaurant, like K-Paul's or Antoine's. But at the mention of those, he just turns up his nose. "Only for tourists," he says. And what exactly are we? Instead, he leads us to a local shack with six tables and a small stage where three grizzled jazz musicians are trumpeting out amazing riffs. Owen orders for us and I don't know exactly what I'm eating, but it's all delicious. The dessert is a gooey mess of white chocolate, bread pudding, whipped cream and whiskey sauce. Just the kind of over-the-top concoction I make on my show. I ask for the recipe, and the chef happily comes out and scribbles it on the back of a napkin.

Back out on the street, we make our way through throngs of revelers, packed so tightly it could be New Year's Eve in Times Square. Above us, half-dressed and fully drunk men and women are hanging from intricately iron-worked balconies, trying to attract attention by dropping strands of colorful beads on passersby below. If the beads don't work, the women resort to another means of getting attention— they flash their breasts. The men are less subtle. They drop their shorts.

Maybe I haven't had enough bourbon to fully appreciate Bourbon Street, because the whole scene feels about as sexy to me as the Republican National Convention. But Owen seems to be enjoying himself. He has his arm clamped around Kate's waist and his eyes are wandering all around the scene. Kate decides we should get even more in the spirit and ducks into a store to buy some beads.

I hover on the edge, between store and sidewalk. On one side of me, I hear Kate bargaining to buy three sets of beads for five dollars. On the other, Owen is involved in his own transaction.

"Like these?" asks a large-chested college girl, lifting her cut-off Florida State T-shirt and giving Owen a good look at her naked 36Ds.

"What's not to like?" he asks. The giddy girl wiggles closer and presses her curvy bottom against his flat one. Owen doesn't seem embarrassed—in fact, he doesn't flinch. And when the coed takes Owen's arm and pulls it around her bare waist, he grins from ear to ear.

"You're cute," she tells him.

"Hey, so are you," he gushes.

I know this is New Orleans. You're supposed to leave your morals at the airport, or in our case, the private landing strip. But I have the uncomfortable feeling that Owen's just crossed a line. One thing to step back and watch the crazy scene, another to jump into it so enthusiastically. If he's so in love with my best friend, shouldn't he have eyes only for her?

Kate comes bouncing out of the store with a big smile, swinging the orange and yellow strands above her head.

"Darling," she starts to call out. But then she catches sight of her darling—who has a young woman attached to his hip—and her face drops.

Owen and Miss Florida State are having such a good time that it takes a minute for Owen to extricate himself. She gives him a big wet kiss and as she walks away, Owen gives her one last long parting look.

Kate takes her place again at Owen's side. "Enjoying New Orleans?" she asks, trying to sound chipper.

"Yup," Owen says. And he doesn't seem at all disconcerted about his little flirtation. The man's sense of entitlement is so huge he doesn't even know he should be embarrassed. And Kate's not going to call him on it. She'd rather gloss over the situation than admit that Owen might have disappointed her.

We stroll over to Preservation Hall, where Owen wants to hear some more jazz. The Sunday afternoon line stretches down the block, but Owen whispers something to the bouncer at the front and somehow we get inside immediately. We stay for barely one set before Owen needs another change of scene. Then we're back in the limo and heading toward the plane.

Owen's made five phone calls and flipped through three business reports before we hit ten thousand feet. Then he stands up and stretches, needing yet another diversion.

"Sweetheart, let's take a little nap," he says, though as he heads to the bedroom, he looks anything but tired.

I watch Kate follow him, her hand on his butt, and wonder how many "naps" this makes for today. One thing I've got to say about Kate. She and Owen are doing their part to raise the national sex average.

I don't get to tell Bradford about my gumbo lunch in New Orleans, because for the next three days, I barely see him. He gets home late and leaves early, and the one evening we might have to see each other, Kirk and I are preparing for our next show. I've figured out how to adapt the New Orleans whiskey sauce so it's pretty darn good. And that might be the only thing around this house that is.

Bradford's sleeping in our room again, but you'd hardly know it. We each stay on our own side of the king-sized bed, and the one time I try to cross the border and make peace, Bradford's asleep. Or pretending to be.

Thursday morning, I call Bradford's office, thinking we should go out to a romantic dinner and try to forget about our fight. But his assistant won't even put me through.

"He's in a meeting," she tells me apologetically. "Important one. I really can't disturb him."

I hang up, pretty disturbed myself. This is the first time Bradford's given instructions that he can't be interrupted, even for me.

Well, damn him anyway, this whole fight was his fault. Or maybe it was mine. I tried one morning to tell him how sorry I am, but when he asked "What are you sorry for?" I realized I didn't know. I can't be sorry for having a demanding job and an ex-spouse. Though I am pretty sorry that he has a demanding job and an ex-spouse.

After school, I help Dylan with his homework and take him to the diner, where he gobbles down mac and cheese and gets to play the video games on the machines in the back. He has almost identical games on his computer at home, but somehow they're more fun when you have to put a quarter in the slot to play.

At home, he falls asleep on my lap, watching a show about constellations on the Discovery Channel. Why we don't just step outside to look at the stars in the real sky is another matter. Maybe tomorrow night I'll pull out blankets and get Bradford to come outside with us and point out the Big Dipper.

I manage to carry Dylan into his bed and turn on the Harry Potter night-light that matches his Harry Potter pajamas and sheets.

Instead of going to bed myself, I head to the kitchen to catch up on the stack of *New Yorkers* that's been piling up. For some reason, even the Roz Chast cartoons aren't making me laugh tonight, and I keep looking at the clock. It's after eleven when Bradford finally comes in, looking tired.

"Do you need something to eat?" I ask him, trying to get things back to an even keel.

"No, thanks, I got something at the office," he says. "I had a long day."

"I noticed," I say, and I hope I'm sounding sympathetic, not angry.

He takes off his jacket and hangs it over the back of the chair. His tie is already uncharacteristically loosened and his white no-crease Brooks Brothers shirt is wrinkled.

"I have some news," he tells me. "Don't get upset. I'm leaving Saturday for Hong Kong."

"Hong Kong?" I repeat, letting the syllables sink in.

"It's a business trip," he says. "A lot of important things are happening in my company over there."

"How long will you be gone?" I ask, biting my lip. Sure, it's a long flight but I hope it will be a short trip.

"Three months," he says quietly.

I sit down and stare at the open *New Yorker,* but everything is blurring in front of my eyes. I'm not going to remind Bradford that I bought tickets to *Madame Butterfly* for next week. Bad opera to have picked anyway. Isn't that the one where the soprano is abandoned by her lover and kills herself?

"Three months is a long time," I say carefully. I won't think about James, I won't. And I won't wonder what it is about me that drives men to leave for exotic places.

"It's business. A good opportunity for me. I've been thinking about it for a while."

"You have? This is the first time you've even mentioned Hong Kong."

"It's been on the table at work for a few weeks," he says, shoving his hands in his pockets. "At first I said no. But I finally decided it might not be a bad thing for us to spend a little time apart."

"Or it might be a very bad thing."

"I'm not really seeing it as a trial separation," Bradford continues.

And until those words tumble out of his mouth, neither was I.

I sit very, very still. Maybe if I don't move, my world will stop turning upside down. "We just had a silly little argument the other night," I tell him softly. "Couples have those. It doesn't mean you need to run off to Hong Kong and disappear."

Bradford comes over and rubs my shoulders. "I'm not running off and I'm not disappearing." He gives a weak smile. "Hong Kong isn't Patagonia."

"Might as well be," I say.

He stops rubbing my shoulders and sighs. "Sara, please, we're back where we started. You have to be able to trust me."

"I didn't feel that much trust when you complained to me about James and Kirk," I say. And then I realize we're about to start rehashing the same argument all over again. So softening, I say, "I still love you."

Bradford doesn't say anything, but he gently kisses me. When he kisses me again, I melt into him, letting myself relax in his strong arms. I feel the barriers dropping between us. More urgently now, Bradford unbuttons my blouse and drops his lips to my neck. He leans me against the kitchen counter and pulls me closer. It's not an aluminum sink at thirty thousand feet, but it's still pretty fantastic.

Chapter THIRTEEN

"SO YOU AND BRADFORD MADE LOVE *after* he told you he was leaving?" Berni asks me Sunday morning, as I'm sitting in her sunroom.

"After he told me he was going to Hong Kong," I correct her.

"Do you think he'll come back?" Berni asks, absentmindedly folding some of the babies' tiny T-shirts. "I mean I know he's not going to stay in Hong Kong forever. But how'd you guys leave it when he went off yesterday?"

"He wouldn't let me drive him to the airport," I admit. "He had a car service pick him up." I bite the side of my thumbnail. For some reason, his ordering a cab upset me more than anything. I thought driving him to Kennedy would be a loving gesture, proof that I understood this was a business trip, not a breakup. He said my driving him made it too dramatic, and he wasn't looking for a good-bye scene. We shared the same sentiment, but had different ideas about how to express it.

"If you had sex, you know he still loves you," Berni says, trying to be comforting.

"You know better than that," I say. "The sex was great, always is. But I can't figure out if it was makeup sex, I-love-you sex, or good-bye-forever sex."

"Any of those are better than I-just-had-babies-so-stay-away-from-me sex."

I force myself to smile, but I'm not feeling very lighthearted today. I keep picturing Bradford in his Hong Kong hotel suite. Is he spending as much time thinking about me as I am about him? He couldn't be or he'd never get any of his work done. He left a voice message saying he'd arrived, but that was it. I've picked up the phone and put it back down about fifteen times without calling him. We didn't set up the rules for our time apart and I'm not going to be the one to call first. Before he left, Bradford kept saying that the trip would be good for both of us because we needed a break. He said it gently, but to me a "break" doesn't sound very gentle—it evokes images of smashed china, windows blown out by Hurricane Ivan or a horrible accident that lands you in the emergency room.

I blow my nose and stuff the Kleenex back in my pocket. "Allergies," I tell Berni, but she knows I'm lying.

"Look, I know you're heartbroken but no crying until after the photo shoot on Tuesday," says Berni, switching hats from love counselor to career coach. "And no salt. Can't have you showing up on a bus ad with puffy eyes."

"Fine," I say, thinking that after the shoot, I'll let myself have one heck of a good time sobbing for hours and stuffing myself with potato chips. If Bradford hasn't called by then it's going to be three bags of Lay's Sour Cream & Onion. Or maybe garlic, since I'll be sleeping alone.

Berni takes her babies' folded laundry and I follow her into the nursery where Dylan is currently babysitting. At least he thinks he is. Baby A and Baby B are sound asleep in their cribs, but Dylan is perched on a chair reading them *The Very Hungry Caterpillar.* From the number of baby books at his feet I can tell he's taking his assignment seriously and clearly enjoying it. He's having fun being a big kid and reading books where he recognizes all the words.

Berni ruffles Dylan's hair. "You're the best babysitter I ever had," she tells him.

Dylan beams. "This is my first job," he admits.

"I'll never find anyone better. You're such a good reader. The twins are lucky to have you here."

"Thanks," says Dylan, whose little boy chest seems to have puffed out under the praise. Who knew Berni would be this good with children? Having her own babies has clearly opened a whole new world to her. I'm not sure that before the twins Berni had a whole lot of interest in anyone under twenty, unless he was a teen actor starring on the WB.

Berni puts the T-shirts into one of the dresser drawers and pulls out a stack of tiny embroidered smocks and crocheted sweaters that still have the tags on them. "The babies have outgrown these already and they never even wore them. Such a waste."

I rifle through the stack of precious clothes that must have cost a fortune.

"All gifts," Berni says.

"What are you going to do with these?" I ask.

"I could donate them," says Berni. "Who wouldn't want to get such beautiful things, even if your baby can only wear them once?" She looks at the items thoughtfully. "But maybe there's something even better I can do."

"Isn't this the one Tom Cruise sent you?" I ask, fingering a suede fringed vest in a size 3 months. Too small for Berni's big babies fifteen minutes after they were born. "Useless, but I'd take Tom's present just as a souvenir."

"So would most people," says Berni. She pauses and refolds the suede vest with yellow tissue paper, so it won't get creased. "Can I run an idea by you?"

"Sure."

"I mean a serious idea. Or maybe it's silly. I can't tell," says Berni hesitantly.

"Hit it," I say, curious now. I've never heard Berni uncertain before.

"I've been thinking about a project I could do from home. I'd still be right here with the twins. In fact, they could watch me and they'd probably be proud."

I wait, not sure where she's going. What more could Berni do to make the twins proud? I'm guessing it's not my new contract at the Food Network.

Berni takes a deep breath. "So here's the point. My twins were born lucky, but there are a lot of needy babies out there. If I sell all this show-offy stuff, I could use the money to buy things for other babies that they really need."

"Nice idea," I say, impressed.

"And then I'd try to get more things to sell. I could call all the stars I know in Hollywood and see if they'll contribute their over-the-top baby gifts, too," Berni says enthusiastically. "If I sell just one pair of crystal-encrusted booties, I could get enough stretchies and Pampers for three dozen kids." As evidence that she's not making up that extravagant fashion item, Berni opens another drawer and pulls out a pair of shimmering silk blue booties, so heavy that any baby wearing them would probably never be able to take his first step.

"If anybody can get the stars involved, you can," I say encouragingly. So now it's going to cost me to get that Tom Cruise vest. But it'll be for a good cause.

"Do you really think this will work?" Berni looks at me so intently that I realize the plan means a lot to her. Instead of being a Hollywood agent, she wants to become an agent for change.

"Anybody who made a TV star out of me should be able to save the world," I say. And then I grin. "And I really mean it."

Berni smiles. "Thanks." But her next words are drowned out by her housekeeper, who's been vacuuming in the hall and now opens the nursery door. I wave frantically to signal that the babies are sleeping and she should leave, but Berni motions her in.

"Don't worry, I have her do this every day," Berni explains. "I figured out that if babies get used to noise they'll be able to sleep through anything. It's only when you make everyone whisper around them that they wake up at the drop of a pin."

Dylan covers his ears but I notice that the babies barely stir. Maybe Berni's onto something. She seems to be figuring out a lot of things about her babies—and her life. I wish I were doing as well.

* * *

"How are your sex toys working out?" community queen Priscilla asks when she calls me a week later. I guess the news about Bradford's leaving hasn't spread around Hadley Farms yet. What's the use of living in a small town if nobody's going to gossip about you?

"Not well," I say, for some reason confiding in my neighbor. "Bradford left for Hong Kong." Look at that, I'm gossiping about myself.

"He did? Without you? Oh, you poor dear," Priscilla gushes sympathetically. Then getting an inspiration, she asks, "Are you putting the house up for sale? I'd love to show it. I've had my real estate license for two months now and I'm already the best in town. But for you, I'll drop my commission to four percent. I can get you an appraisal this afternoon and have buyers there in the morning."

Priscilla rushes along with her plans at such breakneck speed that in another minute or two she'll be filing my divorce papers—and I'm not even married.

"Bradford's just away on a business trip," I say, trying to haul her back to reality and convince myself at the same time.

"What a shame," Priscilla says. But she's resilient and shakes off her disappointment. "So the reason I called is I'm throwing a little Hadley Farms party."

Another one? I have so much whipped cream left over from her last get-together that I might as well use it on my chocolate mousse.

"Boys and girls at this one," Priscilla says, and it takes me a moment to realize that she's not referring to our children.

"I'll be there," I say, thinking that maybe a party will cheer me up. And only when I put down the receiver do I realize that being the only single person in the room is just going to depress me more.

As per Berni's orders, I keep from crying too much until the photo shoot's finished. It goes off without a hitch, even though this time Berni can't be induced to come. She's too busy making plans for her new project, which she's named Celebrity Kids' Clothes. Or at least that's what she's calling it today. Yesterday it was Designer Duds. The day before that, it was Why the Hell Do People Buy Such Expensive

Stuff When They Could Buy Things People Really Need. Actually, I don't think Berni ever really planned on using that one because she couldn't get the initials on a button. But she'll make a final decision after she has the results from the focus group and phone survey she's commissioned.

From time to time during the week, Priscilla's party crosses my mind. The Lilly Pulitzer ladies already surprised me once at the Newcomer's Club. Do their R-rated afternoons turn into X-rated evenings when their men are around? Or do the guys have the opposite effect and turn Hadley Farms' sex-crazed wild women into doting, proper wives?

The morning of the party, Dylan and I are supposed to meet James at the Museum of Natural History, but I'm too down about Bradford to cope with being upbeat for an entire day. For the first time since James reappeared in our lives, I tell him he can pick up Dylan and take him out by himself. Once they're gone, I wish I'd joined them, because I don't even get out of my bathrobe. Actually Bradford's bathrobe—which seems to be the only connection I have to him at the moment. He hasn't called in three days. And the last time he did, we only talked for a few minutes because he had to run off to a meeting. Bradford says he's working round the clock, but who doesn't have time for a phone call?

James thoughtfully checks in with me twice during the day, once to ask if it's okay for Dylan to eat three hamburgers and four servings of fries for lunch. And then to ask if Dylan often complains of stomachaches. Later, I talk to Dylan, who's eating ice cream and floating on cloud nine, and I agree that he and James can—as usual—stay out longer than we'd planned.

I pull myself together to get dressed before they get home in the evening and even put on eyeliner, lip liner and a pale peach cheek gel. I'm getting so good at coloring things I could become a cartoonist.

"You look fabulous," James tells me, appraising my low-cut pink cashmere sweater and black leather boots, all borrowed from Kate for the photo shoot. Apparently they're mine now, because the clothes are from last season and she doesn't want them back. She did, however, ask that I return her Ralph Lauren lapis lazuli belt since it was a gift from Ralph himself. I'm thinking I might wear it a few more times—and then get her to donate it to Berni's charity.

We all sit down for a snack because for some reason Dylan is hungry again. The babysitter, who happens to be Priscilla's sixteen-year-old son, joins us and then whisks Dylan off to play catch by the lights in our backyard.

"You're all dressed up and you've got a babysitter," James says. "What are you doing tonight?"

I look down at my low-cut top, wondering if I'm showing too much cleavage. No, for once I'm like Kate. Just right.

"I'm going to a party," I say dispiritedly.

"You don't seem in the mood," James says. And then risking being too personal, he asks, "Anything going on? Can I help?"

I don't feel like having a conversation with my ex-husband about my current fiancé. Or at least I hope he's still my current fiancé. So I just say, "Bradford's on a business trip, and I don't love going to parties alone."

"Then let me come," James offers with his endearing shy smile. "I'm pretty good at social events. If things get dull, I can always do my card tricks. Remember that Christmas party we threw?"

Despite myself, I smile at the sweet memory of James mesmerizing a room full of happy guests in our tiny apartment by pulling the king of clubs out of somebody's ear. I haven't thought about what a charmer he is in a while. And what the heck. I'm not feeling very charming myself tonight so I might as well bring him along.

"Sure you can come," I tell him. "For some reason, everybody's always happy to have an extra man in a room." Though frankly, I don't know why. Who needs extras? Dealing with one man is usually more than enough.

James stands up and rubs his hands on the back pockets of his Levi's. "I'm not really dressed for a big evening out. Can I go like this?" he asks.

I have to admit that in his jeans, hiking boots and work shirt, ruggedly handsome James doesn't look like the typical Hadley Farms husband. Not at all. He looks a lot better. So I tell him we're good to go.

We say good night to Dylan and head out into the unexpectedly cool evening to walk over to Priscilla's house.

"What's this crowd going to be like?" James asks as we stroll down the quiet street. "I don't know how good I'll be at talking about stock funds, soccer games and SUVs."

"You're not up to date on your suburban stereotypes," I say, laughing. I don't mention that around here, sex toys are the big topic of conversation because I can't bring myself to say the word "sex" in front of James.

But Priscilla has no such inhibition.

"Hello, sexy guy," she says, opening the door for us and giving James a bold once-over. "Who are you?"

"I'm the extra man," James says, with a big grin.

"How thoughtful of you to bring him, Sara," Priscilla says, leaning in to throw an air-kiss to my cheek. "Most people just brought a bottle of wine."

Priscilla's husband comes up to introduce himself. He's a head shorter than Priscilla, slightly round, completely bald, but wearing a very expensive suit. I'm guessing she didn't marry him for his dashing appearance. And glancing around the room, I realize that the Hadley Farms husbands must have all wooed their wives with the only assets they had available—their bank accounts. In this community, you've got to hope that the kids get their mother's looks and their father's money. Another reason to support DNA research.

A waiter comes by with a tray of mixed hors d'oeuvres and carefully describes each one.

"I'll take the crabmeat and Sara will have the mushroom quiche," James says without thinking. Then we catch each other's eyes in surprise. "I mean, you can have whatever you want," he hastily amends.

"Actually, that's still my favorite," I say, reaching for the minitart. Have my tastes really not changed in all these years? I'm oddly uncomfortable realizing how well James still knows me, and I walk away from him and sit down on the sofa. I spot Berni and Aidan outside on the deck, but I don't have the energy to rouse myself and go join them. Berni waves and in another minute rushes inside.

"Did you hear what our not-prissy Priscilla has planned for tonight?" she asks me excitedly.

"A refresher course on handcuffs and whips?" I ask nonchalantly.

"No, but I'll suggest that for next time," Berni says. She's momentarily stopped in her enthusiasm when she sees that instead of paying attention, my eyes are wandering across the room to James.

"Who's the hunk?" she asks, following my gaze.

"James. My ex."

"James?" she repeats, turning to me in amazement. She seems more shocked than if I'd told her I'd just given up shopping at Target.

"He's cute but what the hell is he doing here?" she whispers to me as James saunters over toward us.

"I invited him," I say trying to keep my tone casual. What other explanation can I offer? Let's see, my fiancé is in Hong Kong and I'm terrified that he'll never come back, so why shouldn't I hang around with my ex-husband who I *knew* would never come back but now somehow has? More comings and going in my life than on the cast of *Law and Order.*

When James joins us, I make introductions, and it doesn't take long for Berni to warm to James's easygoing style and comfortable banter.

"He's delightful," Berni whispers when James goes to the bar to get all of us fresh drinks. "I don't know how you ever let him get away."

"I seem to have a knack," I say, shrugging my shoulders.

Priscilla comes over, her arm tucked around James, who's somehow managing to balance three glasses in his one available hand.

"So you've all heard the theme of tonight's party, right? Everybody ready?" asks Priscilla.

"I can't believe you're doing this, Priscilla," says Berni, the only one in our group who knows what our hostess has planned.

"Hard to keep topping myself, but I always do," says Priscilla proudly. "And I expect everyone to join in. Remember, dears, it's not every day you get invited to a key party."

"What's a key party?" James asks.

"My question exactly," I echo.

"You two are such innocents," Priscilla says, putting her arm around each of us. "I used to read about key parties in the eighties. I think Warren Beatty started them."

"So what is it?" I ask impatiently.

"A sexy little game," Priscilla says with a laugh. "Every man tosses his key into a big container, and each woman closes her eyes and fishes one out."

She flits away and the three of us stare at one another.

"What happens after you get your key?" I ask innocently.

Berni looks at me, surprised that I don't know. But she's a lot more sophisticated than I am. She spent her time in L.A. hanging out at Le Dome and lunching with Sharon Stone. I haven't learned as much as I thought I would at the Olive Garden.

"It's simple," she explains. "You have a man's key, and then you know who you're going home with."

James tosses back his head and roars with laughter. But sure enough, Berni's not making this up. Priscilla is now strolling around the terrace collecting keys in a heavy cut-glass bowl that's probably been passed down in her family since the *Mayflower.* If her great-great-great-grandmother had known what kind of feast her precious bowl was going to be used for, she probably would have smashed it on Plymouth Rock.

The less than *GQ*-quality Hadley Farms husbands are gamely tossing in their keys. Priscilla is heading in our direction and I'm wondering what to do. Talk about peer pressure. I'm new to this community and I want to make friends. But not such close friends. On the other hand, I've always been a good sport. I'm not a party-pooper. I even play charades if I have to.

James reaches into his pocket and takes out his keys. "Now I see

why you moved to the suburbs. This is a lot more interesting than anything that goes on at Lincoln Center."

"You're not really planning on playing, are you?" I ask in horror.

James makes a show of studying various women around the room.
He shakes his head a couple of times as if considering and then reject-
ing the possibilities. "Nobody here I'd like to have come home with
me," he says thoughtfully. "Except one person." He unhooks his house
key from his lanyard chain and holds it out for me.

He can't be serious. And even if he is, I can't take his key. I don't
even know where he lives. Besides, I'm engaged—or at least I think I
am. Bradford says we're on a "break," but just how broken are we? I
look at the silvery key and shake my head. This isn't the way to find
out.

"I'm going to pretend you're joking," I say, pushing away his hand.

James pockets the key and gives me a hug. "Of course I am," he
says lightly.

But was he? I don't even want to think about it. "I'm going home
alone," I say stalwartly. Though I'm hoping that won't be the case for
the rest of my life.

I start to leave, but then I see that Priscilla has finished her rounds
and the game is about to begin. I'm not going to play, but at least I can
watch. More fun than reading a John Cheever novel.

"Who's first?" calls Priscilla brightly, holding out her bowl and
waiting for the first woman to step forward. "Time to grab a key from
one of these handsome men."

Either Priscilla's good at compliments, or she collected the keys at a
different party.

A bubbly redhead bounces up to the bowl.

"I'm ready!" she says. "I'll pick while the picking's good."

Priscilla pulls out a purple eye mask and places it over the redhead's
eyes. I wonder if the rules say she has to stay this way for the whole
night. Might be a plus—at least she won't have to look at the guy.

"No cheating," Priscilla says.

No? Then what's this whole game about?

With a well-manicured hand, the woman digs around to select her party favor. So much more creative than the potpourri guests usually go home with.

"Let me see what I got," she says, pulling off her blindfold. She studies the key in her hand then squeals with delight. "Ooh, I hit the jackpot! Look, the key to the Maserati!"

She waves the key around triumphantly and Priscilla looks equally excited.

"The Maserati!" Priscilla exclaims. "Who's the lucky guy who threw in this key? Don't be shy."

But the Maserati owner isn't just shy—he looks downright worried when he hesitantly steps forward. Given that the redhead's gorgeous and he's as round and bald as Priscilla's husband, I'm not sure why she's jumping up and down and he's shuffling his feet.

"Do I really have to go through with this?" he asks.

"Yes!" says Priscilla, who's never taken no for an answer.

"She really gets to drive my car?" he asks.

It takes a moment for that to sink in, and then Berni bursts out laughing. So does James. And so do I. Maybe Hollywood is still kinkier than Hadley Farms. At this key party, you don't go home and sleep with your neighbor. You just drive his car.

The Maserati owner offers to come along with the redhead. Not in the hopes of having a wild night, but in the interest of avoiding scratches on his high gloss paint job. Poor Warren Beatty. How was he to know that his sexy key parties would turn into a game where you switch cars instead of partners? Though maybe he'd understand. After all, the guy's married now and has four kids. He probably doesn't even get to drive a convertible anymore.

One by one, the women go up to the bowl to find out what motor—not whose—they're going to rev for the night. James comes over and squeezes my hand. "See, in the end there was nothing to worry about. Sometimes you just have to go with the flow."

I look at James's twinkling blue eyes and the confident set of his jaw. "Still want to give me your key?" I ask him.

James's mouth drops open.

"Because I'm ready to play. It sounds like fun. You stay here and I'll take the Prius for a spin."

A few nights later, Dylan and I are working on his incredibly tedious homework. I'm trying to be upbeat about my second grader copying the entire alphabet in Palmer method script twenty times. But I don't understand why a school that has a computer keyboard for every kid still makes such a fuss about handwriting. It must be so the children can sign checks when they grow up. Although if the school doesn't get around to teaching them some more practical skills, they'll never have bank accounts.

We're finally up to the M's when Skylar appears in the room and we both jump.

"You scared me," I say, my hand flying up and hitting my chest in surprise.

"Why?" Skylar asks, popping the top on her bottle of Snapple and flopping down on an overstuffed chair behind us. "This is my house. And it's my week to be here."

It never occurred to me that Skylar might show up when Bradford was gone. He had taken her out to dinner to tell her he was leaving, and I just assumed she'd stay with Mimi during his three-month business trip. Or however long he's away.

"I'm glad you're here," I say, recovering quickly. Though I'm wondering what's up. I never got the feeling that Skylar craved my company.

Skylar gets up from the chair and wanders over to us. "You have to do that dumb homework, huh?" she asks Dylan, standing over his shoulder and looking down at his white-lined paper. "Want me to show you how to get the computer to do it for you? I have a program that prints script and I bet your teacher won't be able to tell the difference."

"Cool!" says Dylan, jumping up, ready to follow Skylar into her room.

Another day, another moral dilemma. Skylar's plan sounds pretty reasonable to me, but I know I can't agree to it. It's my job to preach honesty and integrity über alles. No shortcuts, no flimflams, no deceptions. Unless of course Skylar's absolutely sure that the teacher won't be able to tell.

I go to see what they're doing on the computer. But instead of loading a script program, Sklyar is busy showing Dylan how she downloads music onto her iPod. From a legal site, of course.

"Skylar's really smart," Dylan tells me with an innocent grin as I come in.

"I know she is," I say. "But you're probably keeping her from her homework."

Instead of giving me a hard time, Skylar for once agrees.

"Yeah, I got a bunch of English to do," she says. And listening to her, I'm hoping the homework isn't grammar. Or maybe I should be hoping that it is.

After Dylan's gone to bed, I check on Skylar a couple of times and she's actually studying *Romeo and Juliet*. Which she tells me is almost as good as *Shakespeare in Love*. Given that I have a good excuse for calling, I dial Bradford in Hong Kong to let him know that his daughter is here—and turning into an Elizabethan scholar under my tutelage. But as usual, I only get the voice mail on Bradford's cell phone and when I leave him a message I don't mention Skylar. I just tell him how much I love him.

The evening passes calmly and I realize that this is the first time Skylar's been around when she hasn't tried to push my buttons. Maybe we're making some headway. At close to midnight I see the light still on in her room and I go in to tell her it's time to get to sleep. She won't be missing anything. *Romeo and Juliet* ends badly, anyway.

But Skylar's already abandoned Shakespeare for *Teen People,* and she doesn't budge when I come in.

"I'll go to sleep when I want to," she says snottily.

"You have to get up early so I can drive you to school," I tell her, trying to be reasonable. Though fourteen isn't necessarily the age of reason.

"I don't want you to drive me to school. I don't want you to do anything for me," she says, not deigning to look up from the magazine.

"You need to get to sleep anyway," I say, getting irritated and wanting to go to bed myself.

"You can't tell me what to do. You're not my mother." Skylar glares at me, ready for a confrontation. Well, then, dammit, I'll give her one.

"When you're in this house you follow the house rules," I say.

"I like my mother's rules a lot better than yours."

"Then why didn't you stay with her?" I ask, finally losing my cool.

Skylar slams shut the magazine. "Because she's never there," she says defiantly.

I start to answer, but then go over and sit at the edge of her bed. Skylar's a teenager and I'm a grown-up. Hard as that may be to remember sometimes, she's still a kid. And probably doesn't know how to ask for help.

"I know there've been a lot of changes," I say quietly to Skylar. "It must be hard for you. Maybe even confusing." Skylar doesn't say anything, she just stares at the back of the magazine, with its ad for Cover Girl lipstick. So I go on. "I don't know why your mom's not home a lot, but I do know your dad's in Hong Kong on business. That's hard for me, too. Maybe we can make it all a little easier for each other."

Skylar sighs and uses her finger to trace the outline of a heart over and over again on her quilt. "Yeah, okay," she says. She seems to be waiting. But what else can I tell her?

"Anything you want to talk about?" I ask.

Skylar looks at me for a long minute. "Maybe sometime," she says finally. And then kicking back her covers, she climbs into bed and turns out the light.

Chapter FOURTEEN

I'M GLAD Kate's got her guy, but on the scale of demanding lovers, Owen is turning out to be a ten. Now that they're living together, it's not just Tuesday afternoon trysts and the occasional quickie that Kate has to make time for. Her schedule is packed at work, but Owen still expects her to be available to shop for his Hermès ties, attend boring client dinners and fly off with him whenever he gets the whim.

"I hate to whine about being dragged to the Bahamas again," Kate wails, "but all we do there is walk around the luxury resort Owen's trying to buy."

"A luxury resort," I say, trying to work up my sympathy. "No fabulous dinners and amazing sex?"

"That, too," Kate admits. "But it's getting old—and so am I. You should see the wrinkle I suddenly have from being so tired."

"The wrinkle? Most people get those in the plural. In fact, most shirts get those in the plural."

"All right. But I am feeling stressed. Being with him all the time isn't quite what I expected."

"Why not?"

She pauses. "How can I explain it? Owen's used to owning things, and now that he's moved in, he sometimes acts like he owns me. It's like I'm one of his buildings. I'm supposed to be perfect or he demands immediate repairs."

"Repairs? On you?" Maybe that wrinkle's deeper than she's letting on.

"Are you ready to hear this?" Kate asks. "The other night, Owen asked if I'd ever considered a butt implant. He said mine is lovely but he prefers slightly rounder."

A man who pays attention to details. Let him worry about the flying buttresses on his buildings and leave the butt on my perfect Kate alone.

She sighs. "Anyway, he's still a wonderful guy. I shouldn't be complaining."

"Sure you should. That's what I'm here for."

"I do love Owen, you know," Kate says, backtracking just in case I'm getting the wrong impression. Now that they're together, she's allowed to complain about him, but she wants to make sure I don't.

So I don't. "I know you love him," I say.

"Anyway, Owen's away this weekend looking at some property to buy near the Grand Canyon. Or maybe he's buying the Grand Canyon. I wasn't paying attention." She chuckles. "Since I'm on my own, I have a few beauty treatments planned. Give him some nice surprises when he comes back."

"You're not doing the implant," I say worriedly.

"No way. I have too much work to do on my face."

"Bravo," I reply. I can't imagine what Kate could possibly do to improve her face. But who knew that no butt implant would be the good news of the day.

As soon as I hang up with Kate, I head into the city to meet Kirk. Our bus ad is supposed to be debuting today, and we've decided to catch the premiere. Since the bus isn't rolling down the red carpet in front of the Ziegfeld Theater, we're going to watch for the first ads from a bistro on Lexington Avenue. Kirk is waiting when I get there, and he's already claimed a table by the window. He's wearing dark sunglasses and he hands me a matching pair.

"Now that your picture's going to be everywhere, you have to travel incognito," he says, kissing me on the cheek when I join him. "You don't want to be mobbed by screaming fans."

Yes I do. That's the whole point of my being here. Having just one person recognize me would be as exciting for me as not having blackout dates on my frequent flyer miles. And just about as likely to happen—because we see lots of buses go by, but not a single one with our picture. As we make our way through one cappuccino after another, I see buses promoting the downside of drug addiction, the upside of Viagra, and six Christmas movies about the end of the world. Promises to be a cheery holiday season at a theater near you.

"All these buses and no ads for *Afternoon Delights* anywhere," I say, playing disconsolately with my plastic stirrer. "Aren't you disappointed?"

"How could I be disappointed when I'm with my beautiful cohost and having a delightful afternoon," Kirk says, leaning back in his tipply metal chair.

I shake my head. "You're impossible," I say affectionately. "You can't turn off that charm spigot for a minute."

Kirk laughs. "Being charming is part of the job. But with you it's not hard work."

I take aim and flip my stirrer at him. Kirk good-naturedly wipes the foam off his chin and leans over to dab it on the tip of my nose.

"I'm impossible but you still love me," he says.

"I do, and you'd be my best friend if I didn't already have two," I say with a grin. "But they at least tell me about their love lives. What's going on with yours?"

"Not much," he says, unwilling to make any commitments. He may use an unusual amount of hair product, but he's a typical male.

"What about your costar Vanessa Vixen?" I ask. "*Soap Opera Digest* has been reporting all about your steamy affair with her." I've hit a new low admitting that I read that rag. On the other hand, I'm admitting it to Kirk, who's always in it.

Kirk laughs. "Our dating was all a publicity stunt. Got a lot of attention for the plotline where Dr. Lance Lovett fell in love with Vanessa's character after he found her wandering through the streets naked."

So that's what a woman has to do these days to get a man. No wonder everyone always says it's tough being a single girl in New York City. Kirk stares out the window, maybe hoping to spot his next girl-friend.

"You really don't date your soap costars?" I ask him.

"Never," he says. He turns back to me, and catching my dubious look he adds, "Okay, sometimes. There's always some pretty actress available for dinner and a movie. Finding sex has never been the problem. What's tricky is finding a relationship with some meaning."

I keep forgetting that he's a philosophy major.

"So what gives a relationship meaning?" I ask.

"Honesty. Sincerity. You've reminded me what it's like to be with someone who's down-to-earth. The genuine article. Unfaked, unfeigned and unfanciful."

"And what about that do you find attractive?" I ask, interrupting him before he gets to the part about my being twenty-four-carat dyed-in-the-wool boring.

"It's so different," he says. "For one thing, I had to drag you to get some blonde highlights. I can't imagine anybody in the business who doesn't have them. And then you nearly collapsed when you heard someone was getting her pubic hair dyed." He shakes his head. "I don't often meet women with such lofty values."

Lofty values? An aversion to hydrogen peroxide and all of a sudden, I'm in a league with Nelson Mandela.

I finish off my third cup of cappuccino and my second lemon–poppy seed muffin.

"That's another thing I like about you," Kirk says, looking at the few crumbs left on my plate. "You eat absolutely everything and you're not even bulimic. The only other women I know who scarf down that much food scarf it right back up."

"I think I have to start introducing you to a different sort of woman," I say, thinking that if Kate doesn't last with Owen, Kirk might be a good choice. She did say he was cute after they met at the Food Network. And she has an impressive metabolism.

"Introduce away," he says. "But now it's your turn. Is Bradford still in Hong Kong?"

"Yup," I admit, wishing my turn were over.

"But you two are still together?"

I hesitate. "The party line is that he's just away on business and we're getting married," I say, flashing him my engagement ring. "But I guess I'll find out if Bradford still wants me when he gets back from his trip."

"Bigger question is whether you still want him," Kirk counters.

"Of course I do," I say quickly.

"Think about it," Kirk says, leaning forward and putting his elbows on the table, ready for a deep talk. "You've told me all the stories. The guy works impossible hours. You're worried about his ex-wife. And now he's run off to Hong Kong. I'd say there are a couple of problems."

I want to tell Kirk that none of those things matter. I love Bradford. When he was around, I convinced myself that all our silly problems were making me unhappy. But maybe I was just making myself unhappy.

"I'm lonely without him," I admit.

"Lonely isn't the reason to stay with someone," Kirk says. "If you need something to do at night, come visit me."

I groan. "Are you ever going to stop that flirting?"

"You better hope not," he says with a wink. "Our fabulous chemistry is what pulls those viewers in every week. That and those disgusting desserts you keep coming up with."

I laugh. "But what's going to pull Bradford in?"

Kirk rubs his fingers across his stubbled chin. I've never figured out how he manages to keep that perfect two-day growth every single day. "Let me be serious for a minute," he says. "If you want Bradford back all you have to do is go get him. You can have whatever you want, Sara. My advice is that you just have to figure out what that is."

I pick up a crumb from the plate, lick it off my finger, and look out the window. I think I know what I want. But for now, I'd settle for seeing a bus with our picture on it.

* * *

Kate calls Sunday morning and asks me to come over because she can't leave the house. Her Owen-free beauty weekend has gone awry and she's all but hysterical.

"Everything's red and swollen. You won't even recognize me. My face looks like I went through a car wash in a convertible."

I'm prepared for the worst, but when I get to the house, it looks to me like all Kate needs is to comb her hair.

"I know beauty is in the eye of the beholder but you look fine to me," I say, coming into Kate's darkened kitchen with the special strawberries I've brought to cheer her up. Since starting my show, I've gotten a little too creative. After dipping the imported berries into a honey glaze, I probably should have quit instead of swirling them into a cup of multicolored sprinkles.

"I look awful," Kate says, taking my gift plate and skeptically eyeing my latest masterpiece. "And these look as bad as I do. Did you pick them off the rejects pile at Dunkin' Donuts?"

I'm slightly hurt, but then again, Kate's clearly out of her mind. She's taking critical thinking to a new extreme.

"So what happened to you?" I ask, starting to pull up one of the shades to get a better look at her.

"Don't let in any light!" Kate cries, pulling me away from the window.

Why is she sitting here in the dark? Kate had told me she had a bad injection. Hadn't occurred to me it was a shot of vampire blood.

"Light sensitive?" I ask.

"Sensitive to being seen," Kate says. "My left cheek is so puffy I could be storing nuts for the winter." If I look carefully enough I can make out the slightest bit of swelling on one side. But Kate's response is more inflamed than anything on her face.

"Who did this to you?" I ask, not quite sure what it is they've done.

"Idiot chief resident," Kate says grimly. "Didn't I teach her anything? I've given hundreds of Hylaform shots and nothing's ever gone wrong. It's a natural substance, for god sakes. Plumps out your wrinkles. You inject it as a gel and it draws fluid to the skin to fill out your smile lines. I don't know how much of the stuff she injected but I've got so much water that I could live in the Gobi desert for six months."

"And why were you doing this in the first place?"

"That wrinkle I told you about," says Kate, glumly. "I believe in taking immediate action. Let one wrinkle go and pretty soon you have two."

"Which is reason enough to kill yourself," I offer. Before Kate can. "But help me out here. I thought you were supposed to use Botox to get rid of wrinkles."

Kate shakes her head at my ignorance. "Botox if I had wrinkles on my forehead. It paralyzes the muscle. But you never use it for filling in lines. That used to be collagen. Now we use the hyaluronic acids, like Hylaform or Restylane, which last a lot longer. And half a dozen new ones are coming down the pike." She sighs. "Maybe I should have waited for those."

"Will they be better?" I ask.

"Who knows," Kate says. "Everyone's charging a fortune now for Juvederm. It's got two things going for it. One, it's French. And two, it hasn't been approved by the FDA. Makes it much chicer."

If it's chic and French it must be okay. Has anybody ever had a bad word to say about brie, Beaujolais or Gauloise? No, wait a minute. I think Gauloise are cigarettes. Still, I'd rather the FDA spent time looking at a cure for the common cold than focusing on face fillers. But I may be the only person in America who feels that way. More women seem to be upset by a wrinkled face than a runny nose.

"So what else did you do on this beauty weekend before the great tragedy?"

"Just the usual. Salt sea scrub, green tea mask, and Pudabhynga foot ritual."

"I don't know if that's a toe massage, a new sneaker or a country not yet recognized by the UN," I say.

Kate laughs.

"And can you spell Pudabhynga?" I continue. "Because I'm betting not. And if I've learned anything in this world, it's that you should never have any treatment that you can't spell."

She laughs again. "Okay, okay, you've done your job," she says. "Make fun of me."

"Can I convince you to get dressed?" I ask, although I'm not sure why I'd bother. Her strappy silk Eres nightgown is elegant enough for the Black & White Ball. Except it's blue.

"I'll put on clothes, but I'm still not going out," Kate says, obviously feeling slightly better. We amble up to her bedroom and she disappears into her dressing room. I nosily poke around the pile of books on her bedside table. Some light reading. Two hefty dermatology textbooks, a stack of the *New England Journal of Medicine,* and a deluxe illustrated copy of *The Art of Sexual Ecstasy.* I guess she's making a point of keeping Owen happy.

Though keeping Owen happy may be harder than I think. As I go over to the table on the other side of the bed, I notice that his reading includes a one-page real estate newsletter—and a stack of photographs of beautiful women with their bios tacked onto the back. Maybe he's doing a casting call.

"Owen bankrolling a play?" I ask Kate when she emerges in a sheer blouse and a pair of Seven for All Mankind jeans. The brand is so low-cut that they're apparently meant for All Mankind except me.

She pauses, and then seeing the photos in my hand she snaps, "What are you doing? Put those down!"

Instead, I turn over the picture of a luscious, long-haired brunette and begin reading from the bio.

Svetlana. Five-foot-eight beauty, PhD, speaks five languages, former gymnast, very flexible. Available for interesting encounters. Prefers threesomes.

Kate snatches the page from my hand and the rest of the photos go flying across her thick Oriental rug. She bends down on her knees to pick them up.

"Now see what you've done?" she says, sounding more agitated than she did about her chipmunk cheek.

"I haven't done anything," I say. "But what are you and Owen planning on doing?"

Kate stands up and furiously puts her face an inch from mine.

"A threesome!" she says vehemently. "Have a problem with that?"

I let the information sink in and then ponder her question for a moment. "A threesome," I say slowly.

"You think a threesome's disgusting, don't you," says Kate accusingly.

"I didn't say that," I reply carefully. "So I can only guess there's a little transference going on here and that's what you think."

"Thank you, Ms. Freud," she says snippily, turning to walk out of the room.

I race after her and grab her arm. "Hey Kate, wait. If you and Owen want to have some perverted threesome it's your business. But why are you getting so mad at me?"

Kate shakes my hand off her arm and glares at me. "Because you were snooping."

"Mea culpa," I say, spouting Latin, which is what I tend to do under pressure.

"Apology accepted," Kate says, calming down slightly. "Now let's go on to something else."

"Okay," I say agreeably. "Next topic. Which girl did you pick for your threesome?"

"Leave me alone," Kate says. But instead of sounding angry, she covers her face with her hands. I'm not sure if it's because the sun is filtering in from the skylight directly above her and she wants to hide her face. Or if she's crying.

Kate's shoulders are shaking and I go over to put my arms around her. She moves her hands away, revealing a tear-streaked face and red eyes considerably puffier than her Hylaformed cheek.

"Oh honey," I say, wondering how I can possibly comfort her. "What's wrong?"

"I want to keep Owen, but I don't want a threesome," she says, gulping back her tears.

"Is that what it takes to keep him?"

"I don't know," Kate admits. "This all came up the other night when he brought home the pictures. He was so casual about laying it all on the table that I was almost too embarrassed to object. And then he was disappointed that I didn't immediately jump at the chance."

"He's done this before?" I ask, thinking just how naïve I really am.

"I guess," she says, wiping her eyes on the sleeve of her sheer blouse. "He says he likes variety now and then. Threesomes. The occasional fling. When he and Tess were married, they had a little understanding. But I'm not so sure I really understand."

"If he likes variety, why did he move in with you?" I ask.

"Because he loves me!" she wails. "More than he's ever loved anyone in his life! But just because you've finally found your filet mignon doesn't mean you can never again have a cheeseburger."

I know she's quoting him. But this isn't about burgers and steaks. It's about Owen feeding her a whole bunch of baloney. "Maybe when you're as rich and powerful as Owen you think you can do whatever you want. But I do think it's disgusting. If he loves you, he shouldn't be treating you this way." I stop myself, not wanting to give her a lecture. "Anyway, what are you going to do?"

"I haven't decided," says Kate, who seems finally to have realized that she wasn't Owen's first affair. And she probably won't be his last. And then, looking at me with hurt, mournful eyes, she asks, "What would you do?"

I may have trouble making sense of my own relationship, but this one is crystal clear to me.

"I'd be out of here in a split second," I say without missing a beat. "A guy like Owen may want filet mignon, but he doesn't deserve it. I wouldn't even let him eat cake."

I'm walking briskly to school on Monday morning when I get a call from James.

"I can't believe you're right outside my window!" he practically screams into my cell phone.

"I'm not. I'm on my way to my art class at Spence," I say, striding along the Upper East Side and knowing that James's new apartment is at least thirty blocks away.

"But I'm looking right at you," he says. "A bus is stopped in front of my building. I'm staring at your beautiful face."

Instead of being pleased, I'm irked that the Food Network must have switched our ads from the Lexington line to First Avenue without telling me. If only I'd known. Kirk and I could have found much better cappuccino over there.

"This is really exciting," James says, before we hang up. "I'm so proud of you."

At school, I pull out the art supplies for my fifth graders. Today I'm having them draw in the style of Mondrian. With everything else going on in my life, Mondrian's simple blocks of color are about all I can handle.

But the girls rush into my classroom with something else on their minds.

"You didn't tell us you're a star!" says one girl named Sadie, jumping up and down and shrieking, as only an eleven-year-old girl can.

"I watched your show yesterday," another announces, joining her in front of my desk. "Your costar is hot."

"Is he your boyfriend?" asks a third.

"No, Ms. Turner's engaged to one of my dad's partners," says Sadie. "But he left her to go to Hong Kong."

"Then if he left, she can definitely hook up with that hot guy," says another in the know.

"You can get him," says one of the girls, turning to me. "You're blonde now and you're famous. Boys like that."

"We like it, too!" says Sadie. Who I now know is the daughter of Bradford's partner. And who I'm hoping isn't about to report to her father that the lovely art teacher Ms. Turner is hooking up with the day-time soap stud. "Now that you're famous you're our very favorite teacher."

My, my. Apparently the girls are a lot more interested in my class than I'd thought. Although I'm not sure they're learning the right lesson. I went into teaching because it's a noble profession. But in terms of getting the kids' respect, being on television wins hands down. You don't get much money or recognition for influencing young minds. And you certainly don't get a good table at the Four Seasons. But make a Snickers soufflé on a cable channel and the world is your oyster.

I try to get the class settled down with their red, blue and yellow paints so they can make their faux Mondrians but they have other things on their minds.

"Is it fun being a celebrity?" asks one of the girls.

It's hard to think of myself as a celebrity. And I want the girls to know that making a change in the world is what really matters. Like James tried to do in Patagonia. Or Berni is doing right now.

"I am having fun," I blurt our exuberantly. "I love working with Kirk. I loved the photo shoot. I love the phone calls when friends recognize me. I love being blonde. It's just the best." I certainly have my values in order, don't I?

The girls giggle. Truth is if I said anything else, they'd know I was lying. I'm not the only celebrity in the school.

"But I also love art," I tell them. "And what I really want to talk about today is modern art, Mondrian and minimalism." Amazingly, they're willing. We get into a spirited discussion of art that's about art. Pretty highfalutin for eleven-year-olds. But if they're mature enough to be talking about hooking up, they're ready to wax philosophical about painting.

The girls take out their paper and gouache paints and start creating their Mondrian interpretations. I watch them, feeling pretty good. I give a few autographs, but I also manage to teach something. Best of both worlds.

I'm making my way down the school steps at the end of the day when a man calls out to me from the lobby.

"You look even prettier in person than you do on the bus," I hear him say. I do a double take and almost trip on the bottom step.

"James, what are you doing here?" I ask in total surprise.

"I just wanted to bring you a little something to celebrate your TV success," he says. "I'm so excited for you."

I walk over to him, seeing the pleased smile on his face. A gaggle of girls gather around us as James hands me a package wrapped in hand-stamped brown paper, tied with a raffia bow.

"What is it?" I ask, wondering how I can shoo our audience away.

"Dumb question!" calls out one of the girls. "Just open it!"

She has a point. Why ask what's inside a present when the answer is one tear of a ribbon away? At least in most cases. I go to rip into the package, but this ribbon isn't budging. The girls are peering and I'd like to cut the scene short, but I know nobody's leaving to go home until I get the gift unwrapped.

"Can you help me?" I ask James.

"Of course," he says, pulling out a Swiss Army knife that has so many gadgets it could probably do everything from cutting your nails to clearing a forest. And knowing James, he's probably used it for both. With one swift motion, he disposes of the raffia and hands the package back to me.

I carefully remove the brown wrapping and pull out what looks to be an oversized book written on heavy parchment paper. I flip through the pages, and while it appears to be recipes, I don't recognize a word, never mind a measurement.

"The most famous cookbook ever written in Kawésqar," James says proudly. It takes me a moment to remember that was the Patagonian language he'd been trying to save.

The book is totally and absolutely useless to me. But like the clumpy clay necklace Dylan made for me last Mother's Day, I realize that it has a different kind of value. To James it's precious, and he wants me to have it.

"Thank you," I say, genuinely touched, and rising onto my tiptoes to give him a kiss. It was meant to be a peck but James holds me for a second and it lasts a little longer.

"Ooh," call out the girls.

"He's cute," I hear one of them whisper.

I hold the book as carefully as if I've just been given the Ten Commandments and call out my good-byes to the girls. James is at my heels as we walk to the sidewalk. Behind me the girls are giggling. All but one.

"She's supposed to be engaged," announces Bradford's partner's daughter Sadie importantly. "And she kissed him. I'm telling my daddy."

Chapter FIFTEEN

IF SADIE'S PULLED OUT her binoculars, she'll have something else to report to her father, because James comes home with me after school to see Dylan. When we walk in the door together, Dylan seems pleased but not too surprised to see James.

"Are you living here now?" he asks James directly, as only a seven-year-old can.

James just laughs and we all sit down for a quick catch-up on the day. Dylan reports that he played third base at recess and caught two fly balls, had a math test and got a hundred, and was given a note with heart stickers on it from the freckle-faced girl who sits behind him.

"That's my boy," says James proudly. "Math genius, great athlete and already the girls are after you."

"The note wasn't really that good," admits Dylan. "It said 'You stink.'"

James nods sagely. "That's what a girl says when she's seven and in love. You have to know what she really means, not just what she says."

Dylan looks a little bewildered. "What do girls say when they're older and like you?"

James looks at me. "Sometimes they still don't want to admit it."

Dylan jumps off his chair and heads toward the backyard. "I'm going to go play," he says. "Anyone want to come?"

"In a minute," James says. "Just let me grab something to eat."

Dylan's now so used to having James around that he doesn't mind running off without him. And James is becoming so comfortable in the house that he casually goes over to the refrigerator, peruses the contents and pulls out an apple. He heads to the sink to rinse it off, then grabs a paper towel.

"Can I get anything for you?" he asks, taking a juicy bite.

What a cozy domestic scene. Is this what my life would have been like if James had never left? We'd been so happy before he disappeared to Patagonia. At least I'd thought so. But maybe if he hadn't gone off and followed his dream, our marriage would have fallen apart anyway. He wasn't ready to be tied down then, or to be a father. Still there's no denying now that he's changed.

Watching James munching his apple, I have an odd sensation we could just pick up where we left off. But it takes me a moment to realize that this house, this kitchen, this world I have now isn't where James and I left off. This is the life I've made with Bradford. Instead of fantasizing about going backward, I need to figure out how Bradford and I can move forward.

Apparently, Bradford has been thinking the same thing, because our housekeeper Consuela bustles in with a FedEx box with labels on it from Hong Kong. James looks at it inquisitively, but I put it aside.

"Go ahead and open it," he says. "I'm curious what the perfect man sends from China."

"Me, too," I say, excited to have a package from Bradford. And wondering why everyone's giving me presents when it's not even my birthday.

I tug at the string on the FedEx box, which breaks off after half an inch—and for the second time today, James comes to my rescue with his Swiss Army knife. He slices easily through the thick cardboard box, and when he hands it back, I reach inside and find a note in Bradford's messy scrawl. *Saw this and it made me think of you. Miss you. Love, Bradford.*

What could have made Bradford think of me? Excited, I plunge my hands into the deep box and feel for my treasure—which seems to be large, cylindrical and cold to the touch. I wrestle it out of the packing and find myself face to face with a shiny metal pot with holes. I do a double take. A wok. How romantic.

James thinks so, too. He picks up the gift and can't help snickering. "A wok. Way to go, Bradford. What girl could resist?"

"I think it's very thoughtful," I say defensively. "Bradford's supporting my career."

James rifles through the FedEx box. "Maybe there are some Teflon muffin tins you missed."

I grab the box back. But it's empty. Doesn't matter. I'm thrilled that's Bradford's gone to all this trouble to send me anything. Although as long as he was shopping, I've heard that Hong Kong has very nice jade.

James stands up, tosses his apple core into the basket, and looks over at the well-chosen book he gave me earlier. "I'll leave you alone now to think about Bradford and sauté some vegetables," he says. "I'm going out to play with Dylan."

He grabs a baseball glove and when he's gone, I start making a salad for dinner. I don't bother with radishes since Bradford's the only one who likes them. I'm slicing nice ridges onto the side of the cucumber when James comes rushing back. He's slightly breathless and lets the screen door slam behind him.

"I can't find Dylan anywhere," he says, beads of sweat popping out on his forehead. "He's not in the backyard, and I checked the pool and the shed. Anyplace else he goes to play?"

"Not by himself," I say, immediately on alert. We make a quick check of the house, but Dylan hasn't come back inside. I call my two next-door neighbors, who haven't seen him, and then punch in Berni's number on the off chance Dylan has gone over to read to the babies.

"Dylan's gone?" Berni asks, snapping to attention.

"Don't say that!" I cry, my voice trembling. "Dylan always plays outside alone and it's supposed to be safe here. He was running around and he was happy as a lark and then James couldn't find him." I'm babbling, but I can't stop myself.

"James is there?" Berni asks. And before I can answer she says, "Put him on. Maybe he'll be more coherent than you." Without thinking I hand the portable phone to James, and he briefs Berni quickly on the situation.

"Sara and I are going to look for him," he tells her. And then after a pause for Berni to speak, he says, "If you think you should, sure. And tell the guard at the gate to check all cars before anyone drives out." Then another pause, and James adds, "I don't mind. I don't think it's necessary, but I don't mind." He hangs up.

Berni's on the case but I can't even think about what she's planning.

"My god, what should we do?" I ask James, noticing that my hand is shaking. "Dylan could be hurt. He could be lost. He could be dead."

"And he could be playing with a puppy down the street," says James. "Calm down."

"Calm down?" I nearly scream. "Are you crazy? My child's missing and I'm supposed to be calm?" I can practically feel the adrenaline coursing through my body. Right now I could go outside, pick up my car and hurl it down the block if it would help Dylan. But instead James just picks up my car keys from the table. He comes over and gives me a reassuring hug. "It's okay. This is a safe neighborhood. Let's drive around and see if we can spot him."

James leads me by the hand to my Volvo and automatically gets into the driver's seat. We tour the usually quiet streets of Hadley Farms. Lots of children are playing in yards or bicycling on the sidewalks, but none of them are Dylan. I'm suddenly wildly jealous of every mother I see whose child is happily within her view. In front of Berni's house, I see neighbors starting to gather and Berni pointing them off in various directions. A search party? Instead of being comforted that my neighbors are rushing to help, their concern just fuels my anxiety. By now, I have enough adrenaline to toss a sixteen-wheeler.

James keeps driving slowly, craning his neck in both directions, hoping to catch sight of Dylan's blue shirt. "Not that many places to go around here," he observes as he peers through the windshield. I see the veins in his neck tightening, and I can tell he's not as unruffled as he's making himself out to be.

I try to put out of my mind every horrifying story I've ever read about lost children. Not Dylan. He knows all the rules. We've gone through the Safe on the Streets instructions a thousand times. Finally James stops the car and sits back in his seat. "Everybody's running around looking for Dylan," he says, staring straight ahead, "so let's take a minute and think. Be rational. Where would a little boy go?"

I'm completely blank. We've already checked the soccer field and playground. And the ice-cream truck left an hour ago.

"Are there any woods around here?" James asks.

"Down back toward our house," I say, gesturing in the general direction. "But Dylan never goes near them. Bradford tried to take him once but Dylan said he was scared."

James turns the car around. "Let's go check it out anyway. Boys and woods are a natural. It's where I spent most of my time as a kid."

"He's not you," I say. But then I stop. Because it's at least half true that he is.

We park at the end of the street and venture into the cool forest, the one spot on Hadley Farms that hasn't been paved over by developers' plows. Old oak trees and thick pines loom overhead and our feet crunch on the fallen leaves and acorns that carpet the ground. James grabs my hand as I stumble on a tree root.

"He's not going to be here," I say, ready to burst into tears and angry that I've allowed James to drag us off the main road. Why the heck are we in a place where the only living things seem to be squirrels scampering over branches and the birds soaring overhead.

But James sees something else in the scene. He ventures forth a few feet, and looking off to his left he calls out, "Dylan!"

At first my precious son's name just echoes hollowly in the air. Then from not too far away I hear his voice.

"I found a frog!" Dylan calls out cheerfully.

I turn abruptly as our little boy, squatting on a rock at the edge of a trickling brook a hundred feet from us, swings around, a huge smile plastered on his face.

I let go of James's hand and rush over to my baby. When I reach him, I hug him so tightly that I almost send both of us tumbling off the rock. I want to tell him I love him. I want to tell him I'm going to kill him. I want to tell him that we were terrified and he's never ever to do anything like this again.

But all I can say over and over again is, "My baby, my baby, are you okay?"

"I'm not a baby," Dylan grumbles, pulling himself away from me. "I'm an explorer." And even in the midst of my relief I can recognize that my little boy is growing up and testing his mettle. He's ready to start having his own experiences.

James also seems to understand Dylan's need to break free. And why wouldn't he? A moment later he's crouching on the rock next to him, gazing into the brook.

"Show me your frog," James says.

Dylan gleefully jumps up, his soaking sneakers squishing underfoot, and points toward the water. "The one with the spots. Maybe it's a poison dart frog. Like the ones you saw," he says hopefully.

"Very cool frog," James says solemnly. "Not a poison one, though. A very nice bullfrog."

"I also saw a grasshopper and a snake. One of those little water snakes you showed me before that I don't have to be afraid of," Dylan says, as proud of himself as I've ever heard him. "I'm being adventurous, just like you, Daddy."

James looks Dylan squarely in the eye. "Adventures are great," he says. "In fact, they can be the best thing in the world. But your mom and I were worried about you. We didn't know where you were."

"Sorry," Dylan says.

"Next time, tell someone where you're going," James says, making sure Dylan's got the point.

"I promise," Dylan says, standing up and brushing off his muddy jeans. "But I had fun."

"Fun isn't any fun if it hurts other people," James says, looking at me now, not Dylan. "But maybe you need to be older than seven to understand that," he continues quietly just for me to hear.

James takes both our hands to lead us from the brook, and once we're out of the woods, he reminds me to call Berni and let her know Dylan is safe.

"Maybe you can catch her before she calls in the National Guard," he jokes.

"How come she hasn't brought in helicopters?" I laugh, looking up into the still blue sky. With Dylan at our side, we're both feeling giddy again. The panic has lifted so quickly that I hardly remember that five minutes ago I would have been grateful if the entire U.S. Army had parachuted into Hadley Farms.

When we get back to the house the neighbors Berni had gathered are there to greet us.

Berni throws her arms around me and Dylan and then kisses James lightly on the cheek.

"Our hero!" she exclaims, holding onto James's arm. "Good work."

Everyone gathers around to listen intently as I tell the whole story of how James knew to look for Dylan in the woods. James keeps a suitably modest smile on his face, but it doesn't escape Berni that he has exactly the right square-jawed look to play the leading man who saved the day.

"I wish I were still an agent so I could discover you," she sighs, kissing him again and granting him her highest praise.

Not wanting to be out of the center of activity, Priscilla rushes toward Dylan in her pink slit pencil skirt and gold high-heeled mules. Perfect outfit for a search party.

"Where were you, dear child?" she asks solicitously, somehow hugging him without ever touching him.

"Following my heart, but I didn't know my heart was at home," Dylan intones solemnly.

There's a surprised silence in the backyard, and then a few people chuckle. Doesn't sound like a seven-year-old talking. Doesn't even sound like most thirty-year-olds. But it takes me barely a moment to realize where Dylan got that lyrical line. From the corner of my eye I see James blush slightly and dip his head away. So that's how James explained his long absence to Dylan. My ex-husband has a way with words. How nice that at least he came up with a poetic excuse.

Even though Dylan's safe at home, I'm so wound up by his adventuring that I check on him every couple of hours all night long. Dylan might be ready to start testing his independence, but I'm ready to follow two paces behind him for the rest of his life. I notice that for the first time ever, he's pushed his teddy bear Bunny to the floor. I pick up the stuffed animal and hold him for a minute, then finally tuck him into Dylan's arms.

Kate gets to hear about the whole ordeal a couple of days later. She's relieved that Dylan's okay but gives me a gentle reminder that I'm going to have to face it—children grow and life changes.

"I'm not that good with change," I tell her.

"I've noticed," she says.

"By the way, how are the changes going in your life?" I ask.

"Horrible," says Kate. "A major trauma. Mr. Rich is behaving badly."

"Mr. Rich? Is that what you call Owen now?"

"Not to his face." Kate laughs. "But in this case, Mr. Rich is Owen's dog. You wouldn't think something so small could cause so much trouble, but he's peeing all over and tearing up the furniture. He doesn't seem to be adapting well to the new living situation. I guess being a dog of divorce is never easy."

"What are you going to do?"

"We're looking for a therapist," Kate says.

A therapist? I guess once people are putting their dogs on Atkins, it's not such a reach to put them on an analyst's couch. "I'd recommend family counseling," I offer. "Or maybe group therapy. You, Owen, the dog and that Russian gymnast he wants for a threesome."

"Forget about that," Kate says quickly. "Owen said if I was upset, we could drop the whole thing. So we're back to just the two of us."

For now. Every time Owen does something wrong, Kate seems willing to give him a pass. But I have a feeling that problems like Florida State coeds and swinging Svetlanas don't go away. Or maybe they do and Owen just brings in other girls to replace them.

But at least Kate and Owen have been honest with each other about their current trauma—Mr. Rich. Nothing as simple for them as putting a dog gate at the bottom of the stairs.

"Owen's insisting on a Jungian therapist," Kate tells me. "He's opposed to a behaviorist who'll just change the dog's actions without dealing with the underlying psychological issues."

"Talk therapy for a dog?" I ask. "Why don't you just slip some Prozac into his kibble and pretend it's a treat?"

"Outrageous. Lie to your dog once and he'll never trust you again," Kate says with mock righteousness.

"Then tell him the truth and let him know he has a problem," I suggest.

Kate nixes the idea, pointing out that Mr. Rich deserves professional help. And though she hasn't yet found a mutt miracle worker with a PhD, she has something else in mind. A doggy day spa, offering full services.

"Is Bradford's dog free this afternoon?" Kate asks hopefully. "I think Mr. Rich would appreciate going with a friend."

"I'll check Pal's schedule," I tell Kate, who's assuming that while Pal might be occupied with his busy social life, I of course am available.

And I am. So two hours later, Bradford's well-behaved black lab is sitting at my feet on the corner of 16th Street and Ninth Avenue when Kate and Owen's neurotic cockapoo comes running up. The frenetic white ball of fluff is pulling hard against his Louis Vuitton leash and tugging in so many different directions that for once Kate can't keep her stilettos planted firmly on the ground. Of course Owen has a cockapoo—the cross between a cocker spaniel and poodle that's the latest chi-chi breed. What's Owen going to do next year when a new designer dog comes along? Trade in Mr. Rich for a newer model?

We head into the pale pink lobby of the French-sounding doggy day spa, Le Beastro. We're given the day's menu and I study it, but Kate's already preregistered Mr. Rich for a massage and a late afternoon hot oil bath.

"You might consider doggie liposuction for Pal. I hear they're experts at it here," Kate says, running her fingers over what I consider his beautiful shiny flank. He's supposed to have that little bulge, isn't he?

"He just needs a haircut. Besides, nobody in my family is having lipo before I do," I deadpan.

I look around the multifloored facility and realize we're the only dog owners here. All the others have dropped their pets and gone off to work—presumably so they can earn enough money to pay for their dog's lifestyle. But they're missing so much. We walk down a corridor past the Doggie Hall of Fame, featuring pictures of Lassie, Rin Tin Tin, Toto, and Beethoven—the movie-star Great Dane, not the composer.

"Mr. Rich, with a little effort, you can be on that wall, too," Kate says, bending down and trying to direct his gaze to the inspirational portraits.

But instead of striving to achieve the greatness of Huckleberry Hound, the crazy cockapoo jumps up onto a low-lying table and pees on an orchid plant.

"No, no, no," Kate says, grabbing him. "You'll get us thrown out of here." Turning to me, she says, "We'd better get him to the swimming pool."

I hope the dogs shower first.

I pick up a few doggie breath mints that have been carefully laid out in a silver bowl and feed them to Pal. Maybe he'll meet a female pooch and want to make a good impression. I reluctantly skip the perfume atomizer, figuring that not every lab alive loves Chanel No.5.

At the Olympic-size pool, a team of shapely swim instructors who look like they wandered off the set of *Baywatch* take Pal and Mr. Rich.

"First a little test to see if they can go into the deep end," explains one, swatting down Mr. Rich, who has the edge of the instructor's tight red Speedo clamped between his teeth. "Then we'll assign them to the proper class."

Kate and I take seats in the bleachers, and I watch proudly as Pal shows off his proficient doggie paddle. But I'm embarrassed when he gets put in the beginners' class because Bradford and I never helped him master the backstroke.

When the classes get underway, Kate spends a few minutes worrying about Mr. Rich, who's been outfitted with two bright orange water wings on his front paws. From the way he's flailing around the shallow end, it looks like he could use them on his back ones, too. But then Kate decides he's in good hands and she can spend some time worrying about me.

"Have you used your wok yet?" she asks, checking her manicure, which has somehow survived the leash lashing from the daft dog.

"Don't be nasty," I say. "Any man can send you diamonds. It takes real effort to find something as original as a wok."

"Especially hard to find a wok in Hong Kong. Probably took Bradford—well, minutes to come up with one," Kate teases, but then glimpsing my grim expression, she pats my knee. "Seriously, I think it was very cute and sweet of him."

"Do you really?"

"I do," Kate says, playing with the diamond bracelet on her wrist. I'm not going to ask her where she got it, because I'm pretty sure I know. "I've always liked Bradford. He's smart. He adores you. You have great sex."

"How do you know that?" I ask.

"You've told me enough times," Kate says, poking around in her purse. "Here. A little something for when he gets home."

She hands over a clear plastic lipstick container that says Lip Venom on it.

"Venom," I say, studying the name. "Interesting idea. Kiss and kill?"

Kate laughs. "It's for lip fullness. Increases the plumpness by one point seven millimeters over twenty-eight days."

"I don't usually look for things that increase my plumpness," I remind her.

"But this one's special," says Kate. "Gloss it on and it feels like you've been stung by a thousand bees."

228 ——— Janice Kaplan and Lynn Schnurnberger

"And how long did scientists work to create this?" I ask, holding the tube as far away from me as possible.

"Probably decades in the making," she says. "It's a real break-through. Makes the blood rush to the surface of your lips so they feel all hot and tingly. The best part is that it hurts. That way you know it's working."

I usually know my lipstick's working by looking in the mirror. And fifteen dollars to buy a vial of pain? Just add it to all the plucking, pulling, piercing, and plastic surgery women put up with for beauty. But this one apparently has a secret bonus.

"Owen loves it, too," Kate confides. "Drives him wild when I kiss him with my hot lips. You have to try it with Bradford when he gets back."

"I don't know what's going to happen when Bradford gets back," I tell her, putting down the tube.

Kate eyes it, then rubs my arm sympathetically. "You have to stop worrying," Kate tells me.

"I'm trying," I say. "And you know what? I've actually been feeling better lately. I'm not as scared about what might happen anymore. Bradford went to Hong Kong, and I didn't fall to pieces. Maybe James's being back has been a help. I suddenly realize there are options in my life."

Kate looks at me worriedly. "Is James an option?"

"James is back and so some of that old pain is gone," I say slowly. "And I realize the future can be whatever I want. Who would have thought that I'd have a whole new career in TV at forty-one?"

"Aren't we thirty-eight?" Kate asks.

I smile. "You may need to be thirty-eight. But I'm happy with what I am. So many things seem possible now. You know what? Getting older and smarter and more confident isn't that bad."

"I like the way that sounds," Kate says, nodding.

"I'm feeling pretty good," I admit. Without thinking, I squirt a dab of the Lip Venom onto my pinkie and swipe it across my mouth. Within seconds, my lips are burning, my eyes are tearing, and I feel like my face is on fire.

"Oh my god, this hurts!" I say, letting out a yelp and frantically searching for a tissue. There are lots of beauty options out there as you get older, too. But you have to be careful about your choices. This is one I wish I hadn't picked. Next time I'm sticking with my own Clinique lip gloss.

Well after midnight, the newly primped and pampered Pal pushes open my bedroom door and places his front paw on the edge of my mattress. Usually he just barks when he wants something, but this is a very Lassie-like move, so I think the day at the spa has been good for him.

"What's up, Pal?" I ask.

Great, now I'm talking to the dog. He curls up on the floor next to the bed and stares at me with his big brown eyes. But I don't care how cute he is, he's not spending the night. A rule I've tried to enforce with all males who pass through my life.

"Come on, Pal," I say, leading him back downstairs to the kitchen, where he has his very own monogrammed L.L. Bean bed. And maybe Pal did have an ulterior motive in coming to fetch me because I smell something burning. I go over to the Viking stove, where a pot of milk is scorching on a high flame. I quickly turn it off. Then looking around the dark room I notice Skylar huddled on the windowseat in the breakfast nook. She has a chenille throw pulled around her, and she looks miserable.

"What's going on?"

"I couldn't sleep," Skylar says. "I wanted some hot chocolate, but I wasn't sure how to make it."

"Let me do it for you," I say, pulling a new pot out of the cabinet and going to the refrigerator for some soy milk. The only kind, I've learned, that Skylar will drink.

"Don't bother," she says, squirming around on her perch. "I don't care about the cocoa anymore. I don't care about anything. Life sucks."

I think about going over to her, but decide to stay at the stove and give her a little space. I stir the milk, keeping my back to her, and cautiously ask, "Anything particular that sucks?"

"School. Boys. Friends," Skylar ticks off, hitting the big ones immediately. And then because she's fourteen and everything seems like the end of the world, she adds, "I gained two pounds. I got my period during gym. My math test was hard and geometry is just the dumbest thing ever. And I spilled ketchup on my Dolce & Gabbana skirt and it will never come out. Never."

I mix a little bit of sugar into the Droste cocoa, put in a dab of vanilla, my secret ingredient, and pour the mixture into two mugs. I bring one over to Skylar.

"Yup, that qualifies as a lousy day," I say.

"You're not supposed to say that," Skylar says, taking the mug and blowing on the top. "You're a grown-up. You're supposed to tell me that everything will be okay."

"It probably will," I say. "But it never feels that way when you're in the middle of it."

"How would you know? Your life is perfect."

"My life is pretty good, and so is yours. Some things make me happy and some things don't."

"Now you do sound like a stupid adult," Skylar says. "You have no idea what it's like to be fourteen. And don't tell me you were once my age, because everything's different now. Nothing like a million years ago when you were in high school."

"More like a million and a half years ago," I say.

"Right. And in those days, if somebody had a party, she probably had to invite the whole class, right? So nobody was left out."

I flash on all the nights I stayed home watching reruns of *The Love Boat* while everybody else was at parties, but I don't mention it, because that's not really what Skylar cares about.

"Who didn't invite you?" I ask.

"A girl at school. She's having a party Saturday night in the city with a DJ and everything. I asked her why I couldn't come, and she just walked away. I'm the only one in the whole school not going."

I'm betting that's an exaggeration, but Skylar doesn't need to be challenged on details. Not when she's feeling like her entire universe is falling apart.

"Maybe she's jealous of you because you're so pretty," I venture. "She doesn't want the competition."

"No, she just hates me. Everybody hates me. The whole world hates me."

I could commission a Gallup poll right now to prove how many people love her, but it wouldn't matter. Skylar still wouldn't be convinced. So I offer something better.

"You can't go to the party anyway," I tell her, sipping a bit of my own hot chocolate. "You have something more important to do on Saturday night."

"Oh right," she says, sarcasm dripping. "If you want me to baby-sit for Dylan, it's not happening. I don't care what you pay me."

"Actually I want you to come with me to L.A. and meet Tobey Maguire. You know, the cute one from *Spider-Man*."

"Don't make fun of me," she grumbles.

"I'm not. I need your help. I don't know a thing about him, and I just found out that Kirk and I are flying out to shoot an episode of our show in his kitchen. He's going to teach us how to make hot fudge sundaes. Though maybe I should cancel it because I probably make better sundaes than he does."

"Don't cancel!" Skylar screams. "Tobey Maguire's the hottest! Are you dense?"

I grin at her and Skylar suddenly realizes that I was teasing about calling it off—but serious about the trip. She jumps up and throws her arms around me.

"Could I really come with you?" she asks exuberantly. "I have the prettiest yellow Versace skirt I could wear."

I guess the ketchup stain on the Dolce wasn't the end of the world after all.

"Having you there will be the best part of the whole trip," I say, playing affectionately with her hair.

"I can't believe it!" Skylar gloats. "Nobody's even going to care about Delia's stupid party and her stupid DJ. I'm going to have the best stories in school on Monday. The best stories for the whole year."

"You can be my official assistant on the trip," I say. "We'll even put your name on the credits."

"Sara, you're the best," Skylar gushes, hugging me again. "You're so cool. Nobody's cooler. I hope my dad's still marrying you."

I grin, completely thrilled. Skylar actually wants her dad to marry me. And I'm even more delighted by something else. A fourteen-year-old girl thinks I'm cool.

Chapter SIXTEEN

OUR CALIFORNIA TRIP TURNS OUT even better than I could have hoped. Skylar spends the entire six-hour flight to the west coast chatting, and I'm thrilled to be her confidante. In L.A., we check into the Regent Beverly Wilshire and have a first-night pajama party, complete with room service snacks and a Julia Roberts movie marathon.

"Are you sure I can come with you to the shoot tomorrow?" Skylar keeps asking me.

"You're my official assistant," I tell her.

And I've never had such a good assistant. In fact, I've never had an assistant before at all. The next day, Skylar hands me a carefully thought-out list of interview questions I can ask Tobey Maguire.

"These are really good," I say, surprised as I read through them.

"You don't have to use them," she says modestly. But she's obviously pleased.

At the shoot, Skylar is poised and helpful. And over-the-top delighted when I end up using three of her questions verbatim. At the end of the interview, Tobey Maguire gives her a signed picture and a kiss on the cheek, and Skylar looks at me—not Tobey—like I'm the most amazing person in the world.

Right after we get back, I tell Berni all about the trip.

"Congratulations. Your first big celebrity interview," she says.

"Even better. My first real connection with Skylar."

"That's great," says Berni. "And did you hear that your show in Spiderman's kitchen got the highest ratings the network's ever had? Ken Chablis's so thrilled he's sending you and Kirk each a hundred dollar gift certificate for dinner at the new Per Se."

"Terrific," I say.

"Not really," Berni admits. "Prix fixe there is three hundred dollars."

"Then I can't thank him enough," I laugh. "By the way, you deserve some congratulations, too."

While I was away, Berni had her first online sale for her Celebrity Kids' Clothes project and netted an unbelievable forty-five thousand dollars for underprivileged tots. One of the tabloids had a two-page spread of pictures of the star-studded items Berni had for sale, including Gwyneth Paltrow's old diaper bag and her baby Apple's old diapers. Cloth, of course.

And Berni's just getting started. There's not a new celebrity mother in town who's safe from Berni's zeal. If her target's not a former client, a current friend or the second cousin twice removed of somebody she once met at a party, Berni still finds a way to hunt her down. Her latest prey is Teri Ann Thomas, nickname "TAT," the rising young movie star who was almost nominated for a Golden Globe last year.

"Teri brought in a ten-pounder three weeks ago," Berni says as if she's reporting on a fly-fishing contest. "That's one big baby." She shakes her head. "Bad news is she must have had a helluva labor. Good news is the baby's probably outgrown plenty of things by now."

Preparing to ambush the ambitious actress, Berni drags me to the Equinox Fitness Club on the Upper West Side. Reports are that having delivered her baby, Teri is now delivering on her promise to be hard-body ready for a new action flick. She's coming to the gym three times a day and working her tush off. Literally.

We change quickly in the locker room, and as I pull on my mesh shorts and T-shirt, I realize that I no longer have to go to a chic New York restaurant to feel unfashionable. I can look oh-so-last-season right here in the gym. All these other women must be training for the Olympics, because they're decked out in the latest performance-enhancing apparel that takes twenty minutes to haul on.

"Amazing that I ever exercised in plain old Lycra," I hear one slim woman telling another, as she squeezes into her new breed of workout wear. "You really should try this. The corrugated panels compress the joints and relax the hamstrings. I only wear the muscle-hugging Italian brand."

I wouldn't mind a muscle-hugging Italian. But I don't have twenty minutes to get into one. And as far as relaxing my hamstrings, I'd rather do that in a hammock.

We spot Teri Ann in the locker room and follow her as she strolls into the gym toward a room marked "Hard-core Training." Berni starts pushing forward but I'm reluctant. I don't even go into the hard-core room at Blockbuster. Could be why I've never seen any of Teri Ann's early movies.

The well-built instructor in the front of the room bounds over to Berni and me and looks us up and down dubiously.

"Newbies," he says, sounding like a gleeful Marine drill sergeant facing virgin recruits. "You've picked the toughest class, but you've picked right. I call this Cardio Combat. We'll get your heart rate up, your stress down, your aggressions out. You'll want to kill me while we're doing it, but you'll kiss me afterwards, because your endorphins will be flying."

I look around at the intimidating kick-ass cardio machines and the unbudgeably heavy weights. The instructor comes over and clamps his strong hands around my breasts.

"Heart rate monitor," he says, as I realize it's not his hands, but a black, stretchy strap that's now embracing me. "Get started on the exercise bike over there and remember, max heart rate for you," he pauses, barely missing a beat, "one hundred forty-three."

"How do you know that?" I ask.

"Simple formula. Two hundred twenty minus your age. Then you work at eighty percent of that. I figure your age for forty-one."

"You do?" I say, surprised. "I thought I looked younger."

He motions me toward a machine. "Everyone thinks they look younger," he says dismissively.

As I head toward the bike I realize he's right. Who doesn't have a picture in her head of what forty looks like? But it's a black-and-white image left over from an earlier era of women with aprons, aging skin and bouffant hairdos. When I look in the mirror now, I'm proud that somehow I've escaped. And I feel superior until I realize the whole generation has escaped. It would be much more satisfying if everyone else looked matronly—and Michelle Pfeiffer and I were the only ones still supple and sexy.

Teri Ann climbs on a bike and Berni scrambles to grab the one next to her. She directs me to the bike on Teri's other side, so we can surround her—but I'm busy adjusting my heart rate monitor and a moment too slow. Before I can grab the empty seat, somebody else does. It takes me just a moment to realize that the woman speed pedaling away is Berni's former arch rival agent, Olivia.

"O-LIV-EE-AH! Imagine seeing you here!" Berni calls out to her.

"What a surprise!" Olivia intones insincerely, feigning delight at encountering her longtime nemesis. "Wonderful to see you. I'm glad you're here."

"You are?" asks Berni.

"Absolutely. We've all felt so bad about your awful saddlebags for so long. And if the lipo didn't work, maybe the gym will. Worth a try, anyway."

Berni purses her lips and pedals harder. "I like to be in shape," Berni says.

"Oh come on, darling. It doesn't matter what you look like anymore. No clients and I'm sure those little rug rats of yours don't care. Though they might drown in those huge breasts."

"At least they're all natural," Berni says.

Teri Ann Thomas has no reaction, even though rumors were a year ago she was having breast implants. Or as the *Star* headlined, "Tits for TAT?" Now she just looks straight ahead, pedaling hard and ignoring the barbs being lobbed over her head. Which isn't unusual for her, because from what I've heard, most things go over her head.

"Anyway, those babies won't be embarrassed by you until pre-school," Olivia says, panting on her bike as her heart rate soars toward a measly hundred. "If they get accepted anywhere. You looking like you do and all."

"I'm thinking of homeschooling," Berni says, even though I know she's not. "If you ever have a baby, darling, I wouldn't recommend you try it. Only for smart people."

I shake my head and try not to giggle. Love these two. Berni might not be fighting Olivia tooth and nail for clients anymore, but their competitive spirit lives on. Though Olivia can't be having as much fun as a Hollywood agent now that Berni's not there to one-up.

"Oh my goodness!" Olivia says, pretending to suddenly notice the star sitting next to her. "Is that the beautiful and famous Teri Ann Thomas?"

Now I get it. Berni's here to procure Teri Ann's baby clothes and Olivia's trying to sign up a new client. And I thought the only approaches attractive women had to deflect in gyms were from sweaty men hitting them up for dates.

But before TAT can acknowledge Olivia's greeting, the instructor comes over, taps Teri Ann on the shoulder and leads her over to the free weights area. He hands her a bar with a hundred pounds and spots her as she starts hauling it over her head.

"More! Faster! Harder!" he directs.

Berni and I exchange a look and try not to laugh. "Usually you hear those orders in bed," she whispers to me. Then quickly adds, "At least as far as I remember."

The drill sergeant now turns to the three of us, who are standing around watching.

"Get moving!" he barks. "You don't keep your heart rates up by yapping!"

I guess he's never heard Berni talking to Olivia.

Succumbing to pressure, Olivia grabs the forty-pound bar next to Teri Ann's and after lifting an inch, immediately drops it at her feet.

"Ouch, my back!" she exclaims, rubbing her gluteus muscle. But pain is no match for professional goals, so Olivia reaches for the bar again and pushes it closer to the star she's trying to impress. I wouldn't be surprised to see Olivia throw Teri Ann to the floor and wrestle her into a half nelson. Anything to get what she wants.

But what she wants isn't what I'd expected.

"Look, Teri Ann," Olivia says, struggling with ten-pound weights now and too tired to be anything but direct. "I have a new charity or something. I don't remember the details, but I'm collecting baby clothes. Then I sell them. And it's all really good. So I need all yours."

"WHAT?" Berni's startled cry echoes across the room. Olivia looks up happily and watches in satisfaction as her opponent gets off the bike and walks determinedly toward her.

"What are you talking about?" Berni asks. "I'm the one who collects baby clothes. Me. Not you."

"Anything you can do, I can do better," Olivia says slyly.

"Since when did you become charitable?" Berni asks.

"Yesterday," Olivia says. "When I found out what you were up to. Why should you get all the glory? I could always beat you at getting clients. I can beat you at getting their clothes."

Berni stands in front of Olivia, hands on hips, fuming for a long moment.

"So you're doing exactly the same thing I am?" Berni asks. "Selling stars' baby clothes to raise money for poor children?"

"Yup," says Olivia, making a mental note of the actual plan. "If you're doing it, I'm doing it."

Berni takes her hands off her hips. I'd expect her to explode about now, but instead her anger disappears. "Well, good," she says. And she actually seems pleased.

"Good?" asks Olivia. "You must be furious at me. Don't you understand I'm beating you at your own game yet again?"

Berni just smiles. "I'm not playing a game anymore. I'm trying to help people. And the more of us helping, the better."

Olivia opens her mouth and then closes it again. The whole point of her project was obviously to get a rise out of Berni. If that's not in the cards, helping people is about as high on her list as trading in her Mercedes for a minivan.

"If you're going to have such a fit about it, maybe I'll just let you do it all by yourself," Olivia says, trying to wriggle out of the whole thing now. "Gotta go. I'll just be off to sign Jude Law up for another movie. You collect your little booties. We'll do lunch."

Olivia scurries from the gym and when she's gone, I notice the instructor giving a thumbs up to Teri Ann. She grins and pulls out her earplugs. No wonder she was so unruffled: she didn't hear a single word.

Finally finished focusing on her intense exercise, Teri Ann starts to reach for her bottle of Poland Spring and notices us gawking at her. Probably not an unusual occurrence. But now she looks excited.

"Aren't you Berni Davis, the famous philanthropist?" she asks, now pumping Berni's hand instead of her own body. "I've been meaning to call you. You may not have heard, but I had a baby. I have some things to donate to you already."

"That's marvelous," Berni says, oozing agent charm. "But I can't believe you just had a baby. I never would have dreamed, not the way you look!"

"Thanks," says Teri Ann, pleased, and probably preparing to double her donation.

They exchange a few more words and when they part, Berni's careful not to catch my eye. She knows exactly what I'm thinking. She may be done with the business, but she's not done giving stars the business. At least now it's for a good cause.

When we're finished exercising, Berni wants me to come with her to check out a storage warehouse. Her basement is overflowing with baby goods and she's scouring Long Island City for space. But I've crossed enough bridges in my life, and I don't need to go over another one. Especially to an outer borough.

Still, the whole project has Berni so reinvigorated that the whole world looks rosy to her again.

"Aidan and I are going out for a romantic evening, just the two of us," she giggles. "A real date! And you know what happens after a date!"

I rack my brain to remember. Ah, that's right—he kisses you. And then? The rest is becoming a dim memory.

"Have fun," I tell her.

"I'm finally starting to again," she says gleefully.

We're just saying our good-byes when I get a call on my cell phone from Skylar.

"My mom's going out tonight. Can I stay at your house?" she asks.

"Sure," I tell her. Am I the only one not going out tonight? But I'm glad to have Skylar who's more and more fun to have around now that we're getting along. And, joking, I add, "You're definitely welcome if you let me touch that autographed picture that Tobey Maguire gave you."

"Okay," she says, laughing. "If I can borrow your LA Works sunglasses to wear to school."

"Deal," I say, smiling into the phone.

Skylar spends a few more minutes on the phone filling me in on her "Almost maybe not just yet but I think he could become my boyfriend because he really likes me and I think he's cute Justin." I listen carefully as I walk quickly from the gym to Central Park, since I'm supposed to meet James for drinks at the Boathouse. We made the plan after he said he had something urgent to talk to me about. But when I hang up with Skylar, I start to wonder if I'm ever going to find the Boathouse. I make three loops around the park before I realize that all the trees look the same—and I'm lost. Discouraged, I flop down on a park bench. I slide off my shoe to rub the blister budding on my heel and try to figure out which path to take next. But then a minute later, James sits down next to me.

I look at him, stunned. "I ended up in the right place?" I ask. "This is the Boathouse?"

"Nope," James says with a little smile. "But when you didn't show up, I figured you were lost. And I always know where to find you."

"You find everyone," I say, glad that he was able to rescue me as easily as he did Dylan. I don't really care which GPS system he used to locate me. I'm just happy that he's here.

"I know you better than anyone," James says, slipping his arm around the back of the bench. "After all, we're married."

"Were married," I say, automatically correcting him and looking out at the pond in front of us where people are sailing model remote control boats. A square-rigged replica of a nineteenth-century ship is gliding by a three-masted schooner.

James starts to say something, and then pauses.

"Would you hate it if we were still married?" he asks.

"That was a long time ago," I say.

"What if it weren't? What if it were right now?" he asks. "Theoretically. How would you feel?"

"Might get in the way of my marrying Bradford," I say flippantly.

"Yes, it might," James says. "Definitely might."

Something is tugging at the back of my mind, but I let it pass and stare beyond the boats to the huge trees framing the scene, their brilliant red and orange leaves at the peak of their bright beauty. I fasten the top button on my sweater and cross my arms against the crisp autumn breeze.

"You need something warmer," says James, already draping his rugged flannel jacket around my shoulders.

"Thanks," I say, not moving away as he slides a little closer to me. We sit side by side as two more sailboats join the fleet in front of us, all of them moving quickly, but managing to avoid a collision. It's such a tranquil, serene setting that I'd like just to stay here all day. But then I remember.

"You said you had something urgent to discuss," I say to James.

"I did. I do." He reaches over to the jacket that I'm now wearing and takes an envelope out of the inside pocket. He puts it in his lap but doesn't open it.

"First thing is that I went to a lawyer to talk about setting up a college trust for Dylan. I'm funding it. I don't want you to have to worry. Not at least about that."

"That's really kind of you," I say. Whatever else James did wrong, he always tried to keep things right on that score. In the early years when he was gone, he sent regular checks to my bank account. I never spent a dime of the money—just shuttled it into an account for Dylan. In those days I couldn't appreciate his generosity because all I wanted was my husband back. Now I know that in some way, James was always trying to do his part.

"Anyway," says James. "There's something else. While the lawyer was handling all the paperwork, he made an interesting discovery." He pats the envelope in his lap. "You filed for divorce at some point. But neither of us ever signed the final papers. According to the lawyer, we're still married."

I go to speak, but I can hardly catch my breath. In front of me, the sailboats are whirling, faster and faster, cutting unexpected paths through the water. My head is spinning just as quickly. It had all been so complicated back then. Who wanted to deal with a convoluted legal system when I could barely deal with my own emotions? Once I finally accepted that James was gone forever, I somehow assumed that the New York State courts understood that, too. Maybe it was wishful thinking. Or maybe, just maybe, I was still hoping that forever wouldn't be forever.

James holds out the envelope with the unsigned divorce papers, and I reach for it.

"You don't have to take it," he says, holding onto it tightly. "We could rip it up. And just start again."

I pull my hand back, but it's trembling.

"Sara, there's got to be a reason this has happened," James says. "You've let me be Dylan's father again, and I'm grateful for that. But there's one other role I'd like to play in your life. If you'd give me the chance, I could still be your husband. I can't imagine loving anyone else the way I love you. There's never been anyone else in my life. Not seriously."

I swallow hard, and when the words finally come out, it's only the tiniest squeak. "But I have someone serious in my life," I say.

He nods. "I know that. But these last few months being with you again have felt so right." And he doesn't say any more, because he leans in and kisses me, his strong chest pressing against mine. He draws the flannel jacket tightly around both of us and for the briefest moment, all the years fade away. But then I pull back.

"I have to go," I say, trying to untangle myself from the jacket—and from James.

"Go," he says. "But take the jacket. It's chilly." Then he leans forward and strokes his thumb under my eye, wiping away a tear.

"You're crying," he says.

"I know," I answer. And I leave James's jacket on my shoulders and rush from the park.

Two blocks later, I call Kate. I know she's in the middle of office hours, but she doesn't rush me as I try to explain what's happened. Despite my sobs and hiccups, she gets the gist.

"Unbelievable," Kate tells me. "You really never got divorced?"

"That's what James says. We're still married." I hiccup again, making it almost impossible to say the word.

"Look at the bright side," says Kate, trying to cheer me up. "You didn't have to plan a wedding."

"This is serious!" I scream into the phone.

Kate sighs. "I know it is, sweetie. Come on over. I'm almost done seeing patients."

As usual, Kate's waiting room is packed, but her longtime assistant Nina ushers me immediately toward a room in the back I never knew existed.

"Kate said you're upset," Nina says in hushed tones, "and she prescribed thirty minutes in the Serenity Room."

That stops me. The Serenity Room? Are the walls padded? Is Prozac piped in through the air ducts?

"This is your relaxation chamber," Nina explains as she opens the door for me and we step into a softly-lit taupe room. "Now that all the spas in town are offering dermatological treatments, Kate figured her dermatology office better start offering the comforts of a spa."

Nina goes around the room lighting half a dozen aromatherapy candles—which are labeled Calming, Healing and Harmony. Given their strong individual scents of ylang-ylang, yling-yling and geranium, I'd christen the combination Nauseating.

"You'll love this 'Garden of Peace' CD," Nina assures me, as she turns on the Bose surround sound system and the room fills with the annoying melodies of soulful guitar and piercing flute. "It uses brain-wave technology and subliminal suggestion to bring bliss to body and soul."

Subliminal suggestion? I listen carefully, and I'm pretty sure that when the harp starts playing, I do hear an undercurrent murmuring— "Shop at Barney's."

I settle into a low-slung couch wishing I had a set of earplugs. And nose plugs. But Nina has one more remedy in her serenity arsenal and she hands me two capsules and a mug of tea.

"The tea is an infusion of cinnamon and eucalyptus and the Zen capsules contain magnesium, lithothamnions, and . . ." Nina pauses, having forgotten the rest of the magic ingredients. "Well, anyway, it's all good stuff that will battle the negative forces in your life."

I swallow them whole. Given the state I'm in now I'd rather have the Force be with me than against me.

"One last thing," Nina says, putting something into the microwave. Could be this whole process is working after all because I finally stop thinking about James for a second and focus on whether Nina's making me a bag of popcorn? But instead she pulls a floral blanket out of the microwave and hands it to me. "My very favorite. The 'Dream Time Herbal Hug.' All the comforts of a warm embrace."

I wrap it across my arms and true to microwave form, most of the blanket is toasty warm but it's unevenly heated. Sure enough, I imme-diately feel a hot spot burning into my left wrist. Is this a metaphor for my embrace from James? Feels good at first, but I have to be careful.

Nina leaves me to soak in some more serenity, but as soon as she's gone I jump off the couch and fiddle with the sound system, switching off that damn soulful guitar and finding an FM radio station that's blar-ing Led Zeppelin.

"What are you doing?" asks Kate when she rushes in a few minutes later and catches me stamping my feet to the rocking rhythms. She turns off the music immediately and frowns. "You'll destroy the sooth-ing vibes in the room and I'll never get them back."

With the music off, the quiet balance seems restored, but Kate opens a window, as if I've puffed a pack of Marlboros and she needs to bring in some fresh air. Ah yes, honking taxis and polluted air from Madison Avenue should restore the right vibes.

"So James," Kate says, circling back in front of me. Doesn't she realize that saying that name in here right now could wreck the feng shui a lot faster than Led Zeppelin? "Did you really have no idea?"

"No wedding band," I tell her. "How was I supposed to know?" I spin Bradford's engagement ring around on my finger, make a fist and feel the diamond dig into my palm.

"You knew," Kate says firmly. "Somewhere in your heart or your head or wherever you keep this information, you knew. And I'm even guessing that's why you never made any headway planning your wedding with Bradford."

I unclench my fist and look down. "I would have sworn to you that all the divorce papers were taken care of. But maybe I'm not so surprised to find out that they weren't," I say slowly. "I guess my story with James always felt unfinished. No matter what else I told myself."

"So now how do you want to finish the story?" Kate asks.

I slump down in my seat and then arch my back. Whoever designed this to be a comfortable sofa obviously never sat in it. "I felt something when James kissed me," I admit to her. "But maybe what I was feeling was just the rush of the past."

"Or the exhilaration that the guy who hurt you so badly by leaving now wants you back. What a triumph. You should have just stood up and thrown your arms in the air and screamed 'Yes! I win!' "

I give a little smile. "Despite all the awful things he did, we had so much fun together when we were married."

Kate nods knowingly. "Bad boys are always good."

"And when he came back, he stopped being a bad boy. He's been really solid."

"Like a Patagonian rock?" Kate asks.

"No, really. I mean it. He still has that wonderful adventurous streak, but now I know I can count on him."

Kate doesn't say anything now.

"I'd said my life with James was over. I'd moved on. I got engaged to Bradford. But somehow, all the unresolved business was gnawing at me. There was always that empty spot in my heart."

"And do you want James to fill it?" Kate asks softly. She's uncertain which way I'm going with all this, and she looks worried.

I put my hands over my chest, as if I'm feeling for that empty space. "I think he already has," I say slowly. "Having him back has let me comes to terms with the past, and I guess that's what I needed to do. But I'm not the person I was back then. I'm never going to be twenty-five again. And I can't be James's wife again, either."

Kate nods. "So who do you want to be now?"

I think about it for a long moment. And keep thinking. I hope there's not a patient in the next exam room waiting for Kate to come wipe the glycolic acid off her face.

I look up at Kate and finally smile. "I want to be just what I am. A teacher who's also a TV star. A mother who's totally smitten with her funny, frog-chasing son. A lucky woman with great friends." I pause and go over to close the window since I'm pretty sure the Serenity has been restored. "And I also want to be Skylar's friend and confidante. And her stepmother. And Bradford's wife."

Kate comes over and gives me a big hug. "Then you should have everything you want."

"If I don't, it will be my own fault," I say, surprising even myself with my resolve and striding to the other side of the room. I stop with my hand on the door and turn to Kate. "I know I want Bradford back. Enough time wasted. I have to go try to get him."

Chapter SEVENTEEN

I'M FIVE HOURS over the Pacific Ocean when it occurs to me that the Rolling Stones may be right—you can't always get what you want. Other than Bradford, what I want right now is sleep. Unfortunately, having bought my ticket to Hong Kong at the last minute, the best seat I could get doesn't even recline, since it's the middle seat in the last row. The man to my left is so overweight that he snores even when he's not sleeping, and my companion on the other side is a compulsive knuckle cracker. If I were given an eject button for just one of them, I don't know how I'd ever pick.

I squirm around in my cramped quarters and close my eyes. Hello! Who's suddenly lying in my lap? Oh, I see. The seat in front of me does recline, and I'm glad to note that the little five-year-old in it has figured out that if she bounces hard enough, she can get it fully extended.

I look at my watch, even though "real time" has become an abstraction. Fifteen-hour flight. Thirteen-hour time difference. Leave New York at three in the afternoon and arrive in Hong Kong at seven at night. So what if I skip a day or two in there? Actually, I'm looking forward to the return flight, when I arrive home a day younger than I leave. If I do that enough times, maybe I'll start getting carded in bars again.

After I left Kate's office, I was determined to get to Hong Kong as fast as I could, and barely a day and a half later, I'm on my way. I called everyone in the world to make arrangements. My school classes are covered, Dylan's staying with Berni and the twins, and instead of the weekly installment of our cooking show, Ken Chablis has scheduled a "Best of" special. Who would have guessed that Chocolate Surprise would make it to reruns?

But there are two people I didn't call. James and Bradford. I know I won't call James right away because I need to go to Bradford first. Bradford, who doesn't know I'm coming. I play with the AirFone on the armrest, picking it up and putting it down in its cradle enough times to give the knuckle cracker some competition in the obsession department. Bradford's going to be so darned surprised and pleased to see me. At least I hope so. I'm pretty sure I've locked down the "surprised" element, anyway.

If I'm going to show up in Bradford's hotel room unexpectedly, I want him to see me at my best. I rifle through my carry-on tote for Kate's emergency flight kit and pull out her melatonin jet lag pills which come with a two-page timetable on when to take them. It's so complicated that—forget jet lag—I get a headache just from reading the instructions. First problem is that one side of the paper is if you're going west, and the other side is if you're traveling east. What do I do since I'm traveling west to get to the Far East?

For the rest of the flight, I doze on and off and spray my face regularly with the Evian Kate provided. "No moisture in the air on a plane," she'd explained. "So spritz, drink a lot of water, and keep rubbing on Oil of Olay. If you get a chance, pull down the oxygen mask and sneak a couple of breaths. It'll really plump up those lines around your mouth."

When the flight attendant isn't looking, I make one surreptitious attempt to find the mask, but instead I hit the call button.

"Everything okay?" asks the beautiful young Asian woman who appears at my side immediately. Her skin is so perfect, she must be knocking back some oxygen in the galley.

"Just fine," I say, trying to think what I could need. Kate said to drink water, but doesn't wine have water in it? I order a small bottle of merlot and use it to wash down the large bag of Twizzlers I bought at the airport. Mmmm. Taste good together. Maybe because they're both from the red food group.

After being on the airplane for what feels like days, I stagger off, collect my luggage and lumber through customs.

"What's your business here?" asks the immigration clerk, looking from my passport to me.

"Trying to get my fiancé to marry me," I say, too tired to come up with a more subtle answer.

He makes a big checkmark on my form. "We'll call that urgent business," he says with just the trace of a smile. Then he takes one more look at my passport photo before handing it back to me. "Good luck," he says. "And nice change. I like you better as a blonde."

With that assurance, I throw myself into a taxi and look out the window as the driver weaves wildly through the crowded streets. The city is a blur of movement and neon lights, and when we pull up at the Peninsula Hotel, I'm immediately greeted by a white-gloved doorman. My luggage magically makes its way inside the grand lobby, and I follow, slightly overwhelmed by the majesty of my surroundings. Pillars and palms reach toward a high gilded ceiling that looks as if it belongs in a Parisian palace rather than in a businessman's Hilton. From the balcony above, an eight-piece orchestra serenades me, graciously providing a Haydn concerto as check-in music.

At the registration desk, I have a long rambling story ready as to why they have to let me into Bradford's room. I'm prepared for a fight since I'm not Bradford's wife, I'm not expected, and looking around the lobby, I'm pretty sure that I don't even have the right luggage. At first the young man in charge is pleasant but unyielding. So I plead, show him my engagement ring, give him pictures of Dylan and Skylar, and start to open my bags to pull out the nightgown I bought especially for the occasion. Either I've convinced him of my bona fides or he's worried that the rest of my lingerie is going to end up sprawled across the lobby floor, because he quickly hands over a key and I rush off to the elevator and hit twenty-seven before he can change his mind.

Outside Bradford's door, I take a deep breath and slide in the key card. The door opens effortlessly and I step in, ready with the line I've been practicing over and over since I got on the plane.

"Hi, sweetheart, it's me!"

Now Bradford's supposed to look up in happy surprise and rush over to kiss me on the corner of my cockeyed grin. At which point I will start taking off my clothes. Talking will wait.

Only Bradford isn't here. I spot the initialed gold Tiffany cufflinks that I bought him and see his familiar Canali blazer draped over the wingback chair. I go over and rub my hand across the jacket and smell a trace of his Burberry cologne.

The lights in his oversized suite are dimmed and soft music is playing. Clearly the housekeeper has been by for her evening turn-down service. I walk through the elegantly furnished living room filled with fresh flowers into the bedroom, where I catch my breath at the floor to ceiling windows, providing a spectacular panoramic view of the Hong Kong harbor and twinkling skyline. This is better than anything I ever saw on the Travel Channel. Next to the bed, a pair of fresh slippers has been placed on a white linen cloth spread on top of the lush carpet. If this is meant to provide a touch of homey comfort, nobody's ever been in my house. On the night table, I notice two long-stemmed glasses and a large bottle of sparkling water. You'd think that after all the time Bradford has been here, he would have told the housekeeper that he just needs one glass.

The bedside clock says eight-thirty. Good thing it's dark out, or I wouldn't know if that meant A.M. or P.M. I lean back briefly against the thick pillows and sit back up again. Damn, they're that expensive goose down that makes me sneeze. I'll have to call the concierge for nonallergenic foam ones. I wasn't built for luxury.

But apparently I fall asleep before I can reach for the phone, because the next thing I know, I hear a door opening—and somehow the clock now says nine forty-five. Bradford's here. I try to rouse myself and lightly slap my cheeks. Have to wake up and get some color back. Where's that oxygen mask when you need it? For what that flight cost, I should have taken it with me.

I haven't turned on any lights in the bedroom, so Bradford doesn't know I'm here yet. But I can see a lamp flick on next to the desk in the living room, and my heart skips a beat because in another moment, I'm going to see Bradford.

And then it skips another beat. Because the person at the desk isn't Bradford. I can make out a slim, dark-haired woman in a form-fitting beige suit and matching high heels. She's leaning over the desk, writing a note, and she seems awfully comfortable in the room. I sit frozen for a moment as I watch her, and I panic that she's going to come into the bedroom. How will I explain why I'm here? No, wait a minute. How will she explain why she's here?

The woman seems to have brought Bradford a little present, and I see her adjusting a bow before putting the gift down on the desk. She wriggles her hands down the side of her skirt to straighten it, then glances around the room, smiles to herself, and leaves.

Maybe leaving is what I should do, too. Immediately, before Bradford gets here. I get up and walk over to the wall of windows, staring out at the city lights. I can take the next flight back to New York, and then I don't have to be embarrassed when he comes in and starts to explain why he doesn't want me anymore. What an idiot I am. I've blown the best thing I ever had. I'm in love with Bradford, and I let all my damn insecurities get in the way.

Then I suddenly stop. I'm not insecure anymore. Not the hurt Sara who panicked that once she had something she really wanted she was going to lose it. I'm not going to let myself worry about the woman in the beige suit or anything that's happened before. I'm not jumping to conclusions. But I am going to take a stand. When Bradford walks in that door . . .

"Sara?"

I look up, stunned because suddenly Bradford is standing two feet away from me. The tape playing hysterically in my head was so loud that I didn't hear him come in.

"I love you, Bradford," I say, in a rush. "I don't care what else is going on in your life. I forgive you for everything. I hope you can forgive me, too. We've been hurting each other, and that's just silly. We're in love. I want to be married to you. Only you."

I pause. No, now's not the time to explain that being married only to him will take a bit of legal work.

"I'm in Hong Kong to tell you to come home. I miss you and I want you and we belong together. Every second that we're apart adds up to a minute wasted. Enough. It's time to start our life together."

I finally stop and blink hard, and Bradford is looking at me with a dazed smile.

"You really came eight thousand miles just to tell me that?"

"Yes. And now that I've said it, I can leave."

"Don't you dare," Bradford says. "I've missed you. Much more than I ever would have thought."

"I missed you even more," I tell him. I wait a moment, then practically holding my breath I ask, "Do you think we can work everything out? I mean, we kept having all those stupid fights before you left."

Bradford smiles. "They didn't leave any permanent bruises on me."

"On me, either," I say, holding out my arms as if to show off my un-bruised skin.

"Good," Bradford says. "Then all that's over and we'll never fight again."

"Of course we'll fight," I say with a little laugh. "But we'll know how to do it better."

"I love you, Sara," he says, coming over and kissing my lips and my hair and stroking his hands down my body. "I never want to hurt you."

I hold him tightly, not wanting to let go.

"All this time apart. You're sure I haven't been replaced?" I ask lightly.

"Never," he says firmly. "Not in my bed and not in my heart."

That's enough for me. Despite the dark-haired mystery woman, I don't even have to try to convince myself to trust Bradford anymore. I just do. Something deep inside me has finally clicked and I know that our bond is real and can't be broken.

"I can't believe you're here," he says, his warm embrace creating a space where only the two of us exist.

"This is exactly where I want to be. With you, forever," I say snuggling against his chest and resting my head in the nook of his arm.

"You will be," Bradford says. He picks me up and carries me over to the bed. We kiss for a long time, and I feel a dizzying haze of relief and excitement and pure exhaustion. We sink into the soft bed together and as he whispers over and over to me how happy he is, I pull him closer. I feel a stir of desire, but despite my best intentions, all I can manage tonight is using Bradford's great body as a pillow. For the first time in weeks, I fall into a deep, peaceful sleep.

My body clock is totally out of whack, and I wake up full of energy at four in the morning. In the bathroom, I think of taking a bubble bath in the enormous tub, but I don't want to be away from Bradford—even if he's sleeping. The Twizzlers on the plane didn't do it for me, and as usual I'm hungry. I don't know if I want breakfast, lunch or dinner so I decide to check out the minibar in the living room. Macadamia nuts are the right choice for any meal.

On my way, I notice the gift that the brunette left behind and the note sitting next to it. Bradford hasn't seen it yet, and I'm certainly not going to read it. I pause briefly, impressed by my new high-minded spirit. I trust my fiancé. I have no reason to be jealous of anyone. No, no, not me.

But look at that. The woman slipped the note into an envelope, but never sealed it. And how do I know that? Because somehow the envelope is now in my hand.

Dear Mr. Lewis,

Thank you for being such a loyal guest of the Peninsula Hotel. As the assistant manager here, it was a pleasure to meet you at the cocktail party last evening. My apologies for any embarrassment I may have caused by my approach to you. I certainly understand that you are about to be married and wish you all the best.

Do enjoy the remainder of your stay.

Sincerely,
Jennifer Scott

I slip the letter back into the envelope. So my honey said no to her come-on, and she left him a bottle of wine to apologize. A win all around—except maybe for Jennifer, who's going to lose her job anyway if she keeps harassing the hotel guests. Still, I feel a surge of gratitude that my deep-felt trust in Bradford is deserved. Clearly, he's stayed steadfast despite our separation. And that should win him my complete honesty. Now and forever.

I grab the macadamia nuts, munch a few, and get back into bed.

"Sweetheart, darling, love of my life," I whisper into his ear.

Bradford rouses slightly as I nuzzle my lips against his.

"Mmm, you're delicious," he says, obviously tasting the salty nuts.

"Honey, don't be mad at me. I just found out James and I never got divorced, but I'll take care of it as soon as we get back."

"That's nice," he replies in a groggy stupor, licking the corner of my lips.

"Do you still want to marry me?" I ask.

"Marry me," he says. And he falls back to sleep.

If Bradford had plans for the next morning, he cancels them before I wake up—and we stay in our plush suite rediscovering each other until nearly noon.

"I'm never letting you out of my bed," Bradford says, rolling on top of me yet one more time.

"Yes you are," I joke, pushing him away. "I've never been in Hong Kong before. I want to explore the city."

"I want to explore you," Bradford says, kissing each of my fingers, slowly and sensuously. He pauses at my pinkie. "For example, I thought I knew everything about you. But I never knew you had this hangnail."

I giggle. "Then take me out for a manicure."

"I'll get you anything you want," Bradford says, making small circles in the palm of my hand. He's quiet for a moment and then, as if in afterthought, he adds, "By the way, you never said much about the gift I sent."

"Um, I liked it," I say.

Bradford stops and pulls back slightly.

"Liked it?" he asks.

"Definitely," I say with vigor, having told myself since the day it arrived that a wok sent Federal Express from Hong Kong was exactly what I always wanted. "It was very sweet of you. I even told Kate how sweet it was. And I'm thinking of using it on my TV show. Just as soon as I can dream up a dessert to make in a wok."

Bradford breaks into a grin. "You haven't used it yet, have you."

"Not yet," I admit. "But I'm going to really soon. Maybe I can make Thanksgiving turkey in it."

"But if you didn't use it," Bradford says, ignoring my holiday plans, "I'm guessing you never even opened the lid. Or looked inside."

"Maybe not," I say slowly, wondering where he's going with this.

Bradford starts to chuckle, and then to laugh. And then he's laughing so hard he rolls off me and lies next to me, leaning on his elbow.

"So you flew eight thousand miles to find me in Hong Kong and you thought all I sent you was a wok?"

"I didn't come because you sent me a wok," I say.

"Not many women would," Bradford concedes, starting to laugh again.

"I didn't come because of some present," I explain. "I came because I love you. And it's what I said last night—whatever we've done wrong in the past, we're going to do right now."

"I know, sweetheart," Bradford says kissing me. "And I love you for that. But when we get home, you'll find out I didn't do as badly as you think on the shopping."

I'm just starting to imagine what I could have missed inside the wok when Bradford comes closer and my mind turns to my immediate pleasures. For the next twenty minutes, I don't mind being distracted at all.

When we're both sweaty, exhausted and totally giddy, Bradford finally concedes that a little lunch and sightseeing are in order.

"Promise you'll still be here if I leave you for five minutes to take a shower?" he jokes, getting up and stretching.

"Right here," I promise, not taking my eyes off my taut, firm fiancé as he strides toward the bathroom.

But once I hear the shower turning on, I scoot to the other side of the bed and grab the phone to call Berni. "I need a big favor," I tell her, after finding out that Dylan's doing great and assuring her that Bradford and I couldn't be better. I explain what I want her to do.

"I'm supposed to go to your house, look inside some wok and call you back?" Berni asks in disbelief. "Don't you have something more interesting to do in Hong Kong?"

"Not for about five minutes," I say. "Hurry."

Bradford has finished his long, luxurious shower and is shaving at the sink when the phone rings. I grab it before he can even hear.

"South Sea pearls," Berni says, practically breathless, the moment I say hello. "Double strand. Gorgeous diamond clasp. Huge and luminous. Never seen any this perfect. I'd value them at thirty-two thousand dollars."

"Really? That's what was in the wok?" I ask, slightly stunned. And wondering how Berni got them appraised so fast.

"Right there in a beautiful blue velvet box. Next to the instructions for the wok—which, by the way, is guaranteed for a year."

"So he bought the good one," I joke feebly.

"You have no idea how good," Berni says. "I rubbed the pearls across my teeth to make sure they're authentic. Little trick I learned. Imitations feel smooth and real ones have rough spots. Just like men. The best ones aren't all polished surfaces. They have something underneath."

"You're a wise woman," I say with a laugh. "I see how you've stayed married so long. I don't even mind that you stuck my new pearls in your mouth. Just keep them away from the babies."

"Don't worry, the twins aren't on solids yet," Berni reassures me.

Through the crack in the bathroom door, I see Bradford putting away his razor and I rush to get off the phone.

"Maybe you should take the necklace home with you to keep it safe," I say to Berni, suddenly worried about the jewels I didn't know I had.

"Are you kidding?" asks Berni. "I'm bringing all my jewelry to your house and putting it in the wok. What thief in his right mind would look there?"

I hang up quickly as Bradford strolls out, freshly scrubbed and sweet smelling. I jump out of bed to throw my arms around him.

"I just had my spies check out the wok," I say, shaking my head but unable to contain my excitement. "South Sea pearls with an unbelievable diamond clasp. That's so extravagant. What were you thinking?"

Bradford gives me a big smile and takes my hands. "I was thinking about how much I missed you. And I was thinking that I want us to be together for a lifetime."

"Absolutely the gift of a lifetime," I say.

He hugs me. "Does that mean I'm off the hook for Christmas?"

"Definitely. You're covered for Christmas, Valentine's Day and St. Patrick's Day through 2014. There's only one more thing I want from you."

Still holding him, I tumble back onto the bed and pull him toward me. Bradford doesn't seem to mind. Even though he's obviously going to need another shower.

When we finally get outside into the sunny afternoon, Bradford and I amble along the promenade hugging the harbor.

"Two famous tourist attractions here," Bradford says, sounding like a proper guide. "The Star Ferry. And the tram that goes up Victoria Peak."

"You've probably done both of them a thousand times already," I say.

"Actually not even once. All I've been doing is working."

"I'm here, so it's time to play," I tell him, taking his hand.

We take the tram and spend an hour at the top of the Peak, looking out at the breathtaking views and the multimillion-dollar mansions dotting the mountaintop.

"Stunning," Bradford says, looking out and shaking his head. "Look at all I miss when you're not with me."

"You'll never miss anything again," I tell him.

On the way down, I get the sense that we've been in the one tranquil spot in all of Hong Kong. Back in the crowded streets, the city is in nonstop motion, and we make our way past shops selling Levi's jeans, Nike sneakers, and every electronic device imaginable. I examine the Gucci bags, deciding they're much better fakes than I can find on the streets of New York, but pass them up anyway. Farther north, we walk through an outdoor market crammed with vendors selling herbs, Chinese lanterns, embroidered slippers, and even goldfish and songbirds. I find a quilted pink vest trimmed in white fake fur and tell Bradford we should get it for Skylar.

"You think it's something she'd wear?" he asks dubiously.

"Definitely," I say confidently. "I know her pretty well now. We've been spending a lot of time together."

Bradford looks at me in surprise. "That's great," he says, pleased.

He goes over to a table displaying the latest whizmo-gizmos. He quickly buys one and then another.

"And what are those?" I ask.

"Boy stuff for Dylan. Trust me. He and I will play with them some night when you and Skylar are busy doing your nails."

I stick my tongue out at him and we both laugh and kiss again. Over the last twenty-four hours we've now kissed at least ten times for every day we were apart. I guess there's something to be said for absence making the heart grow fonder. Even if you do end up with chapped lips.

As we continue on, a jade vendor tries to reel us in, but I assure him that I have the most beautiful necklace in the whole world waiting for me back home. Then we get drawn into a spirited conversation with a ginseng wholesaler, who tells us his product is good for energy and vitality. And a lot more.

"You have a bad memory? You remember to take ginseng, it's okay," he tell us, speaking rapidly. "Need to lose weight? Get smoother skin? Buy ginseng. Need a better night's sleep? Take a whole case. Don't like your job? Ginseng helps you find a better one."

I'm waiting for him to get to the part where ginseng vacuums the living room. But what the heck. I pull out my wallet, figuring I can always find a use for it. Caramel-Ginseng Soufflé, here I come. I'm just taking the package when I notice two teenage girls gawking and pointing at me. They motion to a few of their friends who join them, and in another minute, the entire group is rushing toward me.

Bradford hesitates, and puts a protective arm around my shoulder, wheeling us around in the opposite direction. But the crowd is growing—and persistent.

"Disgusting lady! Disgusting lady!" they start to scream.

Bradford and I pick up the pace and start to walk a little faster. But the gang is too quick for us. And before we can get out of the market, we suddenly find ourselves surrounded. Maybe I should drop the ginseng. The wholesaler didn't mention that it also gets you attacked by angry throngs.

But they don't seem angry. And a few are waving notebooks and pens in my direction.

"Is disgusting lady from TV!" scream several more people excitedly. They turn around, pointing from me to a poster hanging on a nearby kiosk. I look over and stare at the life-size image of Paris Hilton in her ad for Guess! jeans. She definitely is a disgusting lady from TV, but I don't think anyone could confuse the two of us.

And that's when I spot it. The eight-foot-tall billboard, with a picture of Kirk and me, cooking.

"My gosh," says Bradford, following my gaze. "I didn't know you'd become so famous. Your show's on in Hong Kong!"

"I had no idea! And people actually know me!" I say, suddenly feeling the thrill of celebrity I missed on that bus-watching day with Kirk.

Bradford grins. "Go ahead. Don't deny your fans an autograph."

Heady with excitement, I sign my name several times in a large, loopy scrawl. I'm having the time of my life. I only wish I knew how to write the Chinese characters for "Keep cooking! Keep watching!"—which is what I'd decided to write if anybody in America had ever asked for my autograph.

Finally, the crowd starts drifting away, but one of the first girls is still lingering. She starts chatting shyly with me in perfect schoolgirl English.

"I'm so happy you like my show," I tell her. "But I have to ask. Why did you call me a disgusting lady?"

She points again toward the poster, where the name of the program is written in Chinese. "We translate the title of your show here as 'Disgusting American Desserts,'" she says proudly. "We love you. Everyone watches to laugh at the funny food you Americans eat."

For a moment, I'm taken down a peg. But then I laugh, too. Wish we'd thought of using that title at home. I never really expected to be famous. But hey, being known as the Disgusting Lady has a certain ring to it.

Bradford spends the next two days closing up his Hong Kong deals and I have one piece of unfinished business, too. But I don't manage to do anything about it until the last possible minute.

When I dial James's number the night before we're leaving, I've rehearsed what I'm going to say to him a million times. But when he answers the phone, my practiced speech goes out the window, and I blurt, "I'm in Hong Kong, James. Bradford and I are back together."

"I know," he says calmly. "Dylan told me. I saw him at Berni's yesterday. And I'm happy for you, Sara. I meant what I said in Central Park that day and I wish I could be the one you're in love with. But I guess we're just meant to be connected in a different way than before."

"But still connected," I say. "I'll always love you for giving me Dylan."

"I feel blessed that we still have each other at all," James says with deep felt emotion. "I told Dylan that he'll always have me in his life. And you. And now Bradford. The more people who love you, the luckier you are."

"How wonderful of you to say that," I tell him, admiring his graciousness. Dylan really is very lucky to have him. But now I feel bad.

James has turned into a good guy, and I hope it doesn't take him too much time to get over me.

"James," I say comfortingly. "You're such an amazing man. Any woman would be thrilled to have you. I know you're going to find someone very special. Really soon."

"You're right, I will," James says, moving ahead as only a man can. "Did I tell you I got a job as an interpreter at the UN? The woman who hired me just asked if I want to go out for drinks."

Am I the only one worried about harassment in the workplace? But anyway, that was fast. Word gets out that there's a handsome single man in the city and he's a hotter commodity than a rent-controlled apartment on Riverside Drive. I guess James is going to be just fine. And I can happily take on the role of friend, advisor, and supportive ex-wife.

"If you want to impress her, tell her what a great dad you are," I say conspiratorially. "Women like that."

James laughs. "Thanks for the advice. Anything I can help you with over there?"

"I think I'm okay," I say, really meaning it. "See you when I get back."

"Yup, you will," James says. "Dylan and I are planning to build one heck of a Mars lander. Right in the middle of your living room."

Chapter EIGHTEEN

THE FLIGHT BACK FEELS about half as long and twice as comfortable as the flight over because I spend it sleeping contentedly on Bradford's shoulder. And then there's that little bonus of our being in first class, where the seats don't just recline, they turn into beds. When we get home, Bradford takes a whole week off from work and so do I. The kids complain that they want to be on vacation, too, so we take them for a special day in the city where we cover two museums, three streets of shopping, a carriage ride through Central Park and a night at the Big Apple Circus, which Skylar doesn't complain about. Maybe because one of the clowns comes over to flirt with her and brings her into the ring.

"I knew I'd think the men she dated were buffoons," Bradford says, leaning over to whisper in my ear. "But who thought I'd actually be right."

Afterward we go to The Carlyle so Skylar can feel sophisticated drinking an alcohol-free piña colada in the elegant Bemelmans Bar while listening to the dulcet piano music. She marvels at the whimsical murals on the walls, and she's delighted when we tell her they were created by the man who wrote the Madeline books.

"The bar was named after him, and he lived in the hotel," I explain.

"I could live here, too," she says, contentedly twirling her drink with her swizzle stick.

Dylan admires the ice-skating elephants painted on the walls for a while, but he's less impressed by the intimate, romantic room than Skylar, and he falls asleep in Bradford's lap.

"A perfect night," Bradford says, when we're back at Hadley Farms and he's carried the still-sleeping Dylan to bed. Skylar, on the other hand, is wide awake. She pulls a colorful Post-it from the pocket of her Cynthia Rowley jacket. "Do you think it's too late to call the clown?" she asks. "He gave me his number."

"How dare he do that!" Bradford says, quickly falling into the role of furious father. Predictably, his ire just makes Skylar that much more interested in the whole idea.

"He had floppy shoes, but he was kind of cute," she says, like any teenage girl trying to test her limits.

And for once, stepmom-to-be can do better than dad.

"General rule I've found useful," I tell her with a wink. "Never date a man who wears more makeup than you do."

Sklyar laughs, probably just as happy to be off the hook. "But he could have taught me so much about eyeliner," she says, tossing the Post-it into the wastebasket and heading off to her own room.

When she's gone, Bradford gives me a hug. "Stop giving me new reasons to love you. I have too many already."

Two nights later, Bradford and I are back at The Carlyle, this time sitting at a table with Kate, waiting for Owen to show up. We had so much fun the other night, we decided to come back. But trying to replicate a great evening never works.

"I'd like to tell you that Owen will be here any minute, but he's never on time for anything," Kate grumbles, halfway through her second cranberry juice and vodka. I always think drinking cranberry juice in public takes a brave woman. Either she really can't live without the taste or she has a urinary tract infection.

"I'm sure he's very busy," Bradford says, glancing sideways at me and obviously wondering how often I've made the same complaint about him.

I put my hand reassuringly over his. "You're worth waiting for, honey," I say.

"I'm not sure Owen is," Kate says, delicately squeezing a wedge of lime into her drink. And then tossing the rind into her hors d'oeuvre plate so vigorously that it bounces across the table.

I was never a great fan of Owen's, but ever since Kate told me about his needing occasional flings, I've been trusting him less and less.

"Owen still thinking about wandering into other pastures?" I ask Kate.

"Not that I know of," she says tightly. "It's just hard to be at his beck and call every minute. And now he wants me to cut down on my office hours so I can be even more available to him."

"Not exactly why you went to Harvard Medical School," I say.

"He loves it that I went to Harvard," Kate says, correcting me. "That's part of my appeal. It gives him some cachet since he went to C.W. Post."

"So this is always about him, not you?" I ask.

"It's starting to feel that way," Kate admits. "I didn't mind before because it was so new and romantic that I wasn't seeing straight. But now I'm thinking long-term, and I'm realizing there's a difference between a fling guy and a forever guy."

I turn to Bradford. "You're the forever kind of guy," I tell him, in case he's stymied trying to decode girl talk—or wondering where he stands.

"I'll take that as a compliment, even though I prefer to think of myself as a sex god," Bradford teases.

"Did I hear someone say sex god?" calls out Owen loudly, strutting toward the table, Blackberry in hand. "Because Mr. Sex God himself has arrived."

Despite herself, Kate laughs and stands up to give him a kiss. She introduces him to Bradford, and when they shake hands, I notice Bradford carefully taking Owen's measure. Women check each other out when they meet to see who's prettier, thinner and has the better shoes.

How do men judge each other? Owen's got the bigger wallet, but Bradford's got the better body. My man wins.

"What are we doing in Bemelmans?" Owen asks. "Who picked this place?"

"It's pretty," Kate says. "Nice music. Great drinks."

"Don't be cheap," Owen says. "Woody Allen's playing in the other Carlyle bar across the lobby. What's the matter, you guys can't afford the cover charge?"

Kate looks humiliated, Bradford looks amused, and I'm pretty sure I can get the same Diet Coke in either place. Though it probably costs more a hundred feet away.

Owen's made an executive decision and he's not waiting for a vote. He officiously tells the waiter to move everyone's drinks to the Café Carlyle.

"I don't think there are any tables available, sir," says the waiter.

"They'll find one for me. Tell the maître d' it's Owen Hardy. And give him this."

I'm not sure whether Owen hands him a hundred-dollar bill or the phone number for the madam who arranges threesomes. But a few minutes later, we're sitting inches from the stage, waiting for Woody and his group to start their next set. I'm glad he's got this gig. His clarinet playing's got to be better than his last few movies.

Woody comes back from his break and everyone in the room immediately falls silent. Except for Owen, who chooses that moment to make a call on his cell phone.

"Don't tell me you couldn't make the deal!" he barks. "When I say to buy it, you buy it! Get it?"

The problem with a cell phone is that he can't slam it down. Best he can do is jab his thumb at the little disconnect button. And then pound out another number.

"Hello. Are you listening to me?" he demands loudly to his next call.

"Keep it down," Bradford says evenly. "People want to listen to the music."

Owen, not used to being questioned, glares at him and leaves the

table, presumedly to make a few more calls outside. Kate looks discon-
solate and I pat her hand comfortingly.

"Something big must be up," I say consolingly.

"Something big's always up. Screaming into the phone is just part
of his usual routine," Kate admits, shaking her head. "He's all about
conquest. No matter what he's doing, there's something more important. The next building he can buy, the next business he can swallow
up. Once he gets what he's after, it's just not interesting to him anymore."

I nod and don't ask the obvious—whether now that he's captured
Kate, Owen is out looking for another challenge. All the traits that
make him a successful billionaire add up to his being a lousy boyfriend.
Kate knows it and she probably even gets the irony. She's not laughing,
but she's not crying either.

"I'm getting so fed up with him," she whispers to me.

"I can see why," I admit. "This was supposed to be fun. The first
time the four of us are getting together."

Kate makes a face, and then turning to Bradford, she says, "I'm
sorry about Owen. Don't be offended. I can't even make an excuse for
him."

"You don't have to worry about me," Bradford says. "At the moment, I'm more worried about you."

Kate sits up a little straighter and adjusts the diamond stud at her
ear. "I'm going to be okay," she says. "I'm glad you guys came tonight.
It helps to look at someone through your friends' eyes. I can only imagine what you're sitting there thinking."

No she can't. Because I've already moved on from what an ass
Owen is and I'm thinking about how to get Kate to break up with him.
And whether I should really be concerned that she's drinking cranberry
juice.

Kate keeps glancing back, looking for Owen to finish his deal outside and turn his attention back to the table. But when he doesn't reap-
pear, Kate starts to get annoyed.

"I'm going to the ladies' room," Kate says, grabbing her Fendi
clutch and standing up.

"I'll come, too," I tell her, half suspecting that she's really heading off in search of Owen. I give Bradford a little kiss. "We'll be right back."

Sure enough, out in the lobby, Kate immediately spots Owen still yammering on his cell. She walks over decisively and taps him on the shoulder—but when Owen turns around, he waves her away without missing a syllable. She stands in front of him for a long minute. And boy, can a minute be a long time when you're being ignored.

"Are you coming back inside?" she finally asks.

He pulls the phone away from his mouth. "No," he says. "Sorry, babe. This is going to take a while. And I've got something big going on tonight. Not going to make it home."

Kate spins around and comes back over to me.

"Listen, I'm going to leave," Kate says. "You and Bradford just stay and have fun."

Before I have a chance to argue with her, Kate's striding out of the lobby and smiling graciously at the doorman who pushes the revolving door for her. I run outside to try to talk to her, but she's already getting in a cab. I walk slowly back inside and notice that Owen has been watching the whole scene—but hasn't bothered to do anything about it. I sigh and decide to make the most of what's left of the evening. Bradford's waiting for me at the table, and there's nothing I can do about Owen. He's a jerk, but unfortunately, at the moment, he's Kate's jerk.

The invitation to the Daytime Emmys comes bright and early the next morning. Regis Philbin himself calls—and I don't believe it's really him until I ask him to say "Is that your final answer?" Yup, the voice is unmistakably the one I've heard on morning TV and making millionaires at night.

Regis, charming and ingratiating, tells me that he's the host of the show and has great news. *Afternoon Delights* had premiered too late in the season to qualify for a nomination, but Kirk and I have been chosen to be presenters at the live awards telecast.

"We can't possibly do the show without you," he says ingratiatingly. "How can you have the Daytime Emmys without daytime's two biggest stars?"

I go blank for a moment. Does he really mean us? "Kirk and I are daytime's two biggest stars?" I ask, practically squealing in delight.

"Not really, that's me and Kelly. But we had a last minute dropout and our producers have called everyone else on the list. Show's two days away. Can you do it? Can you save us?"

"I don't have anything to wear," I say.

"Yes, you do," says Regis. "Our stylist has a whole rack of size fours sitting right here."

"Great. Maybe I can wear two of them."

Regis laughs. "We'll take care of you. Just say yes."

"Yes! Yes!" I say, a little too enthusiastically. Maybe I should audition for an Herbal Essence commercial.

"Terrific. Rehearsal tomorrow at two o'clock. Come to the stage door at Radio City Music Hall."

Right after we hang up, I call Kirk to tell him the news. A moment later, Kirk's other line rings and he puts me on hold, then quickly comes back.

"Can't talk," he says excitedly. "Regis Philbin's on the other line. Did you know he can't do the Daytime Emmys without daytime's two biggest stars?"

I'll let him find out for himself that Regis doesn't mean us.

The next day when I arrive for rehearsal, I'm immediately ushered inside by a young intern and introduced to the eternally impish Regis himself. The man looks awfully good for someone older than the Constitution. If he's on TV at this age, he must have had plastic surgery. Kate told me to look for scars behind the ears, and I crane my neck oddly as we shake hands, trying to get a good view. All I get is a crick in my neck.

Another producer, a cute guy named Bill, whisks me away and the next few hours are a whirl of fittings, script readings and flubbed lines. When I get onto the cavernous stage, I just can't seem to say, "Our next nominees are the wittiest, wiliest women around." I keep saying "awound," imitating Barbara Walters without meaning to. Sure

Barbara built a whole career on that little speech tic, but what are the odds of lightning striking twice?

Bill breaks up laughing every time I mess up the word, but he won't change the line. "That's the funniest thing in the whole show," he tells me.

Kirk, my copresenter for the evening, has just rushed over from his soap set and has a solution. "Want me to take that intro?" he asks.

"Absolutely not," says Bill. "Get your own comedy material."

From the stage, I look out at the audience, currently consisting of large photographs of the stars, propped against the chairs where they'll be sitting. Seems to make sense. Other than Kirk, most soap stars I've met really are two-dimensional. Right now, the pictures are set so the cameramen know where to locate the stars tomorrow night when their names are called. Too bad it can't stay this way. The photos are a lot less likely than the real people to pitch a diva fit if they don't win.

The next night, I'm in the dressing room before the show, wishing there was a cardboard photograph of me that I could send out. I'm worried that I'll be uncomfortable on stage and I know that I'm uncomfortable in my getup. I had only one requirement for the stylist—he had to find me a dress I could wear with my South Sea pearls. But I wish I'd made some other demands. It never occurred to me that a dress could weigh more than I do. I'm thrilled to know that every bead was hand-sewn, but the dress is so skin-tight stiff, I can't possibly sit down. And then there's the whole matter of my hair, which isn't just in an updo— it's been wrapped around a wire cage. I protested mildly to the hair-dresser, but he assured me I'd look like a star. He didn't mention that the star was Marge Simpson.

Kate appears backstage, effortlessly glamorous in a lighter-than-air pale chiffon Armani with her hair casually pulled back in a ballerina knot.

"You look fabulous," she says.

"I do?"

"Glamorous. Dramatic. The dress is gorgeous. Just one little thing about your hair." Without any fuss, she takes two minutes pulling out all the bobby pins and wires that the hairdresser spent two hours putting in. She tosses my hair so it cascades freely around my face and arranges some tendrils softly across my forehead. "Better?"

I look in the mirror. "Your patients are right. Whatever you charge, you're worth it."

"You bet I am," she says with a big smile.

Kirk wanders in then and takes in both of us with one sweeping glance.

"The two most gorgeous women in town," Kirk says admiringly.

"You look pretty good yourself," says Kate, eyeing his buff, tuxedoed bod and going over to adjust his tie. Not a bow tie of course, but a long one that to the untrained eye appears to be exactly the same shade of black as his shirt. But Kate's eye is anything but untrained.

"I love that you've mixed the pitch-black and midnight," Kate says. "Very chic."

No wonder I couldn't tell the difference. I always thought it was pitch black at midnight.

Kirk offers an arm to each of us. "Ladies, may I escort you toward the stage?" he asks.

Kate adjusts her backstage pass, which says BERNI DAVIS, AGENT. The laminated card had apparently been sitting on Berni's desk for weeks, and when Kate mentioned that she'd never been to the Emmys before and would love to accompany me, Berni quickly handed it over.

"I've been to way too many award shows," Berni had said. "And I'd rather be home with Babies A and B than sitting in the audience at ABC."

I'm glad to have Kate with me but I'm a little surprised when we make our way to the wings and I find Owen standing there with a pass around his neck that says VIP PROCTOR & GAMBLE. Did nobody come as himself tonight?

"Change jobs?" I ask him.

"I won the pass off my tennis partner this afternoon," says Owen, patting the fake ID. "I didn't really care about coming but he did, so it made the game interesting. Good incentive to clobber him."

"And you knew your beautiful Kate would be here, so that was an even better incentive," Kirk prompts gallantly.

"Ah, so nicely put," says Kate.

Owen, in old-fashioned bow tie and white shirt, glares at the cool Kirk.

"Who are you?" he asks.

"You haven't met?" asks Kate. "This is Sara's partner. The *Afternoon Delights* guy."

Owen blinks. "I've always liked an afternoon delight myself," he says. I don't know if Owen's being funny or honest, and it would certainly never occur to him that Kirk's just my partner on a cooking show.

With the Emmys about to begin, backstage is suddenly abuzz with a bevy of beautiful soap stars rushing to take their places for the opening number. Several send air-kisses Kirk's way and wish him luck.

"Quiet please!" says the stage manager. Then, pointing at Owen, he says, "I need that space clear. Move away from there. Whoever you are."

Instead of stepping backward as requested, Owen looks like he's going to move forward and deck the guy. Despite what his backstage pass might say, he is, after all, Owen Hardy. And everyone should know that.

One woman apparently does.

"Owen, darling!" calls out a leggy brunette who's walking by. She's obviously decided that the more formal the occasion, the shorter the dress—and tonight's about as formal as she gets. "Whatever are you doing here? I thought I wouldn't see you until tomorrow night!"

· She comes over to join our little group, giving Kirk a peck on the cheek and then planting a long kiss smack on Owen's lips. What could she be thinking? She's smearing her lipstick right before she goes out on stage.

Owen pulls back uncomfortably. "Hi, Vanessa," he says noncommittally.

The actress looks familiar—and then I place her. Vanessa Vixen, Kirk's much-publicized costar. Her long dark hair is stick straight and I can't tell if she's had Botox because her forehead is covered with a fringe of thick bangs. But I will say her eyebrows are very highly arched.

Vanessa tucks her arm into Owen's. "Isn't this cute?" she says. "I'm here with the two men in my life. Kirky, dear, you may be my pretend lover on-screen. But Owen's my real lover off-screen."

"QUIET PLEASE!" repeats the stage manager.

He doesn't have to worry, because none of us could say a word right now.

Producer Bill rushes over to say that Kirk and I should get ready—we're the next presenters.

"Wait a minute," I tell him, much more concerned suddenly about Kate than my career. "We've got a little problem here that we need to fix."

"We're on live," Bill reminds me.

But nothing can match the drama playing out back here. Kate goes over to Owen and plants her hands on the arm that Vanessa hasn't hijacked.

"Darling Owen," Kate says, shaking her head and speaking in calm, measured tones. "You're an absolute fool. I've been thinking that for a while now. And I just keep getting more confirmation."

"Vanessa was just making a little joke," Owen says feebly.

"I don't care about Vanessa," Kate says, not deigning even to glance at the actress. "I care about you. Or I cared about you. And that's why you're a fool. You're so used to chasing after things that you don't realize when you have something precious right in front of you."

Vanessa tosses her head, hoping she's the precious commodity but figuring out pretty quickly that she's not.

"I gave you a great gift, Owen," Kate continues, her voice quiet but laced with steel. "Myself. I don't give that easily. If you're too blind to realize what that means, you don't deserve me anymore."

Owen, figuring he deserves everything he can get, disentangles himself from Vanessa. A good businessman, he realizes when the deal of a lifetime is slipping through his fingers.

"Honey, you're misinterpreting. I love you. You know that."

"That's the sad part. I think you really do love me. But only in that limited way you know. When we were having an affair, my friends tried to warn me about you," Kate says, nodding toward me, "but none of us realized then that the affair was the best part. You don't know how to stay with anything and appreciate what you have. I've learned a lot in our time together. Mostly that I should have someone a lot better than you."

"Kate," Owen stammers. "Let's go somewhere private and talk about this."

"No," Kate tells him. "I don't have anything more to say." She leans over and gives him a little kiss on the cheek, then adds, "Good-bye, Owen. I wish you the best. I don't think you'll find it. But I know I will."

Kate turns to walk proudly away, and I look after her in awe. She's just given the breakup speech of the year, and she deserves an award for leaving with dignity and marching forward with her life. After her exit line to Owen, she glides off with head held high. But she must be slightly more shaken than she lets on, because instead of walking out of the hall, she turns in the wrong direction and doesn't realize that she's walking straight onto the stage. The huge, brightly lit Emmy-decorated stage of Radio City Music Hall.

Kate keeps moving boldly ahead until she's halfway to the podium. And then she suddenly realizes what she's done and gasps audibly. She freezes in place and squints into the blinding lights ringing the stage, panicked by her position and unable to move. It's too late to turn and rush back to the wings because the audience, cued for entrances, has started to applaud. They don't know exactly who she is, but if she's on stage, she must be somebody. The cameraman comes in for a close-up and Kate looks like she might faint from sheer terror.

Backstage, all hell breaks loose. The show has been timed to the second, and everything meant to look spontaneous has already been written in. Unexpected moments are unwelcome on live television. And so are unexpected people.

"Who is she?" screams the stage manager. "Should I go out and get rid of her?"

"I'm stronger, let me go," hollers an overeager stagehand.

"Wait a minute, she's got a nice dress. Maybe she's supposed to be there," yells producer Bill, flipping madly through his script book, wondering if he's lost a page.

Now the director rushes toward us, flapping his arms but trying to look unflappable. "Is that woman supposed to be out there alone?" he asks.

"No, she's not," says Kirk, suddenly gearing into action and moving forward. "She needs some help. Give us thirty seconds out there and cue the band."

For some reason, the director does just that and music fills the empty space as Kirk walks briskly onto the stage and offers an arm to Kate, who gratefully accepts. But instead of escorting her back to the wings, he leads her the rest of the way to the podium. The audience falls quiet.

"Ladies and gentlemen," says Kirk assuredly, his voice resounding through the hall and on television screens across America, "I want to take this moment to introduce America to someone everyone here already knows. Dr. Kate Steele—every actor's secret weapon! Actors read the lines in our scripts, but she takes the lines off our faces. To the woman who's made daytime television a beautiful thing. Doctor Kate, we salute you!"

He steps back and leads the audience in rousing applause. Kate, having entirely regained her composure, smiles, bows slightly and gives Kirk a kiss. He takes her hand and they walk back to the wings.

"That was good!" says Bill. "My idea, right? I forgot we were doing that."

Kirk smiles and nods but he hasn't let go of Kate's hand. Owen has taken his bruised ego and left the building, but the rest of us give Kate and Kirk a backstage round of applause.

"Thanks for saving me," Kate whispers to her rescuer as the show continues out front. "I don't know what happened. I guess I got turned in the wrong direction."

"Now you're heading in the right direction," Kirk says, taking her hand in both of his. "Got rid of the guy who doesn't deserve you. And now you need to find somebody who does."

"Somebody like you?" Kate asks, joking.

"Exactly like me," says Kirk. And he's not joking at all.

Chapter NINETEEN

"DID YOU GET TO KEEP the dress from last night?" asks Skylar, as we sit in our sunny kitchen having a casual family breakfast. She's already told me that she watched every second of the Emmys. She thought Kate looked like a princess and I looked like a queen. It occurs to me that sounds like I could be Kate's mother, but I know Skylar means it as a compliment.

"I gave it back. Complete with the wine stain from a party we went to afterward."

"The parties must have been amazing!" says Skylar, wide-eyed.

"We definitely had fun," Bradford says, smiling at me. He'd been sitting in the audience and then joined Kirk, Kate and me for a night of postshow celebrating. If Kate was in mourning for Owen, she managed to hide it pretty well, dancing with Kirk and accepting accolades everywhere she went for her impromptu TV appearance. At one point when I asked her how she was, she whispered that she was feeling relieved. Makes sense. Kate had seen the end coming for a while—Vanessa Vixen was just the final straw.

"The parties were fun," Bradford repeats, "but Sara kept me up way past my bedtime. We didn't get home until two."

"Oh Daddy, you're just a wild and crazy guy," Skylar says.

"Tell Mommy how crazy!" says Dylan, jumping up and down in his chair. "Tell her what we're doing today that's crazy."

"We're not telling yet," Skylar hisses to Dylan, giving him a warning look.

I don't know what they're talking about, but I'm not worried. Ever since Hong Kong, I feel like a cloud has lifted. I wake up every day feeling exhilarated. Despite getting home late last night, I rushed downstairs early this morning, full of energy to squeeze orange juice and make fresh muffins and omelets for breakfast. I'm just as wild and crazy as Bradford. Today I used whole eggs instead of just the whites.

Dylan jumps up again and runs over to whisper something in Bradford's ear, and Skylar, who's never seemed concerned before about getting anywhere on time, keeps checking her watch.

"Some place you need to be?" I ask her.

"Nope, just staying here today," she says, trying not to smile. "Nothing special going on."

What am I missing? There's more covering up going on here than at a Revlon counter.

A few minutes later, Berni and Aidan stroll in, each of them holding a baby. And what's going on? One of the babies has on a little pink dress, and the other's wearing a blue sweater.

"Don't tell me you've given up on one-color-fits-all," I say, going over to give each of the babies a kiss on top of the head. "Isn't this against your plan for an egalitarian upbringing?"

"We only dress them this way for special occasions," Aidan says, smiling.

"Don't give it away," says Skylar, trying to shush Aidan. "Daddy hasn't told Sara yet."

"Told me what?" I ask, looking at Bradford.

Bradford hesitates, and then comes over to me.

"I haven't told you that we're getting married," he says putting his arms on my shoulders.

"Yes you have," I say, taking a gulp of my coffee.

"But he hasn't told you that you're getting married today!" Dylan says, unable to keep his secret for one more minute.

"Nice work, Dylan," says Skylar, rolling her eyes.

I look from one grinning face to another, trying to understand what anybody's talking about. How could I be getting married today? We don't have a cake. I don't have a dress. And I was going to spend the day alphabetizing the spices in the pantry.

"I couldn't wait another day," says Bradford, hugging me tightly. "I know you never wanted to plan a wedding. So the wedding is coming to you."

"He did everything," says Berni admiringly.

"But I got your dress," says Skylar. "I bought it at Century 21. That really cool discount store down by daddy's office."

Skylar knows what she's doing. For herself she shops at Bergdorf's on Fifth Avenue. For me, it's a bargain at Century 21.

"I'm the ring bearer. I bear the ring," chimes in Dylan proudly. "Bradford says that means I carry it. And I can't lose it."

He looks briefly worried and Bradford comes over and ruffles his hair. "You won't lose it, Dyl. You're my very responsible big boy."

I'm still flabbergasted. So I have a dress, a ring bearer and an eager groom. But I'm no fool. I've read *Brides* magazine. You can't get married without a three-tiered cake and four-tiered bridesmaids dresses, a bouquet made out of exotic flora that cause anaphylactic shock in only five percent of the general population, a band leader who croons "Sunrise, Sunset" even though you've begged him not to and a high-stepping horse and carriage to take you to the ceremony. Though check local regulations—many municipalities require the steed to be Pampered.

"It's a nice thought, honey," I say, kissing Bradford. "But we can't possibly do it today."

"We can do anything we want," says Bradford. Then stroking my face, he adds, "Sara, I really want to be married to you."

"I do, too," I say, and I know that I mean it. I have no doubts or hesitations anymore. No fear of shadows from either of our pasts eclipsing our bright future. I'd love to marry Bradford today. If only I didn't have bags under my eyes from staying up so late last night.

"Then we're doing it," Bradford says, kissing me. "This afternoon. Right here."

"Here?" I ask, looking around the splattered, pot-and-pan strewn kitchen.

"Of course here," says Bradford. "This is our home. What better place to celebrate our future together."

The Plaza Hotel is one possibility. But despite myself, I'm completely thrilled. The day's going to be wonderful. I'm having a wedding and all I have to do is show up.

"You're keeping it simple, right?" I ask Bradford.

"Very simple," Bradford says. "This is just about us. And how much we love each other. Nothing else."

But a few minutes later, two trucks pull up in front of the house, and I realize the whole family has been busy making secret preparations. Skylar runs expectantly to the door.

"Right this way," she says, ushering in two burly workmen who start dragging in gold-leafed stanchions, round tables, a stack of gilded chairs and a half dozen white-stained planks of wood. I know today is only about how much we love each other, but maybe Bradford measures passion in two-by-fours.

"You forgot the velvet ropes," Skylar says, frowning as she looks over the bounty.

"They're in the truck," says one of the workmen.

That's a relief. I'm sure we'll be needing to hold back the throngs. I hope the bouncer's in the truck, too.

Before he can go back for them, the driver of the second truck traipses into the living room, carrying huge, long flower boxes. In a minute, the pungent scent of calla lilies overpowers the room.

"Those smell disgusting," says Skylar, wrinkling her nose. "Can you get rid of them and bring in something else?"

"It's what you ordered, lady," says the florist.

"Fine. Then let's put them outside the front door. They'll look pretty," says Skylar, sounding less like a teenager and more like a little executive. Planning a wedding can definitely age a woman.

The florist dutifully moves the vases of lilies and Skylar descends on the other boxes. Then she turns to me. "I want you to be surprised," she says. "Go upstairs."

But there's already another surprise at the door.

"It's me-e-e-e," calls out an inimitable voice that I haven't heard in a long time. But not long enough. "It's me-e-e-e. Mi-mi."

Mimi bounces into the room in a tight Hérve Léger cocktail dress and a white fur shrug. Just what the average woman wears on Sunday morning. Especially if she's coming from her Saturday night date.

"I heard about your little wedding," Mimi says, and she actually comes over and gives me a hug. A piece of white fur lands in my mouth, and when I blow it away, Mimi thinks I'm giving her a kiss. Which, amazingly, she returns.

"Sweet little Sara," she says, taking my hand. "I don't know why Bradford loves you, but he does. And if he tells me one more time how wonderful you are, I'm going to puke."

"Thank you," I say. Because it's the nicest thing she's ever said to me.

"Skylar's been busy-busy planning this wedding with her daddy. Isn't that cute?" She glances over at Skylar, who's carefully unpacking streams of white garlands and starting to loop them through the banister on the staircase. "So I'm here to help. We're all family now."

I look at her dubiously. Either she's here to spike the punch with knockout drugs and ruin the wedding—or her motives really are pure. And maybe they are. In some odd, modern way we really are family. And for the first time ever I'm secure enough with Bradford—and myself—that I don't even mind having her in the room.

"That's very thoughtful of you," I say.

Mimi goes over to help Skylar with her garland-looping, but after one twist she gets bored and wanders back to me.

"I don't mind giving Bradford to you," she says with mock benefi-cence. "I tried every trick I know, but he wouldn't take me back. So no matter."

She drops her voice and moves us both a few steps away to make sure Skylar's out of earshot. "Anyway, I've met someone new," she con-fides. "My Bikram yoga teacher. He has some moves I never thought were possible."

Given all of Mimi's moves, that's some accomplishment. But even if Mimi can stand on her head with her legs wrapped behind her ears, how long is the guy likely to last? And what happens when he's gone? When the finagling CEO didn't work out, Mimi wanted Bradford back. So what happens when the affair with the yoga teacher falls flat on the mat?

"That's great. I hope this works out for you," I say. "But if it doesn't, I want to be clear. You're done playing win-back-your-ex-husband. Right?"

"Right," Mimi says with a flip of her white shrug. "Never look back is my motto."

Obviously a new motto. I bet she hasn't even had time to stitch it on a pillow yet. But I like it.

"Come on, Sara," calls Skylar, from her place on the staircase. "You're supposed to go upstairs."

"Yoo-hoo," calls someone new at the door, before I can take a step. "It's me, Priscilla. I saw you're having a party. I thought I could lend a hand."

Priscilla comes in followed by a troop—literally—of little girls. About a dozen first-graders wearing beanies and Brownie scout uniforms parade in behind her. The only Priscilla parties I've been to involved sex toys and keys, so do I really want her hand in my wedding? At least her gift to Bradford and me will be something more interesting than a toaster.

"We're out looking to do good deeds," says Priscilla, wending her way through the boxes and the still unconstructed wood panels cluttering the floor. "You look like you could use some help."

"I think we're just fine," I tell Priscilla, figuring she and her girls must have better things to do. Don't they have some four-square knots to tie or some cookies to sell?

"We need badges!" pipes up one of the pip-squeaks. "And I'm tired of walking."

"Good, then we'll stay," says Priscilla, checking out the room, and obviously making a mental list of all the things that need to be done.

"Are they any good with hammers?" asks Skylar, waving vaguely toward the wood. "We're building a canopy for my dad and Sara to get married under."

"Sure, we'll do it," says Priscilla, who must figure that if one of the girls pounds her thumb, there's always that first-aid badge to go after.

Bradford wanders back into the room and surveys the scene with a big smile. But then he sees Mimi and his face falls. He walks toward her.

"I thought we had an understanding," he tells Mimi pointedly.

"I understand, I understand, I understand," Mimi says, waving her finger like a metronome. "You're getting married. Our family has changed. I'm supposed to be nice. And that's exactly what I'm being."

Bradford looks at me dubiously.

"It's fine," I say. "Mimi is being nice. And a little later, she might even show us some yoga moves."

Mimi looks delighted. All she wants is for someone to appreciate her. And if I take her with a grain of salt, she's a little more palatable.

Dylan comes in, holding blue-sweatered Baby B, and staggering only slightly under the robust infant's weight.

"Berni says he's all dressed up," Dylan says to Bradford. "But he's not wearing a blue blazer. How come I have to wear mine?"

"Because you're not a baby," I tell Dylan, figuring that Bradford has already set the dress code for him. "And think how handsome you'll look."

"But I don't want to wear my blazer," Dylan says.

"Then you don't have to," Bradford says, coming over and putting his arm around Dylan. "This is the whole family's special day. You can dress however you want."

"Yay!" says Dylan enthusiastically, screaming his delight directly in Baby B's ear. I brace myself for the baby to start crying, but he just gurgles. Bless Berni and her noisy vacuum cleaning.

At the far end of the room, the Brownies are busy observing the workmen construct the canopy. Is there a badge for watching? Skylar has finished putting flowers in the stanchions and she unrolls a long bolt of white fabric, forming a center aisle down the living room.

"Would you please go upstairs, Sara, please?" Skylar entreats.

"You're going to see everything, and I want it to be a surprise." She brushes back a strand of hair from her sweaty forehead. I'm touched. I've never seen her work this hard. Those teenage hormones are pretty impressive when they're put to this kind of use.

I finally go upstairs to our bedroom and try to catch my breath. My wedding day. But I've really got to do something about the puffiness under my eyes. I sneak back downstairs for two tea bags, steep them and come back up to rest for five minutes with the warm, wet English Breakfast bags on my face. I've been reading about this cure for years. Though maybe I should have used a different flavor. If it doesn't work as a beauty treatment, I'd rather have a mug of Constant Comment waiting for me.

"Sara?"

There's a little knock on the bedroom door and I sit up, but the tea bags seem stuck to my eyes. It takes me a moment to peel them off, and when I look in the mirror, I do a double take. I should have read the fine print. The puffiness is gone, but it looks like the tea bags are still attached because the skin all around my eyes is now stained a pale brown. I sigh. At least I won't need as much eye shadow. Nothing's going to get me upset today.

I turn away from the mirror, and realize the person at the door has walked in and I'm face-to-face with the last soul in the world I expected to see today. The surprise wedding didn't startle me. I was cool and collected in the face of Mimi and the Brownie scouts. Not even the little house being constructed in my living room got a rise out of me. But now I'm caught off guard because James is in my bedroom.

"What are you doing here?" I ask my ex plaintively. And I know he's my ex, because we took care of the legal work right after Hong Kong.

"I wanted to see you," James says. But did he want to see me this way? I catch him looking curiously at my raccoon eyes.

I take a deep breath. "You can't see me. It's my wedding day."

"I think technically it's the groom who's not supposed to see you. At least once you're in your dress."

"Then my luck should be holding," I say. "Even I haven't seen me in my dress."

"Great. Then we'll all get to see it at the same time," James says.

"You're staying?" I ask, panicked that James's showing up this way will spoil the day for Bradford. But apparently not.

"Bradford invited me to the wedding," James says with a smile. "He thought it sent a good message to Dylan that we're all friends."

"He invited you?" I ask. So Bradford was thinking about more than the cucumber sandwiches in planning today. He was considering everybody's feelings. And suddenly, I have a warm glow from head to toe. If I had any doubts about marrying Bradford—which I don't—this would have wiped them all away.

"He called me last week, and we had a good talk," James says. And then he pauses. "Sara, this time you picked the right guy."

I smile. "Maybe you were the right guy, too. Just at the wrong moment."

James fumbles in his pocket and pulls out a piece of lined paper that I immediately notice is covered with Dylan's crayoned scrawl.

"What's that?" I ask.

"Something I wanted to show you before the ceremony. Dylan gave it to me last week."

I take the paper hesitantly. With everyone back from Hong Kong, we've had a happy household. And Dylan has seemed on top of the world. He's repeated over and over James's comment about how special he is because so many people love him. But who knows what really goes on in the head of a seven-year-old.

"Read it," James says as I unfold the slightly crumpled paper which James himself has obviously opened and closed a dozen times.

Dear Daddy, I read out loud, hearing Dylan's little voice in my head.

Mommy's getting married and I'm happy. Mommy said I can call Bradford whatever I want. I want to know if it's okay with you if I call him Daddy. He loves me just like you do. I love him, too. And I'm helping plan the weding.

Love,
Your son Dylan

He's carefully signed his name in script for the first time and I look up with tears in my eyes.

"You okay?" James asks, smiling at me.

"Dylan spelled wedding wrong," I say, because I'm too sentimental right now to say anything else.

James laughs. "He's a good boy. But in case you didn't notice, he spelled 'married' wrong, too."

I reach for a tissue to wipe the tears. I guess everybody cries at weddings. The good kind of crying. And this is definitely a good cry, because when I finish wiping my eyes, I notice the tea stains finally coming off. Tears with benefits.

James gives me a hug, wishes me luck, and leaves the letter behind as my wedding gift. Priscilla will never be able to top this. No matter what kind of vibrator she buys.

I wash my face and quickly put on some makeup. Given how sentimental I'm already feeling, I choose the waterproof mascara, just in case.

"Ready to get dressed?" asks Skylar, bursting in, holding a white plastic garment bag.

"I can't wait to see what you picked," I say. "I know it's going to be perfect." Oh damn, I'm going to start crying again. Already.

Excited, Skylar rips open the bag to pull out her idea of a dream wedding gown.

"Look," she says. "Dolce and Gabbana."

The skirt is exquisite—layers of peau de soie satin with delicatedly appliquéd flowers and just the hint of a swirling lace train.

"I really get to wear this?" I ask. "I've never had anything this gorgeous."

"I'm glad you like it," says Skylar, thoroughly pleased with both herself and my reaction. "And you'll be really happy. It was on sale." She's got my number. And I hope she has my size. Last time we went shopping together, she was a size 0. Which already puts me in the plus category.

But I slip into the skirt, which remarkably, is a perfect fit. I'm spinning around in front of the mirror admiring how beautiful it is—when I realize there's a little something missing.

"The top," I say, looking into the now-empty garment bag. "It did come with one, right?"

"It did," Skylar agrees, "but it was way too matchy. Nobody does that anymore. I had a much better idea."

Skylar pulls out a small shopping bag from a teen store called Razzle-Dazzle. Not a place where most brides shop. At least I hope not.

"This is going to be so-o-o perfect," she says, practically jumping up and down in anticipation. "Try it on."

She hands me a garment so small that I can't imagine what part of my upper body it's possibly supposed to cover. I hold the white stretchy fabric in front of me by its teeny spaghetti straps. It's a T-shirt, and it's mine—which I know because across the front, emblazoned in rhinestone studs, is the word BRIDE.

"I love Razzle-Dazzle," says Skylar triumphantly. "They'll write anything you want on a T-shirt. I thought this would be appropriate."

I can't argue about the appropriateness of the word—but the teeny T is another matter. Still, Skylar has worked on this outfit so intently that I can't disappoint her.

I pull on the T-shirt and look in the mirror. Yup, it's form-fitting, but mercifully, my navel isn't exposed. And even though the top is tighter than anything I've worn before, I stand up a little straighter and smile. Maybe the real point isn't how I look but how I feel. And right now, sure and secure and surrounded by people I love, I'm convinced I don't look half bad. In fact, I look pretty good.

"This is spectacular!" I say to Skylar.

"Magnificent! Perfect! Unbelievably . . . like . . . so cool!" she exudes. "I'm going to go get dressed, too. I'll send Kate up in five minutes when it's time for you to come down. Sara, I really love . . ." She stops, suddenly embarrassed by her own emotion. "I really love all of this."

"Me, too," I say, and I give her a kiss.

I walk around the room, looking in every mirror I can find, and for the first time in my life, I don't see anything at all about myself that I want to change. Did I always have such nice shoulders? Probably. I just never thought to show them off before.

As I'm preening in front of the mirror, Kate rushes in, carrying a huge bag containing makeup and heaven knows what else. But when she sees me standing all aglow, she tosses it aside.

"There's nothing I could possibly do to make you look any better right now," Kate says admiringly. "If everyone were as happy as you, I'd be out of business."

She's right. But then I look at my friend, who less than twenty-four hours ago broke up with her billionaire. "You look suspiciously good yourself," I tell her.

"I'm happy, too," she says. "You wouldn't expect that, right? But I'm looking forward to the future. I don't know exactly what it's going to be, but I'm ready for it."

"Whatever happens next, it's going to be great. I'd bet on it."

"I'm betting on it, too," says Kate. And then she gives me a little smile. "By the way, your friend Kirk is terrific. He's funny and he's been so supportive. Something Mr. You-Know-Who never was."

I'm glad we reached the point so quickly where we don't even say Owen's name out loud. And as for Kate and Kirk—well, I kind of like the idea. Has a certain ring to it.

Downstairs, I hear someone starting to play the organ. I didn't know we had one. I look worriedly at Kate.

"What's going on down there?" I ask. "I thought this was just us."

"It is just us. All the people who love you," says Kate.

"Okay." I give her a kiss. And then trying to keep my voice from breaking, I say, "You've been the best friend in the whole world. Thank you for being with me every step of the way."

"Just one more step we need to take," Kate says, linking her arm in mine. "You ready?"

"Finally, I am," I say emotionally.

I start to follow Kate out the door and wonder why she seems so much taller than usual. I look down at my feet. Maybe it's because I'm not wearing any shoes.

"Um . . . Kate," I say, coming to a complete halt. "I can't go."

She turns around. "Come on, honey. Don't worry," she says. "You're fine. It's just cold feet."

"Very cold," I tell her, pointing to my toes.

Kate looks down and starts to laugh. "Well Skylar's only fourteen. She can't think of everything. Let's just grab something from your closet."

I think about it for a moment, but I have a better idea. Today's my day to be just me. Comfortable with myself. And who's ever really been comfortable in satin-bowed Jimmy Choos?

"I think I'll stay like this," I say.

"The barefoot bride," Kate agrees. "I don't know why, but it's you."

As we walk down the staircase, the music goes from organ to cello. Then a violin. And I swear that's a French horn.

"Do we have a ten-piece orchestra in there?" I ask.

"No, Aidan brought over the Baby Magic Keyboard. He's pretty good at it. We just told him he couldn't play any Raffi songs."

When we get to the closed French doors to the living room, Kate gives me another hug. "All you have to do is walk down the aisle when the doors open," she says. "I'll be sitting inside."

Kate disappears and I wait anxiously for my cue. Aidan plays "The Wheels on the Bus" and "Pop Goes the Weasel"—which sounds particularly good on the cello—but clearly those are the warm-up songs while everybody takes their seats. Because then Aidan stops and there's quiet for a moment. Someone pushes open the French doors, and just then, from the CD player, comes my entrance music. My eyes fill with tears as I hear Louis Armstrong croon "What A Wonderful World."

Bradford couldn't have made a better choice. And I couldn't have made a better choice than Bradford.

I start to move slowly forward down the aisle.

"You look beautiful," whispers Berni as I walk past. Baby A apparently agrees, because she gurgles approvingly from her spot in Berni's arms. Next to her, Aidan is cradling Baby B. And on the other side, Berni's mother Erica is holding the hand of a handsome older man who I'm guessing is her new beau, Doug.

I turn my head to the other side of the aisle, where Dylan is sitting up very straight. He's wearing his blue blazer after all and clutching a small box in his hand as if it contained the enchanted ring from *The Lord of the Rings*. He's right. To us, these will be just as magical.

Skylar is sitting next to him, grinning and looking exquisite in a long flowing skirt and a T-shirt that matches mine. With one difference. The rhinestones on hers spell out DAUGHTER. As I walk by, she points to the sparkly word, then points to me. I gulp. I'm glad I thought to wear the waterproof mascara.

The Brownie troop has decided to stay, and the girls are throwing rose petals into the aisle. Not a bad idea since the white runner is now decorated with a few tic-tac-toe boards that they must have drawn earlier. Nearby, James is sitting on the edge of his gilded chair, flanked by Priscilla on one side and Mimi on the other. Poor man. Even seven years in Patagonia shouldn't require that kind of penance.

I raise my eyes to the end of the aisle and see the now beautifully decorated canopy, covered with tulle fabric and garlands of flowers. Bradford, unbearably handsome, is standing in front of it, looking straight at me and smiling. We lock eyes for a long moment, and when I demurely look down, he follows my gaze—and sees my bare toes peeking out from under my elegant swirling skirt. He laughs, then comes partway down the aisle to get me. Offering an arm, he takes me toward the altar and the minister—a man in a white robe trimmed with gold braid who's preparing to perform the ceremony.

"KIRK?" I say, a little too loudly.

I glance over at Bradford. I know Kirk plays a surgeon on TV, but how does he get to play the minister at our wedding?

"Don't worry, this is all legit," Kate whispers to me. Then she adds admiringly, "Kirk can do anything. He's very smart. He takes courses all the time."

That's good enough for me. I can't worry. But just in case I might, Bradford points to Kirk's Internet-earned official state license, now pinned to the side of the canopy.

Kirk graciously starts the ceremony, then calls on Skylar who comes forward and recites a poem she wrote. It happens to be about this great land America, and for a moment I can't figure out why she's reading it.

Then I remember. She composed it for a class assignment last month and one poem a year is enough to ask from any teenager. Besides, she got an A on it.

Dylan steps forward nervously, holding the rings. Kirk leads us through the vows and Bradford and I slip the gold bands on each other's fingers and say our I do's.

"Is that all?" asks Dylan when he sees Bradford and me kissing.

"No, that's not all," says Kirk, smiling at us. "The ceremony is over. But everything else is just beginning."

"Here's to new beginnings," says Kate, popping the cork on a champagne bottle. She comes over and gives a kiss to the bride and groom. And one to the minister.

We head into the dining room which is bursting with enough food for a week's worth of shows on the Food Network. And maybe that's where it came from, because Ken Chablis is standing at the table looking proud.

"I told everyone at the network to invent a Chocolate Surprise for your wedding," he says delightedly.

And they've done it. The table is laden with chicken in chocolate sauce, chocolate-chip stuffed potatoes and sandwiches of bread-and-chocolate. As for the desserts, I may be out of a job soon, because it looks like Ken's staff have come up with more disgusting chocolate desserts than I ever could have imagined.

"Wow," says Dylan. "I love getting married."

Me, too, I think. Skylar is piling Dylan's plate with food and I don't worry about his getting dizzy from all that chocolate—because all of us are already flying high. I look around the room at Berni and Kate, at new friends and old. Bradford comes over and takes me in his arms. Everyone around us is talking, but I don't hear most of it because I'm too busy thinking how lucky I am. Louis Armstrong is right. It's a wonderful world.

Between them, authors JANICE KAPLAN and LYNN SCHNURNBERGER have published eight books, including their previous collaboration, the hit novel, *The Botox Diaries*. They've written hundreds of articles for just about every major magazine in America and have appeared regularly on television shows including *Today, Oprah,* and *Good Morning America.* Kaplan has been the executive producer of prime-time television specials for FOX, ABC, VH1 and other networks and was formerly deputy editor at *TV Guide* magazine. Schnurnberger is the author of *Let There Be Clothes: 40,000 Years of Fashion* and the founder of the nonprofit mentoring organization Foster Pride. The authors live in neighboring towns in Westchester County, New York, with their husbands and children.

This book was set in ITC Berkeley Oldstyle, designed in 1983 by Tony Stan. It is a variation of the University of California Old Style, which was created by Frederick Goudy. While capturing the feel and traits of its predecessor, ITC Berkeley Old Style shows influences from Kennerly, Goudy Old Style, Deepdene, and Booklet Oldstyle, all of which were also designed by Goudy. It is characterized by its calligraphic weight stress, and its x-height, now described as classic, is smaller than most other ITC designs of the day. The generous ascenders and descenders provide variations in text color, easy legibility, and an overall inviting appearance.